Photo © Nuno Bernardo

Irish writer and producer Triona Campbell
is a two-time Emmy-nominated producer of
transmedia, film and TV projects. She is the
creator of Ireland's first TV series on videogames
Gamer Mode (RTÉ) and a producer on the ground-
breaking and iconic UK teen drama *Sofia's
Diary* (Channel 5 / Sony Pictures Television).
A Game of Life or Death is Triona's debut novel.

Published in the UK by Scholastic, 2023
1 London Bridge, London, SE1 9BG
Scholastic Ireland, 89E Lagan Road, Dublin Industrial Estate,
Glasnevin, Dublin, D11 HP5F

SCHOLASTIC and associated logos are trademarks and/or
registered trademarks of Scholastic Inc.

Text © Triona Campbell, 2023
Cover image © Adobe Stock, 2023

The right of Triona Campbell to be identified
as the author of this work has been asserted by her under
the Copyright, Designs and Patents Act 1988.

ISBN 978 0702 31788 0

A CIP catalogue record for this book
is available from the British Library.

Printed by CPI Group (UK) Ltd, Croydon, CR0 4YY
Paper made from wood grown in sustainable forests
and other controlled sources.

1 3 5 7 9 10 8 6 4 2

www.scholastic.co.uk

A GAME OF LIFE OR DEATH

TRIONA CAMPBELL

■SCHOLASTIC

To those we lost, who lit the way for us.

Especially my Dad, Eugene Campbell.

*Saying goodbye during a full lockdown never felt right.
This dedication feels like something you would have
enjoyed more. Miss you, love, always.*

1

London, near future.

I know it's bad when I realize the nurse is leading me towards a room and not one of the cubicles.

Her pace is unhurried. The frantic Saturday night chaos is all around us, but she doesn't want to reach this destination any more than I do. The police officer who gave me a lift to the hospital shuffles alongside us. Plainclothes, white, middle-aged, middle everything, with the overconfidence to think that the too-small leather jacket he wears is retro-cool. The nurse ignores him, eyes multitasking. I watch them darting into the cubicles we pass, each with its own slice of drama inside. It's like I can see the numbers moving up as she mentally tallies the patients, the trolleys, the staff. Every time we fail to stop at one of those beds, my fear worsens.

The air is heavy with a mix of alcohol and disinfectant: hushed voices, monitors, occasional groans, perforated by loud, drunk talk. My palms are sweaty now, so I wipe them on my jeans as we move along. My head feels dizzy as we pass underneath the flickering strip lights. The hum of air purifiers signals we are in the "clean" area.

The door she stops outside has one chair beside it along with a strategically placed small box of tissues, hand sanitizer, and a prominent display of organ donation leaflets. "The doctor will be right with you." A sympathetic, efficient nod. A final repeat of her last question: "You sure there is no one you want us to call?"

I shake my head again. It's always been Maya and me. No one else.

The nurse leaves. The police officer sits down in the chair while I lean against the opposite wall. I stare at the ground, numbing out, counting the square pattern on the linoleum floor. If I let the feelings in, will I drown? I keep seeing her blue lips as I pushed against her chest over and over again, trying to get her heart to restart. I block out the image. I create a fantasy in my head while we wait. When the door is pushed open, Maya will be sitting upright in a hospital bed, an embarrassed look in her eyes. Some doctor beside her, talking about not overworking herself so much. Stressing the need for fluids, the importance of self-care...

This can't be happening. Not the hospital, not me arriving home late from work. Not the weird smell in our apartment when I got there. That sharp aroma of burnt food from a pot left too long on the cooker.

"Maya?" I had dumped my bag and jacket by the door and trudged to the kitchen, the boredom of eight hours working in Sam's local fast-food outlet and the smell of fish and chips pooling off me. I hadn't wanted to work at Sam's – Maya had called it character building; I called it a lot of other things. There was irritation in my voice at what smelt like another forgotten veggie culinary disaster. "Mai..."

I saw it then. The TV screen flickering, casting a pale blue light over the sitting room area. It's on a pause screen for a video game: some web banner advert for an eSports tournament plays on the top. My sister hates those events despite her job. I looked down, and the world stopped.

Maya wasn't answering because she was lying on the floor a few feet away. Body painted in the cold tones of the monitor's images. Eyes hidden behind a VR headset the size of a small pair of glasses. A tiny blue light blinking on the frame, confirming her connection to some online game. A controller in her hand. Fingers wrapped tight around it. No movement. Completely, terrifyingly still.

The rest of the night is just fragments. I called the emergency services. The questions started over the phone. "Is she breathing? Was she sick? Did she take something? Can you see any sign that she was attacked?"

I looked around. Nothing. Nothing out of the ordinary.

Just her and some game that had switched off when I removed her glasses.

There was no breath – no rise and fall. The voice talked me through the chest compressions. My tears started streaming down my face as a horrible thought entered my mind – am I too late? I pushed against it, clinging desperately to hope. One, two, three. One, two, three. The ambulance crew and a detective arrived at the same time. It took ten minutes and all eternity for them to get there. They took over. One paramedic wearing blue quickly talked to the officer and a dispatcher on his radio. The siren not blaring as the ambulance took off. Me walking past our neighbours' eyes; they all watched from their own doorways, none of them meeting my stare.

"Is there anyone I can call for you?" the police officer asked.

"No."

"Other family?"

"No."

"A friend?"

"No."

A sigh. The realization that there was no one to hand me off to. "My name's Murphy."

***

In my mind, I keep processing what I know. That the doctor isn't going to come back with good news.

I slide down the wall and sit on the floor. Head buried in my knees, trying to make myself smaller. From a distance, all that is visible is slightly torn denim, dark trainers, and a mop of long brown hair. How could this have happened? Maya wasn't sick. I go back to my last memory of her, searching for clues.

**

The frustration in her voice. "I called them. You never sent the acceptance forms."

I stared at the ground.

Her tone changed, became more pleading. "They said they can still give you a place..."

I didn't look at her. It was the same argument we'd been having for weeks. Maya pushing me to take up an early offer for an engineering course miles away. I knew why she wanted me gone. Maya worked for Zu Tech, the leading company in VR technology. Among other things. Their logo is on every platform, game, smart and wifi-enabled device; they are the biggest hardware-software corporation on the planet. The company who only hired the best of the best and then worked them hard. Maya didn't have time to look after her kid sister any more.

She lost patience and snapped at me. "We've talked about this..."

She had dark circles around her eyes. I remember that now. She'd seemed tired. But then, she'd been looking exhausted for weeks. Was that a sign I should have spotted?

I had lost my temper too. "You got me out of the system so we could be together, and ever since I got here, you've been trying to get rid of me. That college is in the middle of nowhere, Maya!"

"It's one of the best. They're offering you a full scholarship. Everything is covered, including rooms. And with my salary, I can take care of anything else you need."

"Why can't I stay here in London with you? Finish regular school. Do college in two years' time like everyone else. Why are you trying to get rid of me?"

"Not everything is a game, Asha. You can't just spend all your life alone in your room escaping into the metaverse."

"You never even went to college. You said it was a waste of—"

"I don't want you to end up like me. This is an opportunity, Asha. I didn't get one handed to me."

I had looked away, ignoring the feelings that curled in my stomach. "You didn't get one because of me."

"No, that's not what I meant."

"But it's the truth, isn't it? You could have gone to college if it wasn't for me. If you weren't stuck with a little sister to look after? I'm sorry I'm such a burden. That you giving me a home and taking that stupid job meant you never got to go. Once again, Saint Maya needed to do the right thing. But you could have just left me in care. I didn't ask you for any of this."

I had turned towards the door.

"Asha, please. Don't leave like this."

But I had. I slammed the flat door behind me, and now that stupid argument and me walking out is the last memory I have of my sister.

***

Murphy shifts uncomfortably on the hard plastic seat while the world of the hospital moves around but doesn't interact with either of us. I watch him fidget with his phone and notebook before he stands up. "Let me see what's keeping them…"

I'm too numb to respond. I am not a people pleaser, and that isn't going to change. Maya was the one who cared about manners and being nice.

Murphy returns after a few minutes with the doctor. Thin hands covered by surgical gloves. "Maya Kennedy's next of kin?" Then a pause, a look at Murphy. "No adult?" she asks.

I stand up. "I'm her sister. It's just the two of us."

Her eyes are sympathetic. I guess this part of the job never gets easier. She looks at her notes. "I'm sorry that I can't give you better news. Your sister died between ten and eleven p.m. The ambulance crew couldn't revive her at the scene." A pause. Of course Maya was dead. I knew that all along, but now it becomes real, and I can feel myself shutting down. "We'll need to do an autopsy to determine

7

cause of death. She'll stay here with us till the Health Plus morgue opens in the morning. If you need to call anyone, you can use our phone."

I blink at her. "Health…?"

The doctor glances up at me and then back at the chart. "Your sister worked for Zu Tech. They offer private healthcare. The dispatcher on the scene notified them of her death; it means your sister will be processed faster. If she had company life insurance, they will help you with the paperwork. All I can say for now is that the scan doesn't indicate any biohazard. I am sorry for your loss. It's always a shock when it's someone so young." Another pause, and then she says, "You can see her if you like? Say goodbye?"

I swallow.

"After that, the team here will need some information. Her doctor's name, and there are some forms you and the social will need to sign. She was your older sister, is that right? You're around fourteen, fifteen?"

"Sixteen. My birthday was a few months ago." Maya had made a vegan cake. *This can't be happening.*

She nods and catches the eye of a nurse standing to one side. "The hospital needs someone eighteen or over to sign. We'll make the arrangements for you. Someone can come and collect you from here."

The words don't sink in at first. "Someone can come and collect you." The doctor ushers me towards a room – before the door shuts, I catch a glimpse of Murphy outside, notebook open. The nurse is talking to him. The logo of social services is visible on the back of the documents she holds out.

My brain wakes up. Maya was my sole guardian. My only family. Without her, they're going to try and put me back into the system.

The doctor leads me to the bed and then leaves. I look at Maya's still form. It's her, and yet it's not. What made Maya special was her energy, her smile. I take a moment to breathe and say goodbye. Talking to her in whispers and tears about what I need to do next. Out of everyone, she would understand. We always said we would never go back.

She would be the first to tell me to run.

An hour later. Drizzle is washing the pavements clean. I cling to the shadows, hoodie up, head down to avoid the cameras. Keys laced through fingers, my ears searching for any sound behind me. Heart thumping whenever a car passes by. Cold wind wiping the tears away. Stupid – there's no reason to panic. The social system is fast, but not that fast. I have time. Focus. Emotions lead to mistakes.

When I get back to our building, it's quiet. I stay in the shadows for a while and check the perimeter – old habits. Count the number of lights, check the cars parked outside. Look for anything out of place. It helps me not to think about Maya. What comes next? Pack, erase, trigger the surveillance system. Leave. I wait for a few moments and then enter the building, making sure the communal door catches behind me.

Inside the apartment, I listen to the silence. The smell

of burnt food mixed with something else still lingers. My jacket and bag sit on the floor. Everything looks the same until I glance at the sitting room and see the forgotten plastic glove from the ambulance crew on the floor, the small black electrode sticker from the portable EKG. I can't look inside that room without seeing her lying there so I close the door. Breathe. Think. I grab a sports backpack from the hall cupboard and go first to my hidden stash of cash and codes. What next?

I hesitate outside Maya's bedroom door, feeling the chrome of the handle before I push it open, forcing myself to go in. Her make-up is scattered on her home office desk/ dressing table/dumping ground for lost things. Books and clothes lie on the floor. The smell of coconut body lotion from an open bottle. She never used to be this untidy. A yoga mat with a daisy on it, her favourite flower, is rolled up in a corner by her gym bag – I wonder when the last time she went to a class was. Then I stop. Quick. If I'm quick the feelings can't rush in. I make a pile of her things on the bed to take with me. Handbag, mobile phone, which I remove the SIM card from, laptop powered off. On impulse, I grab the cheesy snow globe with the picture of us together and her favourite perfume, her "signature" scent, the good one she rarely uses because it's expensive. Precise motions. No time to waste.

When I've finished packing, I take one last look around, glancing back at her unmade bed. It has clothes, pillows, a hairbrush strewn across it. I go to the right-hand side and slide my hand underneath the mattress till it finds the square edges of a book. I pull it out. *World Myths and Legends*: the dog-eared copy that Maya has carried with her ever since I can remember. The only thing left from the time when we had parents. My eyes well up, but there is no space to let go now. I hug the book and then push it towards the bottom of the bag before zipping it shut.

I move fast. The last thing I do is take my phone and dismantle it. I place it in the microwave and hit start. I don't want to leave a trace behind me, nothing that might be saved to the phone's internal memory, some random bit of data that might lead someone to where I am going next. It rotates inside, sparks, a few small flames that die as the microwave stops, leaving a black, bubbling, melted mess. I lock the door behind me. Will I ever be able to go back? Don't think. *Run*.

I don't stop till I get to the takeaway a few blocks over. Sam paid me off the books, so they won't know to come here right away. The streets are empty as I disable the alarm and slip in the side door and into the back room, a sort of office with camera monitors, files, storage. Normally employees don't have access, but Sam didn't hire me for my people skills. If I'm honest, the main reason he hired me was probably to impress Maya when his Portuguese charms didn't work, but the other reason I got my Saturday/part-time job was tech. My ability to upgrade his security system for a fraction of the cost.

Within a week of installing the cameras, they caught

11

someone doing credit card skims on the night shift. By week two, I had made his shop impenetrable, both online and physically, rigging a silent alarm and introducing a lockdown protocol for maximum security. Now I use it to seal myself inside the closed takeaway. The clock on the wall says it's one a.m. By six a.m., I need to be somewhere else. To *become* someone else.

I can't break; that can only come later. Fear can either destroy you or drive you. It's the only choice people like me get to make.

2

I start with creating a new ID and opening a bank account. I can't rush this part. I need just enough cash so that it won't attract attention. Money from my old life. I need to be careful not to leave digital fingerprints behind. While I transfer the funds, I think about the social.

The doctor would have thought nothing of calling them. She was trying to help, and they were the only option. But for Maya and me, the "social" was twelve years of living hell. Maya was seven and I was three when our parents died and we started bouncing from care home to care home. A bin bag for our belongings. Maya's book *World Myths and Legends*, the only thing from our parents, the corners always cutting through the thin plastic. With each move, they would try again to separate us. We'd had to stay alert. Aware that we were now stuck in a system where no one cares if you live or die. We were a number on a spreadsheet, a statistic that would simply disappear once it turned eighteen.

"Once we get out, Asha, we never go back." Maya's eyes had held my gaze when she said it. That memory is one of my earliest ones. I must have been about four or five. Maya holding my small hand tight in hers, her eyes bright. *"Sister promise. Once we leave, we never let ourselves get taken back. We never let go of each other."*

Click. The bank account is done. Credit history and scores, fake ID, vaccination records that mirror mine. Nothing traceable.

I find a place near the London Eye. A small temporary rabbit hole, a single-bed studio in a buzzy part of Embankment. An area busy enough that I can blend in. I transfer the funds to cover a short stay and get a code to open the door.

Then I hack the street cameras. Disabling them would draw the attention of a tech crew and questions, so instead, I angle them ever so slightly to create a blind spot around the apartment block entrance.

I wait for the changes to process. Without warning, I think of Maya on the floor. No. I need to block my mind from going there. I can't fall apart yet. Social systems are more advanced now. Once I get listed as missing, the file will go to surveillance. The algorithms there will link everything on my file and open a search. One bank transaction from my real account, one glance up at the wrong street camera, and I'll be spotted.

I'm not going back, not ever.

Cameras re-routed. I secure a code for a nearby ATM for a cash card linked to my new bank account and start to repack. I load a large takeaway foil container with my old ID, travel cards, bank cards – anything with a potential electronic tag or strip that could be used to trace me – and wrap them up using some gaffer tape. I go through Maya's handbag, doing the same. Moving fast, keeping hold of the slender, fragile thread that is keeping me anchored, stopping me from falling into that ocean of loss.

I pack both containers into the bottom of my backpack. It's five a.m.; dawn is at five thirty-eight. Deep breath. Next: I wipe the computer drives, including the CCTV files and history. In my mind, I imagine Sam cursing when he comes in later and finds all the camera feeds and employee files deleted. My fingers hover over the keyboard. No choice; my index finger presses the delete key.

In the back office is an old black puffer jacket and a grey baseball cap. I take them and tie my hair up. Then I am out, moving swiftly away. Just another teenager out late.

I force myself to walk at a steady pace. Speed attracts the wrong sort of attention on an empty street. I can't risk public transport or a cab, and that will cost me time. Shadows frighten me. Footsteps behind me, cars that pass by too slowly make my feet want to run. My heart keeps

15

hammering so loud I'm sure it can be heard. By the time I reach the apartment on Embankment, dawn has already broken, and the first of the morning fitness fanatics are out exercising. I glance over my shoulder – no one seems to be following me. I slow down, looking at the apartment block numbers, counting them as I pass.

"Morning."

Too close, the voice is too close. A copper, security? I glance up and see a guy dumping recycling into a nearby bottle bin with a crash. I keep my head low and my feet moving.

"You lost?"

He's white, male, broad shoulders – and with a phone in his hand. Don't look, don't engage. Keep counting the flat numbers, breathe, walk, don't run.

Footsteps. The voice is coming closer. "I said..."

The sweat cools on my forehead. He's getting too close. I look up and see the door: Apt's 1900–1970. I punch the code into it. Please work, please. It swings open with a slight creaking sound.

I slip inside and shut the door, then duck into the stairwell, eyes fixed on the enforced glass panel of the door. A few minutes later, I hear the muffled sound of the guy passing, the distorted image through the glass of the pods now in his ears, lips humming something out of tune. He doesn't stop. He keeps walking. My hands are trembling. I struggle to catch my breath.

The apartment is on the fifth floor, up a small fire exit

stair and down a rabbit warren of tiny airless corridors, past a dozen identical doors. The place is clean, but it smells of bad ventilation and takeaway food. I punch in a second code at number 1929 and wait for the reassuring click. Go in, look around. White, tiny, characterless, anonymous. I pull the deadbolts across from the inside. There are no other ways in or out. Not ideal, but safe. I am safe. They can't get me if they can't find me.

I put my backpack down and sink on to the floor. A weak ray of morning sun hits my face as I listen to the sounds of London waking up outside. The cars, trucks, voices, the beep of the nearby pedestrian crossing. Deliveries being made, shops and restaurants opening. Normal life. Not mine, not now. Not ever. No more safety net. I am alone.

Something inside me breaks then. Maya was my world. Blood. The only family I had to hold on to. No one came to claim us after our parents passed. No known extended family that we could remember. Nothing. Just us. We'd promised each other to never let go, and now she has. I cry angry, ugly, violent sobs that I try to muffle with my coat. I close my eyes and cry and cry.

Nothing will ever be the same again.

***

When I wake, there is a moment when the world seems OK. Half asleep, listening for the sounds of Maya's movements — brushing her teeth, humming under her breath, the snap

17

of her hairband, the faint smell of coconut. A vague hope that she might have made something normal for breakfast, something not revolving around lentils.

Then I remember.

I sit up slowly, my neck stiff and sore, payback from sleeping on the fake wooden floor. There are no more tears left inside now – just emptiness. It doesn't make sense. How is she dead? Could she have been sick and I didn't realize? If I had gotten home earlier, could I have saved her?

Maya's gone. No – it still doesn't feel real. She was "the nice sister", the one who kept trying to figure out the system when we were little. To understand it so it couldn't separate us. She'd encourage me to apply for schemes, funding, mentorships, to hustle for a better life. Even then, I kept asking her why. What was the point? Happy endings were for others, not us. I kept my expectations low. When you don't have dreams, it can't hurt you when they don't come true.

Maya was my world, my family, the one who pushed me. She started telling me stories in our first group home. I was three, scared, clinging to her, too frightened to close my eyes. So, she crawled into my bed after lights out and whispered stories to me about the parents I couldn't remember, every night a different one till I fell asleep.

"They loved us, you know," she would say. "So much."

"Then why did they leave?" I would ask.

"It wasn't their fault. The virus doesn't discriminate."

18

It helped when the nightmares were bad. But as years passed, even her memories started to fade.

So, Maya came up with another story to keep us both from breaking as we navigated the "system": "our plan".

Late at night, we'd snuggle up together in a single bed, her voice barely a whisper. "Once I'm eighteen, I'll get a job. Then I'll get a place. After that, I'll come back for you. They have to release you then. Once we're out – we never go back."

Nine years. An eternity and yet… "Promise?"

"Sister promise. We will always be together."

Maya broke her promise, and now I have no idea what to do next.

***

I shower. The silence of the studio apartment adds to the feeling that everything is wrong. Afterwards, I look at the clothes lying on the bathroom floor and can't bear to touch them. When I last put them on, Maya was alive.

I go out. Cash card in my pocket, shades to hide my red eyes, baseball hat pulled down. There's a busy Sunday street market nearby, where I pick up food, clothes, hair dye. I buy a new SIM card, phone, metal tape for a better Faraday cage, and a laptop in the small Chinese store close by. No one gives me a second glance. The best place to hide is always within plain sight, deep inside the crowd. I walk back to the apartment, past the happy couples and friends heading out for late Sunday brunches. When I get back, I take out my new phone. I have no one to call, but I needed data. My hands start shaking again, so I eat, and then I set up. I need to find out what happened to Maya, and the system gave me one skill I can use.

The outreach programme run by the Zu Tech Corporation was designed to "create the workforce of the future". Attendance from low-income state schools was compulsory. The classes taught primary coding languages that employers could use. Skills for the world outside. After a year, there were tests that led to more advanced courses, but for only a select few. Both Maya and I made it. The thing about the social was that we had nothing else to do. So we practised, played, and advanced faster than anyone else around us. We were taught by the best of the best. Software engineers, network technicians, cyber security experts, and we absorbed it all. Operating systems, maths, AI and machine learning, security and cryptology, networking. But where I did best – ethical hacking, cloud computing.

Maya encouraged me but, despite her people pleasing ways, she wasn't as much of a die-hard as I was about our new courses.

"It's Zu Tech, Maya," I'd say, and she'd just shrug.

"I want more for you. University, joining some start-up that gets sold for a billion quid. Then you can keep us in a lifestyle we could get accustomed to. Remember, Asha, nothing ever comes for free."

For Maya, tech was a means to an end: a way to get an

apprenticeship at eighteen that would pay enough to get us out. For me, breaching firewalls, finding the things others liked to keep hidden gave me a sense of control and an addictive adrenaline rush. By twelve, I was on my way to building a different reputation from the one she wanted for me. I'd started hacking public records, searching for our parents, their past. The thrill of being places I didn't belong led to me skimming from banks, not the public ones, but the private ones. The places only those with old or vast sums of money use. I built a stockpile of emergency funds. My *just in case cash* that I could never tell her about without revealing where it came from.

I log in to my new laptop and go to the NHS server – security is minimal. The file notes the transfer time to the Health Plus morgue – the autopsy is scheduled for early Monday morning. I swallow. It takes a few minutes before I can read the rest. Cause of death: Unknown. Scribbled on one of the scanned pages underneath: *"Respiratory failure?"*, then another single question mark written beside her blood results. I scroll through the other pages. No visible bruising to the skin, no cuts, no sign of any virus. Maya was healthy: no history of long-term illness or disease on record. So why and how did she stop breathing?

They don't know any more than I do about how Maya died. No break-in, no one else in the apartment. No signs of a struggle. Maya was a yoga-practising, *refined sugars will kill you* person. I kick the table. She promised. "Sister promise. We will always be together."

Anger starts to flow — at her for leaving me alone. At myself for not knowing at sixteen what I am supposed to do now. Do I stay hidden for two years in the shadows till I turn eighteen and age out of the social system's reach? This is a mess.

A sudden buzzing noise makes me jump. I search around me, eventually finding the source: Maya's handbag. The low humming of an incoming alert. My chest tightens. I searched it last night; I thought I'd got all her electronics. What did I miss? I flip the bag upside down, and the contents spill on to the table. Gum, make-up, hand sanitizer, swipe cards for work, winter mask, and then a collection of Maya's favourite hair ties, crystals, hippie stuff. A necklace. Bracelets.

One of them is buzzing. A slender pink fitness tracker designed to look like a bangle. Incoming message alerts. The band looked like the gazillion other feng shui type items she liked to have on her wrist, so I'd missed it. Zu Tech must issue them. Damn. *Damn.* Messages mean it must have a clone of her SIM chip inside; someone could get a traceable GPS signal. I am better than this.

My heart starts to pound again. Emails from her job at Zu Tech, text messages, lots of them from a private number. I look for an off button, but there is none — fingerprint tech. I take the bracelet and plunge it into water. It keeps buzzing. Waterproof. Damn. I need another Faraday cage to block the signal. Bathroom. The rubbish bin is metal with a plastic lining. I take the metal tape and cover any joins, then I put the bracelet inside and seal the top shut. The buzzing stops, the cage instantly blocking the electromagnetic radiation and wifi signal. Like a switch has been flicked, the room is again silent. My breath starts to return to normal. I have to be more careful.

I go back to the table to sweep the rest of Maya's stuff back into her bag, when I spot the small pink crumpled Post-it note. It must have been stuck to the lining at the bottom of the bag. The writing isn't Maya's; the letters are sharp, unlike Maya's looping fluid style.

When can I meet Asha?

No initials, nothing else. Just this.

I sit down at the kitchen table and stare at it. Creepy. Maya never mentioned anyone wanting to meet me. That's when it starts. What else don't I know? The feeling in my gut twists. Something isn't right. There is a puzzle, pieces that don't fit, a picture I can't see. The problem is where to begin to find answers.

3

I start with what's easy: the home security system I set up in our apartment. Tracing back through the last twenty-four hours to look for anything unusual.

Using the new laptop and a few virtual servers, I log in remotely and rewind the footage until I see Maya arriving home. The image makes my breath stop. Everything seems so normal. Focus, I need to focus.

Maya has a bag of groceries with her and her work bag. She must have gone into the office after we argued. Working seven days a week had become her thing recently. She checks for post in the letterbox outside the apartment. Then she takes her mobile out, and her expression clouds when she sees the caller ID. She accepts it, almost reluctantly, distracted, but then I see her listen, and her look changes. She starts to talk fast. She's angry, I think.

She ends the call, jamming the phone into her bag. I check the timestamp. 19:20:03. I was at Sam's takeaway, and I didn't call Maya that night. So who did?

I watch her enter our apartment, a slight jump as the CCTV cameras switch from exterior to interior. She pushes the code into the keypad by our door to open it. The system disarms immediately, switching off, and the screen goes black. That's all there is. I'm about to sign out when I notice other new log entries. Three separate longer video files from the security system stand out, all triggered by movement, longer than the usual ten-second burst when someone walks past our corridor. All recorded just after I left. More interaction than we've had the entire time we've been living there if you discount food deliveries. Why? The digital files start to download.

I scroll through the first file. The timestamp sends a shiver down my spine. 00:18:02. A visitor less than half an hour after I left the apartment and rearmed the system. "Pete's 24-hour call-out service" is stencilled on the van parked outside. An average-looking white guy wearing gloves and carrying a toolbox gets out. He uses a device to open the building's door and then the door to our place. He's inside. Touching our things. Walking on the spot where Maya was lying. The search is professional, measured. Like he knows what he is looking for. He keeps his cap over his face and his gloves on.

My stomach starts to knot. Anger and fear battle each other. Anger wins. He pauses when he gets to the microwave. He takes a pen from his pocket and pokes at the congealing mess of black plastic, searching to see if any part of the phone is retrievable. It isn't, but "Pete" seems even more careful after that. Eventually, he leaves empty-handed. The timestamp reads 01:03:10.

Why was there someone in our home? What or who were they looking for? Then a new fear takes hold. Was this something from my past? Is what happened to Maya my fault?

I take some deep breaths and start to screenshot as much info as possible, creating a digital file. Running searches on the company name tag, the van in the parking lot, city traffic cameras. They begin to ping back with no returnable info.

I recognize the next visitor. Murphy, the police officer I ran out on at the hospital. He arrived at 07:04:10. this morning. I lean forward and stare at the screen. Cops aren't known for their follow-up on social kids. He's let in by a neighbour when he flashes his badge. Then he bangs on the door for a while before writing his number on a card that he shoves through the letterbox. Curious, I zoom in on the details and set up a second search. His records start to return almost at once – single white male. The small portion takeaway charges on his bank records suggest he lives mainly alone in his flat. His listed next of kin is a sister, nurse, Mary Murphy, paediatrics.

I drink some coffee and watch as the footage continues to play. The corridor outside our door is empty, apart from the occasional neighbour who walks quickly past.

Then at 12:03:27, something changes. An elegant but dishevelled black woman slips into the building behind a young mum struggling with a stroller. Once in, she runs to the front door of our two bed and starts to pound on it. She looks twenty-something, well dressed in casual but expensive clothes. She starts to kick the door. She must be loud enough for one of the neighbours to come out. The woman pauses a moment, hair falling in front of her face, then she turns and leaves.

I grab a screenshot, but it's impossible to see her features clearly – only enough to know I've never seen her before and that she doesn't look like she's from social services. A friend of Maya's, maybe? Only Maya doesn't have friends, just colleagues I've never met.

I save the info. I need to widen the search using the street cams, but I'll need more bandwidth and storage space for that. I also need more leads, a proper plan.

I know who would know where to look next. *Dark*. His faith in his instincts meant he would start a search before he knew what was hidden. Endless analysis of the elements already in his possession till he found the right thread to pull. I sigh and reheat my coffee. Evaluate. I need to look at what I have.

I use my fake IDs to buy some hard drives, a router, USD adapter and a few single board computers for the apartment. Within a few hours, the walls are covered with paper as I map out what I know.

19:20:03	Maya arrives home from work, checks the mail and takes a phone call from someone. She doesn't look happy.
22:00:00	approx, something happens to Maya, and she dies on our apartment floor (from causes unknown).
22:17:23	I arrive home and call the paramedics while trying to revive Maya.
22:27:15	The paramedics take Maya to the hospital, where she is pronounced dead.
23:32:56	I arrive back at our apartment, pack and re-trigger the alarm system.
00:18:02	Pete's 24-hour call-out service arrives and enters looking for something or someone. He leaves at 01:03:10.
07:04:10	Murphy, the policeman from the hospital, arrives and leaves a business card.
12:03:27	A female stranger arrives at our apartment, creating a scene outside.

I pin printed screenshots of all three people who came to the apartment, followed by more question marks. Then I add the note from Maya's bag. *When can I meet Asha?*

I examine Maya's laptop and phone, both issued by her work. I don't turn either of them on; they'll both be fitted with tracer tech, given Maya's job as an engineer and Zu Tech's paranoia about intellectual property. I need a clean room to open them and search. A place where signals can't be intercepted or tracked.

I know where I need to go. I just don't want to go there.

4

I need to find Dark.

People act like it's hard to find him. It isn't. He is always in the darkest place, surrounded by, but never interacting with, vast crowds.

Commuters walking past the small dodgy-looking tech shop in the gap between Paddington train and tube station barely give the place a second glance. It's an oddity – a throwback to times past when small shops could survive. From the outside, you can't be sure if it's open or not. The window is filled with old electronic items and faded neon discount signs, all designed to ensure you can't see inside to the uninviting countertop and the crowded, dusty shelves. For a moment, I stand outside, suddenly not sure if I should walk through the door. Then I remember he's probably already watching. The longer I stay outside, the more of an idiot I'll look.

When I push it open, the door jingles as it hits the bell hanging on the wall – an unnecessary touch. The street, train, and tube cameras feed into the shop's security system. He knows when you are coming.

Bill, the heavily built, twenty-something enforcer covered in tattoos, sits behind the counter and cracks his knuckles. He hasn't changed.

"Evening, Asha. Haven't seen you in ages."

"You remember?"

Bill shrugs. "I never forget. You got taller; the hair is cool."

I pull the black beanie off my newly dyed red hair. So much for trying to change my appearance. Then I spot the pad he's playing on and recognize the watermark logo.

"Gait recognition software?"

Bill offers me a grin that reveals a newly missing tooth. "Yeah, got them installed a year ago; dead handy. Your walk is the new facial recognition. Not that he needed it; he spotted you miles away."

I can feel the blood drain slightly from my face, imagining him watching me as I faltered outside. Then I pull my shoulders back.

Bill leans over the counter and nods behind him. "Mr Dark will see you if you want to go on through to the back. He's downstairs, the door's in the maintenance panel."

I step into the back room. A wall of screens monitoring activities in the area and a few in other places Dark must use. One is near Jones's Tower. Dark's old employer. He's still keeping tabs on the competition: some things never change. I glance at the images of the people rushing past on the tube, never knowing their every move is being captured, their digital footprint checked and measured. The only other glow in the room comes from a cracked, dirty exit sign hung over what appears to be a fire door. I go to it and hear a click before I reach the handle. It swings wide. I ignore the fire escape in front of me leading up and instead turn to the opposite wall's large maintenance panel. Another click. It opens, and I step through and wait for the panel to seal again and the emergency lights to flicker on. I'm in a narrow space, with only a small circular iron staircase leading down into the darkness.

I mumble, "so much for disability access" and hear a chuckle from somewhere deep below. Great, the space is rigged for sound and vision. My feet clang on the metal steps. The only other noises are the trains and muted public announcements. The brick walls are a discoloured grey, covered in the grime of centuries of London traffic. The air is recycled, smelling of things I don't want to even think about.

When I reach the last step, I follow the narrow, dimly lit tunnel to a large dark, studded door. I step through it into a vast, vaulted brick chamber as the door silently closes behind me. Warm lighting mimics natural daylight. High ceilings, space. All in contrast to the tiny staircase outside. The architecture has an early twentieth century vibe: black steel industrial beams and exposed red brick. The aroma of coffee and expensively filtered clean air fills the room. The floor is clean, black and white tile, with a careful scattering of thick rugs. One side of the room is outfitted like an old-fashioned bar. Mirrors, sparkling heavy cut glasses and coloured bottles. The long bar counter is a dark polished wood. The brass fittings gleam, along with the chrome coffee machine. The rest of the room is fitted out with oversized leather chairs, small tables, and couches. It feels like an expensive 1920s gentleman's club with no visible tech on display.

Sitting alone at the end of the bar, drinking tea, is Dark. On the counter beside him is a china cup of freshly made black coffee – the steam and its aroma wafting in the air.

"Nice place. You expanded fast," I say, glancing around.

He says nothing for a moment. "I had some lucky breaks when I struck out on my own." A pause. "I wasn't sure if you still take milk, so I didn't pour."

He gestures towards the small silver milk jug that drips condensation down its cold metal surface while fixing his dark shirt sleeve that is rolled up over his elbow.

So that's how we are going to play it. It's been years, and we are going to pretend like we're just two old friends reuniting. I join him at the bar. It never fails to stun me how wrong people get it when they make streaming dramas. The iconic image of the evil genius hacker is a reclusive figure in a sloppy T-shirt, energy drink in one hand, endless rock music blaring as they hack past firewalls, creating waves of chaos just before the government forces blow the door down. Whereas Dark has always chosen calm, pristine spaces. Quiet. He creates confusion that is untraceable. Like in the old quote about the devil, the greatest trick Dark plays is convincing the world he doesn't exist. He is an urban myth, a figure from the edges of the Web, a hacker, an invisible "fixer". At least, that is what he is now.

I take my seat beside him and look at his reflection in the mirror. Seventeen, eighteen maybe. Young, even when life expectancy is short. Impossibly pale skin. He's more well-built now, taller. His eyes are focused on his teacup as I sit down. He doesn't look up at me when he speaks.

"Happy belated birthday. I would have sent you something, but I wasn't sure you'd want it. Given that you didn't accept my last offer." There is an edge to his voice.

I take a moment to pour the steamed milk into the coffee, stirring it in slowly, taking a tentative sip. "Circumstances have changed."

He looks up then, hand pushing his black hair away from his pale blue eyes. "I'm sorry about your sister."

I look at him and see the sympathy in his eyes and wait for the rush – that familiar surge of adrenaline that comes just from being around him. It's still there. Then a thought.

"You knew about Maya? Did you have a trace on me?"

Dark looks away again. "You're one of the few people that know who I am."

"You disappeared. You left and never contacted me afterwards. I kept your secrets, and yet somehow you didn't think you could trust me?"

Silence. Dark takes another sip of tea. Maybe this is a mistake, but I need to know.

"Did you..." I struggle. The words don't want to come. "Did you send someone to my flat? A sweeper?"

Dark's eyes move back to mine, and this time they don't leave. His voice has an edge to it. "No. And for the record, Asha, I never contacted you to keep you safe. You knew where I was; you didn't reach out."

"You left." I take a breath. Nothing to be gained from revisiting the past now. I need to focus. "There was a man who came to our place after Maya. I saw him on the security system. He was looking for something or someone, but he didn't find it. I thought ... I mean, it's been a while, but could he have been connected to ... what we used to do?"

Pause.

Dark takes a moment to answer, but his eyes are still locked on me. "I scrubbed everything that could connect us. I didn't send anyone to your place. You made your share on the hacks we did back then, and that was all you wanted, right?"

"But you had surveillance on me. Why? You must have thought someone might connect us."

Dark puts down his cup. His eyes are bright. "I had my reasons. It wasn't full monitoring, just an alert."

The old anger starts to rise inside. Why does he always succeed in getting under my skin? "So what did you need to know that warranted a trace…?"

He blurts the words out in a rush. "That you were safe, OK?"

There is a silence then. I don't trust myself to speak. Eventually, Dark drains his cup and looks away.

"You want something, or you wouldn't be here." Not a question. A statement.

"I need access to a clean room to go through my sister's files. Something about her death doesn't make sense."

"Maya worked for Zu Tech?"

I glare at him. "Yes, but you already knew that if you had a trace on me."

"Just confirming."

I sigh. "She got an internship when she aged out of the system. A while after that she was promoted to engineer in their VR games division. She was in crunch mode for some new release. Exhausted. Twenty-hour shifts to iron out the bugs and glitches. The launch is about eight weeks away."

Dark gives me a look. "Just what the world needs, another Zu Tech VR game."

His voice drips with sarcasm, and I wonder why. Is he thinking of our old Zu Tech–sponsored coding classes, or is it Zu, the man? Zu Thorp is a legend now. He made Britain the centre of the engineering science world again, at least in relation to virtual reality. The future's Guru. The founder of Zu Tech: the unicorn start-up that began pioneering new VR for remote teaching and business meetings during the lockdowns. A few years later, Zu made the leap into VR immersive games using the tech he created and, almost overnight, they grew into one of the world's major tech giants. Straddling hardware and software. Everyone wants to be part of the Zu Tech metaverse, and it reaches everywhere. Maya had been lucky to get her internship there at eighteen, and she knew it. No one had worked harder than my big sister.

Dark looks at the leaves in his thin porcelain teacup, trying to seem as if he is considering the situation. I feel like a fly about to become trapped in a web. One who can see the spider but knows it has no choice.

"OK. I can get you a clean room to access your sister's data. But I will want a copy of what we find."

"It's a personal matter."

Dark smiles vaguely. "Isn't everything? Leave your number with Bill, and I'll send you the details."

"I didn't agree yet."

"Yes, you did. When you stepped inside the door. I know you."

"No. You used to know me."

I get up and leave, heart pounding. Dark watches me go.

"Take care, Asha. I'll see you again tonight."

Dark's message comes later.

Under St Mary Magdalene's, Regents Park. You'll know
when you see it.

His sense of humour and melodrama hasn't changed. The
evil tech lord using London's gothic structures against the
new world order. It helps, of course, that the stone from
that time is solid enough to offer natural barriers on top
of the ones he uses. That most churches are empty now.
But the symbolism isn't lost on me. He is using places
that represent old London to destroy the parasites of the
new. Despite everything, Dark is still the angry kid whose
world fell apart during the pandemics. First when he lost
his mother to a mutant virus strain, then his father to a
preventable cancer.

Perhaps if I had been alone when I entered the system,
if Maya hadn't been there to protect me, I would have
turned out like him. I was eleven when we met. We
weren't friends then; we were students at Zu Tech's
special coding in-school project, rivals. Dark had a head
start on me. He had learnt to code when his dad worked
maintenance in a university before becoming a floor
manager for Environ. He had tagged along with his dad
then, always looking at things and asking not "what is
it?" but "what can I make this do?" Eventually, someone
at the school noticed how bright he was, and while his
father worked, he was allowed to sit quietly at the back

of a computer lab, soaking up every bit of information he could.

By the time we met, Dark seemed intent on learning how to gain some lucrative retribution by hacking the 1%. The ones linked to the politicians whose inactivity he blamed for the deaths and the poverty that followed the lockdowns and the surges. The people who made money while others died. But with Dark, it's not just political – it's personal. His drive is revenge for his father's death. The only difference between him and hundreds of others who were disenfranchised by what happened? Dark has the tech skills to be the worst terrorist in history. To destroy governments as easily as he reduces the wealth of hundreds of billionaires by skimming their accounts and releasing an avalanche of secrets few can crawl out from under. He does it with no empathy for anyone caught between him and his targets. And, when he is done, Dark will just disappear as if he never existed.

It's past ten p.m., and the sun has just set when I get to St Mary's. The building is locked up for the night, empty. Faded signs outside promote tours of the church, a children's playgroup, and a weekly service it hopes people might attend. Like all churches, it's in decline now. I look around and spot the small hidden side entrance near the overgrown hedges and trees that leads directly to the crypt. The clean room is there, down a series of small broken cold stone steps. No electricity wires or lights, just me and the torch on my phone as I descend. It smells of dust and damp.

The beam catches a cobweb that flutters in the breeze that blows through the stairwell. The first room houses stacks of coffins and stone sarcophagi. My fingers trace the inscriptions. I think of Maya.

The air smells stale and of decay. I hurry up and follow the footprints in the dust that lead to a large oak door. No visible handles, levers, or doorknobs. A solid sheet of thick aged wood with a single brass plaque: "Family Only".

I hate Dark. I pound on the door, but there is no response. I can almost feel his imagined laughter on the other side of the soundproofing. It annoys me so much that I forget to panic. I search using my phone's flashlight for a small black box, one with a thin coating of dark film on its side. I eventually find it on one of the shelves beside a dusty disintegrating coffin. I press my finger against the film and let it scan. There is a slight whirring noise, then a silence, followed by a sharp click as the door swings open. A wall of freezing air and bright blue light is visible on the other side. I'm in.

Clean rooms are exactly what they sound like. The walls are thick and reinforced. Nothing can penetrate them once you are sealed in, no matter how hidden the tracking device or software. Once inside, you and the tech you bring in are off-grid. No wifi, no bluetooth, no data, no GPS, all frequency and EMF signals become blocked. The only information that can leave a clean room is what you choose to take out.

They're also surprisingly hard to find in overcrowded

cities where our every movement is monitored. In London, Dark's clean rooms are the best. Part of the empire and the reputation he built after he disappeared from the care system at fifteen to become a ghost. When he left me behind.

I shiver as I cross the threshold and the door glides shut behind me. It's freezing.

"Apologies for the location, but this is the most secure room."

I glare at Dark. "You couldn't install a heater down here?"

He shrugs in his thermal clothes and coat. "I find if it's cold, my clients don't tend to linger."

The walls of the room are coated in some sort of sound-and-signal-proofing polymer. In the centre is a black steel table with two chairs on one side, facing a large flat touch screen that fills the entire wall opposite. Dark is seated in one of the chairs, a small leather notebook in front of him, which he quickly closes.

My eyes go to the notebook and pen. "I see some things haven't changed."

"You can't hack paper. In this line of work, that's a plus."

"You think anyone would be stupid enough to try and mine you for information?"

Dark gives me a small smile. "You'd be surprised."

A pause. "How's it going?" I ask.

His voice is low, quiet, "I never replaced you, if that's what you're asking. Also, don't believe everything

41

you hear."

A beat. And in that second, I know he means the other stories about him. The ones that say he is ruthless when it comes to rivals. "I never did gossip. I like to make up my own mind."

The air between us is still, the silence growing. Dark playing his favourite trick. Letting it get uncomfortable in the hopes that I'll fill the void first. It doesn't work.

"You know..." he says, "you could come back."

"My sister died." I stare at him. Deep breath. I want him to understand; of all people, he should. "I need to know what happened to her."

He considers me. "You don't think it was natural?"

"I don't know. She could have been ill and didn't realize. But Maya was this yoga-loving vegan. She was tired and stressed but not sick before it happened. Then someone searched our flat. I think they were looking for something. I found a note in her bag that doesn't make any sense. I need to be certain."

"OK." He hits a button, and two sections of the table open and keyboards rise from underneath. "Shall we?" He holds out his hand like it's a formal invitation to dance. And then we begin.

There is a rhythm to hacking, to the ones and zeros that flow like music across a screen. An elegance to the binary code and encryptions. With Dark, it's almost a perfect duet as we hack into Maya's personal computer and phone. Past the firewalls, past the deeply buried company tracers and security protocols. Dark isn't a script kiddie just pasting code or automated tools into a system. He identifies and then creates ways to exploit each weakness. Sculpting each section and then passing it to me to finalize and implement it. Just like before. Time passes unnoticed. With each element unlocked, Dark places the files on the giant screen across from us until Maya's tech is brought back to empty factory settings. A shell. Everything in my sister's life is now on the screen glowing, her phone history, her emails. Data files that will require more decryption but which are now tracker free. Her texts about meetings, reminders to buy oat milk on the way home. Her bank details, browser history detailing endless searches on the universities she was making me apply to, and a thin list of contacts which all seem work-related. Tons of work project notes and a goofy video diary I never even knew she kept. Details on some holiday trip she was thinking of, a TBR pile of ebooks she must have been saving for when she had the time to read. Yoga reminders for classes she didn't go to. She never had time during the last few months. Maya was a life unfinished that exists now only as pure data. A life that revolved around work and me.

It's too much for me. I do the one thing I didn't mean to do. I try to stop it, but I can't. I start to cry.

Dark does something unexpected. He gets up and goes to me. He pulls me into his arms and places them around me. The elegant artifice gone. The walls between us down. A human gesture in a society where you rarely touch anyone outside of your own. I sink into it, my head against his chest.

"Asha, it's going to be OK."

But that somehow just makes it worse. I try to pull away, to quickly compose myself, but he doesn't move.

"Don't," he whispers. "Just let it go."

So, I cry. His arms are comforting, all that is holding me up. The hollow inside me and the cold of the room recedes because of him. That feeling of being held. The clean smell of his clothes. The vaguely citrus and wood scent of him. The sound of his heart beating fills my head.

Then my brain kicks in. This is Dark. Darkness consumes everything.

I pull away. He slowly removes his arms, leaving just a hand holding mine. We stand there. Facing each other, silent. He is unmoving. His face lit by the flickering screen that casts shadows over it. Eyes bright.

Then Dark goes to the wall and bends down, removing two small drives from a port. He puts one on the table.

"Your data."

"What will you do with your copy?"

"I'll mine it for information on Zu Tech. Their security systems have proved ... problematic. I need information into how they work."

"I guess you always get a return on your investment."

"No. I don't. But insider information on Zu and Zu Tech is lucrative, so this is useful. People don't normally live to talk about him or his corporation."

I start to shiver, either from the cold or from his words.

"What does that mean?"

"Just a theory. You know it is possible, Asha, that just like you, your sister had her own secrets. Stay safe."

With a click, the door behind me swings open. I take the drive and go.

5

Maya's face is frozen in time. Exhausted. Circles under her brown eyes, long black hair tied up with a pen in her typical messy bun. The date stamp on the file is from a few months ago, April 13th. She looks directly into the camera, straight at me. My heart aches, my eyes start to well up, but I blink back the tears and keep watching the screen.

"OK, so vlogs are supposed to help deal with stress. Stress." She gives an awkward laugh. *"We're beta testing; there are some glitches, things that don't make sense. Everyone is on edge. I'm so tired now I keep forgetting things. I need a break, twenty-four hours of sleep. But – I can't have that, so maybe talking will help."*

Her eyes are bloodshot. Hand fidgeting with her bracelets, nails bitten.

"Maybe … saying the words out loud will make this easier." A sigh.

"I'm worried about Ash. I know now I didn't do the right thing making her move in with me. We don't connect. We fight all the time, and it's making this harder. I know she's keeping something from me, and I can't push her because I'm lying to her as well." A pause. A deep breath. *"If I'm right about what's happening, I'm going to have to find a way to protect her without her knowing why."* Maya looks directly at the camera. *"One of us has to survive."*

I hit pause. I search, but there are no more videos after that, just evidence of deleted entries. I recheck the dates. April 13th. Maya recorded this a week or so before I got the scholarship offer. The offer that would have taken me out of London to a summer school and then university, the offer she was so keen for me to take. She wanted me out of the way. Why? What was she trying to protect me from?

One of us has to survive. My stomach twists. Even if she had tried to tell me something, would I have listened? I had been too wrapped up in my own drama. I should have known something was wrong.

I shut the file down, remove the drive from my laptop and put it back on the chain I wear around my neck. An old habit; when you're not sure how long you might be in a place, you keep the things you value on you at all times. Or you keep them hidden. Scrunching up my eyes, I walk towards the window that overlooks the street. Watching the people outside move. Fingers playing with the chain of the necklace. I need to find out what Maya meant. The problem is, how?

I pour some coffee in the studio's tiny "cooking" area, consisting of a microwave, small sink, mini-fridge, and a drip coffee maker. It's been twenty-four hours since my encounter with Dark, and I am no nearer to finding answers. The phone log was a bust. The little social life Maya had before this seems to have stopped months ago, around the time she became obsessed with the new video game launch and I moved in. All her calls since then were either me, my school, food deliveries or work. The only one that stood out was the last number she called. *Unknown*, but when I cracked it, the info was for a pay-as-you-go phone, a burner with no name.

I glance at the larger files being decrypted on the desktop, all relating to a VR game, "SHACKLE", and the "special projects division". The symbol on one of the folders I'm trying to open for "special projects" looks strangely familiar. On a hunch, I flick through the pages of Maya's book on ancient myths. A black ouroboros, a snake eating its own tail – life, death and rebirth – great, some video game marketing executive being dramatic.

I start to pace. No leads on who wrote the note. No mention anywhere of any relationships. There are no casual "meet-ups" for coffee or lunch or after-work "drinks" in her calendar. Not that I expected any. Maya and I were always outsiders looking in, afraid to get too close to anyone. I go back to another screen and hit refresh on the search of the coroner's office server. Health Plus still hasn't uploaded Maya's autopsy result. So much for the private service being more efficient. The hospital report clearly said it was to be carried out on Monday morning. Even factoring in delays, it should be live by now.

As I stare at the blinking screen, I realize that at least I can do something about that.

***

Health Plus is in what was Westminster's public coroner's office. An old, red-bricked building hidden behind leafy green trees. It's also easy to break into because the dead, even those with private corporate health insurance, have little left to steal. During lunchtime, a white coat and a clipboard are all you need to wander past the few coroners, admin staff and porters who linger. I enter the building, and all I can think of is one thing. Maya is here. In the basement, near the servers. Lying in a drawer, looking like she did in that room. Soon I'm going to have to start making arrangements. Do the adult things I don't want to do, or she'll end up like our parents, buried in a mass grave. But right now, I can't – won't – think about that. I head towards the basement.

While the morgue itself has some security, the door to the server room has nothing but a Yale lock. I wait till the corridor is empty and the security guy has started into his lunchtime sandwich before jiggling the keyhole with a paper clip. The interior is the disorganized mess that shows its pre-privatization history of municipal council wiring. Layers of patches and wires where updates were made on top of and without stripping out old connections. Easy to hide a small bug inside. A generic-looking cable, undetectable in the old system. Unremarkable. Ironically, because they haven't updated their servers or networked them to the internet, supported their staff with secure VPN logins that I could then hack, this internal system was in some ways more secure. I needed to do this the old-fashioned way, in person. To inhale the cloying fumes of the industrial-strength cleaner that seeps throughout the building. To drift past the funeral directors and morgue workers. Death is always a busy business, even when you're "closed for lunch".

When I'm done planting my bug, I go to leave from an emergency side entrance where the alarm has been turned off to allow workers out for their breaks. I almost reach the door when I hear more voices in the corridor. Close. I lean back into one of the old door frames and wait for them to pass.

"I need to see her. It's very important. I can't come back later. Please? It must be now." A woman's voice, youngish. Her tone is pleading, but something about it sounds … off. A monotonous quality to it.

"As I said, we have rules." The other voice is bored, impatient. "Come back at two and make your request to my supervisor."

A slight pause then. "Is there no way I can see her now?"

The voice in the lab coat becomes louder. "As I said, unless you are family or the police, I can't let you—"

"I'm family. I'm her adopted sister."

"Name?"

"Asha, Asha Kennedy."

My breath stills.

"You got ID?"

"Yeah."

My instinct is to barrel out and confront this imposter. But then it hits me – I can't. I scrubbed my identity; all that is left is some ID cards back at the studio. I have nothing on me that would prove who I am, several items that will instead point to me being someone else. Currently "Heddy Lamarr", but now, hearing someone else use my real name, I want it back. Who is this woman?

Up ahead, I see a worker head towards the exit door, lighter in hand. I disappear further into the door frame. I hear the scratching of a pen on paper.

"I am sorry for your loss, Ms Kennedy. This all seems to be in order. Come this way." The footsteps are echoing away from me down the well-worn laminate corridor floor.

I go to follow and almost run into another figure. A burly security guard.

"Can I help you?"

Damn, damn, damn. I turn away, but the voice follows me.

"Miss?"

Crap. All the blood drains from my face. My heart starts to pound. I'm in the system already as being MIA from the social. If I turn up with a breaking and entering charge in a morgue, I won't see daylight.

I keep moving. Eyes down, I say, "Que? Onde é o banheiro?"

Sam at the takeaway taught me roughly six sentences of Portuguese; now seems like a good time to use them.

I keep moving away from the owner of the voice. Up ahead, there's an entrance that backs on to a loading bay. It has a keypad on one side, but I don't have enough time to bypass it.

The old security guard behind me starts to speed up.

"Miss. You can't be back here without an escort."

My hands start to get clammy. I think about bolting for it – but that would be a mistake. I need to play this out. His pace is uneven, his breath comes fast, he's unfit. I accelerate. I play dumb. Please let him underestimate me.

"Miss. Stop."

My hand reaches the chrome of the main exit door. It's a wide loading dock – big enough for trolleys. I push it, and it doesn't budge; the security guard is gaining on me. Then, a click and the door releases. An ambulance has pulled up outside. I slip out, and a man with a gurney runs through behind me, blocking the security guard.

The guard starts shouting, but I'm gone. I raise my hand in thanks as I leave. Manners cost nothing. "Tchau. Obrigada."

I exit. I don't stop moving until I am at the next intersection. Coat and clipboard discarded in a nearby bin. I pull on a beanie hat and lean against the alleyway's brick wall, hidden by the shadow. My heart is pounding. What if he suddenly decides to become efficient and checks the server room? Notices the bug, makes a report? I push out a long breath, willing my pulse to steady. He won't notice it. It's too small. I'm panicking over nothing. Too close, way too close. Breathe. I look back, hair and beanie now covering my face. The security guard comes as far as the door to look for me before a call on his walkie-talkie directs him elsewhere. I breathe out again and wait. I need to be careful. If I had been caught, I have no one to call.

Half an hour later, fake Asha Kennedy comes out, and I follow her. She heads up the street in the direction of the tube station. I recognize her as the elegant woman from the apartment surveillance footage the morning after Maya died. I pull the beanie down further and keep my eyes on the ground as I follow her through the air-filtered entrance. When the tube arrives, I take up one of the designated standing area inside the HEPA-filtered carriage. Right underneath the security camera, natural blind spot. She gets off at Oxford Circus, and I realize where she is headed before she arrives – Rathborne Place. The brightly lit tech building doesn't need a name outside it; everyone knows which company operates from there – Zu Tech. Fake Asha Kennedy works at the same company as Maya.

6

I watch her from the safety of the green area outside. She uses a swipe card and then a fingerprint scan to enter. What the hell is someone from Zu Tech doing pretending to be me to see my sister's body? Did the company send the guy who searched our apartment too? What are they looking for?

I scope out the security for the building. The guards, the biometric scanners inside, the security cameras. There's no way I can follow this woman in without an invite. Then the phone in my pocket starts to vibrate.

Need to meet.

The message is anonymous, but only one person has the number: Dark. As I stare at the text, another appears.

Now.

Followed a few seconds later by a new one.

Please.

The "please" is so unlike Dark that I wonder if it is someone else. I shrug and get back on the tube. How much weirder can this day get?

***

"You want me to walk away from this?" I'm staring at Dark in disbelief – and anger. We stand facing each other in his gentleman's club office beside some overstuffed chairs and a polished wooden desk with a laptop on it.

When he speaks, his voice is quiet. "I do, yes."

"I am not paranoid. There is something wrong here. I have to know what happened."

Dark's voice has an edge to it even though it's gentle. "Asha, it won't change the fact that she is gone. Maybe the past should stay in the past?" He looks up at me again. "Maya wanted you to be safe, right?"

I can't believe that he – of all people – is saying this to me. "How did that work out for you? Letting the 'past stay in the past'?" I take a breath. "You've seen the data we gathered, I assume. If she was involved in anything, it must be connected to her work. She didn't have a life outside of it."

Dark's hand runs through his hair in frustration. "Your sister's death had nothing to do with you. Isn't that enough?"

When I arrived here half an hour ago, Dark had shown me his findings from his deep dive into Maya's online interactions, personal and professional. There was nothing to indicate that our hacks had anything to do with her death. No demands for cash from companies or banks we'd once skimmed. No links between our associates then and Maya's work life. Her only life. Then I realize why he's so agitated. "You watched her video diary entry?"

Dark doesn't answer, and I know it's true.

"You shouldn't have looked at that," I whisper. "But if you did, you understand – I need to know what happened."

We stare at each other, arms folded. We had always argued, tried to score points against each other, competed – as Zu Tech class rival, and as best friends too. When Maya left the system, Dark was all I had. Both of us were alone. We looked out for each other. Had fun. Did things Maya would never have let me do. Stupid stuff like a non-official gaming tournament for cash at the old factory that led to an offer for me to join an eSports team. Something I declined in case Maya found out. Not that it amused Jones. The eSports manager running the Tower, among other things. "People don't normally say no to me," she'd said.

56

Dark was my only friend. I thought we could get through anything together. Jones's other sideline was finding information for her clients. Anything from someone's whereabouts to official secrets can be bought for a price. *"Information is power,"* Jones said. And she was a power broker. We drifted into doing some small hacking jobs for her and playing more VR to unwind online. We made a good team. I was the healer and Dark was a sniper intent on taking out everyone in the game. Then Jones made another offer – one linked to her lucrative information-sourcing side business.

Dark was in straight away. He was starting to build his reputation on the Dark Web; he was ambitious. But unlike Jones, Dark also had a cause. Determined to change things and this was his next step. Even though I loved what we did, I still had Maya, and part of Jones's deal meant going off-grid. There was no way to balance both worlds.

I thought that even if I passed on the offer, we'd still be close. We'd swapped our stories by then, the ones you don't share with outsiders. I knew about Dark's dad. About "Environ" – the company he had worked for that disposed of toxic e-waste after third-world countries stopped accepting it from the UK. About Dark's theory that they had killed his father.

The first big global pandemic was still a recent memory when the new one hit. Environ saw an opportunity. The inspectors had stopped. Protocols disappeared around the mercury, lead, cadmium and other waste they handled.

They said it was safe. Time passed, and people in the facility where Dark's dad was a manager started to get sick. Most of the workforce was diagnosed with the same rare, terminal cancer within a year. Then Environ disappeared overnight. No compensation, no questions, no follow-up. One day they were there. The next, the building was empty, the company wound up, and shareholders paid off. Dark was a kid looking after his dying father before he ended up in care.

His sole purpose after his dad died became about finding revenge. He knew that Environ had murdered his father. That they would never face consequences. That those with enough wealth could just get away with things. Environ shaped Dark.

When Jones sent Bill to us with her offer, Dark was ready.

I remember his excitement that day.

"We'll need to disappear," he had told me, eyes shining. "Leave everything and everyone behind. Fresh start, Asha. Us against the world, together. This is the beginning of something big, I know it."

And I knew in that moment that I couldn't do it. "I can't," I had said, thinking of Maya. Maya, who was working hard to get me out, to get us a life outside of the system. "I can't go with you."

Dark had said nothing. He left. Later I found out he had erased anything that connected us, including his history in the care system. I waited. I hoped. I told myself that in time, he'd reach out to me. I found out as much as I could about what he was doing. I waited some more. But I never heard from him after that, and it hurt. Dark became the rumours everyone talked about – he left Jones's operation after a year and set up his own, taking Bill with him. He went into the shadows. People started to say he was responsible for things I knew he would never do. A rival disappeared after a "disagreement". Another vanished, and then Dark took over his holdings. A few private banks collapsed overnight. He created an empire, one that didn't include me.

And now, here we are, again. Arguing. Like no time has passed.

"Fine," he says. "But don't do this alone."

I stand taller. "I am doing just fine by myself."

He gives a faint smile. "No, you're not." He takes a step closer. "Did you get the autopsy report?"

"Not yet." Hopefully, soon, if my bug on the server in the morgue comes good.

"You won't find anything, Asha."

"How do you know?"

"Because the autopsy report was never uploaded to the system. You can't hack what isn't there."

"How on earth would you know that?" Then a thought occurs to me. "Did you pull the file?"

Dark walks to one of the bookcases and pulls out an envelope. "No, I didn't. But when I saw it wasn't there, I called a source."

The envelope carries the crest of the public coroner and

then the details of the body underneath. Maya's details. Typed up, impersonal, black and white. Factual. I can't take my eyes from it. The world around me is slipping away.

"Sit."

I comply without thinking, but my eyes don't leave the envelope. Dark takes a seat opposite me.

"How did you…?"

"The file was never put on the system, Asha. There were two copies. One which the technician was supposed to log but which was 'lost'. One a copy the examiner kept in his office. The one I acquired."

"I see."

Dark runs his hands through his hair in frustration. "No. No, you don't see. You're out of your depth, Asha. This isn't an illegal tournament for cash or some private bank hack like we used to do." He studies the table for a moment. When he speaks again, the tone is different, soft. "I don't think you realize what you're up against. And you're trying to do it on your own. No protection."

He's an idiot. That part, I already know.

"Don't pretend to care." I try to be flippant. As if I don't give a damn, but instead, the words come out laced with bitterness.

"I care."

Something about the way he says it, the low tone, the way the words float across the table and stay hanging in the air between us, snaps something inside me. The emotions light me up. Forcing me to feel, to become present. To touch that

60

sharp knife-edge of grief again and open up the deep anger that lives alongside it. Answer a question with a question.

"Why did you acquire the file?"

"I had a hunch I needed to follow. Also, I knew it was something you'd want."

"What's the price?"

"What?"

"You heard."

"We're negotiating?"

"Yes."

He leans forward. "Work with me. Like we used to. Here."

"No."

"Then I keep the file."

"Not happening. But I'll offer you a trade, this for something in return. You want information on Zu Tech's security systems. That was why you went looking, wasn't it? Well, I can help you with that intel."

Dark stares at me. "You aren't in a place where you're thinking straight, Ash. No one can hack past their security. Not me. Not you."

"I have a plan. But to be clear, we're not working together. This is a deal and when it's done, we're done too."

Dark sits in a chair, looking at me, expressionless. Then he pushes the file towards me. "Fine. Tell me what you need."

***

Dark's interest in Zu Tech puzzles me. I'm back in my studio now, hands wrapped around another cup of coffee. Dark always has a reason, but I can't see what this one is.

I sigh and open the coroner's report again. It includes the interim death certificates and the unsigned mortuary release form for relatives. The official cause of death is stark: respiratory failure. Maya stopped breathing. How?

No sign of distress, infection, or disease. No signs of trauma. Her respiratory system shut down. The only other notes are about the levels of natural chemicals in her brain. Her dopamine, serotonin and oxytocin levels were off the chart when she died.

I scan the file and upload it to my drive. There is another way to find answers. I take a deep breath. It's time to pull on the one thread I have left.

7

Like most prominent companies, Zu Tech has departments that deal with all of life's eventualities. Including a subdivision in HR for bereavements.

I scan their website. This morning there's a press junket for their new VR tournament. They always hold it at their headquarters. Zu Tech is everywhere in society: in schools, virtual shopping malls, and workplaces, but nothing quite captures the public's imagination as the place where it all began. Zu Gaming. Immersive, next-level metaverse play. It's what made Zu a modern icon. Any tournament announcement from that division will attract people and some degree of chaos. Even a planned PR junket will naturally stretch security on the ground, creating opportunity.

I call as soon as their lines open. "Miss Kennedy. We've been trying to reach you," says the woman in HR. "We're so sorry for your loss. Maya was loved by the Zu Tech family."

Her voice is warm, but the words are scripted.

"I'd like to come in and collect my sister's stuff," I say. "Today, if possible."

"Today isn't convenient, I'm afraid." Her voice is still kind but firm. "Could you do tomorrow?"

"No." My voice matches hers. "It has to be today, at eleven. I'm leaving the city."

A pause. "Could you hold for just one moment?"

Corporate music plays, and then she's back. "We would be happy to welcome you at eleven today," she says. "You'll need photo ID and a valid vaccination certificate."

I let out a sigh of relief and glance at the foil container from Sam's takeaway wrapped in gaffer tape that contains my old IDs.

"That will be fine. Thank you. I can't wait to see where Maya worked." I wait for a beat, then say, "Maya loved the *special projects* she worked on at Zu."

There is a pause followed by: "So sorry again for your loss, Miss Kennedy."

An email later from HR confirms the time. According to the email, *Zu cares about all his staff, even those who leave.* Like death was an option Maya would willingly choose.

I head out to pull together a "respectable" charity shop outfit, a plain vintage navy skirt and a jumper. Then I get ready. I have one shot at this.

At ten fifty-five a.m., I walk past the giant outdoor posters and projections and towards the entrance to Zu Tech. I've seen these junkets before when I was a young Zu Tech hopeful. There is already a crowd of people outside being kept back by barriers. I move behind a group of press reporters to avoid being caught on camera.

A deep voice comes from my left side. "You here to cover the tournament launch?"

I spin around to see a man in a dark suit, wearing an earpiece.

"No!" I shout back above the noise.

His voice becomes irritated. "Then you need to get behind the other barrier. That's where all the photo ops will be."

"I have a meeting."

"Name?"

I give it as the crowd of people grows around us.

"Wait here. Don't move, miss."

He speaks into his coat sleeve. A string of blacked-out cars starts to arrive. Then the screaming begins – a wave of additional noise and a surge of movement – and I find myself swept a few feet away. Maybe this was a mistake. There are so many people.

"Watch it."

Another rush, and I'm closer to the red-carpet arrivals, swept along in the crowd. I can smell the dampness on their clothes from an earlier rain shower and the overwhelming aroma of perfume and aftershave. The first of the car doors swing open, and a middle-aged YouTuber I recognize gets out, styled head to toe in his own merch. Teeth gleaming an artificial white, hair immaculately styled to look messy, make-up tastefully applied. A younger blonde partner follows a few steps behind, wearing a T-shirt with her channel name. "Helloooooooo, London," he roars in a Texan accent.

The crowd screams as they slam against the barriers for autographs and photo ops. The guy works the crowd like a pro. No hint of nerves as he grins and waves, using his security to take photos for his fans and to hand out pre-signed autographed postcards. An efficient stage manager dressed in black with a clipboard and an earpiece hovers nearby, timing the interactions, moving the entourage along at a steady pace, making sure certain distances are maintained. Carefully prepared sound bites are given to everyone with a recording device.

"I'm excited to be here to hear all the details on the new Zu Tech tournament and, of course, that top secret game we've all been hearing so much about, which will be using new, cutting-edge technology! Everything Zu Tech does is very special."

"That's right. Our live stream will take you behind the scenes at this event. And we will have an exclusive on how gamers can apply online to win a place in the tournament!"

Three more cars appear. I've lost sight of the security

guard completely now. With no other choice, I now have a front-row seat at the Zu PR circus.

The next car holds two British YouTubers. I vaguely recognize these ones. Mates, covered in tattoos, wearing rap gear and talking in hard street accents – amusing, given they are peers with hereditary titles who first met at Oxford. Boys borrowing some working-class street cred till they move on to their inheritances. They work through the crowd faster than car one.

Car three's occupants are the lesser mortals, at least as far as the crowd is concerned. The ones the PR and marketing team have included for diversity. It holds players I recognize. Also programmers, engineers and developers. There are a few girls in this mix, minorities, some younger faces. The entourage that follows is smaller. I glimpse someone tall, ducking their head to avoid the cameras – could it be Jones? But if it is, she moves too fast for me to be sure. After they enter, the crowd starts to thin out slightly.

Then a fourth car turns up – the tail end of the celebrity hierarchy. The ones sometimes admitted as a favour by the PR team to the management company. The crowd shifts, and I take the opportunity.

A press photographer, part of a group who were crouched down to get better shots, stands up suddenly to adjust his angle just as I turn, and he manages to whack me in the face with his long camera lens. I stumble backwards, my hand on my cheek as he starts to shout something about damaging his equipment. There are too many people around. I can't breathe. I'm pushed back: falling, no longer in control. I'm reacting in a losing battle against a sea of faces and body parts, things that all push me the wrong way as I stumble against them. I try to stop and get caught up in the low red rope. With a bang, I hit the pavement, and my face starts to throb, right on the edge of the temporary red-carpet entrance to Zu Tech. A camera person moves to change position, and I see their foot bearing down on me. I go to roll away from it, but there's no space.

"Hey, watch it. Look down."

The foot changes direction. A hand reaches down in front of me. "You OK?" The voice is worried, with a slight accent, somehow cutting through the sounds around me.

I squint, and it takes a second for the sun to move so I can see the owner of the hand. Tall, brown eyes hidden under a baseball cap, brown/blonde hair falling over one side of his face. There's some sort of tattoo on his tanned hand, half-visible under his shirt sleeve. He squats down, so he's at my eye level.

"Can you stand up, or do I need to carry you?"

"I can stand." I say the words, but honestly, I'm not sure I can, and that feeling hits me harder than the fall. I need help. The stranger doesn't move or listen to me as I start to ramble again about how I am "fine". Instead, he helps me up. I'm leaning too heavily; the world seems to be moving. I fall against his chest. Breaking all the norms there are about personal space. This just keeps going from bad to worse. The smell of his T-shirt hits me – coffee and cinnamon.

"We need to get you inside so you can sit, get some ice."

"I'm fine." I repeat the words again, but even I know they're just not convincing.

He looks down. His hands and arms are around me, holding me up. "Those marks on my T-shirt. That isn't my blood."

I follow his gaze and see red drops on his white T-shirt. "Oh."

He doesn't pull away from me. Instead, he just says, "This way."

The crowd parts for him as cameras start to click around us. He maintains the same pace. He helps me inside and then towards one of the chairs in the lobby, which I sink into.

"Carlo, ice," he says to someone I can't see behind us.

I glance back to see a man in his mid-thirties, wearing a suit. Slick, expensively groomed, mobile phone in hand. Unimpressed. "You blew that entrance. You were supposed to do a Q&A. At least allow the cameras to get some good shots. That was the whole point."

"Ice?"

The man shrugs his shoulders and walks towards the reception desk just as the security guy from before enters. "You all right, miss? I told you to stay put."

I make a face. "Yeah."

The guard turns towards the boy whose shirt I have now destroyed with red streaks. "Sorry. We have this, sir."

Carlo arrives back with an ice pack and some water, catching the last part of the guard's sentence. "Thank God." He gives the ice to the security guard as his mobile starts to ring again.

The boy doesn't move. "You're sure you're OK?"

"Yeah." I can feel my face turning red under his stare, the awkwardness of the situation hitting home. This never happens to me. And I bleed on him? Great. "I'm sorry about your shirt." There is a pause, and then I find myself adding: "I'm not normally like this." Why? Why did I feel the need to fill in the silence?

He shrugs and gives a half-smile, eyes still looking straight at me as he makes a joke. "Anything for my fans."

I finally place the face. Augie Santos. nineteen-year-old European eSports superstar. The guy who was supposed to be the next big thing two years ago when he turned pro but then, nothing. I take the ice pack from the guard and hide part of my face behind it, relishing the instant numbness it brings. "I'm not your fan. I mean, that's not why I'm here." I flush again. "But thank you for your help," I finish primly like some heroine in a book from another era. He raises his eyebrows slightly. The smile doesn't leave his eyes.

Carlo finishes his call and circles back. "We need to go inside."

Augie gives him a look. "Are you here for the launch?"

"No."

He glances at my respectable charity outfit. "Job interview? If you are, I'm sure you'll get it."

"Santos." It's Carlo. "Let's get going."

Augie lets out a sigh and gives me a wry grin. "See you."

I watch him walk away while I sink into the chair. When he reaches the entrance to the press conference room across the hall, he stops. He looks back and catches me staring at him. He raises a hand to say goodbye. I look away quickly and try to pretend I wasn't just staring after him.

8

The lobby empties as the press and the last gamer stragglers are herded inside. I look around. So this is where Maya came every day. I try to imagine her walking in through the doors. She'd know all the security guys by name – Maya was the sort of person who would say hi to everyone. The wall behind the reception has the teaser trailer for Zu's next game: a black screen with the launch date on it, July 10th. No other info. Zu Tech is known for suppressing all information ahead of a big new games launch.

My eyes drift up. Logos for the company are projected on every floor. The sound of phones ringing, video requests coming through, voices murmuring. A hologram countdown clock for the new game's release is on the opposite wall. Eight weeks. I shift a little on the leather couch. I start counting the entrances and exits, the security cameras, old habits to try and calm my nerves.

A woman in her early forties eventually appears on the other side of security, holding a small device that she closes when she locks eyes with me. She wears an immaculately tailored shirt, skinny trousers, heels. Expensive but discreet jewellery. Earpiece in one ear. Not a HR person. This is something else: executive. The way the receptionists sit up straighter confirms it.

"Asha Kennedy?" The voice is neutral, polished. Impossible to read.

"Yes."

"My name is Emily, Emily Webber. I understand you were hurt out there – I do apologize. Tournament launches can be intense. Can I call a doctor for you?"

"It's fine, just a slight bump."

Emily Webber. Chief Operations Officer R&D, vice president of … something. Why would someone like her be meeting me? I swallow. Coming into Zu Tech under my own name had been provocative – and it looked like my suspicions that Maya was frightened because of something at work were correct. Why else would they be bringing in the big guns for a nobody like me?

Emily continues. "I'm so sorry for your loss, Asha. Zu would like to see you. Personally."

A ripple passes among the lobby people. There is a quick stare from those around me, particularly the security guard, like everyone's suddenly wondering if I am someone they should know.

Unexpected. For a moment, I feel light-headed.

Zu is a tech genius, a recluse. Someone who only appears in public when the company launches a new "game changer" device or hosts a tournament. Even then, people only see him from a distance. It's carefully choreographed. The lone figure beside some mind-bending tech on an empty stage. Zu is this century's tech guru. A world prophet. What he says affects the stock market. Why on earth would someone like that want or need to see me? My heart starts to pound as my stomach twists.

"Sorry," I say. "I think I misheard you."

Emily gestures for me to follow her and begins walking. "No. You didn't." She leads me to a security desk. "Just a few formalities."

A scan of my face is taken while another security guard studies and copies both my photo IDs. A non-disclosure agreement is placed in front of me to cover any conversations we might have.

"You can leave your phone here."

I look at her. "Is that necessary?"

"Yes. No recording devices are allowed in his office. Zu rarely sees visitors. I'm sure you understand."

I don't, but I have no choice.

Emily leads us to a small private lift. As we cross the main corridor the walls are clear glass, revealing the open-plan offices behind. Zu Tech's London headquarters are vast. Through the glass, I can see more countdown projections on the interior walls. A snack station, breakout rooms with beanbags, small hot desk spaces filled with people on laptops. Some hologram teasers for the game play out as we pass. *Coming soon … the evolution of gaming…* Logline projections followed by monsters with swords that vanish after a few steps. Emily, for the most part, ignores them. Quotes from Zu are also scattered everywhere. On the glass, as decals on the walls that break up departments:

We are the question. Technology is the answer.

All great gains in civilisation come at a cost. One either we pay or the next generation will.

We reach the glass atrium in the centre of the building. The area is flooded with light, and we pause at a small lift marked as *private access*. Emily uses her fingerprint to activate it. While we wait, I look up to see Zu's face on a banner hanging from one of the top floors above me. A black-and-white portrait. Iconic. Intimidating. I look away.

Inside the glass lift, there are no buttons. The doors close as soon as I step through, and it starts to ascend.

Emily tells me the rules as we pass upwards through the upper floors. Polished, practised, slick. "Zu is a genius, and like many of the greats, he has certain habits – quirks, shall we say. Do not make eye contact, he doesn't like it. His suite is dimly lit and minimally designed for optimal workflow. He believes in a clear work and mind space. Safety is also a big concern. This elevator, for example, is also a scanner to ensure no hidden devices are brought in and that the guest is free from illness or contagious viruses." She smiles. "You have none."

"How does that work?" I ask, curiosity finally getting the better of me.

Emily waves a hand. "Heat scan, body temp calculator, analysis of air particles plus a small micro-spray of disinfectant to kill airborne bacteria. If anything were ever to be detected, the elevator would stop, flash red and start to descend to the basement for decontamination and isolation."

I stare at her.

"Flu season is never far off; we can't take risks. You signed permission for this in your NDA."

"Right. And you have this in all your lifts?"

"No, just this one. But the rest of the building has standard virus detection filtration and HEPA filters. We do take safety seriously at Zu Tech."

I digest the information as we glide past a few more floors while Emily checks something on her device. "Meetings with Zu are limited to short information bursts," Emily says. "Probably, he will only interact with you for a few minutes. This is not rude, he's just busy. I'm sure you understand?"

"Is this ... usual? For Zu to meet with the relatives of a former employee?"

She hesitates for a fraction of a second. "No," she says.

"It isn't. Zu usually leaves that to the HR team. They are fully trained to offer support for such things. But, as Maya told you, she was in *special projects*, involved in new research and game design. She got to spend one-on-one time with Zu. SHACKLE is something he is overseeing personally. He has felt her loss." She clears her throat. "Did she ever tell you about what she was working on?"

"No." In fact, Maya had never even told me she'd met Zu. Then again, how much had I really known about my sister since she'd left the system? How much had I bothered to find out?

Emily nods slowly. "You mentioned that Maya had enjoyed working on *special projects* on your call."

I glance at her and swallow. "Did I?" Always answer a question with a question — that was how Dark did it.

Emily nods again. "Yes. All calls are monitored."

A shiver rolls down my spine, but before I need to answer, we arrive.

The doors slide open on to the top floor of the building. Giant tinted floor-to-ceiling windows show a darkened version of the world outside. The floor is a cold black marble. It reminds me of a gloomy empty cave, an expensive one. Emily makes a gesture. "Go ahead."

I stop. "Aren't you coming?"

"No. Once the meeting is over, I'll be here to escort you out."

Not creepy, not creepy at all. I take the ice pack from my face and hand it to her as I step outside. She accepts it.

Discreetly holding it between her two fingers and away from her like it's contagious.

"Where is his office?" I ask.

"This floor is his office. Just keep walking, and he'll find you when he wants to."

The doors slide shut. There is silence in the space. Empty, a world away from the floors below, and cold. Zu must have the same views on heating as Dark.

That is when it hits me, the feeling of dread. The instinct that I should run back towards the elevator. Something here is wrong. I feel it in my gut, but with no logical evidence, I push that feeling down and move forward. I start to walk, eyes adjusting to the inky gloom. I see a few paintings on the walls. The kind of pictures that look like they should be in a museum behind layers of protective glass.

As I move further inside, I see various small plinths scattered across the space. On top of each is an iconic piece of hardware or a retro games console – a museum display of modern tech. I draw closer and examine them. At any other time, I would have been fascinated, but the feeling of anxiety doesn't lift. The knowledge of being watched by cameras dotted around the ceiling. Eventually, I stop by another installation, hand hovering over the display. My fingers are itching to touch it to see if it starts. It looks like...

"Don't touch that." The tone is surprisingly flat, devoid of emotion.

My fingers withdraw, and I turn to see a man everyone recognizes despite his reclusive nature. Tall, white, in his late forties. Zu Thorp, the founder of Zu Tech, wearing his trademark black jumper, dark blue jeans, and white sneakers. Polished.

"It's an Apple 1, right?"

He gives a quick, economical nod of his head. "1976."

I stare at him, and he stares back. Both of us assess each other.

"It's dark here."

"I get headaches. The dim light helps." He seems to look almost through me, beyond me. "Asha. I wanted to meet you. To see if you were like your sister. You are, you know — same patterns, same DNA. Your brainwaves. I am sorry about her death." He steps closer.

"Did you know Maya well?"

Zu stares at me. He lightly touches his forehead. "Does it hurt?"

I swallow. "What?"

"Your face. No damage to your brain?"

Is this guy for real? Maybe he's worried I'm going to sue him or something. "No. No brain damage I am aware of."

He walks past me towards one of the dim windows and its view of London below. "Yes," he says quietly. "So many emotions. Always difficult to process those."

Time to get this back on track. "Emily said Maya did some research for you — *special projects*, wasn't it?"

"Walk with me." It's an order, not a question. "I find it easier to talk when we move. Her work was invaluable. Maya might not have seemed it, but she was crucial to our success. It's regrettable what happened. We had so much more to achieve. She left us at the wrong time."

The flat tone provokes me. I can almost hear my heart starting to beat faster, the blood rushing to my head. Anger. "Maya didn't *leave*. She died."

Zu considers me. His eyes are emotionless, empty. We continue walking further and further into his dark cave, at a distance from one another, him matching my pace. The adrenaline in my system is pumping too fast. It wants me to run.

Zu eventually speaks again. "You could continue Maya's work. Genetically you probably have the same traits. We could test you."

"My traits? Don't you need someone more qualified?"

"Maya had a unique skill set. You are younger, of course, but you share the same basic patterns." His eyes seem to go far away for a moment, struggling to recall something. "I remember – we wrote a reference for Maya to prove that she could be your guardian. You were both part of our outreach coding schools. Yes?"

How does he know that? "Yes, we both were."

"It was such a successful programme. It gave us people like Maya. Hopefully, you will also work for us in the future?"

Answer a question with a question. "Can you tell me more about…?"

Zu nods. "What she did for us. Maya started in beta testing. Then she moved on to new project material and

80

game design. We are sorry she left." Again, that curious, blank stare. "You are different to her — but maybe… We should stay in touch, Asha. You are more like your sister than you realize. I felt it important we meet. Little things matter. I wanted you to know that her work will live on. In the end, that is all humans can achieve. We will be in contact — to show you the work she was doing."

"That's it?"

"Maya's contribution was valuable. Not many get to say that about the work they do. You should be proud of her. You will also need more ice on your cheek." He starts to walk away from me and raises his voice ever so slightly. "Emily, show our guest out."

Zu turns away from me and moves towards the opposite end of the building. He is gone in the shadows in an instant. I'm alone in the dim space. The silence tightens around me. I turn around, and the elevator at the back of the vast room swishes open, giving me a beacon of light. Emily is standing inside with a fresh ice pack.

It's not until the doors close and the warmth of the daylight on the glass hits me that I realize that my heart is still thumping out of control.

"What was he like?" Emily asks in a quiet voice as she hands me the fresh ice pack.

There's something chilling about the way she says it. "What do you mean?"

"He can appear to be different to other people."

"Preoccupied, I guess."

Emily shivers. "The tournament launch is time-consuming. Do you know why he wanted to see you?"

I shake my head. She seems almost as disturbed as I am. But by the time we reach the ground floor, her equilibrium is restored. Her smartphone and screen rejoin us. "This way." We enter a small room with a meeting table and some chairs. A slim stack of documents is on the table.

A tall man clutching a large box labelled "Maya Kennedy" follows us in. Sticking out from a corner of it is something pink, fluffy. With a shock, I recognize it: the pink pom–pom monster I had to make in school. I'd binned it years ago. Typical. I blink to stop my eyes from filling with tears.

We'd been told to make a gift for our parents. Despite that, I had been enjoying it. I'd been pretending. Imagining what it might be like to take the gift home – back to a real home, have a mum or dad say "well done you" or "I love it." To have that feeling of warmth and security.

A stupid daydream that crashed when some well-meaning school assistant said, "Are you giving yours to someone special in the care home?" Then the stares and the whispers of the other kids hit. The slow click in their minds that this must be why my parents never came to school, why I never invited anyone to mine to play. My secret was out. I binned the pom–pom monster as soon as I got back that afternoon. If I could, I would have burnt it. Maya must have seen and rescued it from the bin.

I force the emotions away.

Emily stands at the top of the table. She assumes control. "Can I get you anything? Coffee, tea, water?"

"Water."

"Of course. Sebastian?"

The tall man places two chilled water bottles before us and then leaves.

Emily sits at the table. "Maya was such a strong person. She was family to us. We feel and share your pain, Asha."

Her tone is emotionless, and I wonder if Emily ever met Maya in her life.

"As you know, you signed an NDA before you met with Zu. Those terms will extend to this chat."

"I was hoping to see some of Maya's colleagues," I say.

Emily shakes her head. "Oh no — not so close to launch. Morale is low as it stands since Maya left us. We should keep this between ourselves."

"And what exactly is 'this'?"

Emily slides a cheque face down across the table. "Maya had health and employee insurance, enough to help … ease you through the transition, I imagine."

I turn the cheque over and stare at the amount. Enough. More than enough. I could start a new life away from London. More than any other insurance pay-out I have ever heard of. It's life-changing money. Enough to buy a real place, put down roots, do the things Maya only dreamt of.

I take a moment and just stare at the number. She always said never to look back, that "there is nothing interesting behind us". But our childhood in care taught us a few things. Like the fact that nothing comes for free. I sigh.

"What's the catch?"

"None. You just need to sign some forms."

There's a moment where I think about it. Tempting. But then Emily doesn't meet my gaze. I'm probably going to regret this, but I reluctantly put the cheque back on the table.

"I'm not signing anything today. I'll take the forms with me and get back to you."

Emily looks disappointed. This is not the reaction she was expecting. "No one is trying to do anything wrong here, Asha. We are just trying to help. I know a little bit about your situation."

I stare at her, reading the expression. The empathy in her face that doesn't reach her eyes. She's going to threaten me. I can feel it.

This next part will hurt me far more than it hurts Emily.

I take a deep breath and stand. And then I hug Emily Webber. She freezes in horror. My arms wrap around her immaculate silk blouse. My lungs almost choke on the heavy scent of her expensive perfume. It's probably the first time I have volunteered to touch someone in years. I search for the words. "Thank you, Emily, for being so kind."

Emily remains frozen for a millisecond. Then she can't move fast enough. "What are you doing?" She extricates herself, standing so quickly that her papers, devices, security card, and water all end up on the floor.

I go to help collect the items she dropped while she

moves to the hand gel and sanitizers on the small side table.

"I'm sorry," I say. "You were being so understanding. It's been so hard…"

I continue picking things up from the floor. I put the cheque, phone and screen on the desk.

Emily is not amused; she is blitzing herself with anti-bacterial spray while keeping her distance from me.

"We have a social distancing policy at Zu. We believe in respecting personal space. In announcing our intentions before initiating physical contact." Her anger is starting to show; her voice is getting higher. "It was in the forms you signed."

I grab a tissue from the box and put it near my eyes. "I'm so sorry."

Emily regains her composure with three small breaths. She forces a tight smile. "I think you should sign the papers, take the cheque and go. A fresh start, Asha. It's what Maya would have wanted for you. Unless perhaps there is some service that could help you…"

There it is. The threat. Didn't take long.

"Can't I take the papers and my sister's stuff, read them, and get back to you?"

Emily's face changes then. "Take the paperwork if you want, but you can't remove your sister's effects from here till the documents have been signed. It's procedure."

My eyes, however, are on the pink monster. "Those things belonged to my sister, not the company."

Emily brushes away an imaginary piece of fluff from

her trousers. "When you're ready, Sebastian will have the box waiting for you at the reception desk. Your cheque will be clear for you to cash once you hand over any company equipment Maya may have used for working at home. We take our investment in our IP seriously. She is listed as working on SHACKLE, and using a company laptop. You will need to return it, Asha. It's an extremely generous offer and, frankly, you should be thankful." There is an awkward silence as I hold in the words I'd like to shout at Emily about "being thankful". Emily ignores the tension and rubs some more alcohol gel into her hands. Then she sprays some of her items with a gentle dusting of disinfectant — my signal to leave.

"I should go," I say.

She holds the door open for me. When we reach the lobby, she signs me out.

"Thank you," I say meekly.

"Goodbye," she says crisply. "Oh, and Asha?"

I stop.

"Don't wait too long, will you?" Definite threat.

I keep the meek, worried look on my face till I leave the green space outside the building, clutching the papers Emily gave me in my hand.

It doesn't take long for my phone to vibrate. A text from Dark: *Everything set?*

I turn the corner and reply. *Activate it now. I'm on my way to you.* Send.

I walk, head down. I power off the phone and take the SIM out. Then I toss both into a passing street sweeper. I can't risk using that phone any more, not after it was out of my sight for so long.

I keep moving, hair falling in front of my face to hide a slow half-smile as I remember Emily's horror at being hugged by me. I used that distraction to plant the microfilm worm on her tablet. My instincts were right. Something is off about Zu Tech. And now, thanks to Emily, I have a way to hack in and find out what.

***

"I'll need another favour."

Dark sighs. "What is it this time?" He's still staring at the bruise on my cheek from when I fell.

"Legal. They offered me cash to walk away but on condition that I sign these."

I drop the papers on to the bar in Dark's lair before taking a seat and pouring some milk into my coffee.

Dark closes the two smart tablets in front of him. He's triggered the worm on Emily's device. Everything Emily gets now sends a copy to both clones.

"You know you could."

"Could what?" Part of me is buzzing from the thrill of planting the worm. So much so that I'm not focusing on his tone.

"Could allow yourself to grieve, Asha, to process what happened, before starting anything."

I stare at him. I hugged someone to get this. "You can't

be serious?"

"Asha…"

I'm standing up now. "When people die of natural causes, strangers don't come and search your apartment. They don't pretend to be you at the morgue. Autopsy reports don't go missing. Reclusive tech billionaires don't meet with you." My voice starts to rise, but I am so annoyed now I can't stop. "Companies don't offer you vast sums of cash to walk away. I am not imagining this; something is wrong here. The only lead I have is the place where Maya worked. I can't wait." I take a breath. "She wouldn't leave me, Dark. And I won't leave her."

His hand rests on my arm as he looks at me. There's something in his eyes that I can't read. "I know. I just … I don't want to see you hurt. I…" He stops and changes his mind about what he was going to say next. He takes the papers. "I'll get my lawyer to look at these. But don't disappear, Asha. It's not safe to be alone around these people. Stay in touch and the first sign of trouble, text me. And remember, even with the worm, we are still on the outside looking in. I'm not sure how much we will find." He hands me one of the clone devices and a small black mobile he takes from behind the bar. "My number is on this."

When I leave, it's late afternoon. My cheek stings in the fresh air as I walk. My next step is to track down the woman who impersonated me at the morgue. Emily will have HR emails on her device. It's a tech company. There can't be that many women there. Maya always said there were just a few of them in her division.

It doesn't make any sense. Why send someone to the morgue? I'm missing something.

I cut across Leicester Square and spot the Zu Tech logo and the tournament launch clips playing on e-news feeds and inside various stores.

In Trafalgar, I stare at the old lion statues, the office buildings, and the vertical city farms. The smell of hydroponic crops fills the air as shoppers come in and out with baskets of freshly cut farm vegetables, the latest innovation to fight climate change. The mix of tourists, workers, and Londoners. An excited school group passes by me on their way into the virtual section of the National Gallery. Another of the Zu Tech innovations. The company logo is above the entrance.

He is everywhere.

I take a breath and let it hit me then. London. The place where Zu Tech, the future in all its cutting-edge glory and the ghosts of the past, the ancient buildings, the streets, the public squares that have seen it all, sit side by side in an uneasy coexistence. I get lost for a moment watching it, remembering Maya and me here as kids.

Then I spot my reflection in a bus shelter. I need a shower and a change of clothes. I still have blood on me and a faint aroma of Emily's perfume that is making my stomach turn. I walk towards Embankment and then across to South Bank, watching as the sunlight glints on the water under the bridge. That feeling of being alone as the crowds rush past and the city and the river stretches out and wraps itself around me. Of being part of London somehow.

On the other side of the bridge, the smell of food hits me. I feel hungry. I grab something from one of the take-outs and head back to the apartment.

I access the building through the back stairs as usual to avoid the main cameras. I pause just outside my studio door. My stomach tightens in a way that has nothing to do with food. There is a tiny gap between the door and its frame.

The door is unlocked.

9

No sound comes from inside the studio flat. The hallway is empty. Nothing helpful nearby, not even a fire extinguisher I could use as a weapon. I think about running, but then I remember Maya's stuff is inside. It's all I have left of her. Damn it. I listen again. Silence. I put the food on the floor. Then I push the door open just enough to see inside.

The tiny space is trashed. The images I printed out and stuck to the wall are on the ground. The corkboard I had covered with pictures, words, questions, pins and string is smashed in two. Some of the papers are torn, others floating across the floor on a breeze from the open windows that I know were shut when I left. My rucksack has been upended, lining ripped and destroyed. The Faraday cage lies empty on the floor. The contents – Maya's fitness bracelet, phone, and laptop – are all gone.

I check the rest of the room. My clean laptop is missing too. I hunt through the debris. My shoe hits something that rolls across the floor. Maya's snow globe with the picture of us inside. I pick it up gently. There's a crack on the top and a film of water on the outside. I lean against the front door, shutting it, and fear hits me in waves. I am numb, unable to move. Stuck.

This was my safe space. No one, not even Dark, knew where I was. My brain tries to figure out where I went wrong. The payments were untraceable. I had re-angled the security cameras. I had used cleantech. I had been careful every time I left the building. How had someone found me?

I hold on to the leaking snow globe. The carefully built walls I had erected around myself are crumbling. All the pain I have been holding off hits. I can't be an adult right now. I need Maya to tell me what to do next. I want to be in our home, letting her do the "big sister" thing. Curling up beside her. Sipping a hot chocolate, telling her everything even though I know she'll be mad. Mixed with that hurt is anger – anger at her. She should be here. And I'm mad at myself, too, for feeling that. Because I know she would never have left if there was a choice. She always found a way for us to stay together after our parents died. Whenever we were shuffled from one care home to another, she was the one who made sure we didn't get separated. Now I'm alone, and she isn't coming back.

My fingers trace the crack in the plastic. A jagged piece cuts my skin, causing a drop of blood to flow down the globe.

I wipe the tears from my face with my fingers. I need to pull myself together. Maya would tell me to survive, to get somewhere safe and make a plan. That's what I need to do. I can't stay here.

In the kitchen, there's a drawer with cleaning materials. I place some cling film around the snow globe and then take out a large black bin bag. Exactly like the ones I used as a kid when we had to move. I double bag one and pack what I can. I keep trying to stop the panic from rising as my stomach twists. My ears listen for every sound from the corridor outside. A few minutes later, I pull the studio door closed, locking it behind me.

The fire exit leads into the main lobby. I pretend to read the noticeboard there through my black shades till I see a crowd of people leaving the building. I exit with them, head down, blending into the crowd, clutching my black bag like I'm on my way to the communal bins – nothing to see here. I head to the nearest tube station, past the body temp scanners and the cool invisible gust of air that marks the start of the HEPA filtration. I stick to routes that go deep under the city, the wifi black spots that they can't fix. Keep to the shadows, avoiding the CCTV cameras, hat pulled down. Invisible.

I take multiple lines on the tube, crossing and circling back several times before the ideas in my mind become more than floating fragments. They become a plan.

I run the potential consequences and the possibilities again. Then I exit at Charing Cross. I pick up a different jacket, bag, and hat on the way. From the station, I take a train to Blackheath and exit again. Conscious of every person who walks just a little too close behind me or follows for too long in the same direction.

It's twilight now in the picturesque green space. Underneath is a mass grave from the Black Death. This is where the bodies are buried. Around fifty thousand of them. Beside the heath, a bell tower rises to the sky, attached to the church of All Saints. One of the few to survive the downturn in religion – because of its lucrative tenant, Jones.

The bell tower is the centre of Ma Jones's network. Its height hides a multitude of antennae that she uses. The people coming in and out to buy information and trade secrets pretend they are there to pray. The church of All Saints is always open now. Ma Jones runs a twenty-four-hour business and has her finger in every digital pie there is. Some – like her eSports management company and the teams she puts into high-profile competitions – operate in the light. Others underground, underneath the tower. Her only rule – no unannounced visitors.

Minutes pass as I stand at the small oak entrance door to the bell tower. I try to think positive thoughts, but nothing happens. I stare at the endless darkening sky above. The air is cold, despite it being summer. I wonder if this is possibly the worst idea I have ever had, but there is no plan B. After five minutes, just as I start to lose hope, the door opens, only a tiny fraction. I push against it into the dark, away from the heath, shutting it closed behind me, blocking out the smell of the grass and the lavender planted around the church. Ahead I can hear footsteps coming down a narrow staircase. A sharp click of expensive heels on stone. Jones.

Molly "Ma" Jones is a tall, thirty-something Londoner of Jamaican and Irish descent. To the outside, she looks like the business manager for an eSports team: stylish and fun too – a well-crafted camouflage for a savvy businesswoman. Jones controls a massive chunk of the legal and illegal satellite access points in the city and a sizeable amount of the pro eSports action, taking her cut from the gamers and their tournament prize funds plus the bookies who organize the side bets. She also deals in information, selling data and secrets on the edges of the Dark Web. The authorities decided long ago that Jones knows where too many of their skeletons are hidden and that therefore their best course of action is to leave her the hell alone. In exchange for this, Jones occasionally throws them a bone and sells out the odd hacker.

Jones looks me over. "Twice in one day, Asha?"

I was right. The face in the crowd at the tournament launch. The one hidden behind the glasses. It was her.

"You OK? That was quite a fall you took."

I blush. "It looked worse than it was."

"What can I do for you? I'm pretty sure last time we met, you were going to try going down the straight and narrow."

"Long story."

Jones gives an elegant shrug. "I got time. Come on up to the garden. If it's a good story, I might even agree."

"Agree to what?"

Her eyes narrow. "To help you with whatever has you so scared you needed to come here."

I take a deep breath. "I need you to get me into the Zu Tech tournament."

Because Dark was right. If I am going to find out what happened to Maya, then I need to be on the inside.

The staircase ends just out of sight of the entrance floor, leading to a small, futuristic open lift shaft: the clean-cut metal, glass and light contrasting with the old damp stone. Jones steps in, and I follow her, looking for a moment at the number of floors listed as options on the touchpad screen.

"I see you've expanded the basement section."

She uses a manicured hand to trigger the fingerprint access. "Stick around, and I'll give you a tour."

Jones hits the button. The lift glides upwards, emerging from the darkness of the tower into a stream of light. The garden level is just as I remember it. It takes up the entire top section of the bell tower. The roof is smart glass, allowing a clear one-way view of the sky and the antenna hidden in each corner of the structure. Cane and wicker furniture are scattered in comfortable small groups across the room. The floor is polished wood. A water feature plays somewhere, hidden by the jungle of tropical and colourful potted plants. Screens of living bamboo conceal secret areas. The air is heavily scented with jasmine. Ma's infamous garden.

"Sit." She gestures to an oversized comfy chair. It's not a request.

Jones sits across from me. We watch each other in silence for a minute, then she sighs.

"So how much trouble has my old protégé got you into this time?"

I move in my seat, sitting forward. My hands shake, so I clasp them together to hide it. I have one shot at getting her on board. "It's not him. It's me."

Jones reclines back further in her chair. "Then you better start talking."

When I finish it's late outside, and small solar fairy lights are glowing in the trees inside the room. Jones finished her large mug of herbal tea that appeared during our conversation ages ago, and I take a swig from mine, which has gone cold. It leaves a bitter aftertaste in my mouth, reminding me again why I never liked tea. The silence lengthens, and I can't think of anything else to say to convince her. I've laid myself bare.

Finally, she speaks. "Why go to Dark first?"

I look at my shoes first before meeting her gaze. "I needed a clean room."

"You're smart. You know a hundred places to go to get what you need, but you choose to go back to that brain hacker. And now that someone found you when you

97

thought you were hidden, you decide to come to me. Why? Why not call your boy?"

I look at the floor. Jones sighs. "You didn't want to lead them back to him. But you have no problem landing me in a world of potential trouble. That right?"

There's a kernel of truth to what she's saying. I can't bring Dark into this any further. Something happened to Maya. Part of me doesn't want to put Dark in danger, to risk losing yet another person I care about. Even if it's complicated.

My voice becomes defensive. "I was careful. I wasn't followed here."

Jones shakes her head. "You're a kid dealing with your first real enemy. Your trace won't tell you anything. You only find out about someone like Zu Tech from the inside. They are as big as it gets. Those types of people keep their secrets close. Any intel they don't destroy, they guard on air-gapped data storage devices under heavy security."

I look up from the floor and meet her eyes. "You're right. But if I play in the Zu tournament, I have a way to infiltrate the company. I know you've got a team entering. I saw you at the launch."

Jones says nothing for a moment. "I do need a healer on the team," she says at last. "You know, the prize fund is going to be big. The equipment will be cutting-edge; the whole planet will be watching. With just a few weeks to go, you really think you can qualify? You'd have to win a spot in the open competition before I could add you."

"I'm good. You know that."

"No, I knew that two years ago. Everyone with a console and some basic VR gear will be trying to win a place in this tournament. Have you even played since then?"

Two years ago. Just like that, I'm back in that space. The invite-only, off the beaten path clubs where pros and amateurs battle each other in virtual worlds while organizers charge admittance fees and run bets on the side and off the live streams. I was good then. Playing in the virtual worlds Zu Tech pioneered. Using my prize money to upgrade the standard school edition VR glasses and gloves we used in class for the pro player metaverse-ready ones needed to compete.

"I can do this." I look up and meet Jones's stare. "I'm even better than I was back then."

Jones meets my gaze and doesn't move a muscle. "Positions?"

"Healer. Sometimes sniper."

Jones says nothing for a few moments, deep in thought. "I don't like it. I don't do centre stage. You know that. I'm behind the scenes. And if you go poking around at Zu Tech ... well, it could attract a lot of attention." She leans forward. "You turned me down before. Why?"

I close my eyes for a second.

"Maya." My voice catches, and I swallow before moving on. "She wanted me to go to college, take up a scholarship. Do something long-term. Maya was the reason I turned you down, and now she's gone." A pause.

"Jones, I didn't go to Dark because he can't help me with what I need to do. I have to know what happened to her. I can't find the truth by being on the outside. If I enter the tournament, I get to be on the inside. Launching the new gaming tech means the players will have access to the labs. I have to be there."

I catch my breath for a moment.

"I need this, Jones." I swallow. "I wouldn't ask otherwise. Please?"

Jones reaches a decision in her mind. Her fingers suddenly go still against the armrest on her chair. The tension and atmosphere in the room changes. "If you lose, I gain nothing." She plays with one of her long dangling earrings, thinking. "So what's in this for me?"

"Thirty per cent?"

She smiles. "Asha, darling, we know each other better than that. I will be taking a risk vouching for you. You may have nothing to lose, but I built all of this from scratch. Reputations can go up as well as down. I'm only ever as good as my last score."

"Tell me what you want."

Jones sits straighter in her seat. "Don't confuse me with someone who believes in causes or friendships, Asha. Both can get you killed. Despite what you think you may know about me, I'm a businesswoman."

"You know how I game. Make an offer."

"Sixty per cent?"

I give her a look. "I'm not green."

Jones smirks. "You *are* good, Asha. But you're flat out of options, or else why would you be here?"

"Forty."

Jones shifts. She gets bored easily. "Fine, fifty–fifty. Last offer. And after this, no more favours. Are we clear?"

"Fifty per cent."

"You game under one of my brands. The team places in the top five. If you fail to place, I get to recoup my investment."

"How?"

Her eyes take on a hard look. "Fail, and you work for me until the debt is fully repaid, with interest. You hack what I tell you to. You don't complain when I put your services out for hire or ask questions. You become mine till I recoup."

She knows that would be everything I hate. We've both seen plenty of work for hire black hats. People with no input into how their skills are exploited. Maya would hate this. Me becoming trapped in this web. But then, I made my decision when I was on the train. Whatever it takes.

Jones's fingers start to dance as they rest on the arm of the chair. The metallic sheen on her fingertips catches the last of the light as, behind her, solar fairy lights switch on. She knows she has me.

"All right," I say. "I understand my side of the bargain. What's yours?"

"I find you a team, organize the training and take care of the entry. I'll look after the backstory and new IDs so you don't pop up in any searches related to your previous life. Then there is the little matter of how you look."

I glance down at my baggy jeans and trainers. "What's wrong with how I look?"

"Asha, you are many things, but even you must know that you can't go into an eSports arena looking like … well. I need people to want to bet on you in this tournament. To root for you. They need to want to be you. Image, darling, is everything. Basic won't cut it. Besides, the social will have recent pictures of you, and I can guarantee Zu Tech does, too, by now. You need a new 'look'."

"Fine."

"You stay here where I can keep an eye on you till the competition ends. And, Asha, while you're here, Dark never steps inside my door, got it? He isn't the same guy you knew before. We didn't exactly part on good terms."

"OK." Dark has what he wanted anyway – a way into Zu's data.

I should feel relieved. This is my way of getting inside the impenetrable fortress. Exactly what I wanted. So why do I still feel afraid?

I look up, and Jones is watching me. "Welcome to Tower team, Asha."

10

Bang.

Multiple blasts. A volley of flying daggers. I send a round of gunfire in the direction of QueenMean07. It's my fifth VR match of the day; my fingers are cramping inside my gloves, and my eyes are starting to burn despite the refresh rate on the ultra-thin VR glasses Jones provided.

I borrow from some of the old school tactics I used with Maya when we were kids. Find a high vantage point, then descend with a string of roundhouse kicks. QueenMean07 is having none of it; she ducks and throws a grenade into the fight, which catches me off guard. I make it into the shell of a nearby building just as her explosive detonates. It's a smart bomb. It catches the rest of the players, and we become the only two to qualify from the match.

No time to celebrate. I load immediately into another one.

I've been spending my time alone in a single-player game room in Jones's Tower. Just me, a small lightweight set of VR glasses, some metaverse gloves with haptic feedback and a console that loads and tracks the online matches. Jones hasn't introduced me to any other players on her team, which is fine by me. I need to bring my gaming skills up to speed. And I guess Jones wants to see if I make it through the open online qualifications before she assigns me a spot.

Each match is open player: anyone over fifteen with access to wifi and a Zu console – basically over half the planet – can apply. With the prize pot rumoured to be one of the biggest in eSports history, millions have taken up the challenge. I need to place in the top fifty to have a hope of getting through, and I'm starting with a major disadvantage. A newbie player with zero scores in a competition that closes at midnight in four days. Ninety-six hours to make this work. There are a hundred players in each game – Player vs player. No teams. Just an all-out battle until only two players remain. The winners then advance to the next match. My rankings slowly start to climb, and the rest of the world fades away. I lose track of time, and somehow that helps because it means I stop thinking about everything else.

"Hi." It's Jones, with a tray of food. I hadn't noticed her come in. "You OK?"

I jump at the interruption, but I don't stop playing. "I'm fine."

"When was the last time you got some fresh air?"

"A while."

"Make time. You're useless to me if you burn out."

I try ignoring her, but she stays put, so as soon as I win the next game, I stand and stretch. She doesn't get it, and I'm not about to explain. It's not just the need to qualify that's driving me. It's the fact that when I play, I am switched off from the memories that keep rushing in.

I grab a hoodie from my room first, glancing at the downloads from Maya's data on my way out. The decryption program I'm running on her archive files is working. I scroll quickly through Maya's retrieved text messages. The ones from me with things like: When r u home? and Did you pick up dinner? Please, no more tofu. And hers to me: Ash, the school called, again. You didn't submit? (I hadn't) or Have you seen my new top? (I had, and I was wearing it when I saw her text and replied no).

Then I spot some others. Work reminders about team meetings, beta testing. Names of other Zu Tech employees. And then some messages from "Unknown". Listed under a "work" label – but the messages aren't about work.

Maya: I miss you.

Unknown: Me too.

Then a few minutes later.

Unknown: When can we be together?

Maya: Don't push me. Ash needs time.

Unknown: If she got to know me first, it would be easier to tell her...

Then later.

Unknown: When are you going to be honest about who you are?

I think of the note I found. *When can I meet Asha?* Is this the person who wrote it? The messages and chats flow on. Then it becomes "Unknown" who is holding back.

Unknown: I need some time to think.

Maya: I'm sorry about the other day. I didn't mean to cancel.

Unknown: I'm tired of being your secret. It hurts.

Maya: When this is over, we can talk.

Unknown: That's what you always say, but nothing changes.

Maya: That's not fair. You know I have to think of A.

Unknown: I'm tired of fighting. Please stop calling me.

More silence. The messages end. Then, twenty-four hours before her death, there is one last one.

Unknown: I meant what I said. I deserve more. You're acting weird. And if you can't do what I'm asking then it's over.

Acting weird. Maya *had* been acting strangely. Distracted. Forgetful. More burnt crazy veggie dishes than usual. I just put it down to her working long hours ahead of the launch, but could it have been because of this other life? Does "Unknown" have more answers than me? What was he asking her to do? Is he the reason she died? I try the mobile number that sent the messages, but all it gives me is a disconnected signal. Dead end.

106

I rack my brain, trying to recall whether she ever mentioned anyone. I don't think she did. I realize, too, that I never asked. That the last few months with Maya were filled with fights over school and little else. Both of us trying to adjust to a new life together. Both of us hiding secrets. In her case, a relationship. The regrets flood in again. What if I had asked? If we had opened up to each other, would she be dead now?

Hoodie pulled down, I push the thoughts away and head out to the heath to run. I run with the ghosts in my head until it's time to return to the tournament pre-qualifier. I have seventy-two hours left. If I qualify – no, *when* I qualify – I'm going to track down "Unknown".

Seventy-three hours later, the images of the final rankings are loading in front of me. I'm beyond exhausted, muscles burning, mouth dry. I stretch out in Jones's small single-player room. The last few rounds were rough. Most of the people remaining were pro players. NYLiz, phoenix1, Dragon247 all had styles I recognized from watching old tournaments. I have to hope that the last few wins were enough.

It has to be enough.

"You good?"

Jones is leaning against the doorway. When I look back, the image has stopped refreshing. The final rankings are live. Valkyrie16, my gamer tag, is right in the middle. Number 25. I made it.

I sink to the floor, taking off the VR glasses and

pinching my nose. "I am now." Joy and relief. I'm in. Then something bitter. This would have been my dream when I was a kid, and the one person I would want to tell about it isn't here.

Jones sees my look. "I never doubted you."

She's lying. She must have. I know I did.

Jones claps her hands. "That was the easy part. Take a shower, get your head together, rest. In forty-eight hours, you'll meet the team. That's when the fun starts."

Jones leaves. I lean back against the wall and take a moment. I think I could just sleep straight for those forty-eight hours, but there is something else I need to do. Something I've been putting off.

Forty-eight hours. Just enough time. I can't avoid it any more.

I hack first into the camera network around the chapel at the City of London Crematorium, setting it up to record a twenty-four-hour section to my desktop.

Then I begin to plan Maya's funeral. Or, rather, two funerals.

One will be real – I'll attend under a fake name. And one will just have an empty coffin and a camera feed.

The fake funeral is designed to try and draw out her mystery boyfriend and any other interested parties. If they attend, I'll have footage and camera access to follow. Both will happen simultaneously. With luck, any care officials or police will head to the fake one too. It buys me just enough time to say goodbye alone.

I can't let her go into a mass grave like our parents, and if the body remains unclaimed for much longer, that's exactly what will happen. I write the notice for the fake funeral with enough detail to attract the attention of anyone who's set up a search around me, Maya or Zu Tech. It's brief but somehow devasting.

Maya Kennedy. Video games designer at Zu Tech. Died suddenly at home on June 3rd, aged twenty. Daughter of the late David and Chabi Kennedy. Beloved sister of Asha. Funeral service on Tuesday June 12th at noon in the City of London Crematorium, north-west chapel, followed by cremation. Family flowers only, please, donations if desired to the Children in Care charity c/o Everton's Funeral Services.

Once the notice is online, I make sure it's reposted on all the local message boards.

The second piece is simpler, not designed for publication anywhere except in the funeral directors' listing.

Augusta King, beloved sister, family only.

I stare at the screen. Augusta Ada King, the woman who worked on the first computer in the 1800s.

Maya would have liked that.

***

Maya and I had wondered once what religion our parents might have been. All we knew about them was that they were once engineers. We had been too young to attend their funerals, to be at the mass burial that was the norm during the pandemic surge. After a while, it didn't matter. God wasn't going to save us; we had to protect ourselves. That was our religion. Now here we are, together one last time, but facing different paths.

Maya loved daisies and sunflowers, so that's what I bring her, placing them on the coffin.

The celebrant turns to me and says, "Shall we proceed?"

I realize that I'm supposed to say something. I also realize I can't.

"Miss?"

I still can't speak. Then a quiet voice says, "She needs to say goodbye."

The man nods respectfully to the owner of the voice and steps aside.

"I'll be at the back when you're ready." His footsteps echo on the stone floor of the small church. There are just three of us now in the space. The bearers left once the coffin was in position.

I don't need to turn around to know who the voice belongs to. I stand still, staring at the coffin with the sunflowers already starting to wilt on top. My hands dangle at my side. Useless.

He comes up beside me, his hand reaching for mine. We stand holding hands in front of Maya. He gives a gentle squeeze. A life preserver in a sea of tears.

"How did you know?"

His hold tightens slightly. "I knew you wouldn't let them bury her in the city's unclaimed plot. That you'd have to use an alias, otherwise, they could track you. When I saw Augusta King's name, I remembered. Countess of Lovelace, Augusta Ada King. Maya's favourite historical coder."

"You didn't need to come," I say.

"Yes, I did."

I look at him. "There's something I need to tell you."

"We don't need to talk about anything but Maya now. We have time, I promise."

Maya had liked Dark but never trusted him. Dark is the nightmare that older sisters warn you about. The criminal that can consume you and damage your soul beyond repair. But now, he is all I have.

"You're not alone, Asha."

I wonder then, in a slight moment of madness and grief, if he can hear my thoughts.

"You loved her. We never really lose the ones we love, Asha. We carry a small part of them with us, always."

The words echo around my head. After a while, he asks, "Do you want me to go? To have some time on your own with her."

I look at him then. The black wool coat. The face half-hidden by shadows that come from the dirty lead glass church windows. His blue eyes.

"No."

"Are you ready?"

"No." Then a pause. "But I don't have a choice, do I?"

"No."

I nod, and Dark raises his other hand.

The funeral director comes forward. He pushes the button, and the coffin starts to roll away towards the heavy velvet curtains that lead to the crematorium chamber. "It will be about thirty minutes – you can wait here or outside."

I'm still numb, so Dark answers. "Outside." Then he leads me away from the coldness of the church.

A weak sun shines in the deserted graveyard that surrounds the building. Quiet, except for small bursts of birdsong and the occasional rumble of traffic outside the walls.

"Let's go for a walk?"

I suddenly become aware that we are still holding hands at the exact moment I also realize that I am not ready for him to let go. "OK."

We start to walk through the rambling old graveyard with its blend of headstones, remembrance walls, cracked monuments and marble effigies. A landscape dotted with trees, old vines and gravestones. Some cared for, some abandoned.

I glance at the headstones with their barely visible names, wondering about the lives they represent, watch a squirrel climb one of the trees. We stop in a patch of sun on an old bench near the church. Its brass remembrance plaque is no longer readable. Sitting side by side, my head resting on his shoulder, hands intertwined. I should tell him about the break–in, about going to the Tower and finding Jones, about joining the tournament, but I don't. It's almost as if nothing exists but the feel of the sunlight. The smell of the grass. This small moment. Neither before nor after.

Eventually, Dark speaks, voice low. "I know you need time, and I'm here for you, Asha."

I can't speak. A well–practised polite cough sounds behind us. The celebrant hands me a polished oak box. Augusta King's name is on the top. We stand up. I finally let go of Dark's hand to take it. My sister's ashes. After.

11

Back in my room in the Tower, I put the box on the table. I take a deep breath and sit down at the computer and open the file containing Maya's fake funeral footage. I'm not sad any more. The tears have gone. All I feel now is empty and angry. A rage that burns everything else away. Maya shouldn't be dead – something or someone made this happen.

The images load almost at once.

Maya's fake funeral is a sparse affair, but there is a beautiful simplicity to it. Two elderly women sit in the back pews. I don't recognize them; perhaps they're just there to take a break and say a prayer. For a while, I wonder if they are the only people who will show. Then at eleven forty-five a.m., the doors open.

First to enter is Sam. My boss from the takeaway, whose files I deleted when I ran. He looks around as if searching for me before he sits in the middle section, and my heart breaks a bit. Sam came. His shoulders hunched into a suit he probably just keeps for funerals and weddings. Something I've never seen him in; normally he wears old jeans and T-shirts, clutching an espresso that tastes like rocket fuel. His tanned face is freshly shaven, his black hair slicked back; his brown eyes watery. He looks older than his twenty-something years. He didn't have to come. I guess we meant something to him. He's self-conscious, looking around him, unsure what to do with his hands.

Then the door opens again, and it's Murphy. The police officer from the hospital, still looking dishevelled, still wearing his too-cool black leather jacket. Eyes resting briefly on everyone in the room before he slides into the back row. Beside him is a haggard-looking lady who I know, even before I run the screenshot, will turn out to be from the social.

At eleven fifty-five, a tall white man, wearing black, heavily built, mid-thirties, enters. I start angling the camera to see if I can get a shot of him, but he keeps his close-shaven head down – could this be Maya's boyfriend? I wait for him to look up, which he does when the door opens again at eleven fifty-eight – got you. His frame looks familiar. I start to run the photo through facial recognition while I scroll back to see who arrived.

Emily Webber. Full corporate outfit. Smart black dress

and heels that click expensively on the stone church floor. She sits towards the front, glancing keenly round. Then she discreetly checks her smartphone.

I'm about to fast forward when I notice a moment to the left of the screen. A latecomer, slipping in at the back, clearly trying to avoid being seen. She glances up once, and my breath stills. It's her. The mystery woman from the footage outside our flat, the one who pretended to be me at the morgue, the woman who works for Zu Tech. Except this time, I have a clear image of her, one I can use in a search.

The initial search on the mystery man returns with nothing, so I set up a search via the worm on Emily's device for him and the woman who pretended to be me. Being a woman and a person of colour in a games company means my imposter pings first. Annie Queen. Coder. No priors, no convictions, clean record, and a history of research in AI and machine learning. Legit college transcripts. There is a home address, but when I check it, Annie no longer lives there. She must have moved recently. You can run, I think grimly, but you can't hide. I am broadening the search when someone knocks at my door.

Ma Jones strolls in, and I realize how she got the nickname "Ma". She comes with the demeanour of one herding small children. "Play time's over. Level four. Thirty minutes." Then she hands me a small file.

"I did what you asked. New IDs – by the way, why the name 'Daisy'?" Jones asks.

"It was Maya's favourite flower."

Twenty minutes later, I turn up at Jones's larger games centre. A purpose-built gaming floor in the labyrinth of underground levels that lie under the Tower. Immersive, high speed top-of-the-line specs. Cutting-edge tech. On the floor, already logging on to a VR game, are two others.

One of them scowls as soon as I enter. "Newbie." He's tall. His skin a warm brown, dark hair cut short. His comment earns him a punch in the arm from the girl beside him. She is about the same height. Hair tied in braids back from her face. They both look slightly older than me, probably eighteen. The kind of kids who could be gamers or models or both. Tall, beautiful, and intimidating. The type that makes me feel insecure. But then I remind myself that I'm not "Asha from the care home" any more. I need to stop thinking that way.

The girl nods at me, all business. "I'm Ruby. This is my twin, Josh."

"Daisy."

Josh is already pulling on his VR gloves, ignoring us both.

Ruby nods to another area on the floor. "You're over there. Jones said the last player wouldn't be here for a while. In the mornings, we have tactical training. We're playing all the classics in VR – *League*, *Fortnite*, *Civilization*, *Rainbow Sieges*, *Overwatch* – the idea is to build up reflexes and skills, learn how each other plays. Jones said you were in the rankings; you weren't a pro invited to be in the tournament?"

I nod.

Josh looks up, interested. "Number?"

"Twenty-five."

Ruby's voice is curious. "What was your tag?"

"Valkyrie16."

"Congrats. I remember you from one of the matches."
A thought occurs to me. "QueenofMean07?"

"Yeah."

"Nice gameplay," I say grudgingly.

"Thanks. I'm number nineteen, and Josh is twenty. He
is a bit sore that I'm a place higher than him, but he's more
of a tank than a sniper, aren't you, bro?"

Josh scowls at her. "I had an off day."

Jones gives us a look. "Daisy here will be the healer.
Josh, you're our tank. Ruby is the main sniper. Player
number four will be joining you in a few days. Now, if
you'll excuse me. Play nice. Remember, you will be a team,
so act like it."

"Ready?" Josh looks over and asks.

I pull on my gloves and slide my glasses down. "Yeah."

I log on. No lag time, instant loads. Shooting, puzzling
and running my way through each match and level. This
is home. Ruby and Josh have chosen classic multiplayer
online shooters for our first games. I blot out the world.
Every virtual sword slash, sniper shot, and bomb blast feeds
that place inside me that just wants to lash out at something.
I wield my healing staff as often as my knife. I barely notice
when the timer ends. After that, there's a silence where

reality rushes back in. Josh and Ruby unstrap first and come over to my floor area.

Josh's expression has changed. It's warmer now. "Impressive, newbie."

Ruby punches his arm again.

"Can you stop doing that?"

"Not a chance, little bro."

"You're only older by two minutes."

"Still counts." She grins at me. "Josh is right, for once. Good game. Welcome to the team, Daisy."

I shrug. "Thanks. I guess." Listening to their banter makes my chest feel hollow again.

"Do you want to grab a drink?" says Ruby. "Jones has stocked the kitchen with loads of weird smoothies. We can—"

"No." I cut her off. "I mean, I'm tired. I'll see you guys later, OK?"

I walk off before they can answer. I don't want to see the look of hurt on Ruby's face. But I'm not here to make friends. I'm here to get access to Zu Tech.

***

Jones quickly formalizes our training schedule. I resent her for it as it eats into my research time. She includes blocks for our "mental health", we all need to take some air outside daily, so I start to run, something I haven't done since school. At first, I train in my flat sneakers and ripped jeans. Later, some sleek black training gear appears in my room, along with new runners. I start to clock up miles. Headphones on, face hidden by a baseball hat, body normally soaked by summer showers. Always alone. I run as dawn breaks to avoid Ruby's offers to come with me. Jones doesn't like me being solitary. For her, pre-tournament time is, as she puts it, "bonding time".

"I don't need to be friends with them to win. Besides, I train better alone."

Jones looks at me and shrugs. "You don't know what you need. Also, it wasn't a request. I've added a regular daily group training session to your schedules so you spend more time in the real world together. Resist any more and I'll add a second one."

The twins call the sessions "group torture". eSports players aren't known for their fitness, but Jones has a team that assesses and advises her on each player. They come by at regular intervals, considering us one by one before reporting back to Jones. She knows how physical conditioning impacts reflexes during the game, how lack of sleep leads to inadequate decision-making. Meals become balanced to avoid mental fatigue during battles. Sugar is gradually removed from our communal kitchen. Burnout isn't an option.

Jones follows science like a religion. I wonder how many teams she's running or if we are her only one. If we're all on the same schedule. Where they are. With Jones, this is business. She only ever invests where she feels there is a potential return.

One morning, after a strenuous session, Ruby slumps on to a bench with a dramatic groan.

"I can't do this any more. How do you manage to keep going?"

I look up from the stair master. "I don't give myself the option of stopping."

Josh grins at me. "You could learn from Daisy, Ru."

Ruby answers by throwing a towel at him.

"Bet you were, like, amazing at school, probably won all the sports day prizes. I hated PE."

I focus on my mileage. I never won prizes at school. I was Asha, the misfit from the home. When you have nothing, you live in fear of being asked for anything. School trip money, a costume, bake sale stuff, even a parental permission slip could cause issues. It's easier to be in the background. I followed the rules. I interacted as little as possible. I was a ghost. I doubt anyone from my class even remembers me being there, never mind how I did on sports day in my worn sneakers and second-hand uniform.

"No prizes."

Ruby grins at me. "You would win the lot now, though. Never seen anyone train like you."

Her smile is genuine. Everything Ruby sees is always half full, not half empty. She compliments without expecting anything in return. She's open. Something I could never be.

I avoid her and Josh as much as possible and focus on my training. Two weeks pass, and as the English summer sun tries to shine outside, I start to feel physically better. I embrace the schedule that doesn't allow time to think. At night I decipher more information from Maya's drive and Emily's bland data stream of corporate emails. I find nothing of interest. I keep searching for Annie Queen until I can't keep my eyes open. When I close them, however, the nightmares are there. Always the same. I'm in the flat, trying to resuscitate Maya, only this time, when I look down, it's not Maya who is dead, it's me.

I am having that dream again when the ping from a server jolts me awake. I rub my eyes with my fingers, confused, till I see the red light of the computer. The desktop screen says three a.m. The ping is from keywords I put into my search on Emily's new incoming emails.

Breach of internal security notification. Confirmed. The subject was involved with someone before her death who may have had access. We recommend a full deep clean once located. Please authorize.

Do they mean me? Has Emily found the worm we planted? Or is this about someone else? After that, I don't sleep. Instead, I check my trail, ensuring nothing can connect back to my current IP address. I'm clean. I think.

Around eight a.m. the next day, Jones appears in my room. She waves a cup of coffee temptingly in my direction. "Stage two, Daisy/Asha. Let's go."

And I groan because I know exactly what this fresh

hell is.

Jones leads me out to the garden. "This is Penny," Jones says, pointing to a stylish-looking young woman sitting on top of a heap of cases, taking a selfie. "She's going to help you with your image overhaul."

Penny, who is wearing flares and a crop top, jumps up. "Hi!" she says cheerfully. "I bet you can't wait to get started."

"Oh, I can wait," I mutter under my breath. Jones snorts.

Penny pats a stool. "Sit here, will you?" She hands me an iPad. "Why don't you take a look through these? I've pulled together some look books for you."

She drags forward a rail of clothes and leans in closer. "You have such beautiful eyes!" she exclaims. "You should show them off, not hide them under all that hair."

In the system, people noticing you is never good. I've spent sixteen years of my life learning how to blend in and be invisible. Besides, Maya was the one who liked this sort of stuff – clothes and make-up – not me.

"Come on, Ash, at least brush your hair. You can't wear a beanie all the time."

"Why?"

"Ash! Come back here!"

But I was too fast for Maya that day when I ran out of our room. I never told her about the kid in my class that teased me and pulled my hair, that the beanie hat was my defence against him touching me. She already had enough to deal with.

Now in Jones's garden, I cringe as Penny talks in what sounds like a foreign language. Skin tone, face shape, capsule wardrobe. I'm staring at the make-up boxes, remembering Maya again. Her sitting in front of the mirror in her room, applying lipstick, spraying perfume. Was she getting ready to meet "Unknown" then?

I realize that Penny has asked me a question. She and Jones are both looking at me expectantly.

"Sorry, what did you say?" I ask.

Jones rolls her eyes. "For God's sake, Daisy, just tell the girl what you like!"

I glare at her. "I got out of the social six months ago. I have never bought clothes. I either wore what they gave me or what my sister passed on. So I don't have a clue what I like."

Jones says nothing. Penny, however, brightens. "Awesome. You're like a blank canvas. We can try different things until we find something that's you."

"OK," I say suspiciously, keeping my arms folded across my body.

Penny gives a grin that shows her dimples and makes her look way less scary. "Don't think of this as 'fashion'. Think of this as you finding your armour. Something to protect you while you battle the outside world. Clothes can let you hide, give you comfort, or strengthen you for the fight. We start simple. What's your favourite colour?"

"Blue? Purple?" I'm looking over to Jones for reassurance, but she avoids my gaze, eyes focused on the screen in her hand.

"It suits your skin tone. So, let's start with some lavender balayage. Something that shakes you up a bit. I'll pop on a face mask. Then I'll start bringing a selection of clothes over for you to try on. For the tournament itself, we'll go with coloured contacts. Jones said you wanted something that doesn't look like your 'old self'."

Lavender balayage? I turn hopelessly to Jones, who is suppressing a smile. She translates for me. "Penny's going to start by dyeing your hair purple, Daisy."

"Oh." Fire and pan. For the next three hours, I drink coffee and learn not to move as Penny gets to work.

Later that afternoon, Jones enters my room just as I am getting dressed from a post-gym shower. Her eyes scan my multiple screens, the frozen images from Maya's data, the stats on Zu Tech, the traces I'm running. The wall already covered with photos, clippings, questions and string. All she says, though, is, "You have a visitor."

I snap a little at the interruption. This is my time, and she knows it. "No one knows I'm here."

Jones shrugs. "Clearly, that's not the case. He's outside — been there an hour. I am not inviting him in. If you want to see him, you do it somewhere else."

Jones passes me a screen showing the feed just outside the door of the Tower. Dark. Great, just great. I don't say anything. I don't need to. We both know he's stubborn enough to stay there all night.

I stand and follow Jones out. She pauses at the door.

125

"What is the deal with you two anyway?"

"We agreed to pool some information."

Jones looks thoughtful. "Make sure you don't confuse business with anything else."

"What do you mean?"

She sighs. "After you guys split, Dark changed. He's not the kid you remember. I can't see him helping you unless there's something in it for him."

"Why the concern?"

"You're here to make me money. You're useless to me if a guy gets inside your head, especially that one."

"Noted."

Jones leaves, taking one last look around the room at the fragments of Maya's life. She should know she has nothing to worry about. If anything, this room proves I don't have space for anything else.

When I turn to leave, I catch a glimpse of myself in the mirror. Mentally, I know the image that stares back at me is me. But I don't recognize the reflection. The hollow cheeks are those of a stranger. My hair, thanks to the stylist this morning, is unrecognizable. Once red, it has been transformed into a deep dark purple with scattered highlights. Only the eyes look familiar, the same brown eyes as Maya, and they are surrounded by dark circles despite Jones's order about regular sleep schedules. I turn away from the image and add a pair of canvas trainers to my jeans and T-shirt.

As soon as I step outside, I am blinded by the weak

sun, and goosebumps rise on my arms. I'm yet again underdressed for an English summer.

"Here, take these." It's Dark. His hand is offering a pair of sunglasses. We fall into a slow walk in silence, away from the Tower and around the heath.

After a few minutes, he starts talking. "You were supposed to stay in touch, Asha. You vanished. It's been over two weeks."

I look at him, startled. I start taking in his crumpled appearance, the matching dark circles under his eyes. "You already had access to Zu Tech. I didn't think you'd need anything else."

Dark stops. We stand on the twilight heath, the grass turning brown from lack of rain. "You dropped off the face of the earth. You stopped checking texts. The last time I saw you was at Maya's funeral. I got worried. And what the hell did you do to your hair?"

We stare at each other. I can smell the cut grass. Feel the last rays of the sunlight I've somehow dragged him out into. I push the shades from my eyes. The words don't even make sense as they tumble out into the everyday setting of kite flyers, joggers and kids. A world I have never associated with Dark, and yet...

"You were worried ... about me?"

Dark shakes his head angrily. "Of course. What did you think? You disappeared, Asha. And now you're with Jones? Helping her with the Zu Tech tournament? Like some glorified intern?"

I pause for a second, silent. "Something like that." A shiver runs down my spine as I remember the open door of my studio in Embankment. "Before the funeral, someone found out where I was. They trashed the place while I was at Zu Tech. They took all of Maya's stuff. I knew I needed to disappear, fast."

There is a silence then, filled with all the unspoken words. Dark steps closer. "Why not come to me?"

I can't say anything because there is too much to say.

His voice is rough as he says, "You didn't think I would help?"

I can't lie to him, but I can't tell him the truth. Because the truth is, I don't want him to get hurt. And also: I don't know if I can trust him. He built an empire in the shadows over the last two, almost three, years. I think of what Jones said. *"Dark changed when he left the social, and again when he left my Tower almost two years ago. He isn't the kid you or I remember."*

As it happens, he sees my face and says the words out loud for me, saving me from having to answer.

"You didn't want to get me in trouble, but also, you couldn't trust me? You still don't."

I nod. A single tear starts to find its way down my cheek. Dark carefully, gently, as if afraid I will break, uses his thumb to wipe it away. His hand rests lightly on my face. I lean against his palm.

We stand there for a while. Then he takes a step back, his hand dropping to his side and then into the pockets of his jacket.

His expression is bleak. "We were friends before. We could be again? I'm not as bad as people say, Asha."

And there it is. The other thing we haven't really talked about yet. The reason so many people fear Dark. The incidents that happened after he left Jones to start up on his own. The rumours that put him behind the sudden disappearance of "business" opponents. The reported data breaches into government systems and banks. I've heard those stories, the ones that mean no one crosses Dark now. How he became the one person you don't want to anger.

"I know what people say about you."

His eyes scan my face. "And?"

Everything seems to stand still around us as I meet his eyes. "I meant it, what I said before. I don't trust rumours; I make up my own mind."

He takes a step closer, and I don't move.

"I know you're not that guy."

Dark looks at me again. The doubt is still there. "Why? Everyone else thinks I did those things. Why not you?"

"I just know."

Dark takes another step towards me. "If you believe that, then why stay away?"

I don't move. I can't.

For the first time, I wonder if he was ever interested in Zu Tech. Or whether, all along, he was doing this for me. I look right into his eyes. No secrets.

"I have to know what happened to her. *How* and *why* this happened. And I need to do this alone."

Dark says nothing. Slowly, he reaches forward, and his lips gently brush my forehead. It takes everything in me not to fall into him. To fight the instinct to wrap my arms around him, to demand more. But I stay still and, at last, he pulls away.

A pause where neither of us moves.

"OK." Dark takes an envelope from his pocket. "Before I forget."

"What's this?"

"The paperwork from Zu Tech. Legal looked at it. It's a pay-off, a standard non-admission of any guilt. An agreement that, in exchange for a generous sum, you will never look to pursue a civil case against them regarding your sister. You also can't discuss any aspects of your sister's work. Pretty normal except for one thing. They want you to return the files your sister had."

I frown. "Files?"

"R&D for a new game she was working on. Information her office listed was from the special projects division. It's all pretty vague, but they are convinced that she took some confidential digital files from the building, and they want them back."

I shake my head. Maya's files had contained the odd screengrab and a glitch she'd found in the game, but there was nothing else. "You have everything I have. There are no other files."

Dark rubs his forehead. "They seem convinced you have them. Look at this. *The above files in Maya's possession have*

130

not yet been returned. *Until they are, the agreement will be void.*"

"Nothing you do will bring her back, Asha. Just remember that when the time comes to choose." He turns to start walking away.

"You said 'when the time comes to choose'?"

"Things like this – there always comes a point where you need to make a choice."

I stare at him. "Is that what you did when you disappeared from the social, you made a choice?"

He stops then. Takes a step towards me. He looks like he is about to say something, but a look crosses his face. Something I can't read. He turns instead to go. "By the way, your hair looks good. Purple suits you." Then he's gone.

12

I'm tangled up in emotions I can't process after Dark leaves. He's still him. I'm still me. Yet something is different, and I don't have time to figure out what.

I need to focus. The tournament clock is ticking down; there are just five weeks left. Pretty soon, I will be inside Zu Technology. I need to know everything I can about the enemy I'm facing. I have to block Dark out. Focus. I pull up a chair in front of the curved screen in my room and get back to work.

Emily's feed has given me access to Maya's employee file. It contains the three requests she made to Zu Tech, asking them to write references to social services as part of her application to get me out of the system. The first two requests were ignored, but then the third is acknowledged. At the same time, paperwork is filed confirming Maya's acceptance to join the company's "special projects division".

Special projects division. The division she allegedly took files from.

Various release and personal indemnity forms with Maya's practically unreadable scrawl follow. After that, a reference letter supporting her application to the social appears along with a pay rise and the start of what seems to be regular medical check-ups listed as an "employee benefit". Which raises the question – if she was so heavily monitored, why wasn't whatever killed her spotted?

The implications are clear. Maya was desperate to get me out of the system. And as soon as she had agreed to join this special projects division, Zu Tech had helped her do just that.

And now she's dead, and there's just me and the guilt. I remember all the hard times I gave her over school, over everything, and all along, she was hiding this from me.

I start to search for "special projects division" in Emily's stream. Fewer hits. Some scrubbed files that weren't purged. Financial reports with large transfers of company funds to the division going back years. Then a massive increase in funds dated two years ago. Whatever the division is, seventy per cent of all ZU Tech's considerable resources are now committed to it. Nowhere does it say what this Division does. I broaden the search; they also have their own security detail. Why?

It's getting late, and I need some coffee, something to help while I pull the pieces together. As I walk to the kitchen, I keep running through the information in my head. After a few months in special projects, Maya's behaviour had become erratic. She had seemed exhausted by the time I moved in. And she had also been in a mysterious relationship – with someone who I had never met. Then she started to push me into taking an early uni scholarship that would mean moving away from London.

Was she trying to get me to leave because of this mystery boyfriend? Or was it something to do with what she was working on? Was her death linked to her relationship or her work, or both? The pieces of the puzzle are stacking up, but I can't figure out how they fit together.

I find a cup and push the button for some coffee from the machine.

"If you can't sleep, that stuff isn't going to help."

I freeze. Ruby. She's on the other side of the table: sketchbook, pencils, and an iPad out, a half-drunk mug of hot chocolate beside her. I didn't even notice her when I came in.

"By the way, nice hair. Trying out a new look before the tutorial and the party?"

"What party?"

"I thought that's why you couldn't sleep. I can't believe we finally get to handle the tech we will be playing with. The tournament – it's getting real now! All that's missing

134

is our fourth player. Want to play a guessing game with me on who it might be?"

I am still looking at her blankly. Ruby pulls something up on her tablet and slides it across the table to me. It's a video e-invite for the qualifying players to visit Zu Tech's lab and try out the cutting-edge equipment we'll be using in the tournament. It's a typically slick affair, almost like a promotional video, complete with footage showing smiling engineers in the lab.

Ruby, meanwhile, is pacing the kitchen. "We start with a tour of the lab and a tutorial of the new game. Then there's a party. We can finally scope out the competition and see who we will be facing. We will be in the room with the best of the best. It's..." She stops. "What's wrong, Daisy? You look like you've seen a ghost."

I keep staring at the images on the invite. Zu Tech's London lab, the one I fought to get into, has a symbol above its main entrance: a black ouroboros. And right in the centre of the image, in the midst of a group of computer engineers and coders, holding out her hand in welcome, is Annie Queen. I read the caption underneath – Annie Queen, VR Engineer. Behind her, standing in a shadow, talking to someone else, stands the mystery guest from the funeral. The caption underneath says Theo Smith, Head of Security.

"Daisy?" Ruby interrupts me from my thoughts.

I blink. "Sorry. I was miles away."

"Let me guess. You're worried that Jones still hasn't told

us who player number four is?" Her face becomes serious. "Me too."

"Yeah, that's it," I say coolly.

She narrows her eyes. "Daisy, you need to know something. I came here to win; so did Josh. If something is going on that's going to affect this team, you should tell me now."

I let out a small breath. Something about Ruby makes me want to open up to her, but I can't. Instead, I change the subject before she digs any closer. "We all want to win. What's your reason? Fame?" My eyes flick to her design sketchbook filled with T-shirt graphics. "Glamour?"

Ruby looks at me, and her eyes are clear. "Money." I don't say anything, so she continues: "When you have nothing, it is all about the money. We've got a little sister and a mum who has two jobs. We're here to make sure our mum doesn't work herself to death. That our sister gets to have options. So that every week of our lives isn't a choice between rent and food. Because that's the reality right now. You probably never had to worry about those things, but we do. I'm not saying it because I want sympathy. I'm telling you the truth and not making up some other story because we need to learn to trust each other. You need to know who Josh and I are, and I need to know that you are all in and won't ruin this for us."

I swallow. I've spent the last few days so wrapped up in my own stuff I never really thought about the others on my team. I've never been part of one before. "I grew up in the care system. I know what it's like to have nothing."

Ruby takes a seat beside me. "So, two kids from the flats and one from the social. You want to be the ones they talk about after this is over?"

She should be careful what she wishes for. "I'm in," I say.

Ruby grins. "Good. Because I think we need to make an entrance. Now let's discuss the party."

I give a small, tight smile as I sip some coffee. "What are you thinking?"

"I'm thinking it's all about the branding."

Half an hour later, I head back to my room, having agreed to wear a Tower T-shirt designed by Ruby. But all thoughts about that evaporate when I enter to see a message blinking on my desktop screen. It's an automatic alert, signalling a security breach in my old apartment.

I log on to the system. Someone has been inside in the last hour.

The leather jacket looks familiar. But I still don't place him till he looks up. Murphy, the cop from the emergency room. He used some tools to break in. He's in my home, mine and Maya's, and as he searches each room, my anger grows. That was our place. What the hell is he looking for?

Then he finds it. One of the hidden security cameras, the one I hung up in our sitting room, hidden inside an air duct. I'm impressed he found it – he is smarter than I thought. I watch as he writes something on a piece of paper and holds it up to the lens. Three words: *"I can help."*

I hit pause on the footage and stare at the blurry image.

I can help. But how? Could he have a lead – something I've missed? Can I trust him? No. Of course I can't.

Still, there's no harm in seeing what he wants. I dig up his details from my last search, sending him a message using an anonymous server.

A one-word reply. *"How?"*

Then I try to work more, but my eyes won't stay open. I'm too tired to think, so I hit the bed in my clothes before I fall asleep on my keyboard.

When I dream, my nightmares are a mix of Dark and Maya. Except this time, I lose them both.

13

I sleep late and wake with a pounding headache. I throw my purple hair into a messy bun and then run to level minus three for training, my stomach grumbling from having missed breakfast. The twins are in the games room, but the screens are blank.

"What's up?"

Ruby gives me a look, and I nod back. Josh stands beside her, his fingers playing with a slender silver chain around his neck.

Ruby glances over to him. "You break that, and Amy will kill you." Josh pretends to ignore her, but his fingers stop playing with the chain. Then she says to me, "Jones sent a text. Apparently, we're going to meet the mysterious player number four. Little bro is nervous."

I glance at my smartwatch and see two new texts I must have missed when I ran from my room – one from Jones about the meeting, one from Murphy.

"Be right back."

Ruby throws her eyes to the ceiling, and Josh glares at me. "Daisy!"

I ignore them and duck into one of the bathrooms to open Murphy's message.

Let's meet, and I'll tell you.

I hit reply: Someone searched and trashed this place after Maya died. If you find something here, then I'll meet you.

Then I send him the address of the studio I rented and the access code for the door.

If Murphy goes there, if he manages to find something – a print, a fibre, anything – then maybe, maybe, I might trust him enough to meet with him.

I exit the door. Eyes lowered, watching my wrist for the confirmation that the info has been received. Three stories down, Jones's cell reception tends to disappear.

Bang. I collide with another body, and I'm lying on the floor in a heap before I know it.

"Sorry."

A hand reaches down to me, and a feeling of déjà vu takes over as I notice the half-hidden tattoo. It's a star.

Northern Star. Then the slightly accented male voice. "You OK?"

I look up and confirm my initial thoughts. Yeah, I have just thrown myself at the feet of Augie Santos. Again.

"I'm fine." Purple hair is falling over my face, hiding the flush on my cheeks. What is he doing here? Then I remember. The mysterious fourth player. Please, gods, no. I take a quick breath. I remind myself that the last time I saw Augie was at the Zu Tech press junket, when I had red hair and respectable clothes. We only crossed paths for a few seconds on a day when he probably had a meet and greet with hundreds. He won't remember me. I just need to play it cool.

Augie helps pull me up.

I mumble, "I wasn't looking where I was going."

He gives me that same half-grin. "Well, at least you're not bleeding on me this time. Nice hair, by the way."

He remembers.

I push open the door to the training room, suddenly needing to feel the bite of its air-cooled atmosphere. Inside, Jones is standing with Carlo, Augie's manager, and the twins. Jones gives me an irritated look. Then she turns her smile back on and beams it to Carlo. "This will be Augie's other team member, Daisy."

Carlo looks unimpressed, but I get the impression that's his default setting.

"Daisy," Augie says. "You didn't tell me your name last time." The grin is spreading as he watches my discomfort grow.

That catches Carlo's attention. He looks at Augie. "You know her?"

Augie nods. "Yeah." He turns to Carlo. "You know her too. She was at the Zu Tech launch a few weeks ago."

Carlo gives an exaggerated hand gesture. "There were a lot of fans that day."

Augie says, "I may have missed the outside photo op because I was helping her."

Carlo's gaze now snaps to me while the twins and Jones look on. "You."

There's an awkward silence, then Jones takes a step forward and gives everyone a charming smile. "Now everyone knows everyone else. Let's get started. Let's go through your positions on the team…"

As Jones talks, Ruby leans in, so close I can smell her vaguely vanilla scent, and whispers, "You never mentioned you were at the Zu Tech launch."

My eyes stay on Jones as I shrug. "Nothing to tell. Just a junket."

Jones glares at us, and we fall silent. She runs through the team. Augie will be the captain, the main strategist. Given his previous gaming tournament experience, it's a logical pick, but I see Josh shoot him a look. Ruby squeezes his arm gently, an unspoken message between the two. Jones goes on. "Ruby is our main sniper, and Josh our defence tank. Daisy – you're the healer, scout, and secondary shooter."

I nod. I don't care what position I have. The tournament isn't my endgame. I just need it to get in the door.

"Now," says Jones, gesturing to a woman in jeans, a white T-shirt and blazer to her right, "this is Rachel. She's the analyst who's been watching your gameplay for the last few days. Rachel, if you can start?"

The analyst takes us through our gaming tells, our tics. The way the twins always play as a pair but can self-sabotage when they get competitive with each other. My propensity to play solo even when I'm attached to a team. As a group, we have trust issues (putting it mildly). She suggests a training schedule moving forward that focuses on us training together.

"Excuse me," Josh interrupts. "How come Augie gets to be captain? He's only just got here. Shouldn't we see who is best before assigning that position?"

Jones gives him a look. Augie looks sheepish. Carlo steps in. "Santos is a pro. You don't need to worry. He leads. But I've got a question of my own, if you don't mind."

"Sure," says Jones.

"You two…" Carlo nods to Ruby and Josh. "You two, I get. I've seen your scores at other tournaments. But why the newbie?" His gaze rests on me, and I shift uncomfortably. "You're bringing an unknown into an important match. What if she can't handle the pressure?"

"Daisy is my pick," Jones says smoothly. "I'm not worried about her handling pressure. She was placed twenty-fifth in the rankings overall – I asked the team not to place in the top ten because I didn't want them attracting any attention. Not yet. But believe me, she can handle this.

143

Don't question how I put my team together, Carlo. Your boy will be on the winning side. That's why we're all here. Now, why don't we leave the team to get acquainted while we work out logistics?"

Her tone is pleasant yet firm, and Carlo backs down without another word. Jones takes Carlo and the analyst to the lift, leaving Ruby, Josh, Augie and me alone.

There's an awkward silence, which Josh breaks. "Jones may have picked you, but you're not my captain," he says, then turns and walks out.

Ruby lets out a sigh. "He'll come round. He needs a minute. We'll be back. OK?"

With Ruby and Josh both gone, it's now just Augie and me.

"I told you we'd meet again." He is standing close to me, and he smells nice – like a heavy spice mixed with coffee. Cinnamon.

I gesture toward the machines. "Want to play?"

"Sure, but I get to pick, OK? Let's go old school, consoles."

"Weird choice for a VR tournament pro."

Augie shrugs. "Humour me."

I head to one of the four gaming pods near the back and strap myself into the chair. Augie holds up two wireless gaming headsets from the rack. "Here, put these on so we can chat while we play." He leans over to put it on me, tapping the Bluetooth and pairing it with his. Hands resting lightly on either side of my head as he tweaks it. "You hear me?" he whispers.

I nod.

He logs in on another gaming pod while the screen in front of me loads with the game he picked. "You picked *Donkey Kong*?"

I can hear the smile in his voice as he answers. "Start with the classics. Besides, I wanted something easy. So we can talk."

"About what exactly?" Even as I answer, I can feel the heat starting to slowly spread on my cheeks.

"Let's start with the day we met at Zu Tech. You never gave me your name. Why?"

My hands grip the controller that feels clunky in my hands after so much VR play. I guide my avatar, Cranky, on the platform, grabbing some bananas, smashing a few barrels, and moving up to the next level before answering.

"Why would I have given you my name? I was just the girl who bled on your T-shirt. The wardrobe malfunction. You wouldn't have remembered it anyway."

Augie's avatar, DK, jumps over two more barrels and smashes a third. "I would have remembered."

We reach the end of the first level and move on to the second. Augie's DK character is taking out some cement carts as I climb upwards.

"I went looking for you," he says, "after the junket."

The information is so unexpected that my avatar almost collides with one of the cement carts. Through our headphones, I hear Augie chuckle.

"Why would you do that?" I ask as I focus on hitting everything in front of me.

Augie brings us on to the next level, and I search for the bonus items to up our points score.

"Here's the thing. I wanted to check if you were OK. So I bribed the security guard with some merch and photos for his kids. Nice guy. He checked the visitors' log for me."

The blush is now a burning fire across my face. I used my real name to sign into Zu Tech. I need to buy myself some time to come up with a story.

A question with a question. "So why ask me my name if you already knew it?"

"That's the thing. I didn't get your name. There were no records of your visit to the building. Not even the CCTV footage of my hero moment when I was carrying you inside. Which I have to say hurt my ego."

The sentence hits home. "They scrubbed the security footage of me being in the building?"

"There's only one reason they'd do that. Because you were a private guest – of Zu Thorp. A man who hasn't taken an appointment with anyone not working at Zu Tech in the last three years."

I turn cold as we make the last few jumps, approaching the final level. The sound of the endgame starts to fill the air. Augie speaks again. "So, tell me, Daisy, why were you having an off the books meeting with the most reclusive tech giant of our time? Just days before you enter as a complete unknown into his tournament?"

The "game over" sound effect starts. And then silence.

14

We sit in quiet while I wonder what to say. I go with the truth.

"My sister, Maya, is … was an engineer at Zu Tech. She died. I was there to collect her stuff. I didn't realize I was meeting Zu till I got there. He knew her."

Augie walks over and crouches down by my pod. Gently, he takes my hand. "I'm sorry for your loss." He means it.

I take my hand away and stand. It's time to change the subject.

"How come you're here?"

Augie looks away, and I know I've touched a nerve.

"Because he's all washed up," Josh says. I glance over and see him standing there, Ruby behind him. "Brought his last team down, and now they won't play with him any more. He got kicked off."

"Josh." Ruby's voice is sharp.

"It's OK." Augie takes a deep breath. "Josh is right. I'm here because I'm broke. I blew a few matches and got dropped by my sponsor. My team decided I was all washed up and I haven't played a lot since." He glances at Josh. "Who told you?"

Josh squares up to him. "One of your old teammates said something to a mate of mine. He said you threw a match and got them disqualified from a tournament a year ago. You lost on purpose in exchange for cash." He looks at Ruby and me. "Don't you get it? We can't trust him. We are here to prop him up, to make Santos look 'good' while he tries to stage a comeback."

Augie takes a step towards Josh. "You don't know me. That match was a one-off."

Josh takes a deep breath and swallows. "Yeah, right. Scores don't lie. You. Burnt. Out. You haven't played in any big tournaments since then; you disappeared. Now you're back trying to trade off your former glory days. Like a sad has-been."

Augie's face becomes anxious, and he says nothing, just stares at the floor.

There is silence.

"You should leave, man," Josh says at last. "We didn't work this hard to be brought down by someone who can't handle the pressure."

Ruby looks at Josh, one hand fidgeting with a large gold ring she is wearing on her thumb. Then at Augie. Her voice is low when she says, "Josh is right. This isn't a game for us, Augie."

Augie doesn't say anything. No one moves. The tension is so thick I can feel it.

I take a deep breath. "We should give him a chance."

Ruby and Josh stare at me like I've grown a second head. "What?" they chorus.

"You think Jones didn't already know everything about him? Of course she did. It's Ma Jones. She chose him. She has a good reason for it. Plus, do you want to be the one who goes against her?"

Josh's jaw tightens. Moments pass. I watch as he struggles to control his temper. Then he sighs. "Daisy's right. If I could find those things out about Augie, there is no way Jones didn't. She must have known his rep when she picked him for our team." He kicks at the wall.

I look at Ruby. "I don't know what the game plan is, but I know I'm not going against Jones, and neither should you."

Josh looks at his sister again, and some tension drifts out of his shoulders. Then he turns back to Augie. "If you screw up, if there's even a whiff of you not playing by the rules, you're out – and I don't just mean out of the tournament. Got it?"

"OK." Augie offers him his hand. Josh sneers.

"Don't push it, Santos. I don't trust you."

Ruby gives me a shrug and heads off after Josh, leaving Augie and me alone. Again. "Why did you do that?" he asks quietly. "Why speak up for me?"

I shrug. "Because deep down, maybe I want to believe people can change."

Later we all wait for Jones in a breakout area. She appears eventually, with Carlo trailing behind her. If she notices the tension in the room, she doesn't show it. "Listen up, time for a pep talk," she calls. "Or as much of a pep talk as you'll get. From here on in, you eat, sleep and breathe this tournament. You need to burn off some excess energy or some rage, then use the gym." She glances at Josh as she says that. "You will learn to play nicely with each other. I don't care if you don't get along. This isn't the playground. The prize fund is over ten mill. Add in the endorsement and sponsorship opportunities, and that's a lot of hopes and dreams. From now on, you play as a group – no more solo runs. You will learn how to be a team, or so help me, none of you will be competing ever again because I will blacklist you all." Jones pauses for effect before continuing. "We go to Zu Tech in a few days for the tutorial on the new game. And when we go there, we go with a winning attitude. Got it?"

We nod. But none of us speak. We don't even make eye contact with each other. So much for being a "team".

15

June twenty-ninth, we pull into the entrance of Zu Tech's building. It's quieter today, just the usual people coming in and out — tech graduates in jeans, suited executives, event workers. The sun means that the tiny patch of green outside the building is being used by office workers in short sleeves making summer plans. Augie throws a glance my way, and I ignore it. This isn't the time for a trip down memory lane. Outside the door, an assistant that looks like a throwback to 1950s pop culture clutches a smart device. Blonde hair tied back in a high ponytail, navy pencil skirt, white blouse. A small red silk scarf knotted at her neck. She is beaming and wearing a badge that reads, "I'm a Beth, here to help!"

"Tower team! Welcome to Zu Tech." Beth's tone is annoyingly upbeat.

Josh gives her our details as she leads us to security and gives each of us a smart tablet with pre-loaded NDA agreements.

Ruby looks at me. "What the hell?"

I shrug from behind the brim of my baseball cap. "Standard non-disclosure agreement: you leak anything to the press, they sue you into your next life."

Beth turns her beam on me. "Exactly."

Ruby stares at her. "I know what an NDA is. I'm just used to them being on paper."

Beth waits while we sign, then collects the tablets. "This way, please, you still need to be scanned and checked."

I take a deep breath. Jones and I talked a lot about this part. If my newly created identity fails, this is where everything will end. I keep my eyes down as we go through. Each of our ID cards has a chip that can be scanned through security: beep, beep. Now it's my turn. For a second, nothing, then another beep. The security guy views my fake ID details, including my vaccination status. Augie falls into step beside me. "I liked your brown eyes better."

He's noticed my green coloured contact lenses. "Just felt like a change." I shrug.

Ruby rolls her eyes at him. "Nice way to give a girl a compliment, Santos." She pulls me ahead, leaving Augie looking stricken. "But seriously, why the change?"

"Trying something new," I mumble. I am on edge. I look different: my hair purple, green eyes, Tower team T-shirt, baseball hat. So long as I avoid Emily Webber, I should be OK. And surely she's too important to bother with the likes of us.

I look towards the main reception desk, and I remember something else. Somewhere near here is a box of Maya's stuff. Before this ends, I am getting it back.

We clear security and are brought to the elevators, which take us down to the basement. The walls are white down here, the only colour coming from modern art pieces and large flat screens that show a montage of Zu Tech's history and clips of speeches given by its founder. Everything is pristine – too pristine. Minimal signage points the way to fire exits – and a bomb shelter.

"You have a bomb shelter?" I ask Beth as we walk.

She smiles. "Several. It's best to be prepared. Each shelter has its own independent ventilation systems. This building uses some of the most advanced air filtration systems available to pick up foreign pathogens, viruses, and poisons, but in the case of a ventilation breach or a cyber-attack, the bomb shelter is where people on the list will go."

Josh raises his eyebrows at her. "I'm guessing we aren't on the list?"

"Correct. Ah. Here we are." Beth comes to a stop. "You are all so lucky! Everyone else who has been in has loved the experience."

Ruby's ears prick up. "So we aren't the first?"

153

Beth gives her another overly happy smile. "No, you're the last. You'll be playing the tutorial version of the game. The aim is to test you both as players and at playing the game. This tournament is designed to showcase SHACKLE and Zu Tech's new gaming equipment..."

"So, you want the best of the best at using the new equipment in the competition?" Josh fills in.

Beth smiles. "Exactly. The goal of today is to get you to play the tutorial level. You need to pass the level, either by completing it or by lasting till the tutorial timer runs out."

Ruby stops. "And if we don't?"

Beth gives her a smile. "Then you're out."

"That's not—" Ruby starts.

"Fair? Existence rarely is. The right to choose or exclude players was in the fine print when you signed up. Zu Tech only want the best of the best."

Josh nudges Ruby. "That won't be a problem; there's no one better than my sister," he says.

Beth comes to a stop. We are standing in front of double glass-frosted doors marked with the logo of the black ouroboros. Beth activates the keypad, and they swoosh open. We are in.

The lab is a vast open-plan space. Display screens show data, constantly updating in waveforms, graphs and numbers. Clusters of standing desk work terminals around a small arena – the gamer zone – below. Unlike at the Tower, these are standing pods. A team of technicians stand near them, checking the feeds and connections.

The pods are designed for players to stand at full height inside. All four pristine play pods are linked, and behind them, a giant blank LCD screen covers an entire wall. Each pod is sleek, ergonomic, and motorized. Constructed from glass and white chrome, the floor of each pod is a textured matt black material that looks like the belt of a running machine over a hydraulic base. The side panels have small ventilation shafts. Elegant. Science fiction come to life.

"Welcome to the future." I know the owner of the voice before I even turn around. It's the same flat tones I heard in the morgue. Annie Queen.

She stands at the head of a small team of technicians, all young and wearing white coats, clutching smart tablets, security passes dangling from lanyards around their necks like status symbols. My hands start to get clammy.

"Thank you, Beth 1. I'll take it from here."

Ruby frowns. "Beth 1?"

Annie turns to Beth. "Beth 1, did you explain to the guests what you are?"

Beth continues to beam at us. "They never asked. I am Beth 1, prototype AI assistant."

Josh looks at Annie for confirmation. "You mean she works with robots – or...?"

Annie nods. "She is a robot. As I said, welcome to the future. Beth is one of three prototype 'Beths' in this building for beta testing. They are part of Zu's robotic vision, designed to be part of future healthcare for the elderly and the young. But for right now, she's one of our lab assistants – while we iron out the kinks."

"Oh my god." Ruby is looking seriously impressed. She goes to touch Beth. "She looks so lifelike."

"Don't." Annie's voice stops her. "They don't like it when you touch them. It's one of the kinks. Now, you will need to get changed. For this test, we've assigned you with test names Tower 1 – Captain, Tower 2 – Healer, Tower 3 – Tank, and Tower 4 – Sniper. You'll see your suits inside."

Augie takes a step closer to Ruby and me, voice low. "We've stepped through the looking glass?"

Ruby whispers back, "Yeah, and straight into the twilight zone."

Josh and I ignore them both. But he's freaked out, too, I can tell.

Beth 2, identical to Beth 1, leads us to a changing room with a central space and four large changing areas with curtains. A silver-grey body-con suit hangs in each cubicle, numbered 1 through to 4. "Please change into these and proceed back to the main area. The suit size will stretch to accommodate you." Beth 2 beams. "You're going to enjoy what comes next."

Focus. I need to focus. Behind the screen, the suit moulds on to me once I manage to pull it on. It's cold, full length, flexible, soft. The exterior feels rubbery to the touch and is infused with millions of tiny silver and copper conductor threads with small wearable computer chips embedded into the fabric. It's like nothing I have ever seen.

Outside, Annie Queen is waiting. Another tech assistant hands each of us gloves made from the same material but with rubber around the fingertips, then tiny ear pods and VR glasses that look like high-end light shades. "Please go to your assigned pod so the test can begin."

I stand in my pod as the lab team starts to programme us in. Three to four technicians are clustered outside each pod, each checking different feeds. My heart is pounding. Was this where Maya went each day? Annie Queen looks over in my direction. I think I see something in her glance – interest, maybe – but perhaps I imagine it. The knot inside me tightens. She went to our apartment. She saw Maya in the morgue. Does she recognize me? Can she see through my disguise?

"Try to relax, Tower 2. This is supposed to be fun," Annie says. Her eyes flicking back to the labelled screens in front of her. "You too, Tower 1, you need to breathe. Your heart rate is too high."

Great, the suit is monitoring us. Not creepy, not creepy at all. I let out a deep breath as the pod adapts to me. "Try bouncing up and down," the voice in my ear suggests. I do, and the head clearance area above extends slightly. "Great, now try running normally." I peek over to Augie's pod, and we share a look. He shrugs and starts to run – and the floor moves with him, like a treadmill. I watch for a moment and then copy him.

"Calibrated," Beth 1 says.

"Are you ready?" It's Annie's voice in my ear now. "If so, please give a thumbs-up signal. The game is just loading."

Here goes nothing. I make the sign.

Beth 1 stands near my pod. "Now put on the glasses, please. Remember, you can ask for help at any point."

I comply, and gradually the lab, my pod, everything disappears. The world around me fades away. All I can see is a series of blurry shapes.

Annie's voice speaks again in my ear. "You're wearing contacts. Give the computer a second to compensate. Now."

Slowly the world starts to assemble and come into focus around me. I'm not in the lab any more. I'm standing on a lakeshore surrounded by mountains. There is a mist coming in. On my right, I can see Augie holding a sword. On my left, Josh holding a hammer, a shield on his back, Ruby clutching a bow. It's not like 3D or VR rendering though. Everything looks real. I watch sunlight reflecting off the water. A single ladybird teeters along a blade of grass. It's so perfect, so peaceful. Below my feet is gravel. I can feel a gentle breeze on my face – logic tells me it's coming from a vent in the pod, but it feels natural. Augie was right. We have stepped through the looking glass.

I raise my hand to look at it. It's now wearing a black glove and holding a machete. When I turn I can feel the wood of a short healing staff strapped on my back.

Annie's voice then booms into my ear. "Players, welcome to the tutorial for Zu Tech's newest game, SHACKLE – now let's see how long you can live."

16

"Get behind me." Augie's voice wakes me up. I am still standing rooted to my spot by the lake. Josh and Ruby are in a similar trance. "I said behind me." Augie is moving towards me, sword raised. "We have to get out of here."

"What's happening?"

He grabs my arm. "Move, Daisy, just like on a treadmill, remember?"

Josh is watching the lake, which is covered in mist now. There is a sudden splash on the surface of the lake. Whatever he sees makes him move, and suddenly he is sprinting towards Ruby.

It's then that the creature emerges from the lake at speed. A giant monster with grey scales and gleaming razor-sharp teeth. Eyes a cold yellow, like an old sea serpent's. It emerges fast from the water, slithering on to the shore, mouth snapping – just as Augie drags me away.

"Run!"

We move, all of us. I'm awkward. Tripping over myself and flying hard into the dirt. Augie is there again, pulling me up. "Remember you're on a treadmill in reality, OK?"

We go into the thick canopy of jungle that surrounds the mountains. I'm gasping from running; heart pounding, words come out in spurts. My hands are sore after the fall on the dirt. Everything feels too real.

"What was that?"

Josh is trying to catch his breath beside Ruby. "How did you know about the monster in the lake, man?"

Augie shrugs. "Instinct. Something that looks that peaceful is always the thing that tries to kill you first."

Ruby looks at both of us. "What's going on?"

I survey the jungle. There are Aztec ruins just visible through the green foliage. A mountain tower's overhead. The sound of jungle insects, birds, and a distant waterfall. The sun also seems higher in the sky now that we've cleared the beach and the heat is starting to build. The branches in one of the trees nearby start to rustle in a way that makes my stomach sink. One thing I know for sure is that we can't stay here. "If I had to guess," I say slowly, "this is an extreme challenge. Beth said to pass the tutorial, we need to survive for a certain amount of time, presumably using all the skills available in the game."

"They should have given us more info before throwing us into this. I mean, a tutorial gives you instructions on how to play, right?" Josh's voice is on edge.

Augie looks grim. "Usually. But that's not always how Zu Tech works."

Ruby throws her head back and talks to the sky, her voice loaded with sarcasm. "A little help would be great?"

Beth's floating head and shoulders holo appears so suddenly beside Ruby that she jumps. Beth is slightly blue and transparent now, a projection into the game. "Congratulations, Tower team, on surviving the shore attack. How can I help?"

"Beth – how do we pass this level?" Josh asks.

Beth smiles. "This is a tutorial section designed to introduce you to the key features of SHACKLE. Should you wish to try, you could attempt to reach the highest mountaintop, which ends this section of the game. But you will meet more dangerous animals, hunters, and flesh-eating zombies along the way. Your likelihood of surviving all those elements is negative. So far, no team has even made it to the temple, which is the midway point. It is best just to enjoy the experience. The tutorial will end once you use all the basic skills – moving in-game, defence and attack skills, and have passed the fifteen-minute mark, which is harder than you might think. Best of luck."

Beth's overly cheerful face vanishes before anyone can ask anything else.

"Great," Josh snaps.

"So what now?" Ruby asks, looking at Josh.

Augie answers. "We go to the highest mountaintop, over there. I'll lead, then Josh, Ruby, lastly Daisy."

"Should one of us go ahead?" I ask. "Scout it out?"

Augie shakes his head. "No, we stay together."

I see it then as he turns away. The look in his eyes. Augie Santos – the big tournament pro – looks scared. What the hell is this place?

I trek behind Ruby and Josh as Augie leads. I'm glad I'm at the back. I'm still finding my feet moving through the space and cutting the jungle into a path with my machete. The jungle seems to grow back around us as we move. Almost like it wants to separate us from each other. Augie cuts down the brush, but by the time I get to that spot, it's almost fully grown again.

Just outside my eyeline, I see movement. Faces that flash into frame and then vanish, gruesome heads on spears planted in the ground, giant snakes that slither from tree to tree. God, why does there have to be snakes? How on earth would anyone think that this would be fun?

We keep moving forward. "Watch it." Josh catches my arm just before I lower my foot. I had been so busy looking around at the things that skulk in the bushes that I forgot to look down. The patch of ground just ahead looks freshly disturbed. "What is that?"

"If I had to guess, landmine. We need to move slower."

We become more careful after that as the sun climbs higher in the sky. The temperature increases. My throat starts to feel dry. Then another sound begins to break through the jungle noise. Water. I can hear running water.

We speed up and cut through the foliage to a small pool of water fed by a stream coming off the mountain. It's picture-perfect, a small spring pool surrounded by tropical flowering plants. Peaceful. That word triggers an alarm bell in my mind. Peaceful was what Augie said about the lake, and it was anything but. I see Ruby move towards the pool.

I scream at her. "No, don't."

But I'm too late. As soon as Ruby's foot touches the pool, her image starts to waver. She cries out in pain, and it doesn't sound fake. It sounds like agony. Josh runs towards her, trying to pull her out. Water splashes on him, and he screams too. Then they both vanish into the water.

"Ruby?" I yell. I run to the pool's edge, Augie behind me. "Josh?"

Beth's holo image reappears. "Your heart rate is elevated. Is there a problem?"

"What happened to Ruby and Josh, Beth?"

"They were both eliminated from the game at the 'tranquillity pool of acid'." She pauses. "You seem upset? Is there something I can do for you?"

I take a breath, and my voice is loaded with sarcasm. "Yes, Beth. You can bring them back."

"I cannot bring them back, Tower Team Healer. They have been eliminated from this round. They cannot return till the game is reset."

"Why were they screaming? It sounded ... real."

Beth beams again. "It was. We programmed the suit to trigger some pain reactors in their body so players can feel the consequences of their actions. It makes the experience more realistic. Therefore more fun."

Augie says, "Fun for who?"

"Beth?" I say. I feel embarrassed asking this, but I have to.

"Yes, Healer?"

"Beth, please confirm that both players are OK?"

Beth looks confused. "Yes, both Tower team members are healthy and in the control room, watching the game." I'd forgotten that big LED screen in the lab.

Beth remains hovering. "Anything else?"

I've had enough of this game. "Yes, what is the quickest way to the mountaintop, Beth?"

Beth's smile becomes extra wide. "Through the Aztec temple. But you won't survive that."

"Let's see."

Beth fades away. I turn to Augie. "Want to visit the temple with me?"

He gives me a slight smile, his first since we arrived. "It's a date."

Beth, as it turns out, was right. Neither Augie nor I stood a chance against the game as we got deeper into the jungle. An ambush of cannibals wielding knives and clubs (presumably the ones making art with heads on top of spears) and poisonous spiders that drop from above mean that we are both lucky to be alive when we reach the moss-covered ruins of the old temple. We start to climb upwards, through the ruins, towards what seems to be the mountain path.

We make it as far as the temple when the zombie horde starts to attack. Row after row of the undead moving at speed on broken limbs and rotting flesh. Their teeth gnashing at us every time they get near. Their numbers are so vast I begin to believe Beth. This game is unwinnable.

Augie and I are backed up against each other. "Any ideas?"

Augie looks over his shoulder at me and gives a half-smile. "We go down fighting?"

We take positions, blades raised. The horde starts to surround us as we inch closer to the steps leading to the mountaintop. I do a practice slash with my weapon; my healing staff will be useless here. "Let's do it." My hand manoeuvring is getting better, but I still trip over myself when we have to move.

We dig in. Determined that if we go down, then as many zombies as possible will too. Body parts and limbs start flying as blood splatters across my face and suit. We hold firm, and for a moment, it looks like we have a chance, that we might just break through – and then the numbers increase. We try to change position, but it makes no difference.

Eventually, as our muscles get tired and the game generates even more zombies, we become overwhelmed. I stumble and fall, and a zombie is above me, raising a boulder. I feel a sharp pain and then nothing.

As the world of the lab starts to load around me, I take off my glasses. I feel dizzy, and my eyesight blurs. I look around and can only vaguely make out the image of Augie getting overrun and eaten as the zombies go into a victory dance on the giant LED screens in the lab.

Then, slowly, my focus comes back.

I can hear clapping. A few cheers from the technicians.

"What's happening?" I whisper to Beth 2 as she helps me out of the pod.

"They're congratulating you. You and your teammate lasted longer than the others today. It's a new lab record."

I look over to the screen where Ruby and Josh are standing. I raise my voice. "You OK?"

Ruby nods. She shouts back, "Death by acid sucks. You?"

I touch my head, which is still throbbing slightly. "Death by large rock does too."

Beth 2 goes to help Augie from his pod, and I go to join them. As I walk past Annie Queen's terminal, she stops me.

"Congratulations," she says, in a calm voice. "You did well." She holds out a hand, and I shake it. She holds mine just a beat too long, and I feel it then. The scrap of paper she has slipped into my palm. Then, in barely a whisper only I can hear, she says, "Don't open it inside the building."

17

"Party time."

My heart is racing, and my mind is focused on one thing: the small square of paper now hidden inside my suit.

"Hello! Earth to Daisy!" Ruby waves a hand in front of my face. "I just got killed in an acid pool, and it hurt, so we're going to enjoy ourselves tonight."

I swallow. "I'm not sure I should go. My head hurts." I want to get out of here and read that note.

Josh nods. "We need to skip it and talk tactics. Zu's VR was always cutting-edge, but this is next level."

Ruby shakes her head firmly. "No way! None of you are bailing. How often do people like us get to go to one of these events? Plus, I made T-shirts. So get dressed, now."

Ruby hands me a sports T-shirt. Still a dark blue, with the Tower team logo on it. But this time, the words are printed in glittery block letters and surrounded in a zig-zag line as if it's a comic book sound effect. I'm lost for words. I don't think anyone apart from Maya has ever made me anything.

Ruby shrugs. "When we were growing up, I learnt how to make my own stuff." She hands Augie a shirt. "You too."

He looks down at the shirt in his hands. "You sure?"

Ruby looks at Josh, who grins.

"Yeah," Josh says. "We outlasted the other teams because of you and Daisy."

Ruby laughs. "That was unreal, right? I mean, pain aside."

Josh nods, but when I look at Augie, he isn't smiling. There is a look in his eyes that I can't read. Like he is remembering something else, something painful.

We head into our various cubicles to get changed. I hide the note from Annie Queen on me with a sigh. Her instructions were not to open it inside the building. Guess I'm going to a party before I get to read it.

Annie seems to have left with the other lab technicians by the time we finish changing and go back outside. It's just Beth 1 waiting to escort us to the main hall where the meet and greet is. I take a last look around the equipment and monitors as we walk out. What I wouldn't give to somehow lose Beth 1 and "accidentally" wander to where the data storage units are. The answer to Maya's death is in this building. I can feel it.

"Take your time," Josh calls, and I see they're all waiting for me. I hurry over.

"Sorry," I mutter.

Josh rolls his eyes. "Don't mind him," Ruby says. "He's pining for his girlfriend, Amy."

Josh flushes, embarrassed. "I am not. And at least I have a girlfriend. The last girl you dated – what was her name again?"

Ruby shrugs. "Stacey."

"*Spacey Stacey.* How long did that last again, Ru?"

Ruby grins. "I'll meet the right girl someday, little bro. Till then, I'm here to have fun."

"For the last time, stop with the little bro. You're older by seconds, Ruby, seconds."

"Still counts." She hits Josh with a beaming smile. "So, what are these parties like, Santos?"

"Lots of egos," Augie says. "Some press, photographers. A famous DJ playing a set that you never get to dance to because you're meant to be 'working the room'. Slick, expensive and basically boring as hell."

Ruby looks at him in amazement. "You're kind of a 'glass half empty' type, aren't you?"

Augie looks at her, puzzled. "What exactly does that mean?"

I start to panic, heart speeding up again as another realization hits home. People. Press. I can't do photos, not now. I need to get out of this.

Beth 1 interrupts before I can fake a headache.

"Speaking of press," she chirps, "there won't be any. No press, no managers — at least not at the meet and greet. You will be in a player-only room. Everything you have experienced here today is embargoed."

"That's weird," says Augie thoughtfully. "I've never heard of a party like this with no press before."

I'm relieved — it should make my life easier. But I can't shake the feeling that something is off, all the way to the party.

The event is in the main conference room. The hallways are empty and silent as we pass. Beth 1 waves her hand at the sensor, and the hall's double doors swing wide, letting out a wave of sound and light. The room's interior is decked out like a movie set in a 1980s high school prom. Giant Zu Tech logos hang on the walls like old-fashioned American high school football banners, along with signs for the "principal's office" and the "nurses' station". The edges of the room are lined with old arcade machines which have game noises and lights spilling from them. Around these are raised platform areas with beanbags where some teams are already lounging. Pro players. People I have only ever seen on a screen or from a distance before.

Beverage and snack areas are clustered near the beanbags: retrofitted mini burger bars, milkshake makers and ice cream counters. In the centre is a half-empty square dance floor lit by pressure-sensitive tiles that light up as people move across them. The air is heavy with music, a mix of electronic, '80s and contemporary streams from a

DJ booth. Overhead, the ceiling is a mix of glitter balls and thousands of balloons held back by string nets.

Beth 1 nods. "Enjoy," she says, then leaves.

The panic starts to rise inside me. I have no idea how to behave at a party. The group care home didn't do many; each time they tried, it always ended with a fight breaking out. Proper parties aren't something I've experienced. My instinct is to run. The first person to notice my discomfort is, surprisingly, Augie.

He holds out a hand. "Want to dance?"

I look at the dance floor, which contains a few couples shuffling to a slow song, and the blood drains from my face. "I…"

Augie follows my stare and laughs. "I meant over there." He nods in the direction of the arcade section and the neon lights of what looks like *Dance Dance Revolution* circa 1999.

My shoulders relax. An arcade dance game. That I can do. "Sure. Ruby?"

"Are you kidding? It's pizza time. They have *Teenage Mutant Ninja Turtles*. Meet you guys near the *Ms Pac-Man* game later? Josh?"

"Food first," Josh says firmly. "Taking an acid bath makes you really hungry."

As we stroll over to dance revolution, I sneak a look at Augie's face. He's projecting his eSports pro smile all around, but it never entirely meets his eyes. Nearly everyone we pass seems to want to reach out to him, say hello, and be seen with him, despite the rumours of his recent failures. In this moment, he is still "Santos", the most promising eSports player in years. The one everyone thought would be the next big thing.

It takes for ever to cross to the arcade games, and we are almost there when a shoulder hits me hard as someone barrels between us.

"Watch it."

The owner of the shoulder turns around. He's about nineteen and well built. Straight black hair, dark eyes. I recognize him almost instantly. Thresher. Singapore World Tournament finalist from two years ago.

He ignores me and instead steps closer to Augie. There's an angry sneer on his face. "Want to make something of it, Santos?"

Augie is taller than Thresher, so he looks slightly down on him. "Move it."

Thresher laughs, a nasty laugh, and I can hear the hush building around us as people stop what they're doing and start to stare. "Still the same old Santos. Always running from me."

Augie sighs. "You want me to punch you in front of an audience? We can do that, but why keep repeating the past?"

The guy shifts, uncomfortable that the crowd is now watching. His pride is threatened. He isn't about to back down. "This time, you're going down," he snaps, and steps forward.

Neither boy notices my foot sliding out as Thresher steps forward. He goes to lunge and instead finds himself

172

tripping and face planting on the floor. The crowd starts to laugh and then shifts a little as Thresher gets up, blood pouring from his nose, his teammates rushing forward.

"Are you OK?" I say sympathetically. "There's a first aider over there."

I take Augie's arm and walk him away. As I do, I notice a familiar-looking woman – she competes in all the big tournaments. She looks at me, then at my foot, before she nods and, with a slight smile, strolls away.

Augie leans closer. "How do you know Eliza from the New York team?"

"I don't. I know *of* her, of course."

Augie glances at me. "What happened back there?"

I shrug. "I thought this would be a fancy party. Didn't realize I'd be breaking up fights." I nudge him. "I think I'm starting to feel at home now. Come on. I want the high score on *Dance Dance Revolution*."

It turns out Augie knows all the moves to the game, easily matching mine as we clear the first round and head into the second. The music drives both of us along, accompanied by the cheers of other people in the line. It's fun. I try to think back to the last time I felt so free, so uncomplicated, and can't. Josh and Ruby find their way over to us just as we finish a third high score, and Augie is wearing a grin that lights up his eyes.

"Remind me never to play you in dance battle mode. Want to get something to eat?"

I nod at Augie, and the four of us head to the food

tables and pile our trays with food and drinks. Then we commandeer four comfy beanbags and slump down to eat.

Ruby grins at me. "Nice moves. I didn't realize you had it in you."

I find myself smiling back. "Thanks."

Josh leans forward, spooning an ice cream sundae rapidly into his mouth. "What happened earlier, with that big guy?"

"That big guy is Thresher," says Augie.

"No way," says Josh. "*The* Thresher? And you have beef with him?"

Augie snorts. "I guess."

"Whoa," Josh says, eyes wide. He's so rapt that he misses his mouth, and the next spoonful of strawberry ice cream goes straight down his shirt. "Ah, man," he scowls. "I ruined Ruby's T-shirt."

I watch Josh scrub at his shirt with a napkin, spreading sprinkles and chocolate sauce further, and something clicks deep inside. I can't help it. I start to giggle. A slight low sound that I can't stop.

Augie looks at me and Josh, then he starts to chuckle. Ruby follows our gaze, seeing the shirt she spent hours working on smeared in melted strawberry goo and sprinkles.

"You've ruined it," she says, but she's giggling now too. She throws one of the smaller cushions at him. Josh scoops up a glob of ice cream and throws it at Ruby. It hits her square in the face. Now the four of us are hysterical.

I haven't laughed like that in for ever, not since Maya

and I were little kids. We try to calm down after a while, and then Josh looks at Ruby and gives a snort of laughter, and we are all off again. I don't know how long it lasts.

After a while the DJ makes an announcement. "Everyone on the dance floor for the balloon drop!"

Ruby grabs my hand and Josh's hand. "Come on!" she says. "Tower team on the floor."

Still giggling, the four of us make our way together to the centre of the now crowded dance floor. We start to sway to the rhythm of the music coming from the DJ decks. As the music builds, the DJ counts down.

Five.

Four.

Three.

Two.

One…

The air above us becomes a mass of floating balloons, paper streamers and glitter. I hold my hands up, watching everything as it descends, letting it drift over me. Lost in the moment. Twirling around as the balloons float down. When I stop, Augie is looking at me.

"You look happy," he says. "It suits you."

This is the first time I've laughed since Maya died, I realize. Maybe the first time I've laughed in a very long time. Ruby joins us as she takes a selfie with the still gently floating down glitter streamers and balloons.

Before I can think more, Josh joins us. "Cars are arriving to take us back. You ready?"

Ruby makes a face.

Suddenly I remember Annie Queen's note, tucked into my pocket. "Yeah, I'm ready," I say. It's time to go back to reality.

18

I close my door and lock it. Then I wait a few minutes, just in case. When I'm sure everyone has gone to their rooms I sink on to the bed and unfold the note from Annie Queen.

Asha,
  Maya never got a chance to introduce us, but I recognized you from her photos. What you're doing is dangerous. Come to the address below tomorrow at nine thirty p.m., and we can talk.

I tie up my hair and set to work searching on the drive containing Maya's data. Focused now on items with the words "SHACKLE", "VR Immersive" and "Annie

Queen". I start to ping the area around Annie's address, which is in St John's. There's no way I'm walking into a trap. I look at the location, the escape routes, the roads around the area and the CCTV.

Back to the data. I discard the files I've already looked through and focus on the larger video files. "Annie Queen" doesn't come up at all. Nothing is ever easy. I follow a link to a folder in an encrypted part of Maya's drive to her "special projects" folder.

Most of the files are chunks of code. I won't be able to process the code while I'm so wired on coffee. I go back to the video files. They are segments of recorded gameplay screen captures from a first-person shooter. VR. Multi-player, insurgency shooter game.

The backgrounds in the videos are like nothing I've ever seen before. Despite only being a few seconds long, I am stunned by the clarity and detail. How each background looks like a piece of art.

My attention is caught also by one of the avatars, its sleek design. A modern version of a Greek Fury, the winged female vengeance deities of ancient Greece. Maya was obsessed with Greek legends as a kid. I start watching the screen captures. Swords that slash and cut, blades moving so fast they can deflect bullets. The movements, the fluid style of play, the roll and jump tactics, seeking out the higher platforms to play from — are all oddly familiar.

I realize then — it's Maya. I almost choke on the emotion

in my throat. The avatar is her. A creature fashioned from the pages of her worn copy of *World Myths and Legends.*

But why hide it so deep? I focus more on the images, slowing them down. Then I see it. A jump, a crack in the perfect realism of the image. A slight drop in the frame rate. Maya must have been beta testing the game and found a glitch. My sister was so annoying about not letting go of something until she found the answer. This has to have been a puzzle she downloaded to study at home. What did she find? Where did it lead her?

I fall asleep, still wondering.

***

June thirtieth. The other searches are still running the next morning when I finish tying up my shoes. I am no closer to any answers. I need a break, a run. I get to the door just as Ruby goes to knock on it.

"You up? Super. Jones wants us all in the games room. The analyst wants to see how we play together after yesterday. See what we've learned."

***

After having experienced Zu's VR world yesterday, Jones's set-up seems flat, less exciting. Inspired by the footage from Maya's laptop, my avatar is another vengeance ghost – a Valkyrie. Swords that move like a hurricane, healing staff

179

strapped to my back, and a cry that shatters anything in front of it. The boys have gone for Aztec soldiers with big guns and massive firepower but, as a result, little speed, especially given Josh's additional hammer and shield. Ruby is sticking to her tried and true ninja panther skin, meaning she is faster than us but less heavily armed. She needs to rely on exploding throwing stars and knives. Precision shots along with her sniper's bow and arrow..

The game is a battle for earth. The alien team has a bomb. We have a map that shows all players and five minutes to kill the other side or neutralize the device. The clock is ticking. Augie is leading again. Or trying to.

"Josh, Ruby, take the far-right corner of the map. Josh takes the heavy fire while Ruby knocks out the alien horde. Daisy take out the fighters behind and search for power-ups. I'm going into the temple to find their leader and the bomb."

I can almost hear Ruby sigh on the comms over all the battle noise. "We did that last time, Augie, and you got wiped inside the temple. Remember?"

"I do. That's why this time it's going to be different. I've got this."

Augie starts each match with something to prove. I tune them out as I start a hand-to-hand fight with my opponents. A group of standard mutated starfighters. Each limb I cut feels cathartic. I finish the last one with a sword decapitating alien head stroke to save my ammo supply. Then remembering the alien numbers in the previous attack, I teleport to Augie.

As expected, it's a horde. Augie is outnumbered. I grab two power-ups from my virtual inventory chest and move.

"I told you I have this," he says through the comms.

I ignore him. "Ruby, when you're done, we could do with some help."

"On it."

The bomb is in the middle of a crumbling old Aztec temple. Between it and us is an alien nation. I keep looking around, wondering why Augie would attempt this alone. There is no way you can win this level solo. Overhead are old vines. I use one of them to swing to the opposite corner of the room, throwing Augie a power-up as I pass to boost his health stats. "Meet you in the middle?"

"Fine," Augie says.

We start to fight our way across the room to the centre, where the bomb and the alien overlord lie in wait. Me a whirling furious wave of swords and cries that take down anything around me. Augie a wall of flame and bullets. The timer on the bomb ticks down. We are running out of time.

"Ruby, Josh, where are you guys?"

For a moment, nothing happens, and I feel my stomach twist, then Ruby's stealth ninja materializes and vaults to the other corner of the room. "Josh is just cleaning up."

With the three of us now fighting the horde, we make more progress, but our ammo and life points are running low. I toss my last power-up to Ruby. "Josh, we need you."

I may be losing it, but I think some of the dead aliens are now respawning.

"Now!" Ruby yells.

Josh's super-soldier appears with non–era-appropriate but effective machine gun arms blazing as he shoots into the corner of the room and then raises his shield against the resulting attack.

"Watch it!" Augie yells at him as Josh's fire stream of ammo comes close to him.

Josh changes direction as we push from the four corners into the centre.

"We aren't going to make it," I say.

"I can if you cover me," says Augie.

"Fine, let's clear a path."

Ruby and I vault over to Augie, followed a moment later by Josh. We lay down a fire path. Clearing the horde so Augie's super-soldier can run towards the bomb. Too late, I realize the error. "You're too slow. We should send Ruby."

Augie ignores me or doesn't hear me with the game noise around us. He runs – but not fast enough. His ammo runs out long before he reaches the target. We get a full thirty seconds of seeing the alien leader's victory dance before the horde overcomes Augie, Josh, Ruby and me. We watch our avatars as they get eaten.

"That's gnarly," Ruby says.

I can only nod my head in agreement as the bomb detonates and we all die. "GAME OVER".

"Damn it." Augie smacks the controller on his pod as the rest of us strap ourselves out and stretch.

Behind us, the analyst, Rachel, has reappeared. "OK, I've seen enough." She wears a pained expression and lets out a faint sigh as she tucks a strand of her straight jet-black hair behind her ear and then repositions her glasses. "Come with me."

We follow her slowly into another room set up like a schoolroom with a whiteboard at the end.

"The tournament is less than two weeks away, eleven days," Rachel says. "Let's chat about that first. Then we'll circle back to today. Firstly, you're in. Your tutorial performance was good. You outlasted every other team but one."

Josh frowns. "But one?"

Rachel nods. "One other team outlasted you in the trials – the Dragons."

"But at the lab, they said we were the last to play and we'd outperformed the others," says Ruby.

"They were delayed and ended up taking the test the day after you. They made it past the temple. Secondly, this event will not be like a regular eSports competition."

"So how many teams are there now?" Ruby asks. "What's the format?"

Rachel puts up a slide on the interactive whiteboard. "So glad you asked. While you were at the meet and greet the Tournament team gave us this."

THE TOURNAMENT STRUCTURE:

- Eight teams chosen from the tutorial trial – four players per team.
- Three main rounds, each round a death match. One match, two teams, winner takes all, and each battle lasts until there is just one clear winner. No draws, no best of three.
- By the end of round one, eight teams will become four.
- Those four teams will then become two teams who face off for the final battle.

Ruby looks at Rachel in horror. "You're kidding me? That's insane. They pitched this as a regular tournament. The pre-selection with the 'tutorial' was weird enough. Now they're saying this is a knockout structure instead of everyone playing everyone else like in a round robin?"

Rachel nods. "It's unusual. But Zu Tech wants this tournament style, and with their money, they will get exactly what they want. They are buying time on every main platform to ensure this is the most hyped and viewed event they have ever produced. At the end of the day, this is a product launch for them, for their new tech and this game. The good news is the money, the prize fund has been increased – every one of the final four teams gets a guaranteed one million. Get into the final two, and it's another million. Win, and it's four million each, and that's before the endorsements kick in."

Josh leans forward. The happy go lucky look he usually wears is gone. He looks intent. "So, how do we win?"

Rachel holds his stare. "I can give you tactics and help some of you adapt your VR skills to make you comfortable in the space, but bottom line – you want to win, you must play like a team. You can't play like you just did in there." There's a pause, and then Josh nods slowly. Rachel turns back to her slides. "Now, let me talk you through where you guys messed up."

After the presentation, Rachel asks Augie to stay behind. Josh, Ruby and I head to the canteen for lunch.

"We're not going to win with him playing like that," Josh says as we sit down with our sandwiches. I take a fruit smoothie to keep Josh happy.

"What do you mean?" I say.

"Augie. He's shown that he can't lead. He went to pieces in there."

I can see the worry etched deep on his face. "We trust Jones," I say. "She chose him as leader – she must have had a good reason. Augie's finding his feet. I saw his old gameplay from when he was first on the circuit; he knows how to play. We just need to give him some time."

Josh looks thoughtful. "Time's not something we have a lot of, Daisy."

I meet Josh's look. "Then stop playing with him. You were late into the temple."

"I had an off moment."

"Then stop having those. You want to win. It means we need to support him and each other. You heard Rachel – we have to work as a team."

"She's right," Ruby says. "Come on, J. What choice do we have?"

Josh nods slowly. "OK, I'm in." But the worried look on his face doesn't change.

Just then, my smartwatch gives a slight vibration.

Murphy.

I found the cleaner who was at that studio. We should meet.

19

Murphy's phone rings out the first time. He answers on my second attempt, by which point I am impatient and pacing the room.

"Don't you answer your phone?"

"If it's important, people normally call back or leave a message. I was getting some tea. Where are you, Asha?"

Coppers and their tea breaks, of all the clichés. "Go on, then. You said you found the cleaner. Who is he?"

There's a sigh at the other end of the line. I wonder if he is delaying his answer to try and trace the call. Like I'm some rookie who hasn't even put a scrambler on my mobile.

"I'm not doing this over the phone. You want the information, then you need to meet me."

Fear starts to build in the pit of my stomach. "No deal."

"No meet, no information."

"Why should I trust you?"

Murphy sighs again. "Because you have no other choice."

He's right. Damn it.

"Fine," I say, thinking fast. "Ninety minutes from now; the coffee kiosk outside Leicester Square tube – the exit by the Hippodrome."

I hang up.

***

I get there early, scan the area for anything usual. It's afternoon now. I should be in the gym doing group training. Office workers hurry past, day drinkers hide in shadows, and tourists have started to weave through the doors of nearby cafés and restaurants. The usual public safety warnings light up on LED screens around us.

"I nearly didn't recognize you." Murphy's voice comes from behind one of the trees planted to cool this area of London and makes me jump. How did I miss him? Five-foot-five, still wearing his black three-quarter-length leather jacket that must have been bought when he was younger and leaner. Black shirt and trousers, hair that looks messy, like it needs a cut, but clean. Stubble that says he shaves at most once a week. I tug my hat down over my head and the cheap blonde wig I bought on the way.

He looks at me with concern. "I didn't mean to scare

you. I got here early. This place has doughnuts, and it's been a day. Can I get you something?"

"Yeah. Coffee, Americano."

Murphy buys the coffees and another doughnut for himself while I watch him to see if there is any tell, any glance to where someone else may be watching us. There is none. He's either a great actor, or he's on his own.

I take the coffee, and we start to walk in the direction of Leicester Square and its patch of wild grass, trees, and scattered benches. Green roofs and living walls surrounding the space are keeping the heat and pollution levels low.

We sit on a bench, and Murphy takes a bite of his doughnut. "Are you OK?" he asks.

I nod, although "OK" is as far away from my current state as you can get. Murphy makes me nervous. Being outside like this makes me jumpy. "You said you had information?"

"The guy who went to your studio was a professional cleaner, expensive. Name is Petrov. The type you use when you don't want to leave a trace behind. I've come across him before."

I try a sip of the hot coffee, eyes still scanning the area. "Who hired him?"

Murphy takes another bite and keeps talking. "He now works for just one corporate client." *Zu Tech*, I think. "We had a little chat. He said his client was concerned that an employee had been stealing proprietary information. They gave him that address and asked him to retrieve company tech."

"Maya would never steal anything."

He shrugs. "I didn't say she did. The guy said your place was clean. He was just picking up a company laptop."

"He trashed the place. He was looking for something."

"He said it was a coincidence. An unconnected break-in; he might have been careless leaving the door open."

I look down at my coffee. "My sister is dead."

"From natural causes." Murphy finishes his doughnut and screws the tissue paper into a ball, throwing it into the bin beside the bench. His voice is quiet as he says, "I talked to the medical examiner, Asha. She had some sort of respiratory failure and stopped breathing. There were no drugs in her system, no break-in, no signs of trauma. It's unusual, especially for a kid her age, but it happens. There is no mystery here. No conspiracy."

I clench my jaw. "Then why did you want to meet?"

"Because you're sixteen," he says gently. "You need somewhere to stay."

Silence.

Murphy sighs. "Let me bring you in. It won't be like the last place. I'll make sure of that. Stay in the system, do your exams, finish school."

Back to the social. I am flooded with memories. I do what Maya always told me to do. Breathe, let the pain flow away. "I'm not going back. And you're wrong. What happened to Maya was a crime. Zu Tech are involved. I'm going to prove it."

"Asha, you're a kid. The choices you make now will

affect everything you can do later. I read your file: you're smart. The security you set up at your apartment – that was professional. You could have a bright future. You know that, right?"

I take another sip. My coffee is getting cold. "Why the interest?"

Murphy shifts a bit. "I have a sister. She's got kids, raising them alone. One of them is your age. I see things as a police officer. Sometimes I can't do anything about them. But this, I can do something about this."

I see it then. His eyes dart, ever so briefly, over my shoulder.

"I'm not looking to be saved, Murphy." I stand up. "You told them where we'd be, didn't you?"

"It is for the best. If you're to have a shot at a future, you need to come in."

I don't speak. I don't look back. I just move. The shouts of "wait" echo behind me. I run straight into the nearby cinema, moving past the ushers and security towards the main auditorium that's half full, showing some new animated superhero thing. I didn't just pick this area because it would be busy; I know the escape routes here. Dark's training kicks in. Through the side door, behind the screen, don't look anyone in the eye. Slow it down. Act like an employee. The darkness and the audience will help confuse anyone chasing me. Think.

I block the exit door at the end of the screen with a chair, then head to the employees' locker area. Throw on a bulky, too warm jacket, a beanie that hides my hair. Dark glasses. Ditch the fake long blonde wig. When I emerge, I head towards the National Gallery, blending with the crowds, the tourists taking pictures. I join the fringes of a walking tour group. I never look back.

I go towards the Embankment. Crisscrossing my tube lines until I take the train back to Blackheath. There is no sign of Murphy or the social. He underestimated me, but only just. I can't believe I was so stupid. What did I expect from anyone connected to the system?

I head to my room and sit on the bed, steadying my breathing. Then I take Annie's note from my pocket.

Hopefully, she has more answers than Murphy.

***

It's still daylight when I step outside the tower again and on to the heath – that extended summer light that, in an hour or so, will quickly fade into black. The air still feels warm despite the breeze. People wander through streets free of the frantic day.

All around me, the only thing I see is families strolling across the heath under the streetlights. Couples are holding hands. Parents marshalling teenagers in for bed. Everyone has someone; even the lone guy I see on a bench has a dog who stares up at him. I feel jealous of them all. It isn't fair. I know that my pain isn't unique, but that doesn't make it easier.

I wonder – does the loss inside me make me see the world differently, as someone stuck on the outside looking in, or has it always been this way? These people have lives, routines, loved ones who would care if they vanished. Friends and families who would raise hell if something happened to them. Maya just had me.

"Asha."

I freeze.

"Dark."

He hasn't changed. Black T-shirt, jeans, dark hair that looks like he's run his fingers through it too many times, circles under his eyes, a hint of stubble on his face. He seems more uncertain than usual.

I start walking again. He keeps pace. "You just happened to be passing by?"

"Yes."

He's lying. I know it. He knows it.

"I can go if you want?"

And he would. We've always had that – a respect. If I tell him to go, he will. But I don't want him to.

"Why did you come back?" I ask.

"I know what it's like to be alone."

We stop and face each other. "You can't fix this for me. So stop trying to." A pause. "Tell me something true instead?"

Dark sighs. This was a game we used to play from before. One he always hated. *Tell me something true.*

"I don't like chocolate."

"OK, *Asha, that is just weird, but noted, no chocolate.*"

"*Your turn.*"

"*Fine — I don't like coffee. I prefer tea.*"

I'd grinned at him then in mock horror. "*I'm not sure we can stay friends after that particular confession,*" I'd said.

He'd smiled. "*Think of it another way — I'm leaving you all the coffee, as long as you leave me the tea.*"

"Something true," Dark says quietly. "OK. I don't want anything, Asha. I just want you to know that I'm here if you need me."

I shrug. A beat, then, "Walk and talk?"

His shoulders relax. He holds out a hand, and I take it; a slight smile hovers around his lips when I do. I squeeze it, and his fingers wrap around mine. That familiar smell of citrus and wood. The tension leaves and I feel lighter for a moment. Despite everything, sometimes being with Dark feels like peace.

We stroll through the last red streaks of the day and into the night. People in the park scatter and drift away.

"You owe me a truth," he says.

"I know how it works." A pause. "I missed you."

We walk on. The scent of grass, jasmine, the whiff of alcohol from some outside beer garden. The faraway smell of a hopeful London BBQ. The grass soft underneath, a warm breeze blowing past.

"You have a destination in mind?" he asks.

"Always."

An almost-smile from him. "Lead on."

The streets play out before us, bursting with the usual drama, noise and hustle. Some people are already loud and sloppy, day drinking turning into night drinking. We say nothing; we just fall into an unhurried pace. I lead him towards St John's. I get close to Annie Queen's address, but not all the way. At last, I stop.

"This is me," I say. "Thanks for the escort, but I need to go it alone now."

He nods. "It was harder this time," he says.

"What was?"

"When you left before, I knew how happy Maya made you. I knew that it would be safer for you if I stayed away." He stops, and I face him. We stand under a streetlight and look at each other. His thumb strokes my cheekbone for a moment. I shiver under his touch. "But now, I don't know if you're safe."

I stare back at him, and there's that pull again. That thing that keeps drawing me to him. Somehow, instead of becoming weaker as the months and years pass, it keeps getting stronger.

"I need to find out what happened to Maya," I say, my voice a whisper on the breeze. "That's all I can do right now."

"I know," he says. His fingers brush my cheek again.

"Do you think we can be mates?" I ask. We are now standing so close that we look like one dark shape in the night. The hand that had been holding mine is now on my waist. My hand has found its way on to his shoulder, fingers dancing with electricity. My body leans a fraction forward. I refuse to wait for my logical brain to remind me of all the reasons why this is a bad idea.

His words, when they come, are so close to me that his breath feels like a caress. "We were before." A pause. "If that's what you want?"

I don't know what I want. I just know I'm tired of being alone. Of living with only fear, pain and grief, always running. I move closer. Standing on tiptoes, I lean forward. I kiss him. Our first real kiss. A gentle brush of my lips against his sets something off. He responds. One hand holds my face as the other pulls me against him. My body is on fire. The world and everything around us is gone. It is just the two of us and the endless London night. I'm lost in something that feels inevitable.

He pulls back for a moment. "Asha." The words are a whisper near my mouth, my neck. "I…"

But he never gets to finish those words because I stop them with another kiss.

20

When Dark and I eventually pull apart, we are breathless. His arms are still holding me.

"You kissed me."

I did. I'm drunk on the feeling of Dark's lips on mine, his arms around me. It's overpowering.

It's making me forget what I came here to do.

"I did," I say, my voice firm now. "But I meant what I said before. Until this is over, we need to just be friends." His arms fall away from me. The sudden chill of the night air replaces their warmth, and I miss them. My body gives a shiver, physical rebellion against what my mind is telling me to say.

"All right," he says. "But let me wait for you, at least."

I read his face. The worry in it. And again, a shiver runs down my spine. I know why now, but I don't want to admit it to myself out loud. Dark cares about me. I care about him.

"I need to do this alone." I walk away.

He stands in the street, watching me go. After turning around the corner, I feel my burner phone vibrate with a new message.

Stay safe, be brave. D

The air is sharp now. The street is fully dark. Lights are on as I reach the door to the small block. It's an old building that's seen better days, divided into tiny flats. I take a deep breath. I am suddenly scared about what might be on the other side. Hand buried deep in my pocket, touching my phone. *Be brave*. I push against the bell for flat 1C.

"Hello?" The voice is female, slightly stilted. A camera light flashes on above the bell.

Here goes everything. I keep my voice steady, eyes looking up and into the camera. "Hi, it's Asha."

The buzzer sounds almost immediately, and Annie Queen's apartment door opens.

Apartment 1C turns out to be a one-bedroom flat on the ground floor. The paint is peeling on the door, but the doorstep is clean. There is an old full-length umbrella outside. Her face is backlit from the warm light of the apartment that spills out into the darkness.

"You better come in. I've been waiting to meet you for a while, Asha."

Her voice is calm, even, just like at the coroner's office. I push the fear down and step through the doorway.

The apartment is bright. Pale cream and honey colours, soft textiles. It feels like the home of just one person. It's open plan. Once a sitting/dining room space, the central area is dominated by a play pod and a large dining room table covered by a black cloth and littered with various computer parts, motherboards, processors, RAM and wireless cards. One wall is lined with shelves double-filled with books and different objects like small, recycled glass jars filled with circuits, connectors, pen drives. Two 3D printers occupy the bottom shelves and give out a quiet mechanical hum as they print. Alongside them are some upcycled PC motherboards and a few packing boxes, still full. Annie Queen, it seems, has just moved in.

Annie gestures to stools by the kitchen island where a candle is burning. The smell of mango wafts around the room. "Do you want some tea?"

Is it safe to accept anything from a stranger who impersonated you to get access to your dead sister's body? Probably not.

"No, thanks," I mumble as I sit.

Annie looks at me. "Could you repeat that? I need to lip-read. I'm partially deaf."

"Oh. Sorry. I'm OK for tea."

"Don't be sorry. I'm not." She sits down across from me

with a mug of tea. I can smell ginger and spices. "The code I write doesn't care about my hearing."

I stare at her. Up close, Annie is striking. Her cheekbones are impossibly high in her oval face. She's tall with a kind of effortless regal beauty. A queen, but there are signs of strain. Her eyes are slightly pink. She's dressed in soft grey loungewear, elegant and expensive looking. Her hair piled up in a box braid topknot. Something about her makes me feel at ease, even though the circumstances mean I need to stay alert. This could very easily be a trap.

I scan the room. Ground floor windows, as well as the way I came in. The front door just has a small Yale lock on it. Annie didn't pull the bolt across. Still, just in case, I keep one hand in my pocket, keys through my fingers. A weapon of sorts if I need it.

I clear my throat. "You knew my sister. Maya."

The tears that come to Annie's eyes are quick and fast. "I can't believe she's gone." Her voice is close to breaking.

"You knew her well?" I ask.

Annie looks at me, devastated. "She never told you about me?"

"She never really told me much about her friends and work colleagues," I say.

Annie gives a watery laugh. "Friends? Maya is…" She stops and gulps for air, like the words are stuck, fresh tears filling her eyes. "Was. Maya was my girlfriend."

21

"What?" I say. Yes, I'd seen the messages between Maya and Unknown. But I still hadn't believed it. My studious, quiet, closed-off sister – in love. How had I not realized? How could I not have guessed?

"Maya was my girlfriend," Annie says as the tears stream down her face, and she goes to wipe them away. The nails on her hand are bitten and cracked.

"Here." Annie takes a small photo album from a shelf and gives it to me. On the cover is a photo of her and Maya. I trace my sister's face with a finger. Annie watches me sympathetically. "How about I make you that cuppa?" she says, and this time I accept.

While Annie boils some water, I stare at the cover image

of the hardback album. Annie. She looks less worn in this picture; she's smiling. The person in the photo beside her is Maya, but I almost don't recognize her. Head thrown back, laughing. Not just a half-smile but a not-caring-who-sees-you look of joy. Her arms are thrown around Annie's shoulder while Annie tries to take a selfie of them both. In the background, all of London lies below.

"It was on the London Eye, the day Maya found out you were coming to live with her." She puts a cup in front of me. "She was so happy." She glances towards the cup. "It's camomile, Maya said it was the only tea you drank."

The tears start to well in my eyes. I turn the album's pages. Maya and Annie in various parts of London. Summer shots, at a Halloween movie marathon, winter ice skating, a picnic under pink cherry blossom trees in the park — Maya bundled up against the London spring in two coats. Laughing, smiling, goofy faces. There is no mistaking the look my sister has in the photos. Maya was in love. And she never told me.

"I didn't know..." I say helplessly as I sink further into the stool, eyes unable to look away from the photos on the counter.

Annie shrugs. "Maya loved her secrets." She takes a sip of her tea, her voice gentle. "She didn't trust people easily. Not surprising after ... well, after what you both went through as kids. I take it that had something to do with you changing your name? Daisy?"

I gulp the tea to force down the lump in my throat.

"It was her favourite flower. She told you about how we grew up?"

"A little bit. I'm not close to my family. She was the only person I opened up to. She knew all my secrets, and I knew all of hers." She stirs her tea. "Or so I thought."

"How long were you two together?" I ask.

"Just over a year. When you came to live with her, she was so happy. She said I could meet you; she just wanted to give you time to settle in first. Then, over the last few months, Maya became ... distant. We started fighting. She stopped wanting to go out, kept making excuses, cancelling at the last minute. I thought maybe it was because she was embarrassed, afraid of me meeting you. Or that she'd told you and you'd reacted badly."

I meet Annie's gaze. "She never even told me she was involved with someone. If she was happy, I would have been too."

"In that case, I don't understand," Annie says. That desolate look is back in her eyes. "She was hiding something from me during the last few months. She said she still loved me, but I could feel her pulling away."

I take a deep breath. In my gut, for some reason that I don't quite understand, I trust this woman. I also need her. "How much do you know about the 'special projects' division in Zu Tech?"

Annie puts down her tea. "A bit. I should start at the beginning. I met Maya at one of those weird annual physical check-ups they do at work. We were waiting outside the

203

exam room; someone had messed up the times, so we were there for ages, and something just clicked. I was brought in to work in the lab for SHACKLE. I went to college too early, too many degrees. This job was a big deal for me, my first gig outside academia and the pressure was on. Maya was working in another division in beta testing and new game design. We were around the same age, both new, single and trying to prove ourselves. We decided to go for a coffee one day after work. Then we started to hang out, and it developed into something else. But Zu Tech has a strict policy on office dating. So, when we started seeing each other, we decided to keep our relationship quiet. No one at work knew about us. We could only be ourselves outside the office or when we hung out with one of my few mates from uni."

Annie's fingers start to drum slightly against the cup she's holding. "All Maya talked about from the start was getting you out. It was her whole focus. A few months after we met, Maya saved enough to rent a two-bed apartment. She was engaging daily with the social, jumping through all the hoops. She put in a request for human resources to do a letter from her employer confirming her employment status, salary, all that stuff, and to recommend her as a fit guardian for you. The first request got ignored — she assumed it was an oversight. When they didn't respond to her second request, she went to talk to human resources. They directed her to…"

I take a sip of tea. "Let me guess. Emily."

"Yeah. The mouthpiece of the suits. I call her Zu's

Rottweiler. Emily said she was afraid that Maya hadn't been at Zu Tech long enough for them to in good conscience recommend her as a suitable guardian. She was still on probation. So Maya had two options. Wait another ten months, build up her savings, see out her probationary term and reapply when she was on her fixed contract. Or take the deal that Emily offered her."

"She wanted Maya to work in the special projects division," I whisper.

Annie nods. "Emily was recruiting for a new project – something even better than SHACKLE, which you've experienced first-hand. A new algorithm to *redefine the user experience in VR*. Something even more *revolutionary*, which would keep the company in the number one spot in tech innovation globally. They were impressed with Maya's coding. They said if she joined the team, the hours would be long, but they could expedite her probation period, and she could get her referral letter."

I chew my lip. "You didn't want her to do it?"

Annie shifts a little. "No. I could understand her wanting to get you out, but there was something weird about that project right from the start. People assigned to that section were separated from the rest of us. They worked in the sub-basement near the data storage. Security was tight, the turnover rate was high. People would disappear overnight – burnout, the rumour was. Maya had her whole career ahead of her. I wanted her to stay away. But Maya wouldn't listen to me. She took the deal."

I wrap my fingers around the warm cup. "What happened?"

Annie thinks for a moment. "She started to change. It was almost like she wasn't in charge of herself any more. I'd find her doing something, and she'd have no idea why she was doing it. She was blacking out, sleepwalking through things. Forgetting. She was always so reliable, you know?"

"Yes, she was." Reliable was Maya's middle name.

"But after she joined the special projects division, she started forgetting dates. Standing me up, accusing me of *making* things up. When I confronted her about it, she'd get annoyed, then fly into a rage – and that wasn't like her either. I figured it was exhaustion from the ridiculous work hours. We started fighting over nothing, stupid things. Where to have lunch, what to do for her birthday, the hours she was working. When she was going to introduce me to you. Everything would escalate into a row. Now I wonder whether … she was pushing me away on purpose."

I realize with a jolt that I've stopped clutching my keys like a weapon.

I drink the last dregs of my herbal tea. "What do you think happened to Maya?"

Annie takes another sip from her cup before she answers. "She was overworked, exhausted. And I – I pushed her too far." Tears fill her eyes. "I said I wanted to meet you, and I wanted her to tell people about us. That I was sick of being a secret. She said no. So, I cut her off. I blocked her messages. I thought if we had some time apart, some space, she would realize that we were worth fighting for." Annie's voice cracks slightly. "By the time I came to my senses, it was too late. I don't know what happened to Maya. I only know that something feels off about her death. Like if she was sick, I would have noticed something, right?"

"When you *'came to your senses'*, you reached out to her, didn't you? You rang her that day. She argued with you, so you came to the apartment the next day?"

"I told her that she'd won on the phone. That we could play it her way because I couldn't bear the silence and fighting any more. She got angry at me. The next day I came to say those things to her in person. But I was too late. The neighbours told me what had happened. I searched the hospitals. I just had to see her one last time to say goodbye. I went to the morgue and pretended to be you. I saw her on that metal drawer. I…" And with that, Annie's body starts to shake with sobs, and I go and gently touch her shoulder. She turns and wraps me in a hug, and my first instinct is to move, but somehow, I don't.

"It's OK," I say. A lie.

She shakes her head. "It's not. I loved her, and when she needed me, I wasn't there."

I wasn't either, and I lived with Maya. I should have known. "Those pictures are the happiest I have ever seen my sister," I say. "She knew how you felt about her, Annie."

Annie wipes her eyes with a tissue. "But that doesn't bring her back, does it?"

"No. And I need to know what killed her. I can't say goodbye to her till I do. Something isn't right here."

Annie meets my look. The tears stop. Her face changes. "What do you need?"

When I eventually leave Annie's apartment, it's late. I asked her to find a way to get Maya's office stuff from Zu Tech before we meet again. I think I can trust Annie. As far as I can trust anyone right now.

It's cold when I walk back towards Blackheath and the Tower. Somehow it seems darker than before, less magical. Filled with hidden dangers. When I get to the door, I'm shivering. Hand raised to find the scanner that will allow me to enter. But the door opens before I do. Augie steps out of the shadows.

"Here." He hands me a fleece. "Thought you might need this."

"You were waiting for me?"

He shakes his head. "I saw you approaching on the system. You looked cold. Nice walk?"

I nod cautiously. "Yeah."

"Only Ruby said you texted and you were sick."

"I was." Another lie. "I just went for a walk when I started to feel better. Needed some fresh air."

Augie takes a step forward, and his expression is grim. "But you weren't going for a walk alone, were you? So, new question: how well do you know Dark?"

22

I throw the fleece at him so hard that he flinches. "You *followed* me?"

"I was worried about you! When I first got here, I know Josh wanted me gone. You talked him down."

"So this is payback? You don't owe me any favours, and I don't owe you anything either."

I see the small upward movement of his lips, the slight smile that crosses them. His inability to stay serious for too long. "You owe me a T-shirt."

I scowl. "I can take care of myself, Augie." A thought occurs to me. Dark has been off-grid for almost two years now. "How do *you* know Dark?" Augie shifts uneasily on his feet.

"I saw him at a thing six months ago. Carlo, my

manager, explained who he was. Said he's the kind of guy you don't mess with."

"Like I said, I can take care of myself."

"I never said you couldn't, Daisy."

This time I walk past Augie to the lift. As I press the button, he calls after me.

"Hey, Daisy?"

"What?" My voice sharp, still annoyed.

"That guy is … dangerous."

The doors begin to close. "I worked with him for almost a year, Augie. Tell me something I don't know."

***

When I wake up the next morning, my emotions are scrambled. I kissed Dark. Maya hid the person she loved from me. Murphy tried to turn me in to the social, and Augie — what's the deal with him? I bury my head beneath the pillow. My body wants to stay in bed. My mind has been running in so many circles it's exhausted. I want time to figure out what all of this might mean. Then I roll over and see the neon glow of the countdown clock beside my bed. We are ten days away. And later today, we are going to Zu Tech again for the final fittings of our suits.

I throw on some clothes and head down to breakfast. My black mood seems to be matched by Josh's. His hair is damp from the shower, but he looks like he hasn't slept. His eyes are bright. He keeps checking his phone and toying with the chain necklace his girlfriend gave him as he hangs out by the coffee machine in the kitchen.

Augie is in another corner, eyes fixed on his phone. He doesn't look up when I come in. Ruby sits at the table nearby with a mug of tea. "Daisy!" she exclaims. "What happened yesterday?"

"Sorry. Stomach ache."

Josh puts down his phone. "Seriously? This close to the tournament?"

"Thanks for the sympathy," I say, sliding into a seat. "I'm all better now, promise."

"Is it nerves?" asks Ruby, handing me a coffee. "Because Josh is right, now is not the time." She sits opposite me, her eyes wide and serious. "Is something wrong, Daisy?"

I hesitate. I need allies, I realize. Allies who know some version of the truth. I can't trust anyone completely – but maybe I can let them in some of the way.

I take another deep breath. "Being in Zu Tech, it was kind of emotional for me." I glance around and see that Augie has put his phone down and is listening. "Did I ever tell you how I first met Augie? It was at the tournament launch; I ran into him."

Augie snorts. "Actually, more like I saved you."

I hold up a hand. "Zip it, Mr 'I'm going to try and defeat an alien horde single-handedly because I have something to prove'."

Ruby hides a slight grin. "Way to psychoanalyse, girl. Go on, Daisy."

"There were crowds when I got there," I explain. "I tripped and fell — Augie gave me a hand and got me into the lobby."

Augie looks annoyed at my bald recollection. "When I got to you, you were on the ground in a heap, bleeding. You were about to get crushed by the crowd..."

"I had a tiny scratch on my cheek."

"You bled all over my favourite T-shirt."

"I'm sorry, again, about the shirt—"

"Favourite shirt."

I sigh. "How about I buy you another one?"

Augie brightens. "That would be nice."

Ruby and Josh exchange a look.

"Should we just leave you guys to it?" Ruby asks. "You argue like Josh and his girlfriend."

Josh scowls. "Like you and Spacey Stacey."

I glare at them both. "Do you want to hear why I was there or not?"

"Please," Ruby says. "Go on. You were there for the launch and..."

"I wasn't there for the launch. I was there because my sister was an engineer for Zu Tech."

Ruby and Josh lean in closer to the table. "Does she have access to the game? Can she give us some tips?"

I look down for a second, wondering how to phrase the next part when Augie speaks, his voice quieter this time. "She said 'was', guys, past tense."

"She left Zu Tech?" Josh asks tentatively.

"Daisy's sister passed away a few weeks ago. She was at Zu tech to collect her stuff."

"Oh." Ruby and Josh both move before I can react. The arms come at me in a tangled mess. They surround me without asking, creating a weird human sandwich where I am the filling. Or at least that is what I think as my control starts to unravel. One more act of kindness, and I will be crying in front of them. And I'm scared that if I start to cry, I won't be able to stop.

Ruby speaks first, her arms still around me. "How long ago did this happen?"

"June, June third."

Ruby looks like she is going to cry. "Are you OK? Stupid question. Of course you're not."

"Why didn't you tell us?" Josh asks.

"There was nothing you could have done. Nothing to be gained."

"Idiot, we could have been there for you." Ruby hands me a tissue, and I realize I am crying, and she is also crying. Great. "You don't need to do this alone."

Augie's expression is sombre. "I'm sorry for your loss," he says. "I know how hard it is."

"You lost someone too?"

Augie sighs. "My mum. It wasn't the pandemic. It was old-fashioned cancer, about a year ago." His voice is quiet. "They didn't spot it at first. Thought it was something else. Told her to lose weight because she had this tummy. Didn't realize that her 'tummy' was a tumour. I thought I could buy a different outcome for her. Better treatment. In the end, it didn't matter."

I go towards Augie, wrapping both arms around him and inhaling that smell of coffee and spice that seems to linger always on his skin. Just holding him. Josh and Ruby hug us both. It's cheesy as hell, and I don't care.

"I guess we're all a bit broken and lost," I say into his shoulder.

Augie hugs me back and then says, in a whisper, "I don't want to be lost any more."

When we pull apart, Josh snaps his fingers. "Wait. That's why you took a dive, isn't it? Threw that tournament? So that you could pay for your mum's treatment?"

Augie nods, and it's like watching a weight lift from him. "We'd exhausted every option. Then we heard about some experimental treatment – it was overseas, cost a lot of money. I took the dive – but by the time I'd got the money, she…"

"I understand," says Josh. "If someone came after my family, I'd make a deal with the devil if I thought it would help them."

"Was it just you and your mum, Augie?" Ruby asks. "No other family?"

"Single parent. Her parents threw her out when they found out she was pregnant. She was the one who believed in me. It was always the two of us against the world. I guess when she passed, I got lost. But that's why I want to do this tournament. To make her proud of me again."

The two of us against the world. Like me and Maya. I meet his eyes, and something unsaid passes between us.

"Is that why you entered the tournament too, Daisy?" Ruby asks me. "To make your sister proud?"

I nod and blink back some tears. I feel guilty because it's not the truth — or at least not the whole truth.

23

We spend the rest of the morning training. SHACKLE is next-level immersive. A space I need to get comfortable in fast, otherwise we won't make it past the first round. Rachel, our analyst, sets up some simulations for me while she runs Augie, Josh and Ruby through strategy games.

After a few runs, my movements get easier. The new controller gloves become extensions of me. I rejoin the others, and we go through more live multiplayer online VR battles, tougher ones, trying to outthink each other every step of the way. It's equal parts exhausting and exhilarating. We all lose track of time until Jones comes into our games room to call lunch. I realize she must have been watching us for a while.

As I go to leave, she calls me back. "Daisy? A word. You OK? You missed a session yesterday."

"I'm fine."

For a moment, a look of what might be concern passes over her face. "Because you can tell me if you're not."

"I'm not going to scupper your win if that's what you mean."

Her face changes, the mask goes on. "Good to hear. I have a lot riding on this one. Speaking of which, a package arrived for you by courier, care of the church. I had it put in your room, but don't make a habit of it."

"Sorry." But inside, my heart leaps because I know who it's from. I just didn't expect it to be so soon.

***

After lunch, Augie corners me. "Listen," he says. "About the other night – about Dark…"

I groan. Between him and Jones, I'm feeling seriously under scrutiny.

"He's a friend. Can't you just leave it?" The way he keeps circling back to Dark has me on edge.

"Does Jones know you met him?"

Anger rises up in me, and I cross my arms over my chest. "Is it any of her business?"

Augie looks at the ground as if unsure what to say next. "Look, a few days before I came here, I saw Jones with Dark. It was in a club after an eSports thing. They were arguing in a back room, and I overheard. He said she stole something from him, that he wasn't going to forget or forgive, and that the consequences were dangerous. Jones looked worried."

The room is silent for a moment, just the quiet hum of the machine fans cooling down. That doesn't make sense. Dark is many things, but he owes Jones a lot. He wouldn't threaten her. Augie must be mistaken. He's concerned about Dark's reputation, but I know him. His reputation has been well cultivated, but most of it is rumours, a way to keep people away and avoid having his time wasted. Dark's never had an ego, just a purpose. We both learnt that the hard way when we were little – if someone fears you, they don't mess with you.

Augie somehow seems to sense a little bit of what I'm thinking. "I know you and this guy go way back, but sometimes people change and not always in a good way. Just be careful, OK?"

I know he means well, but still – the rage builds. "I don't need you looking out for me," I snap. "I grew up fast, Augie. I can take care of myself." I turn and move towards the door. His fingers gently touch my arm, and I shrug them away.

"Daisy, please. Look. I'm not good at this." A beat. "I used to be someone, you know? Augie Santos, pro player."

The anger in my chest recedes a little at his tone. "You're still Augie Santos," I say. "The tournament pro, the wins from your past – no one can take those away from you."

Augie shakes his head. "I know I'm not that guy any

more, the bright shiny new thing, and that's OK. I don't want to be. But I do get it, Daisy."

"You get what, exactly?" My voice is laced with a warning.

"I lost everyone I loved too. I understand how rough and lonely it is because I went through it. And, for some stupid reason, I want to be there for you. Why don't you trust me?"

Two boys are offering me help. Like I'm some damsel in distress. Like I didn't survive the care homes. Like I haven't been running for what feels like forever since. I'm stronger than that. I can rescue my damn self. I want answers, and I'm faster on my own. I glare at him.

Augie's eyes search my face, and he reaches out again to try and touch my arm, but I jerk it away from him. The smell of coffee and cinnamon lingers between us. My heart starts to pound. *Alone is safe*, I think. Alone will keep me from getting hurt again.

I move towards the door, and the words when I find them are bitter. "You don't need to worry about me, Augie. I'm not about to jeopardize your big comeback."

I don't wait for a response. I have somewhere else to be. As I walk away, I wonder – if Dark has changed, then have I changed too? Become harder, colder?

It doesn't matter, though. All that matters is what happened to Maya.

***

219

I recognize the brown cardboard box in my room immediately. Once I see it, everything else fades away – it's Maya's work stuff.

On top of the box is an envelope marked with my name in large looping handwriting with a note inside. When I remove it, something shiny and metal falls on the floor with a clink – a large oval silver locket engraved with *"Asha"* on one side and *"I'll always be with you"* on the other.

I read the note.

> *Security owed me a favour, so I got the box.*
> *The locket I found in an envelope hidden in my desk – M must have left it for me to hold on to. She put some holo images and video clips inside.*
> *See you soon. A*

I hold the locket in my hand for a moment – the solidness of it. Simple, apart from the ornate inscriptions.

I load a few of the images from the Bluetooth-enabled chip in the locket. There are clips of Maya's avatar playing. The personalized skin Maya designed of an ancient Greek Fury. A few are photos of Maya, like the ones I first saw last night at Annie's flat. I grab one and use it to do an image search through Maya's data. It comes back with the same photo, in a hidden folder full of other images. Annie and Maya look so happy in these shots it hurts. She should still be here, still be this happy.

Something happened to her just before I moved in.

Something that changed my happy sister into a distant, frightened ghost.

I put on the necklace. Then I open the box.

The pink pom-pom monster I made in primary school is inside along with an assortment of office stuff. Mini make-up kit, pens, notebooks, chargers, a wallet I don't remember seeing before, and a battered friendship bracelet. I put the monster on the side of my desk. Its stick-on googly eyes are already falling off. I can't believe Maya kept this. And yet it's so her. To form attachments to random things. We never had anything from our parents' lives. No photo albums, nothing to show that anyone ever loved us, aside from Maya's battered old book on ancient myths. The one time I walked past Ruby's room, I saw the walls covered with pictures. Parties, girlfriends, family, events and memories I don't have and can never make.

I turn to the investigation board on my wall.

There were two question marks under Maya's name – Unknown and Zu Tech. Now that I know about Annie, that just leaves one thing on the board.

Zu Tech/"special projects".

***

A car meets us outside and drives us to Zu Tech. It's ten days till the tournament. I've copied Maya's files on to another pen drive, along with the autopsy report, and slung it around my neck. My fingers play nervously with it until

I realize what I am doing and force them to stop. I need to figure out a way to pass it to Annie unseen. Breathe. It's going to be OK. I've got Annie in my corner now, at least.

Augie sits beside me, staring out the window. Ruby and Josh are across from us. Josh is silent again. His hand grips his mobile phone tightly. He stares at the streets outside, avoiding making eye contact with anyone. Ruby, meanwhile, has her head bent over her phone. Then she suddenly starts laughing.

"Guys, you've got to see this." Ruby holds up her phone. It's a social media post showing a screen-grab of the online tournament rankings that list our qualifying placements and player names.

Then it cuts from that image to the face of a seven-year-old girl in her bedroom, who looks exactly like a mini Ruby/Josh. Her voice is so excited and high-pitched it's almost out of the range of human hearing as she starts screaming. *"OMG, OMG, OMG, it's Ruby and Josh. OMG, guys, my sister and brother made it!!!"* Followed by what has to be the most acrobatic demonstration of extreme jumping on a bed I've ever seen. She leaps so high and so hard I'm surprised she doesn't hit the ceiling, and she still manages to keep chanting, *"OMG, OMG Rubieeeee, Joshieeeee. Yessssss."*

It's genuinely adorable. I can't help it. I start to grin. Augie smiles. He nudges me, and the tension between us disappears. We are all now glued to the screen of Ruby's phone as her sister's antics continue. We start to laugh out loud. Her energy is infectious. Then the little girl finally stops; she looks thoughtfully at the camera as if suddenly remembering something. *"Oh, and a big shout out to Daisy, aka Valkyrie16 and my other favourite eSports player, Mr Big Time, Augie Santos, who are on Ruby and Joshie's team. I love all you guys."* The image then cuts to a shot of us all from the party at Zu Tech. The glitter strands and balloons floating past; Josh and Ruby are smiling at the camera, Augie and I are just behind them talking, unaware.

Did she just post a picture of me online?

Ruby looks at me, pride beaming even as she wipes a tear from laughing too hard. "Seventy-five thousand views. My little sister is going viral, guys."

Augie, Josh and Ruby don't notice that I've stopped laughing. I mean, no one will notice me in the end comments of some social post, right? I sit back. Hiding my thoughts behind the smile frozen on my face. I try again to convince myself. I should have paid more attention to Ruby that night. She must have sent the pictures to her sister.

Four minutes later, my phone starts to vibrate with incoming messages. Someone's noticed.

24

When we get into Zu Tech, I mumble something about needing the toilet. Once the cubicle door is locked, I check my phone. The texts are all from Dark.

> You're in the tournament? I thought you were going in as Jones's assistant?

> Asha, it's a matter of time before they spot that post and put it together with Maya's employee file.

> Where are you? I'll come to you.

Then the last one. The one that makes me shiver.

Asha, they know about the worm you put on Emily's device. THEY KNOW.

I reread the last message as the banging starts outside the door. "Daisy, are you in there? We've got to go."

It's Josh. Great, just great. I stare at my image in the mirror, the necklace and data drive around my neck. What the heck do I do now?

"Daisy? You OK?" It's Augie now. I hear them speaking outside. Then Augie again. "Daisy, the others are going ahead. I'm here, OK? It's just a fitting for the suits."

I open the door. I feel light-headed. Hands clammy. There is no choice. "I can't tell you why, but I need to get out of here, right now."

Augie says nothing for a beat. Then: "OK. Let's go."

We turn back into the central part of the lobby. There are just a few steps between us and the main door we came through. The blood has drained from my face. I'm scared. Two security guards are by the door. In the background, I can hear someone – Beth 1 – trying to attract our attention from the other end of the lobby. Augie has a grip on my arm now, steadying me. We keep walking. My forehead is damp. Just a few more steps. I can see the street outside. Once in the patch of green, I can blend in and get on to the main street, find the nearest underground. I can feel my phone vibrate again in my pocket. Just a few more steps...

"Santos! You're going in the wrong direction."

I look up, and it's Carlo, Augie's manager.

"Just keep walking. I'll distract him," whispers Augie.

But it's too late now. Both the security guards are watching us and have taken up position behind Carlo, blocking the exit.

Carlo glances from Augie to me. "Why is it that every time I find you late for something, or doing things you shouldn't, this girl is always around?"

Footsteps come from behind. Beth 1 has caught up with us. "There you two are. Please proceed this way. The tech team are waiting, and we have a tight schedule today."

Carlo nods. "Make sure they don't get distracted, will you?" He goes to leave but changes his mind and grabs my arm before he does, voice low so only I can hear him. "Jones vouched for you. It's one thing to get nervous and bail during a match, but if you're trying to bail during a tech run... Trust me. There is nowhere you can go where I won't find you, and I'm not as nice as Jones when it comes to people that jeopardize my investments."

Beth leads us into the lab for our suit fitting. Security guards line the doors, and I have no choice but to follow. I half expect a hand to fall on my shoulder, but it doesn't. The others are standing around talking strategy while we wait for our turn in the fitting rooms, but I can't focus.

I feel a moment of relief when I see Annie in the distance. She's at her desk, checking the signals from each suit as the Beths check the measurements inside

226

the changing areas. I watch her precise movements, and now that I'm looking, I spot the small implant in her ear that allows her to hear. I also remember the way the suits measured our vitals. I start to focus on breathing out and lowering my heart rate.

I wait till she goes to check some data at a workstation closer to us, then I step back, stumbling against her.

"Sorry." I slip the data drive I made from my hand into hers.

"No problem." Under her breath, she whispers, "They are watching, and they know who you really are, so be careful."

I nod. She walks on, and I rejoin Ruby and Josh, who are arguing about what today's game will involve. I barely listen to them. Why haven't I been picked up if they know who I am?

"Good to see you again." It's Eliza. The pro player from the party.

Ruby looks surprised. "Daisy, you never mentioned you knew the New York team?"

Eliza smiles. "We were never officially introduced. I'm just a fan of her ... footwork. Sometimes it's good to have friends. Right, Santos?"

Augie is rooted to the spot. "Eliza, I..."

"Save it for the match."

Eliza ignores him and turns to Ruby. "I'm Eliza, by the way..."

Ruby returns her smile. "Nice to meet you."

Eliza and her teammates leave while Josh looks at Augie. "What was that about?"

Augie doesn't meet anyone's eyes. He is saved by Beth 1. "This way, please, while you try on your suits and we calibrate your lenses." She gives us all her customary beaming smile. "You guys are going to have so much fun!"

***

By the time we get back, it's late, and nothing that has happened makes any sense. Just as I am driving myself wild rethinking the day's events, my phone lights up with a message from Annie Queen.

> Asha, we need to talk. I found something when I tried to access a file at work. Come in early tomorrow. Say it's an issue with your contacts and the glasses. Security will let you in. A

What the hell did Annie find? I lace up some running shoes and pull on a black hoodie. I need to get out of here and get some air. I need to think.

Outside, the sun is setting as I run. Headphones on. Music fills my head, prompting me to process. Going back to Zu Tech is ... risky, to say the least. But I need to hear what Annie has found out. Besides, what happens to the team if I pull out now? Heart pounding, I focus only on putting one foot in front of another. That is, until he steps in front of me.

228

"Asha."

I should have known Dark wouldn't stop at a text.

We stand there as dusk starts to fall in the park. The smell of the grass, the sounds of the city muffled, almost like it doesn't exist.

Dark starts first.

"What happened?"

"Nothing. One of my teammates took a photo at the Zu Tech event. She must have sent it to her kid sister. I didn't notice her taking it."

"Yeah. You looked occupied. You're on Jones's Tower team with Santos? That was your plan on how to get inside Zu Tech?"

I nod.

"Did you even stop to think this through?"

I look up, angry now. "I know Zu Tech had something to do with Maya's death. I needed to be on the inside. Competing was the best way in."

Dark stares at me. "But you're leaving now, right?" When I say nothing, he takes a step forward. "Asha, Zu Tech knows you're here. They intercepted the worm. If you think they had something to do with Maya's death, why would you stay in the competition? Your life *is in danger*."

We stare at each other. Neither of us speaks. Then, at last, I say, "I can't. Not now. I'm too close to finding the truth."

Dark turns away in frustration.

"I can't hide you, Asha. They know who you are. And

229

they still want those files that Maya took. My guess is they will stop at nothing to get them."

His eyes are bright, and he seems sincere. I think back to Annie's text. "No."

Dark takes a step back.

"Take it from someone who knows, Asha. This is the point where you cut and run."

"I'm done with running. I want the truth."

Dark goes very still and swallows. He says nothing for a few moments more. Then: "Please, Asha. Walk away from this. The truth is no use to you if you're dead. Nothing good will come from staying in the tournament."

He just watches me as I leave. I've made my decision. I just hope it's the right one.

***

The next morning I get up early and groan at the Eight Days to Go! marker on the countdown clock as I make my way into Zu Tech. Annie's left a pass for me at the almost empty security desk. Dawn hasn't broken yet. The building's main occupants seem to be the cleaning staff. This time I'm more careful than before. I don't bring anything with me – no drive, no phone, nothing apart from Maya's necklace.

I take the lift to the lab where Annie works. She is alone in the empty room and looks exhausted, anxious. "Ah yes, we need to recalibrate your glasses, right? Let's go to the dressing room."

In the dressing room, she gives me a nod. "We can talk privately here."

"Annie, what did you find?"

"You were right. Maya's death wasn't natural. I think someone killed her because she found out something she wasn't supposed to. I think Maya was gathering information, compiling data so she could become a whistle-blower, but they found out and got to her first. I need proof to verify it. The only place I can think it might be is on an internal data storage device. I need your help."

"How? How did they kill her?" I ask.

"I'll explain everything but not here. Right now, we need evidence."

She hands me a smart tablet. "It's rigged up to the security cams. I need you to stay here, pretending we are doing a fitting and play the pre-recorded CCTV loops. I've hacked the security system. Once you hit play the loop will hide me from the cameras so I can get down to the basement, that's where the servers are. Take this too." She puts a small Bluetooth piece in my ear. "So we can stay in touch. It's linked to my hearing aid." She takes a deep breath. "Can you do this for me?"

My mouth goes dry. Maya would never leave me willingly. I've always known that. Annie's just confirmed it.

"Annie," I say slowly, "I'm not letting you take more risks. I'll go. You direct me. You're more familiar with the security system, so it makes sense that you loop the footage from here. Be my eyes. Maya told you I used to

231

hack, right? I've got this, just point me in the direction of the right place, and I can do the rest. If something goes wrong, you take what you have and go to the police, promise me?"

Annie looks unsure. But I'm already heading towards the door, unwilling to give her any choice. I lost Maya. I'm not about to lose anyone else. "Where are the cameras in the lab?"

Annie shrugs. "OK. Fine. Stick to the edges, the walls are the blind spots. I can talk you through what you need to do via the earpiece. You need to grab everything you can on the 'SHACKLE: origins' project. It's in a stand-alone data storage space. It's air-gapped, not linked to the main servers. The only way to get the code is to physically hack the device." Annie hands me a company USB drive and a small company-issued foldable Bluetooth keyboard. "You'll need these. The system admin protocols are pre-loaded, so the server should accept them. And take this too." She hands me a cloned security pass.

I give her a thumbs-up, and I step back into the lab, this time clinging to the edges of the room, the only blind spots available and then back out on to the corridor to access the lifts.

Zu Tech's secure vault is in the sub-basement. Level minus three. Close to the bomb shelters. Unlike everywhere else in the building, there are no funky light signs with directions on level minus three. No neon-coloured breakout rooms with retro games and sugary snacks. It's a blank white space with hidden electronic pocket doors and sensors. If I run into anyone down here, there is nowhere to hide.

Deep breath. I have to trust that Annie will trigger the right doors and disable each camera until I get to the server. For the first time since Maya, I need to completely trust someone else.

"Asha, I'm looping the footage for you, all security can see is an empty corridor, but you need to be fast, OK."

Door one of the corridor swishes open as I approach. An infrared beam searches for the cloned pass and scans it. Another swish, and a second door opens. One down. I keep moving. Annie's voice comes through my earpiece. "The main server entrance is at the end of the corridor."

Almost there. I wait for a second in front of the blank wall, and then the first set of doors open.

"It will be in a stand-alone section, not networked. Air-gapped so only people in the building can access it. Got it?"

"OK." My hands are clammy now. With one final swoosh, the second set of glass doors opens into a cold, vast dark space lit by rows and rows of server racks, all blinking. I step inside, and both sets of doors seal shut behind me. Judging by the cabling, if it's not networked, the server needs to be on the right side of the room. I start to move and then stop.

Footsteps, not mine, sound in the distance. I'm not alone.

25

My heart pounds. I need to move fast, find a hiding place. I look at the storage banks and spot a gap in the racks, a small break between rows a few feet away. I duck into the gap, then shut down the Bluetooth connection.

The steps continue. Now that they are closer, I realize there are at least two people. Heels on the cold tiled floor. The squeak of sneakers. Two voices: one male, one female. I crouch down lower, my heart thudding in my ears, so loud it drowns out everything else. I hold my breath, begging no one to look closer at the dark servers and their blinking lights. I stay like that as the shadows of Emily Webber and Carlo – Augie's manager – pass by. Carlo's voice carries further than Emily's.

"I'm not happy. You said we wouldn't need to do this any more. I've started lining up deals."

Emily's voice is low. "He's not a match. It's just a check-up. And as for your financial earnings…"

I glance at them as they pass my hiding place. They're too far away for me to hear more. And then I see a third figure, stumbling slightly. Augie. Augie is with them.

Why is Augie down here? How is he involved?

I stay where I am till the footsteps fade away. Once I hear the doors swoosh closed, I reactivate the Bluetooth connection to Annie.

"Asha, are you there?"

"Yes. People were here. They just left; see if you can track them?" Then I scurry towards the back of the room. There are a few separate racks of servers, all unconnected to the primary grid. I scan the labels – "NY 100", "Arkib", "Muto" – until I see one with "SHACKLE UK", and then I insert the drive and use the keyboard to hack in. I need to get out of here. Fast. I hack in and wait, grabbing the origin files and watching the lights flicker on the drive as copy over, waiting for it to turn green.

I dash back to the main door and swipe my pass, but it doesn't swoosh open this time. I try it again. Nothing. I look up at the security cameras, panic starting to rise. "Annie, the doors," I whisper. They don't move.

Then I hear her voice through my earpiece. "Asha, I'm locked out of the system."

Damn it. I knew it was too easy. Think, think. It's

getting late, the building will start to fill up with employees soon. I have to get out of here. I pull open the control panel near the door. I can overload it, but I will have only seconds before security is down here after that. I pull at the metal on the panel, cutting myself on its sharp edges. Then I pull two of the power wires. No choice. Now or never. The wires connect, and the door opens, but a red warning light starts to flash almost at once, a silent alarm.

I run down the corridor to the lift. Arriving just as Annie manages to open the doors for me. I throw myself in and pound on the button for the lab. It starts to ascend just as its twin lift descends. Come on. *Come on.*

When the door opens, I walk towards the lab, heart pounding, hands shaking. Annie is there, but beside her, fitting on a glove, is Thresher.

Annie gives me a wide smile. "Ah, there you are, Daisy. You found the bathroom then? Those new glasses will be ready for you later on today."

I stare at Thresher.

"What?" he snaps.

"Thresher needed his suit calibrated," says Annie. "Oh, and Daisy, leave me your hall pass, will you?"

I hand over the pass along with the drive hidden beneath it. She puts it calmly into a pocket of her lab coat. "Now," she says, turning back to Thresher, "you're concerned about the glove reflexes?"

He grunts. Then as I turn to leave, he calls back, "Hey, Daisy, right?"

I look at him. "Yes."

He gives me a shrug. "Tell Santos I said 'Hi'."

"Tell him yourself."

I make myself walk at an average speed through the building, but by the time I'm on the green outside Zu Tech, I'm gulping in mouthfuls of air. Too close. That was way too close.

My phone vibrates. Annie.

Meet me at my place tonight.

26

Somehow, I get through the day of training at the Tower. I can't meet Augie's eye over breakfast. What is he up to?

In the evening, after training, I lace up my running shoes. Running normally clears my mind, but now all my thoughts come back to just one thing. Does Annie have answers?

When I get to Annie's apartment, it's almost nightfall. She must have seen me approaching because the outer door to her block is unlocked. Out of habit, I almost call out "hello" and then stop myself. Annie won't hear me. Instead, I push the door open and step inside, walking quickly towards her door, which is slightly ajar. A cold feeling starts to wash over me.

I enter the flat silently. The first thing I see is the lamp on the floor lying on its side. No. No. No.

Where is she? My eyes dart everywhere. The room is a mess. The contents of the bookshelves, the circuit boards, the 3D printers and materials are tossed all over the place. Dishes are broken on the floor lying beside the stools from the breakfast bar. Pictures ripped down from the walls and smashed pieces of glass are scattered everywhere. Books are open, and the pages are pulled out. Trashed.

I take a careful step into the room. I see it then. A bare foot, just visible behind the kitchen island, a single discarded slipper near it. I go closer.

She's still. Too still. Her eyes are staring upwards at nothing. Blood has pooled around her head. "Annie…" I whisper.

She doesn't move; her head lies at an unnatural angle. I put my fingers against her neck to feel for a pulse. Nothing. Her skin feels cold. I put my head to her chest. No rise and fall. I start to move her arms so I can begin compressions on her chest. They're stiff.

I grab my phone and punch in 999. But before I can connect, I hear it – a sound. Coming from what must be her bedroom.

Whoever did this is still here.

My mouth dries up. Heavy footsteps head towards the front door – one person. I dart quickly behind the kitchen island. For a moment, I think maybe they will leave, but instead there is a terrifying click of the lock.

I look back at Annie. Her jacket has moved from under

her, and I see it then: a small envelope sticking out from an internal pocket. The same colour and size as the one from her note when she had Maya's work items dropped off. My name is written on top. I shove it into my tracksuit pocket. My eyes scan the room. One of the bottom shelves of the island contains a selection of cast iron pans. I take one from the top as quietly as I can.

I try to creep towards the window when I hear the footsteps returning. No choice. There's a heavy black tablecloth covering the dining room table, hiding all the cables and power cords that dangle down from Annie's computers on top. I crawl underneath just as I hear the footsteps turn back towards the kitchen area.

I take out my mobile and redial 999, making the call silent so the operator can only listen in, hoping that's enough for someone at the other end to look for the GPS and send a car out. It's a long shot, but that's all I have right now. Then I text the only number I've texted on this phone. Fingers are shaking, blood staining the keys.

Help.

The footsteps get closer. I put my phone into my pocket and grip my frying pan. The ridiculousness of it hits me. Why didn't I look for a knife?

Under the tablecloth, I can see large black boots. Then they move past the table. I can hear the sound of the curtains being drawn.

The footsteps stop. There is silence. I wait, listening for any sound — but there is nothing. My grip on the frying pan relaxes. Then a hand shoots under the table and grabs my leg, and I scream.

27

I kick again and again, but the hold on my leg is vice-like. Inexorably, they drag me out from under the table.

I swing blindly with my frying pan, and it connects. I hear a sharp intake of breath, then, "You'll pay for that." The voice is deep, harsh, unfamiliar. I lash out again, pulling down the tablecloth and a computer which crashes down beside me. I roll on to my back and aim both my legs at the area between my attacker's thighs. I catch a glimpse as I sprint to the door. He's white, maybe thirty. Shaved head. Dressed all in black with dark leather gloves.

My hand is on the door handle when I feel his grip again. He flips me easily to the floor, and I lie there, winded. Can't fight against his size and strength. A fist connects with my face, and pain explodes in my right cheek. "You're not going anywhere. Did she give you the drive? The data, did she have it?"

"What drive?" I gasp, eyes watering.

"If you don't have it, you're no use to me." I can feel his breath – the smell of stale caffeine and cigarettes. My hands search for something, anything that I can reach to hit him with, and my fingers wrap around the handle of something narrow with a broad base. I splay my fingers for a better grip. A desktop microphone attached to what feels like a heavy metal base. I grab and swing it with everything I have towards the back of his head. A splatter of blood hits me as it connects. I taste it: metallic iron.

He cries out in pain, but his hands tighten around my neck. I struggle to breathe.

No. Not like this. I can't end like this. Maya *died* for me. I lift the heavy metal tube a second time. I raise it again. My grip is weaker this time, but I push the last of my strength into this final swing. A grunt, and his hands go slack. I go to scramble up – red handprints on the floor. Outside, in the distance, I hear sirens.

Hands grab for my feet, and I kick out viciously, connecting with a sickening crunch.

"My nose!" he roars.

I don't look back: fumble with the Yale lock. Come on, come on, come on—

Click – the latch turns. I run through the door, down the steps and to the entranceway. My feet are slipping. I leave red footprints as I almost slide to the outer door – another latch. I push it open and run into the shadows. His footsteps are behind me, or I think they are. They echo in my head as I run, and I run, and I don't stop. I keep running even though I can't see through the tears and the swelling. I am close to traffic. I can see the lights, the dim shapes. I hear a car swerve and stop. I hear the door open, and I veer off towards the park. Running steps. They are getting closer, faster than mine. I don't even look back; I don't stop until a pair of arms swings around me, pulling me to the ground. A voice in my ear. The smell of citrus and wood around me. Breathe.

"Asha. I'm here."

I sink into the ground, sobbing – a mess of bruises and blood, so much blood.

"It's OK, Asha..." Dark whispers the words. Over and over again. "You're safe. I got you. I got you."

I'm not safe, I think. *I'll never be safe*. Then everything turns black.

28

When I surface, my surroundings are … soft. Silent. That smell of citrus and wood. A hand holds mine tightly. My eyes are closed. I am half awake, half in my dream.

Then the memories flood in, along with a low constant pain that seems to be everywhere. I try and open my eyes, but I can't. My hands find my face. It feels bruised, throbbing, swollen. Emanating its own fiery heat. I can feel the fabric under my fingertips. I start to panic, to tear at them. I need to see where I am.

"Asha, don't." It's a voice – Dark's. "We put those on last night for the swelling. I can take them off. Just give me a second." There are hands, fingers gently, carefully unwrapping the bandages from my eyes.

I squint in the faint light. It takes a second for the world to come back into focus. The first thing I see is Dark. His face is tight with worry.

"How do you feel?" he asks. "Sorry. Stupid question." His fingers entwine instinctively around mine. I try to assess where the pain is coming from. And then my mind flashes on to Annie, lying on the kitchen floor. The blood. Crouching under the kitchen table as footsteps come closer...

"Where am I?" I ask.

"My room."

In all the time I've known Dark, I've never been inside his bedroom. I look around. The room is minimal. Warm white walls with a few pieces of modern art. Wooden polished floors. The space dominated by a giant bed covered in soft cotton sheets, pillows and a duvet. All a uniform black. There is a large, soft grey rug on one side, and away from it, an en suite and a dressing room. Two low modern tables are beside the bed with reading lights. A haphazard stack of books on one. On the other, closer to me, is a framed photo and a glass of water, beside it an old wristwatch I've never seen him wear and a piece of paper with crumpled edges. Even through my swollen eyelid, I can make out that the photo is of a younger Dark. I can see his features in the child who looks up at what must be his parents with a giant smile. The frame is cheap plastic, scratched and battered. I glance down at the piece of paper beside it. Another photograph, a single shot of just one person.

"It's me," I say. It's an image from three years ago before he left. Before he decided to walk away from me. At the old factory where we used to play games. I'm smiling up at the camera.

Dark quickly puts the photo into the drawer underneath. He sits carefully on the edge of his bed. "What happened, Asha? Who hurt you?"

I close my eyes. This is too hard. It hurts too much.

Dark notices. "Take these."

He takes a prescription bag from one of the drawers and hands me two tablets and the glass of water.

"Painkillers and an anti-inflammatory, one every four hours. Dr Brady's orders."

Dr Brady is famous. He's the one the entertainment industry calls when their clients have issues they don't want to become public. He's in Dark's pocket too.

"He was here?"

"I thought it best not to take chances. Besides, Brady is nothing if not discreet."

I take a sip, and my throat feels raw. It hurts to swallow. I force down the water and the pills.

Dark gives me a few seconds. Then: "So? Who was it?"

I sink against the pillows. "I didn't recognize him. I went to my sister's girlfriend's apartment. She'd been looking into Maya's death – she said she'd found something at Zu Tech, and I was to meet her later. But when I got there, she was – she was…" Dark squeezes my hand and draws a breath. "The attacker was still in the apartment."

Dark's arms come gently around me.

I feel myself go numb. It's the only way I can cope. Like after Maya died. Detach, then act. Don't let the pain in. Box it away till later with all the other things. Survive.

Dark leaves me alone with my thoughts for a while. When he returns, he has some antiseptic and cotton wool. His touch is light, gentle as he applies creams and antiseptic to the worst cuts and bruises. I flinch as they sting parts of me that are still raw. Then the pain blockers start to hit. I take a deep breath. "Annie found something, Dark. Proof that Maya was murdered. The guy who attacked me ... he said he was looking for a drive."

Dark stands. "We'll look into it. For now, you should rest." There's something odd in his voice.

"You're not telling me something."

"Asha. It's OK. The rest can wait. You're safe. No one knows you're here."

"Please."

Dark pauses. "The police want to question you," he says.

"What?"

He sighs, takes a screen from his pocket, and opens a link to a news story. A blurry CCTV image of a person leaving Annie's apartment. A police sketch of someone who looks like me. The chyron reads: "Teen wanted for questioning in connection with local woman's murder. Police appeal to the public for help."

"They think I did this? But — but what about the guy who attacked me?"

Dark frowns at the screen. "They haven't released any other images yet. Maybe they will."

"But…" There is always a *but*.

"Your DNA is at that scene, Asha. The police can trace you. The only option is for you to stay hidden."

I shake my head and wince at the pain. "I can't stay hidden. Maya's killer is still out there. And if I don't find them, Annie will have died for nothing. Annie discovered something, and I have to find out what. There has to be a clue somewhere…"

"Asha…"

But I'm distracted. For the first time, I've noticed what I'm wearing. I'm in my underwear but with one of Dark's T-shirts over it. It even smells like him. How did I…? My cheeks feel suddenly hot.

"Who changed my clothes?"

Dark's cheeks tinge faintly with pink. "You were unconscious. Your clothes were covered in blood. Brady examined you, then I got you changed. That was the first thing I could find. I sent Bill out to get some things – they're in the bathroom."

Dark looks away, and the silence grows between us.

"I should go," I say at last.

Dark touches my arm. "No, you really shouldn't. You almost died last night, Asha. You're wanted for questioning. Walk away, Asha, please, before you end up like Maya and Annie."

"This is different."

"Is it?"

The pain throbs, my mind is a mess, but the guilt burns pure. "Yeah. What happened to Maya and Annie is my fault. I have no choice but to keep going."

Dark is standing now, frustration written all over his face. "And what about me? I have to watch you as you do this."

"It's all I have left, Dark."

"You have me, Asha," he says quietly. "But I'm not enough, am I?" There is a silence. He is looking down on me now like I'm some child he needs to protect. Like I didn't survive on my own without him all this time.

"I have to see this through." I kick back the covers and square up to him. He's taller than me. Every step is agony, every muscle aching despite the painkillers. I reach down and use the pain, the hurt, to stand taller. To keep holding me up.

Dark's pale blue eyes are almost glowing with anger. His body is rigid as I come closer. "Don't."

My face is inches from his. My eyes locked on his. "Don't what?"

His voice cracks slightly. It's almost a whisper. "Don't leave."

I realize, then. We've reached that place. What happens next will change us both. Our defences are down. He's the boy that both Augie and Jones have both warned me to stay away from. And yet it was Dark who found me in the graveyard. Dark who saved me from Annie's killer. Dark, who has helped me every time I asked. I trust him, but I don't trust myself around him.

"I won't watch you kill yourself, Asha," he says. "I can't. Last night – your blood was everywhere. I thought you were gone. I can't watch you run towards something that will kill you. I've been there." He draws a ragged breath. "I can't stop you. But I want you to be honest. When you find your answer, what then? How far will you go?"

Something hardens within me. "When I find out who did this? I'll make everyone involved, every last person, pay for taking her away from me."

Something washes over his face that I can't read.

I stare at him. Silence. The emptiness becomes its own answer. Dark turns and walks out of the room.

I am rooted to the spot. Eventually, the pain gets replaced by something else. Something worse. Emptiness. A feeling of drowning on dry land.

I take a deep breath, and then I move. One foot in front of the other towards the bathroom. I run the hot water until it fills the room with steam. I undress and wince at the image in the cloudy mirror, at the bruises all over my body.

I go through the clothes Bill picked up instead. Soft black running gear, my necklaces beside them. Some basic toiletries from Boots left on top. Something falls out from the pile and flutters towards the floor as I go through them. An envelope, small, once white, now stained with blood. Annie's blood. My name scribbled on the outside.

My hands shake as I pick it up. I had almost forgotten the note taken from Annie's pocket. Inside is a single piece of paper with a bunch of numbers – the IP address for a VPS. Annie must have uploaded something to a Virtual Private Server before she died. The question is what?

29

"It's the last favour I'll ask. I promise."

We're in one of Dark's labs. It's an extension of his room – white walls with some modern art pieces. Servers and computer equipment hidden away. A single long desk facing an interactive screen takes up most of the wall. Two leather swivel chairs.

"Please," I say again. In my hands, I hold the crumpled piece of paper containing the code that Annie died for. It's cold in here, and I shiver.

Dark sighs and takes off his jacket without a word, handing it to me. I put it on. "OK," he says.

First, he creates a bounce to hide our IP address. Once the VPN is in place, Dark hands the wireless keyboard to me, and I type in the details Annie gave me, with fingers that shake. A box appears asking for a password. I look again at the paper, but there is nothing else. I try my alias name. *"Daisy"*. Access denied.

I try *"Maya"*.

Access denied.

One more attempt left. I think, then I try the name she had written on the outside of both envelopes: *"Asha"*.

The link takes us to a folder. A video file. I take the mouse and click on the video first, and my heart stops for a moment.

It's Annie. In what looks like a clean room: white walls, sparse. No pictures. Someplace I haven't seen before. She seems nervous, on edge. She sits, clears her throat, and faces the camera, the timestamp in the corner of the frame says 18.30.

It hits me that I'm watching her, but she's gone. She's gone. Maya's gone, and it is like a physical tear deep inside. I can feel Dark watching me, and I square my shoulders.

I hit play, and Annie's voice fills the room.

"I'm making this in case something happens to me. I opened one of the files at work and … and I found something. I think it's only a matter of time before they notice." On-screen, Annie takes another deep breath before leaning in closer to the camera. *"There is no easy way to say this. Maya discovered something when she was beta testing SHACKLE. It sounds crazy, but… You don't play this game, Asha. It plays you."*

A chill runs down my spine. I look over to Dark, who has become still beside me.

Annie continues, looking straight at the camera. *"Its code is like nothing I've come across before. It is designed to hack into your brain like an organic machine. The best way I can describe it ... if you think back to those early brain power games, they used electrodes to register the brain's activity so that your thoughts could control movement in the game. Reverse that process. This code, it connects to the suit and glasses you wear with its electrodes. All of your data goes into the game. The more you play, the more information the game gets on you. Eventually, when it has enough, it can use it to hack your brain. It learns how to control you. Not just inside the game, either. You become a puppet. The game's avatar. The game plays you in the real world. When Maya discovered what it was... She was going to blow the whistle. She'd gathered evidence. Whoever is behind this, they found out, and that's why they killed her."*

Annie stops for a second. Blinks back tears. I glance at Dark, but he is still staring at the screen as Annie continues, his expression frozen.

"I think she was trying to protect both of us. That's why she was pushing us away. Someone hacked her brain, Asha. They hacked in and shut her down when they found out what she was doing. They made her stop breathing. That's why the hospital reports couldn't pinpoint the cause of death. They used her own body as a weapon against her." Annie stops, tries to recover, wipes the tears away.

"I'm not sure how far this goes, who was involved. Emily, perhaps. But this thing, it can't go live. If it does, it will replicate in every console. Once it spreads, I'm not sure how it can be

stopped." She leans forward, gaze intent. *"She had a drive with proof; it's in the notes we got from the server. They knew Maya had proof but not where she kept it. We have to find it. I don't know why or what they're planning, but the effects of this could be catastrophic."* She presses a button, and the screen goes blank.

My face is wet with tears – I hadn't even realized I was crying. All this time, I wanted to know what had happened to Maya. How she died. Now, I am numb. It feels impossible – and yet, if what Annie says is accurate, someone inside Zu Tech murdered Maya, and if SHACKLE goes live, everyone, every player is at risk.

Dark, meanwhile, has started pacing the room. "It can't be true," he mutters.

Alongside the video are some developer code files. I start scanning through them. There is no doubt in my mind, it's incredibly skilled code. And if Maya had proof that Zu Tech was involved, that this code came from them...

"I believe Annie." I study the code. "I think she's right. Maya must have known about this, and that's why they killed her."

"No." Dark looks rattled. "Check again."

I turn to him. "You know it's possible. You were the person who introduced me to those weird games you played with a headset – with the electrodes monitoring your brain."

Dark nods slowly. Then he comes and kneels on the floor by my chair.

"If it is true," he says, "then we need to run, now. We can expose them from somewhere far away, somewhere they won't find us. Annie and Maya died to get you this information – use it wisely. Don't do anything stupid because you want revenge."

His expression is earnest. But if he thinks I'm going to be scared off, he's wrong. "I am not going to run and hide. I'm going to stop this. You're either with me, or you're not. Time to decide. We could find out who the people responsible in Zu Tech are, disable it, leak this so others know. Make them pay. Or you can walk away. Which one is it, Dark?"

He has to be on my side, I think. He just has to be. Dark takes a step away from me. "I can't."

I stare at him. "I helped you," I say at last. My voice is shaking. "I helped you hack into Environ and find out about your dad. Got you what you needed to expose them."

Something flashes in Dark's eyes. "And then what? I needed you. I needed you to come with me, to work with Jones, to take the next steps. You wouldn't."

"I couldn't."

"The truth is, you didn't want to."

We are both angry now. But what he is saying is partly true. I know why I let him walk away. Maya. But also because I was scared of where we were going. I *had* wanted him to contact me after that. A test. He was my only friend. I spent weeks wanting, waiting to hear from him. Checking for messages and texts that never arrived.

Dark was everything to me, then he walked away, and now he's asking me to do the impossible. To do the same. Only this time, I'd be running away and letting the people who killed Maya and Annie get away with it. I'm too close. They deserve justice.

I take a deep breath. I survived the care homes, the attack. I can do this. "I'm not dropping this."

Dark meets my gaze. "I won't watch you kill yourself."

I take one last look at him and shrug off his jacket, handing it back to him. "Then this is goodbye, Dark."

30

When I leave, Bill is standing outside with keys in his hands. "Dark said you'd need a lift?"

He takes in my bruises, and his knuckles tighten. "You ever find out who did that, you call me. Even if you aren't speaking to Mr D. OK?"

"OK."

He drives me back to the Tower in a black electric car. A family mid-range vehicle that doesn't attract attention in a sea of similar ones. This one comes with tinted windows in the back, probably so sleeping babies can take a nap while a parent drives them around town. At least in the adverts, that's what happens. In my case, they are also perfect for a murder suspect to hide behind.

When I get to the Tower, Jones is waiting outside. She looks less than pleased, but I notice concern on her face as well. "Mr D told me to call her," Bill says by way of excuse, then he and Jones share a look.

He helps me out of the car. "Thanks, Bill, for everything," I say.

A moment of awkwardness as I stand there in the clothes he bought me. A pause as the once pro wrestler takes a beat. Then his large, tattooed arms wrap around me. "I mean what I say," he murmurs into my hair. "You need something, call."

Another random act of care that almost undoes me. I can't speak.

"Let's go inside before anyone sees either of you," Jones says, her sharp eyes scanning the area. "No offence, Bill, but I'd rather not be openly associated with Dark, and you picked your side when you left."

Bill simply shrugs and goes to leave. "Business is business. Things will settle. They always do."

Inside, Jones hands me an ice pack. "Straight to your room. When he rang, I thought he was overreacting, but no. You look like hell."

We take the lift down to my level. Once inside my room, she stands against the wall. I sit on the bed. For a moment, my exhaustion hits me and the room dips. Jones's long fingernails, drumming against the wall, bring me abruptly back to reality.

Her voice is firm. "Talk." It's not a request.

I hunch my shoulders. It's the second time I need to relive the story of what happened inside Annie's flat.

I tell her that Annie was Maya's girlfriend, who also worked at Zu Tech. That she had some information on Maya, but someone got to her before she could tell me what it was. I tell her about the attack, about my escape. About Dark finding me. And that's all. I don't tell her about the video or what Maya had discovered, how she was planning to take down Zu Tech.

When I finish, Jones sits on the floor, back against the wall, looking thoughtful. Eventually, she says what I already know. "This is a disaster."

I don't say anything. She's right.

"I took you in because I thought this would be a contained investigation. Look at you, Asha. I invested in you, in the team you're part of. This is a bloody mess."

"I'm sorry."

"You're *sorry*?"

"I could still…"

"Play?" Jones gives a short laugh. "The police are looking for you, Asha. You were spotted on CCTV. A sketch of you is circulating. How long before they put a name to your face? I can't risk having you on the team any more. I owe people." She stands and turns away from me as she mutters the last part. "The people you don't want to be in debt to."

"Please." I swallow. "I need this. I'm so close, I can feel it."

Jones shakes her head. "Get some rest, Asha. We'll talk later." She walks out.

I go to bed, but I don't rest. Instead, I spend the next few hours going through the files on my sister's drive and the ones in Annie's VPS folder.

Now that I know what I'm looking for, everything I find confirms Annie's theory. Maya's notes are there too, careful and thorough for a while – that's Maya all over – but eventually, they become more cryptic. *Security protocol?*

Tournament?

Final test for SHACKLE.

I chew my nail as I read. The tournament is intended as SHACKLE's final test – after that, it will become fully operational.

I debate going to the police. Copying all the evidence I have on to a drive and handing it over with a flow chart to the cybercrime division. But they could never move fast enough. Even if they believed me in the first place, what I have isn't proof that Zu Tech was involved. It is circumstantial at best. It would be one sixteen-year-old kid on the run from the social, wanted for questioning in a violent death, versus the most popular and influential British corporation in years. Yeah, I know exactly how that will play out.

So, two problems. One, Jones wants me out of the tournament that is my only way to get into Zu Tech. Two, I have no idea where Maya hid the drive that supposedly has proof about all of this.

I glance at the time. It's late evening now. I start with problem number one first and head to Jones's garden.

***

"I need to stay in the competition."

Jones raises her eyes up to the dark sky visible through the glass ceiling and puts down her cup of tea. "Which part of *you're leaving the tournament* didn't you understand?"

"Think about it. The best place to hide is in plain sight. The police won't be looking for me at a tournament. If we make the semi-finals, it's at least a million in prize money. My share is yours. Same if we get to the finals. Then I disappear till I can clear my name."

Jones studies my face. "Why? Why take the risk?"

I take a breath. I have to tread carefully here. "I need to do this for Maya. I know what they did and now I need to find out who did this to her."

"I should tell you to drop this…"

"I already made up my mind. Even if I walk, this won't end. You're one of the good guys, Jones. This is the right thing to do. I need you to let me keep playing."

She sighs and looks at the floor before meeting my eyes.

"I want you to play. But I have to know – are you prepared for whatever you find, Asha?"

"Yes."

Jones sighs. "OK. I checked with my source in the police. You're a person of interest, but they're not seriously pursuing you. Other DNA at the scene matches a criminal in the system. A guy with a history of assault. I'll arrange security around the team, just in case. If there is a way I can get my money and you can find your truth, I'm in. Unlike Dark, I never bought into Zu's corporate ethos anyway."

I frown. "What do you mean?"

"Nothing, just that your boy was once a fan."

I think back to our coding classes in the social and shiver slightly. I guess, once upon a time, we both were. "Anything else I need to know?"

Jones studies her nails for a moment. The scent of jasmine fills the air in her garden. Then she looks up. Determined. "Nothing. Let's just say I am starting to feel like I've been played by Zu Tech, and it's not a feeling I am comfortable with." She reaches for a smart tablet. "I'll call my doctor. Get you fixed up. Then Penny – it's going to need to be an extreme makeover to hide those bruises. We have barely seven days."

Hurdle one cleared. Now for another one. "Jones, what do the others know about what happened to me?"

Jones gives me a look. "I told them you got jumped in the park when you went for a run. What you choose to share with them is up to you, but…"

"But?" I ask.

"Sometimes, honesty isn't the best policy. So far, everyone you've connected with has ended up dead. You might want to think about that."

Back in my room, I try to rest. But all I can think about is what Maya discovered about SHACKLE.

Mind control. It should sound impossible — but then again, I'd heard about things like this before, along the edges of the Dark Web as well as in the trusted pages of medical journals looking at ways chips in the brain might help people recover mobility. But this…. Maybe they had it right back in 1957 when they banned subliminal messages in films and TV. Perhaps they should have extended it to games.

Games controlled by your brain are, after all, not new. They've been around since 2017. Algorithms designed to calculate brain signals, translating them into game commands. Dark has always been obsessed with the possibilities of that type of tech. Wasn't it only a matter of time before someone thought about reversing the process? Instead of the algorithm calculating the brain's signal for gameplay, flipping it to control the brain itself. And now Maya and Annie are both dead.

I keep staring at the screen. Dark was right about one thing. The truth isn't the end — it's the start of another bigger nightmare.

***

A few hours later, Ruby knocks on my door. Her eyes widen at the sight of the bruises on my face.

"You had a time."

"Thanks for sugar-coating it." I step out into the corridor, closing the door behind me.

Ruby sighs. "Well, at least it didn't damage your sense of sarcasm. Jones has a medic coming down to give you a once-over. You good if she sends him in now?"

I hesitate, thinking of my room with its investigation board. "Give me five. My room is a bit messy."

"OK." She turns to go, then stops. "Look, Daisy. Jones told me you got mugged in the park. You want to blow off some steam on a game, do some combat in the gym, or just talk over tea, I'm here. OK?"

Looking at her bright, warm face, I am tempted for a moment. But I can't. Jones is right – letting people in will only get them hurt. Maya and Annie are dead. I need to finish what they started. Alone.

"You asking me out on a sympathy date, Ruby?"

Ruby snorts. "You wish. You're not my type." Then the smile disappears. "But we're a team, OK. Josh too." And before I can move, her arms wrap around me.

I tense, then relax. Ruby holds me close, and somehow that's OK. Somehow it's just what I needed.

Jones and the doctor appear a little later, just as I hide the last of my murder boards in the wardrobe. He does a complete physical before certifying me as match ready. Then there are some shots and creams to take down the bruising around my face. After that, he and Jones leave.

"Rest. I'll send one of the others to get you in the morning."

But I don't rest. Instead, I go back to Maya's data and the info from Annie. I have seven days to come up with a plan to expose what happened to my sister and her girlfriend. I work until I can't keep my eyes open.

It feels like I've barely closed my eyes when there's a knock on the door. "Daisy?"

Great. Augie. Not now. Still, I don't have much choice but to make nice.

"Come in," I call. Augie enters the room and then stops. "You … you look…"

I flush. "It might take some time for the bruises to come down."

Augie still hasn't moved. He swallows heavily. "Yeah. Um. We have practice."

He stumbles backwards, knocking the table behind him. The pink fluffy monster I made and Maya kept hits the floor with a sharp crack.

"Sorry, er, let me."

"I got it." I scowl at him. "I'll see you in the training room."

There's a pause. And then: "Did he do this to you? Dark?"

I blink. "NO. Dark would never… I got jumped in the park. Jones said she told you guys."

"Yeah, she told us. I just didn't believe her."

"Never been mugged? It happens, you know."

Augie's eyes refuse to leave mine. "Except it didn't. I hacked the park's security cams to try and find who hurt

267

you. Instead, I saw him carrying you." Augie leans against the wall. Hands shoved in his pockets. "So... Let's start again. Want to tell me what happened?"

My head is pounding, and it's got nothing to do with my injuries. "Not really."

He shrugs. "Tell me the truth, or I'm out."

I stare at him. "You need this. You're here for a payday."

Augie shakes his head. "I made one mistake. I'm not making it again. You can fool the twins, Daisy. They're here for their family and to pay off some debts. It blinds them. They see what they want to see. Jones has her stuff going on. Not me. I don't have anyone left to stay for. So: the truth or I'm walking."

Great. Everyone I confide in ends up dead.

"I'm waiting."

I regroup. "Why don't we start with you instead of me, Augie? How was your trip to Zu Tech?"

"What? You were there – we all were."

"Not that one, the one you took two days ago."

"Sorry?"

"You heard me. Early morning, you and your manager, having a cosy little chat with Emily."

"Carlo wanted me to go in to get my gloves recalibrated." He frowns. "Wait? How do you know I was there?"

I look at the floor, mind racing, spinning. Annie had mentioned something about some other fittings. That's why Thresher was there. Could Augie be telling the truth?

"The tech who did the fittings – she was the one who

died that night," says Augie slowly. "A robbery at her flat. Oh my God." A sudden realization floats across his face. "You were there when it happened, weren't you? That's how you got hurt?"

I can't help it. My eyes fill with tears. I don't know how Augie made the leap he did, and now I can't speak. Augie sees what's happening, and something clicks.

His face is gentle as he says, "Does this have something to do with your sister?"

I nod because it's true, or as close to the truth as I'm willing to admit and, with that, Augie's arms are around me, holding me as I cry.

"It's OK. You're going to be OK. You're safe here, safe, all right?"

I let go of what little control I had left and sob until all my emotions are outside of me.

When I stop crying, we're both sitting on the floor by my bed. The shoulder of Augie's T-shirt where my head has been resting is a mess from my tears.

"You have got to stop ruining my T-shirts."

I try to laugh, but my bruising means it hurts, and I end up making an embarrassing nose snorting sound directly into his shoulder.

"Sorry. Augie, you shouldn't make me laugh."

Augie just holds me tighter. "Noted."

We sit there for a while, side by side, saying nothing. Augie's arms still holding me close.

Then, quietly, he says, "What can I do?"

"You want to help me?"

He sighs. "It looks like we're in this together."

I wipe my face. "Staying in the tournament, making it to the finals. It's become more important to me. Can you help me get into the zone for this?"

Augie's smile lights up his eyes. He scrambles to his feet and holds out a hand. "That I can do. Let's go!"

I smile, which makes the bruises on my face ache. "Give me a minute first." I gesture to my tear-streaked face. "I'll meet you there."

I give him another slight smile as he leaves.

When the door closes, I bend to pick up what remains of the pink fluffy monster. That clunk as it hit the floor – it had sounded heavy. And it feels heavy too.

Carefully, I unpick my sloppy, childish stitching. I know what it is before I see it. It's Maya's drive. It has to be. The one Zu Tech has been looking for that has evidence, the one with the virus. I've had it this whole time. I just didn't know it.

31

"Murphy."

"Asha. Finally … tell me where you are. I can help you."

Right now, I've got a plan A and a plan B. Murphy is part of plan B. Maya's drive, hidden in my fluffy pink monster, was exactly what I thought it might be and more. I've spent the last three days figuring out a plan.

"I have evidence of what's been going on at Zu Tech. Maya found out what was happening, and that's why they killed her. She was going to blow the whistle on everything. I've sent it to you, but the information is dangerous. Be careful. Get someone from cybercrime to examine the code and the software. Only use someone you know is reliable. It has to be someone you can trust with your life – you understand?"

"Why don't you come in and show us?"

"No. You get the code, and you investigate it. I'm not coming in. That's the deal. Take it or leave it."

"You're sixteen, you are not in a position to—"

"Yes, I am. Just do it. Otherwise, things will get bad."

"Is that a threat?"

"No. It's a fact. One you and I need to stop from happening."

He sighs. "Fine. I'll look, but I'm making no promises."

I hang up, then breathe a little.

I glance at my watch. Time for another part of plan B.

*****

"Thanks for meeting me, Bill."

The sun is low outside the small café near the heath, close to the railway station.

"I said I would come if you needed me. I always keep my word."

I can't help but smile at that. Bill is old school, a gentleman despite the waitress's anxious look when he entered. Most people just see his exterior, his massive frame, his muscles covered in tattoos. They don't notice how he scans the café, clocking me and then the old age pensioner in the corner. How he sees her look at the cakes on display and then sigh and orders just a tea with her carefully counted coins. How he orders a Victoria sponge and, with a wink and a quiet "have this on me", leaves it at her table.

That's Bill. He'll help people without making a fuss; it's one of the reasons I like him. Another is because of the time he got Dark and me out of an illegal eSports tournament on the night it was raided, but that is another story.

"I need your help."

Bill nods. "Is it to do with whoever hurt you?"

"Yeah." I slide a small drive across the table towards him.

"What's this?"

I give a half-smile. "It's proof. He'll know what it is about. If anything happens to me, I want you to give it to him. To Dark. But only if something happens, Bill, OK? Not before the tournament."

Bill sighs. "You two still aren't talking? You should give it to him yourself. He hasn't been the same since you left."

I shake my head. Dark meant it. This time he is staying away, and I want him to. I can't afford to lose anyone else. Jones was right. Being around me is toxic.

But if something happens, I need someone to know what Zu Tech is doing. Dark is one of the few people I trust. He's been obsessed with this sort of code for so long that he's probably the one person who could understand what Maya created. The drive contains everything I have on SHACKLE and a video message from me explaining what I know.

I look at Bill with a smile. "I got to go. Remember – wait till after the tournament, OK?"

Bill pockets the drive. "Hopefully it won't come to that. Remember, Asha, you can call me, any time."

273

I stand. The old woman is tucking into her cake a few feet away and smiling. On impulse, I give Bill a quick hug. "Thanks, Bill."

He looks surprised by the gesture. His voice cracks just a little with emotion. "See you soon, Asha?"

"Yeah, see you soon, Bill."

I hope so. I really hope so.

***

We all assemble for training in the afternoon.

Josh stares into the middle distance, looking dazed as I enter the room. His eyes still go immediately to my bruises.

"You OK?"

"Been better, but I got this."

Ruby and Augie are still gentle with me, asking how I am. I don't hate it. There's a part of me that feels warmed by the fact that they care. I don't tense up when Ruby's hand touches my arm as she reassures herself that I'm OK. It's only been five days since Annie died. Yet it feels like a lifetime. Not that Ruby knows that my obsession with my sister's death has claimed another life. My fault. But not just mine. I am going to make everyone who was involved in this code pay for killing them.

Rachel enters shortly after I do, followed by Jones, finishing up a call. She looks tense.

She nods at Rachel, who begins. "Thanks for coming back from lunch so promptly. There's a live stream." She lowers the lights, and the giant screen in front of us fills a countdown for a live stream with one face in view – Zu.

I can feel my stomach curl as I study him. That distant look in his eyes. His clothes are the same as I saw him in at Zu Tech. The trademark uniform of a black polo neck and black jeans. The perfectly cut black hair. The monochrome design of the space behind him, empty, excellently lit. He never seems to age. He continues to look as if he's in his late forties when he must be older?

How much does he know? I wonder. The research and development for SHACKLE must have come from him. But Maya's death, Annie's – was he involved in those?

"Welcome, players."

His voice, the same flat, emotionless tone, fills the room. I take a look and see Augie's face go still while Josh and Ruby share a high five.

"Legend," Ruby says. Once upon a time, I would have said the same. Now? Now I'm not so sure.

The screen cuts to a montage of Wembley Stadium, where the tournament will be held in three days. Zu employees, technicians and security guards are everywhere. "In seventy-two hours, we launch THE game that will change the face of the industry for ever. You will be the first players to enter the immersive world of SHACKLE. You're playing for one of the largest prize funds in eSports history in an event that will be watched by millions live from this stadium.

"Some of you are pro players, the best of the best whose

rankings were high enough to be given an invite. Others are joining us through the online open play. All of you have battled your way for a place here. I can tell you that you were up against thousands of gamers. You represent the thirty-two players we feel have got what it takes to win.

"On Tournament day, eight teams will battle to become four. The four teams who make it through will become two, and eventually, one team, at the end of our all-day event, will be crowned champion. At each stage of the competition, you will be rewarded for surviving. The champions will walk away with four million pounds each. However, any player that impresses us enough could also become the new 'Face of SHACKLE', an annual contract worth in excess of ten million."

Ruby starts almost screaming in excitement in the background, and even Josh looks slightly less miserable. Only Augie seems uncomfortable, and when I look up, I see I'm not the only one watching him. Jones is too.

Zu continues on-screen. "We live in strange times. What we've built can give something unique back to a world that needs a distraction, entertainment, guidance from the horrific events that can engulf us. You're going to show the world the future. Gaming unites us all. So let's begin our live draw and see who you're battling against. Let's start to *play*."

I shiver in my seat as the screen cuts to the tournament draw. "Show the world the future." A world controlled by Zu Tech.

I'm so lost in thought I almost ignore the draw. Until I hear the words "Tower team". The screen cuts for an instant to our player profiles, our online gamer tags, symbols and stats. Against all the other teams, we look like underdogs. Augie is the only one who has professional tournament history. Ruby and Josh have a few amateur competitions but little else. My gaming history is limited to just the online stages and is otherwise blank. We are, on paper, the weakest team. Then they draw our opponents. Augie inhales. Thresher's team, the Dragons. A high-ranking pro player and three of the highest qualifiers from the online section. They have to be the favourites to win the competition. If we want to make it past stage one of the tournament, we need to bring our A-game to this battle.

Afterwards, the room is silent as the last draw takes place. The Phoenix team from New York captained by Eliza versus the Giants. When the live stream ends, Rachel gives us a pep talk, but I'm not focusing on it. My thoughts are the same as everyone else's. We just got drawn against one of the strongest teams in this competition. How do we beat them?

***

Later in my room, I run through my plan. Maya's drive didn't just contain proof of what Zu Tech was trying to do. It contained a way to stop it. She wasn't convinced that an organization as powerful as Zu Tech wouldn't find a way to suppress the truth and carry out its plan anyway. So she created something. What was she always telling me?

"You have to have an 'A' and a 'B' plan, Ash."

She took her own advice, creating intricate, elegant malware. A computer virus that can work on SHACKLE during the tournament's final match. Something no else knew about. A code that if planted in just the right place would be enough to corrupt and fully destroy SHACKLE. Erasing it for ever.

I go back again through Maya's notes from her hidden drive. For the game to infiltrate your mind, it needs to open up access points. Mind control requires a two-way flow and it's intensive. Maya created something that used that flow to send a virus back into the game. It was the only weak point in its operation. SHACKLE spends time gathering your data, analysing your brain's chemistry and reactions before it tries to corrupt/hack you. The further into the tournament you get, or the more you play, the better its chances of taking over the player. Maya used that. A trojan horse of a virus. While SHACKLE was busy accessing your brain, her virus could access the game. For it to work it would need to happen in the tournament, before the game goes live. Wait till afterwards, and it will already have been globally distributed to every gamer with a Zu Tech console and begun replicating, making it impossible to stop the spread.

The problem? Tower team has to make it to the final for me to plant the virus. It's where the game's weak point is.

To do that, we have to beat the Dragons, the hot favourites. I think back to the draw and everyone's reaction. We need a miracle.

***

At our evening training session, I can see I'm not the only one who is nervous. Josh looks distracted; Augie is lost in thought; even Ruby looks worried.

"Guys," I say. Silence. "Hey!" I say, my voice louder now. "The Dragons are just another team. The whole reason Thresher was trash talking at the meet and greet was to rattle us. He's scared."

Josh looks up. "What makes you say that?"

I meet his gaze. "Because he should be. Watch."

I start to load up a VR game. "I've loaded this with moves from one of Thresher's last tournaments and his teammate's data as well. Care to take them on?"

Josh looks uncommitted. Ruby looks apprehensive. I look at Augie, who slowly nods and then stands.

"What Daisy said. Let's go."

We get ready as the gamer stats load into one of our practice VR games. It takes us a moment to zone in, but we start moving in sync with each other when we do. When the game throws a sudden curveball of murderous plants at me, Josh appears out of nowhere by my side. When Ruby runs into trouble with a zombie horde later in the game, I move to her instinctively to help her take them out so we can advance. My movement is better now. Augie's tactics have also improved. We defeat the villain at the centrepiece in under an hour. It feels effortless, natural, like breathing. We play like a team now. Ruby, Josh, Augie. We needed to remember that.

Afterwards, we are silent, but the energy in the room crackles as the game ends.

"You're ready." It's a statement, not a question. We turn. Jones is behind us, watching.

Ruby gets out and gives Josh a high five. "This tournament is going to change our lives."

Augie gives me a look, and I shiver again because Ruby is one hundred per cent right. The tournament will change everything for all of us, one way or another.

32

We train, and I plan. On July 9th, our last day before the tournament, Jones springs Penny on all of us.

Augie gives Josh a wolf whistle when he sees him saunter back into training with a razor fade haircut with what looks like a "greater than" maths symbol.

"Laugh all you want, Santos, but I make this look cool. Right, Ruby?"

Ruby shrugs. "Your girlfriend will kill you, but it looks great. And Augie?"

"Yeah?"

"I wouldn't laugh so much, you're next."

Augie grins. "You can't top perfection."

Ruby grins back at him. "You're dreaming, Santos."

We keep training till late when Penny calls me last.

"Buckle up. This is going to take some time."

Great, just great.

Penny grins at me. "Don't look so nervous. I know what I'm doing."

"And what exactly is that?" I ask.

"Preparing you for war. This is Daisy 2.0."

Several hours later, my long lavender hair has been cut to a shoulder-length bob and lightened to a silvery pink. Side sections have been rolled into space buns with some strands pulled free to frame my face. The make-up Penny applies includes a heavy kohl eyeliner and a sprinkling of glitter around the eyes. Surprisingly, while the make-up and hair is elaborate, the rest isn't. Canvas runners, super soft and flexible skinny jeans with pockets. A black top to wear underneath my Tower team jersey, light but thermal. A black jacket with hidden pockets inside and a collar that hides the bruise marks that are still fading on my neck. My collection of necklaces she makes no mention of, nor does she try to take them off. The "look" feels relaxed, soft but durable, and better quality than anything I've ever worn.

"Thanks."

Penny looks at me. "When you battle, you go in as 'you', not someone else. You fight in what you can move in. You wear things that make you feel powerful. But, last element, you need to wear these in the tournament."

She hands me a small contact lens box. "Blue contacts this time. To change your eye colour for the cameras. In one of the jacket pockets, you'll also find shades. Bright lights can irritate when you wear these things. Oh, and this." Penny hands me a touch-up bag with everything I need to recreate her look. "Follow the steps, and you'll be fine."

I stare into the mirror. I feel more "me" than I have in a long time. This isn't the kid from the social. Or the girl who was lost between worlds when living with Maya. This is someone new. Someone who has survived.

Penny starts to pack up. "Good luck, Daisy. I mean it. I hope you find what you're looking for. Now I'm going to check in on Ruby again before I go – that girl is a pro." Penny gives me a wink. Then she's gone.

***

The following day there is a nervous energy in the air. Outside Wembley, queues of people are stretching around the corner. Security working its way in teams, scanning, checking ID and vaccine bracelets, bags, running swabs on phones and cameras.

The mood is light. The sun is out, and those lucky enough to have a pass are taking selfies and doing live streams. It's like you can almost touch the energy, the excitement. The eyes of everyone in the gaming industry are on this event. The TV crews are already clustering near the entrance for fan arrival vox pops – everyone repeating the little information that has been strategically leaked and the cliches that come with it.

"SHACKLE is the future of gameplay."

"Zu is a genius."

"London is the new Silicon Valley."

"The next evolution in gaming."

Celebrity arrivals are taken through a separate gate, past a waiting horde of hungry press. Black town cars with tinted windows. The occupants herded on to a red carpet with a background wall filled with only one logo – Zu Tech's. A bank of flashlights pops alongside the regular press flashes. A gimmick to save the egos of the corporate VIPs who also use this entrance. The people the press don't care about. From there, they go into their green rooms, escorted by waiting assistants clutching digital clipboards. A divide between air-filtered suites designed for press interviews before the event and corporate boxes overfilled with food and drink that the press will never enter. The place where the deals are made. Our car glides past it all to another entrance, the one reserved for players.

"Nervous?" I say.

Ruby snorts. "Yeah, like, what do you think? I mean, our futures hinge on us playing well in the next few hours in front of a few thousand—"

Josh interrupts her. "Millions when you consider the streamers and TV guys, Ru."

"Thank you, Josh." Ruby elbows Josh's shoulder. "So, yeah. Not nervous at all."

I laugh, and Ruby glares at me. "Don't you dare. And

don't try and pretend you're cool with all of these people watching you."

I shrug in my seat. I have other worries. "I don't care what people think any more. You worry less when you stop caring."

Ruby rolls her eyes. "You care too much. That's your problem, Daisy."

The car comes to a stop.

Augie beams. "Learn from the pros." He whips out his lucky baseball cap, the one I last saw him wear the day we met at Zu Tech and puts it on. Before the driver can come round, Augie opens the door. He steps out waving, calling, "HELLO, LONDON."

Silence. Jones, who has got out of the car in front, watches with her arms folded.

"They don't allow fans or journalists back here, Augie," she says drily. "It's so you can get in the 'zone'."

Augie blushes. "I knew that." Then he walks towards the backstage area while Ruby follows, snorting with laughter.

"OK, that was hilarious. Now I'm loose. Let's win this thing."

Backstage, the corridor is littered with people, more people than I'm used to seeing in one place. I glance again at Jones, who nods at me reassuringly. She checked again with her police source last night. Apparently, Annie's case is getting dropped. Pressure has been placed on the detective in charge to close the case and move on. It doesn't take a genius to guess from whom.

This has Emily written all over it. A dead employee murder investigation this close to the launch is inconvenient.

A motion-sensor triggered projection of Zu greets us.

"Welcome, players," Zu says smoothly. "Today is a proud day for all of us."

I looked up to him, I think. His coding classes gave me the skills that have got me to where I am. And now I need to use them to destroy what he has made.

I follow the others. Josh is distracted and taking a call. I hear his voice, low and urgent. Ruby is two steps ahead of me when she gets hit by a whirlwind of colour, braided hair and a whiff of mango. The little girl from the video. "Dawn!"

"Mum's here too, Ru. They put us in your dressing room. You have a dressing room each! Well, you and Josh are sharing one. How cool is that? There were sweets in there too."

Josh hangs up the phone abruptly. "Wait. There were sweets in there? I told you not to touch anything."

"Yeah, the man said I could have them."

Ruby looks back at me. "Daisy — want to meet our mum?"

Standing side by side, you can see the resemblance between the twins and their little sister. The same eyes and high cheekbones. The self-confidence that radiates from them. Dawn is a mini-Ruby.

I am not adding to the body count. "You haven't seen each other in weeks. Go, catch up, I'll join you in a bit."

Ruby gives me a quizzical look. "Promise?"

"Yeah. Definitely." A lie that is easy to tell.

Ruby pauses, then leans in close, voice low.

"Daisy, I haven't said this before, but you belong on our team. You're strong; you pulled it together after your sister, after the attack. You are one of us. The kids from the social and the flats … it's our time. We got this."

Ruby has no idea I'm about to pull on the string that hopefully unravels all of this. My stomach knots. "Go. I'll find you later." I turn and head towards one of the other rooms. "I just need to freshen up."

But Ruby catches my arm. "One more thing. This isn't brain surgery; we're going to have fun too, healer. It's play."

Except it isn't.

I watch her go. If what I am planning works, this won't be the golden payday Ruby and Josh have been dreaming of. If I bring Zu down, chances are his prize money will vanish in the chaos that follows. I realize my phone is buzzing in my pocket. No one should be calling. Confused, I take it out and see the name flash on the screen. Dark.

A hand grips my arm. Augie. "Hey, can I borrow you for a moment?"

The storage area is harshly lit and smells of grass, seeds, soil – it's a small space where the maintenance crew who look after the pitch store tools. As Augie closes the door, I put the phone back in my pocket. A dusty mirror reflects my space buns, the silvery pink hair, the glitter around my now blue eyes.

I look at Augie. "Care to explain why we're here?"

Augie looks at me. "I saw your phone. You're going to think I've lost it – but I needed to tell you."

"Needed to tell me what?" I say, my heart sinking. Augie is a nice guy, but I hope he's not about to ask for anything more than friendship. Because it's always been Dark – always. That might be the thing that annoys me most of all.

He rumples his hair. "Just hear me out, OK? I had a dream about Dark – a vivid one. I've had it more than once. He's always inside Zu Tech when I see him. And lately, I've been wondering ... well, whether there's something to it."

"Augie. You're just nervous..."

Augie shakes his head. "It's not that, Daisy. It's something else. It's—"

There's a knock on the door. "Santos, I saw you go in there. People are waiting. Let's go."

Augie gives me a look. "Look, I think maybe I saw Dark inside Zu Tech and something about it feels wrong. Just, be careful..."

Carlo bangs on the door this time.

Augie raises his eyes to the ceiling. "That guy has no patience."

"Augie, you had a dream, that's all. Dark isn't someone you need to worry about."

His face becomes more serious. "There's something I need to confirm after this tournament, but until then, I'm asking you, as a friend, please play it safe with him?"

Carlo's voice booms from outside. "Santos, you have one minute."

I sigh. I don't have time for this. "Augie, we have to go."

Augie gives a half-hearted smile that doesn't reach his eyes. "Fine. Time to face the music. And Carlo has that muppet Thresher with him..."

"What's the deal with you two, anyway?"

Augie shakes his head.

"I don't know. When I threw that match, Thresher was the guy who won. Got some major sponsorship deals off the back of it. When what I did on purpose got leaked by someone, he got angry and aggressive. He's been obsessed with beating me ever since."

I think about it for a moment, about the press clips and interviews I'd seen of the Dragons in other tournaments. "You hurt his honour."

Augie stares at me. "What century do you live in?"

I sigh. "This one. Thresher is old school. You offended his sense of honour. This grudge he has against you is personal. It's not about the money for him or the win. You took his honour when you threw that match. He wanted to beat you fair and square."

"Santos!" yells Carlo. "Get out here, now. You get me the key."

I go to leave, but Augie pulls me back. "If we both walk out of here together, it will look like we were up to something."

"Fine. You go first. I'll wait."

289

Augie looks around the tiny room, which has no hiding places. He reaches for me, a look on his face that I can't read as it's half-hidden by his cap. "They'll definitely see you when I open the door. We could always ... fake kiss, just for good luck?"

"That's not funny. What are you...?"

But his hand goes to my cheek, and gently brushes the bruise hidden there. We are too close. His other hand snakes around my waist. And then Augie's lips are near mine, but he doesn't move. Part of me feels something, and it makes me forget where we are. An invisible pull that makes me feel warm. I stop thinking and my body leans into him; our lips touch. Then one thought floods my mind: *Dark*, and it makes me pull away.

At the same time, Carlo succeeds in pulling open the door. Two press people are standing with him, waiting for their exclusive pre-match interview with the one and only Augie Santos. Augie snaps back and a beat later he turns to the press person, his eSports star persona fully in place. "Sorry. We were occupied." A smile for the cameras.

I don't think. I storm off. As I move away, I can already hear some journo ask if it's a "lovers" quarrel.

When I turn the corner towards the team dressing room, I hear a voice. "I didn't know you guys had a thing."

Jones.

"We don't."

"Well, you both missed the tech run through, so I hope whatever that was, it was worth it. We're needed on the floor. Dump your stuff in the dressing room; you can suit up later."

Guilt washes over me. Then my fingers find the chain around my neck, and I think of Maya and Annie. Thinking about Dark or anything else will have to wait till this is over.

33

The excitement in the arena feels like a physical wall around us now. Like you can touch it. It's amplified by the placement of screens, the sound design, and the interactive video walls. The constant roving vloggers and presenters. Even the custom-designed smell of the arena – a celebrity perfume that wafts through the HEPA filters. Streams like this make eSports history, and everyone knows it. The number of eyeballs and views from this will create a new event standard.

A new game is a major event planned years in advance. Gaming giants have business plans that stretch into the next century. That's why Zu Tech's performance, the little company that could, has always raised such interest. It's the exception to the rule. Zu and his investors have gone all out this time, backed by a government determined to place themselves in the "digital economy", but who can't or will never realize that this isn't micro men. That the concept of "country" and "government" ended long ago. This is the era of corporate industry, and games – one of the biggest industries – are running global empires. Zu is an emperor. His face, his logo, interactive holograms of him are everywhere.

We keep walking. Past the screens cutting between the various live streams and the "fan cams" worldwide. Towards the centre of the arena – the kill zone. The players' area. The immersive custom pods we last saw in the lab have been refined into gleaming white ones carrying the Zu Tech logo. Each one is linked to a giant screen dedicated to the players' stats, their vitals as they experience the game, their odds of winning, their world rankings. Win or be eliminated, each match will be sudden death.

All eyes are on this stadium, and the air vibrates with pop music and pre-show commentary as outside the skies darken, and the launch clock counts down. Hours. I have only hours to stop this.

Once the winner is crowned in twelve hours, the countdown clock above the stadium will reach zero, and SHACKLE will go live as a download on every gaming store platform and as a free update on every console that already has Zu games or Zu Tech on it. Spreading like a live digital virus that will create billions of mind-controlled people answering to one company. Zu Tech.

I don't know what they planned to do with that power, but I don't want to find out.

I'm shivering, and it has nothing to do with the air conditioning. My fingers go by instinct to the pen drive and the locket around my neck that holds the virus. Now isn't the time to start doubting myself. Focus.

"Nothing like seeing yourself as a twenty-foot image," Augie says tentatively.

I don't smile. I keep my voice low and say, "We don't ever do that again."

Augie looks towards the floor. "I'm sorry. I don't know why I..." The mask of the pro player slips from his face. His voice is hesitant. "I like you, Daisy. I have since the day I first met you. I shouldn't have suggested that, and I promise I'll never do it again unless ... you want me to."

I glare at him. "We're teammates, friends, Augie. Nothing more."

"Got it. Loud and clear."

A pause while we both stare out at the crowds, neither of us able to look at the other. I would be lying if I said that kiss hadn't made me feel something for a second – and then Dark had flooded my brain with a wave of guilt.

"We good?" Augie asks.

I nod. I move away towards the twins. When I look back, I see Augie look at Carlo, who hovers in the background. They exchange a look. Something about it sets me on edge, but I push the feeling down. Carlo is just being Carlo. An overprotective, ambitious manager. But then I think back to him in the server room with Emily Webber – was Augie really just there to calibrate his gloves? And the uneasiness inside me grows.

"Hey, Daisy, you never made it. Mum wanted to meet you!"

Ruby.

Distraction. "Yeah. I didn't want to intrude."

Josh nudges me. "Next time come, OK?"

Ruby is now rocking glitter and strands of purple in her braids. Her T-shirt with the Tower logo is slightly styled, knotted at the front into a crop top. She looks fantastic, and already I can see several of the boards starting to flip to her profile picture and stats. "Live stream is starting. My little sister said we've got to give the fans what they want."

Augie beams a megawatt smile at her, his pro player mask now firmly on. "Truth."

Josh and I exchange looks, and he rolls his eyes at me. He's his usual self. Or is he? Now I think about it, something seems off. Nerves? "You OK?"

"Yep." Then he points to the screens. "Looks like they are bringing out the big guns for the opening."

I follow his eyeline and see the screens projecting Zu's face. This time with a banner that reads "live from Wembley". He's dressed in his iconic dark jumper, jeans, presenting a calm, laid-back elegance. The camera is feeding live from his private box just above the arena. The buzz is now electrifying. Zu's face starts to fill every screen, all the live feeds, the streams and the traditional TV cameras.

"How many people do you think, Daisy?" Josh asks.

Augie answers before I can. "Everyone that matters. Millions. The only thing bigger than this is the New York tournament and that event in Singapore."

Josh gives him a look.

Augie sighs. "Yeah, I'm a pro player, man. I've been there."

My stomach sinks even lower. So many eyes. My mind snaps me out of it. *You're better than this. You survived the foster homes. Taking down an evil empire is just a walk in the park.*

I beam a fake smile in the direction of Augie, who gives me a small smile in return. "Then let's give them a show," I say.

I glance up at the darkened windows of the large corporate box. Inside, Zu is watching.

There is a deafening roar as the first teams take their places in the arena. Like everyone else, I turn to watch the gameplay.

The first battle loads on the giant stadium screens.

The visuals are even sharper than before. It looks like someone has hand-rendered each pixel on to the screen. The snakes and scorpions that crawl up from under the dunes are textured, unique, grotesque. The feeling of dry heat and emptiness drips from every image. The sound effects come straight from old big-budget movies and arcade games. You can almost feel the knife that slashes with a swishing sound in the air as a player tries to defend themselves from a horde of crawling insects.

The soundscapes, the blood that splatters from a player's avatar when a snake bites into them, the venom that drips from the monster's teeth. It's so vivid I see people, real and those projected into the stadium, having to glance away from the gore. All of us are in this fight. Watchers, fans, teams, managers, coaches, streamers, TV people, technicians. Monitoring, checking. If you close your eyes, it's almost like we are back in Wembley's past with ninety thousand screaming football fans.

"One day, that will be us." That's what Maya used to say when we watched eSports, curled up on a battered old beanbag at some foster home or another. *"They will be playing a game we made."* Now the thing we dreamt of has destroyed Maya. My eyes drift again towards Zu's box. He was once my idol. And now...

A clash of swords on a rock catches my attention. In the arena, the second match of the eight battles is starting. This one is closer to us. Time seems to be going faster now, or maybe that is just how it feels to me. A Scottish team, The Giants, is battling it out against team Phoenix from New York, led by Eliza. Their battleground looks like some alternative universe version of South America. Amazon rainforest, giant lizards, ancient ruins, tribes. The Giants shoot everything and everyone that moves, while the Phoenix team seem content just to wait it out. Conserving their life points until their opponents are at their weakest.

It's the smart move, but not one that seems to be going down well with their supporters who are howling for them to attack.

As time goes on and the crowd grows restless, I realize that the game is changing. Just like with the respawning zombies in the practice game, the AI behind SHACKLE starts to throw more monsters at the Phoenix Team. I see Eliza respond and change tactics. She begins to marshal her team. Her snipers go on the attack, led by their tank player, who absorbs the worst hits. They are being pushed by the game's AI into a battle with The Giants, but now they're not alone. They're both up against a horde of monsters as well.

When I look back again, I see Jones watching the screen, too, her expression serious. "Get ready," she says. "We're up next."

The Dragons. Focused, precise, experienced. High scorers. No biggie.

We each go to our dressing rooms and change quickly into our Zu Tech suits. Ours are a dark blue colour. Our names and roles within the team are written in small writing on the front, like soldiers in an army. Centred on the back is the Tower logo and the tournament's name. We gather backstage and wait for the signal from the technicians.

Ruby looks at Josh. "Thresher and his friends. Basically our worst nightmare?"

"Win or lose. We'll be OK," Josh says.

Augie shakes his head. "We win." He looks around at us. "This is a show. They may have experience, but we have skills. Even with Thresher. We got this, OK?"

"Spoken like a guy who wants to crush it." Ruby grins and gives him a high five. I don't say anything. I need us to win, but not for the reasons she might think.

34

My plan is simple. I need to go deep into the tournament. Far enough to access the source code of the AI that will spread SHACKLE. Then I drop the "bomb", Maya's virus.

Maya's notes, hidden in the drive from the pink fluffy monster I made, have made everything fall into place. The AI they've put in SHACKLE learns your moves as you go. There are no cheat sheets. The game adapts to each player individually, changing as it learns their moves and challenging them. It is the ultimate game. You're at one with it, and slowly, little by little, it learns everything about how your brain works and how you respond. Then it takes you over.

I had time to examine Maya's virus carefully. It's a bomb: a creatively crafted sequence that will wipe everything in the game. Halt and Catch Fire. Code that can spread through every execution thread and live in the memory on the server, corrupting every copy of the code that runs there, and taking down all of Zu Tech's servers before they can go live. Maya knew what SHACKLE was. And she knew how to end it. I just need to find the perfect place to plant the virus in the game.

There is a roar that I hadn't expected from the virtual and live audience as we step out into the spotlight on the stadium floor. Most of the screaming is for Augie, who waves and smiles. The blinding flash of cameras. Each lens is now carrying an image of me that could lead to trouble if it gets cross-referenced with the police database or social services. I have to trust that by hiding in plain sight under a different name, I am in the one place no one will think to check. That Penny's makeover will do the trick. There is nothing else I can do.

My legs shake as we walk to our immersive pods on the main tournament floor. When we get them, the earpieces are more refined, the VR headset even more lightweight than before, calibrating almost instantly to my eyeline. We check that our mics and earpieces are tuned into the frequency that only our team can hear.

Then the pods shut with a click, and all the stadium's noise disappears. Inside the pods, it's just the player and the game. Outside, the feeds for the giant stadium screens are taken from each player's pod directly. What I see is what the audience sees. Viewers can choose between experiencing the match through a single-player, watching a wide-angle shot, or go with multiple views. My vitals: heart rate, body temperature, pulse and respiration rates and blood pressure also start to load on to a screen, a new touch that allows the fans to see how their favourite players react to the pressure. I imagine the crowd's roars outside, and all I can think of for a moment is one of Maya's stories about gladiator battles in ancient Rome.

Game time. The warning bell rings inside the pod, and I strap in. Just the four of us now facing Thresher and the other two boys and one girl who make up the Dragons.

Small holos appear above our avatars inside the game, giving our names.

AUGIE SANTOS
RUBY WILLIAMS
JOSH WILLIAMS
DAISY CHABI

Then the VR world starts to load around us.

"Game on…" I whisper through the headset.

When we load, the first thing I see is the most beautiful rainforest I could have imagined. Light dappling through the trees. Complete silence. I take a moment to almost feel the leaves beneath the feet of my suit. The light breeze and sunlight on my face. They weren't lying. The design of this is next level.

"Daisy, find a vantage point." It's Augie's voice in my ear.

"On it." I look around and start to run towards the highest trees.

"Ruby, Josh – borders."

I can hear them affirming their positions as my avatar picks up enough speed to start using the trees as springboards to run up towards higher land. I am not alone. Somewhere in this game, the Dragons are probably doing the same thing.

From a small mountaintop, I can see the map of the territory our battle covers. We're in a weirdly scaled version of Australia. It's a condensed continent. Outback, Queensland Jungle, a beach that looks like the Great Ocean Road. Everything on this map looks capable of robbing us of life points. Lose too many, and we won't respawn later in the game. As I look for landmarks, tiny captions appear above them for a moment. "Settlement" 50 points, "Mine" (obviously a resources stronghold), "Ocean of Death". I'm currently in "Jungle of Deadly Snakes". Nice. No sign yet of the Dragons. I take screengrabs of all the info using my hands, instantly sending it to the rest of the team.

"What's the plan?" Ruby asks in my ear.

"We take out the settlement first so we have a base, and from there we plunder for resources till we are strong enough to find and take out the Dragons in battle." Augie's voice is firm. Commanding.

"Plunder?" I say. "Does that mean killing the indigenous tribes?"

"Daisy, they are just computer graphics designed by graphics artists and controlled by an AI," Augie says.

He's right, of course, but I still don't like it. It all feels too real, for one thing. "We could hit the mine for resources first, then use the trade/ally option to make them part of our army. Boost our numbers."

"Kill or be killed, Daisy. Don't argue. It wastes time we don't have."

He's right. Augie is the captain. SHACKLE is just a game. I move.

"On it."

The Dragon team seem to have the same mindset, so for the first few minutes of the game, we avoid each other as we move around parts of the map, securing our areas through epic battles with creatures that can kill with one bite. Everything – snakes, spiders, the ocean, the indigenous tribes created by the game's AI – seems to be working against us. Ruby takes some life point hits when a tribal spear strikes her, and a black snake sinks its teeth into her foot simultaneously. I see her face crumple, even as Josh, our tank, tries to protect her.

I break ranks and scout a nearby cave that pings as a mine, searching for health packs. Augie's strategy also means we'll need more ammunition. It's dark inside, the floor rough underneath me. The smell is dank; there is a sound of trickling water. The rock walls, when I touch them, feel damp, cold after the hot, humid sun outside. The VR is so impressive. The temp in my VR pod lowers as I enter the cave. I can feel my body shiver in response. I go further in, and two small yellow spots glow in the distance. My breath stops. I consider how fast I can speed boost myself out of this. A figure approaches. As it gets closer, it solidifies into the image of an old man bent with age.

"Who are you?"

The figure's eyes are yellow, bloodshot. "Harold, Harold Lasseter – have you come for my reef?"

"Your what?"

"My gold." He clutches something in his hand. An old-fashioned gun.

I slowly start to back away. "I just wanted an item stash, a power-up ... medicine for my teammates. I mean no harm."

"You're not drawing your weapons," he says. And he's right. I'm not. Because even if this is a game and the smart move would be to kill the old prospector in the mine and secure his gold, I can't do it. I can't just shoot someone that looks worse off than me. A man, or a game's sim of one, who looks more dead than alive.

I can hear Augie's voice in my ear. "Daisy, where are you?"

I start to back away from Harold, but he gestures with his hand for me to follow him. "I have something for you. But only if you can answer my question first."

Augie's voice is in my ear again. "Daisy, I need you to scout ahead, we've lost visual on two of the Dragons. We have to know if they're planning a rear attack. Are the Dragons approaching? Daisy?"

Harold turns, and for a second, his avatar seems to glimmer slightly. A ghostly Valkyrie shape surrounds him and then vanishes again. Maya's avatar! Was this a part of the game that she was involved in designing?

"My question to you: what was your favourite book as a child?"

I mute my mic and walk towards Harold, my throat suddenly dry. *"World myths and legends.* Who programmed you?"

Harold holds a finger to his lips and then walks down the old mine shaft. Up ahead, there is a faint green glow. We move closer, and it becomes a kart filled with glowing orbs.

"My treasure is yours."

Power-ups, at least 50 extra life points, medicines, speed boosts, armour hardening, special use items.

"Why?"

Harold's image starts to fade away. "Because it isn't always about shooting first. To win this game, you have to be patient. Wait until the time is right. If you remember the stories in the book, it will help you. Be quick after you take this gift. As soon as you claim it, the mine will start to collapse." Then in a blink, he is gone.

A shiver works its way down my spine that has nothing to do with the immersive VR. I stretch out my hand and add the power-ups to my virtual game inventory, and then I run as the walls around me start to shake.

I make it out of the mine just before it collapses and then teleport to find Ruby and Josh.

"About time." Ruby glares at me.

"Your comms were down." This is from Josh as he ninja attacks what looks like a bunyip, and in the crossfire, Ruby takes another hit.

"You strayed too close to the billabong," I say.

"Yeah, no kidding." Ruby dispatches the creature but not before one of its claws hits her, depleting another life bar.

"Good thing I'm your healer." I go into my virtual inventory. "I think I can help you with that."

Augie appears as Ruby's life points are restored. "Where did you get all this?" he asks.

"In the mine," I say. It feels too complicated to explain about Harold.

He frowns. "That's weird, though, isn't it? That it was all just waiting for you."

I shrug. "Lucky, I guess."

"I guess." Then he says, "We're in the end stages. We fight as a group now — battling the monsters, like the Dragons are doing."

The Dragons have taken some major life point hits. With all the land now claimed, we now have no choice but to battle it out. To try desperately to push each other off the edges of the map. The Dragons are strong, but we now have extra power-up's. We out-plot and outmanoeuvre them at every turn.

Midway towards the last round, they stage a comeback. Thresher and his main sniper split from their tank and healer. They drive a wedge between us as we scramble to avoid them, separating all of us.

"Status?" It's Augie's voice in my ear.

I crouch low near an outcrop of red sandstone in front of the jungle. It's a natural maze. The rocky stones drown out all other sounds as soon as I enter them. "I'm in the red rocks. The Dragons aren't here."

"Stay where you are. Josh and Ruby, find a vantage point near Daisy. I'm going to see where Thresher is, then we regroup." Augie's voice cuts out just as I hear a giant hissing sound behind me. I will myself to stay still, but I can't. The sound comes closer. When I look around, everything inside me freezes. Towering above me is a huge inland taipan. Its scales are a kaleidoscope of brown, black and burnt amber, gradually leading to the darker black scales around its head. One of the most toxic serpents on the planet. VR or not VR, I am not staying here to feel it bite me. Why does there have to be snakes? I start to slowly inch away as it advances, somehow exiting the rocky area in a different place – this time, it's not the jungle I see but Thresher and another Dragon isolating Augie near the cliffs. No sign of Josh or Ruby. He's alone.

Augie is pushed closer to the cliffs as Thresher fights him with one of his teammates. His life points are low; indicators are blinking as he tries to battle back. He's injured, outnumbered, his vitals fading fast. I am the closest and use a power-up to teleport to him to boost his life points. I have just seconds to do it before he crashes out.

But before I reach him, something shifts in the game. Before I can touch him, his life points restock, and his weapons are upgraded. Now fully powered up, he fights back, and I join him. Together we push Thresher and two other Dragons off the map in a move that marks us, finally, as the winners of the round. Slowly the game fades away, and as the pod doors open, we become surrounded by the stadium's noise.

"Victory. Tower team wins." And as the announcer's voice booms out, the points beside our names explode. I remove my glasses and struggle to unstrap myself from the pod.

My mic is still live. Tuned to the team frequency that only we can hear, the twins are on it. "Wow, Daisy, that power-up you gave Augie turned the tide. Next time you need to share the wealth. Sick move. What was it anyway? Weapons upgrade? Easter egg bonanza?"

But I don't answer. I hadn't given Augie anything. So who did?

I step outside the pod and am overwhelmed by lights, mics and cameras, each wanting a reaction to the win. We've passed the first round in record time. The underdogs that no one rated have beaten Thresher and the Dragons.

Everyone is excited. I see Ruby start to glow under the camera lights, her dimples showing as she laughs. Augie wraps her and Josh in a bear hug. Only Jones and I stand apart and silent; her eyes meet mine.

"Daisy, come on." It's Ruby, holding out a hand to me.

I hesitate, but Jones nudges me forward, her voice low so only I hear her. "It's going to look suspicious if you don't join them. Go, smile for three minutes. No one is looking at you thinking you could be a person of interest to the police. They just see a new pro player. Be that player for a moment, or people *will* start to ask questions." She shoves me in the direction of the cameras.

Augie pulls me into an interview he's giving to some eSports network.

"Here she is, my protégé, Daisy."

Their attention flickers to me. "Where did you play before? How did Augie Santos find you?"

I bristle slightly. I got here on my own. But then I see it for what it is, an available cover story for the press that's easy to understand. "I guess … this is my first big tournament."

"But not your last, right?"

I give a slight smile. "We need to see how this goes first."

The reporter turns back again to the camera. "You heard it here, folks, this is Mark E with a new rising star of the eSport's scene, Daisy." He waits for a beat before saying, "Cut." Then he turns to Augie. "Aren't you afraid of being outshone out there, champ?"

Augie shrugs. "No. New team, new me."

The twins join us. "This is so cool," Ruby squeals.

Josh looks tense beside her. What is going on with him? But then Jones claps her hands, and I shift my attention to her.

"Let's clear and let the stage crew in for the reset. The interval will be around one hour. No one wander off, OK?"

We all nod and head backstage. I catch up with Augie and whisper, "We need to talk about that last stats boost."

He grins. "Yeah, thanks for that."

"Augie, it wasn't me."

He gives me a bewildered look. "It has to have been you. Who else could it have been, the Dragons?"

"I don't know, but it doesn't make sense—"

Just then, we see Thresher coming towards us.

Augie stiffens and goes to try and step in front of me. I ignore him and hold out my hand to Thresher. "It was a good game. Well played."

Thresher takes a beat and then takes my hand. "Good game," he agrees.

Thresher goes to move past, but Augie clears his throat. "I'm sorry, Thresher," he says. "I need to be honest about what I did, the tournament I threw. I took the easy way – not the right one."

Thresher looks at him in surprise. After a moment, he nods and then turns to me. "I will not underestimate you next time, Daisy. You're a good opponent." He turns to leave but pauses before turning back and secretly hands me a tiny folded note. His voice is low as he leans towards me. "As a gesture of goodwill. Eliza asked me to give you this. She believes in fair competition."

I take the small piece of paper and keep it hidden in my

clenched hand, surprised. My voice matches his. "What is this? Aren't you and Eliza rivals too?"

Thresher raises one eyebrow. "Sometimes. Looks can be deceiving."

He nods at Augie as he leaves, and I quickly open the note so that only I can read it. It's a single sentence:

You have a traitor on your team.

I look up, but Thresher is already gone.

Jones comes up to us. Her eyes have questions in them, none of which I answer as I crumple the note into my pocket.

"Daisy, Augie, there's not much time between matches. If you need a break or something to eat, do it now," she says.

In the distance, a buzzer sounds.

"I need a minute."

Jones nods. "Go. I'll stall if needed. And well done out there."

I shoot her a grateful look and turn towards the players' area. When I enter the dressing room, I let my back slide against the door as I sink for a moment on to the floor and shut my eyes.

You have a traitor on your team.

Who?

Then a voice speaks from inside the room that makes my heart jump.

"I didn't think Santos was your type?"

Dark.

35

I stand up. Angry. "How did you get in here?" Then I remember where we are. The place will be monitored to the hilt. I bring my finger to my lips.

Dark raises his eyes to heaven and points to a small signal jammer he's plugged into one of the wall sockets. "I assure you this is probably the only safe place in the building where we can talk right now."

There's a loud knock on the door, and my eyes go wide, then I jerk my head towards the small en suite bathroom. Dark raises his eyebrows at me, and for a second, I think he will refuse, but then he saunters over. I watch while he disappears inside, then I answer.

"Yes?"

"It's me. Jones."

Jones doesn't even give me a moment to respond. She just enters and then quickly shuts the door on the noise and chaos of the tournament outside.

She glances over to me and then around the room. "You can come out, Dark," she calls. "I saw you earlier."

Dark walks out of the bathroom and nods at her. There's a silence. Neither Jones nor Dark seems surprised to see the other.

I sink on to one of the chairs by the mirrors. "I thought you guys weren't speaking."

Jones shrugs. "I wasn't happy when he left. But water under the bridge, as they say. Anyway, here we all are." Jones takes a seat on the couch.

Dark flinches slightly, but he doesn't say anything.

Jones looks at him and then at me before she continues. "We don't have long, so if I were you, I'd start talking."

I shake my head. "I can't. The less you know, the better."

Dark gives a weak laugh. "You don't have a choice in this, Asha. Tell her."

I turn to him, realization setting in. "You abandoned me again and then you went to Jones?"

"I never left you, not them, not now. I just disagreed with watching you put your life at risk. Bill gave me the drive. I needed to know you were OK." His eyes study me. "You have allies, Asha, use them. Tell Jones about the world-ending event you're here to stop."

Jones glares at him and snaps, "Stop being dramatic, Dark."

Dark just shrugs. "You're going to wish I was."

I glare at him. Dark glares at me.

At last, Jones sighs. "I'll begin, shall I? First off, Dark has found out that Carlo has been taking money from Zu Tech. It didn't show on any of the background checks I ran on him, so I don't know what that means, except that it's something he didn't reveal to me when he bought up my debts and insisted that Santos was placed on this team. For some reason, Zu Tech wanted one of their own on the team. And I don't like being played." She's silent for a moment, then turns to me. "OK, your turn."

"Wait," I say, frowning. "You're saying Augie is a plant? But it doesn't make sense."

"Well, it might make more sense if you hadn't been so busy flirting with him," Dark says coldly.

Just then — at possibly the worst moment — there is a knock at the door, and a familiar voice calls out, "Hey? Are you in there?"

Augie. Dark looks like he wants to punch someone.

Dark crosses to the door. "You won't mind if I let him in, will you?"

Before I can answer, he's at the door, which he opens and then shuts it behind Augie as soon as he steps over the threshold.

Augie swivels round and stares at Dark with a furious expression on his face. "You."

Augie turns from Dark to me. "What's going on?" he asks.

315

"That's what we want to find out," I say. "Jones, how much time do we have?"

Jones looks at her watch. "Thirty minutes."

I go over to my phone and send a text. Then: "OK, Dark, you first. Tell me how you found out about Carlo, and make it quick. I thought you weren't going to have anything more to do with this."

Dark scowls. "I lied. I started digging into the data we acquired from Webber's device before the worm was shut down."

"Webber ... as in the Chief Operations Officer for R&D at Zu Tech?" Augie asks.

Dark glares at him. "No interruptions, especially from you. As I was saying, I followed the money, in this case, payments she was authorizing for 'special projects'. Three recent pay-outs to three names. Two — well, two are to people you don't want to be involved with. And the third was to Santos's manager, Carlo."

Augie sinks back in his chair. "Oh."

"That's right," says Dark. "So want to explain why your manager is taking money from Zu Tech?"

"Wait. Who is working for Zu?" Ruby's voice comes from the doorway, and standing very still behind her is Josh. "I got your text, Daisy."

Dark makes an almost snorting sound when he hears her say my alias.

"Now the gang is all here." I shut the door behind them.

"I didn't know Carlo was anything other than Carlo, I

316

swear. He's a respected manager. I was flattered when he signed me. That's the truth," Augie says.

I want to believe him – but I can't forget the note.

I turn to Josh. "Something's going on, isn't it? You've been distracted. It's now or never, Josh. You have to tell us."

Josh swallows. He looks almost ill, and I can see the tears in his eyes. "Nothing is going on."

My voice is steady as I say, "So you're not working against us?"

Ruby looks at me, lost. "What are you talking about, Daisy?"

I hand Josh the note from Thresher and watch his face crumble.

Josh stares at Jones and me. "It's not what you think." He draws a shuddering breath. "It's Dawn." He looks at Ruby. "It's our sister."

Ruby just stares at him. "What? She's in our suite, Josh. She's fine."

"Start at the beginning," Jones says. Josh looks at Dark and then back to Jones. She sighs. 'You can trust him.' Josh nods.

"A few days ago. When that post Dawn made went viral. Someone sent me a video of her, taken just outside her school. No text, unknown number." Ruby opens her mouth, and he holds up a hand. "I thought it was one of my mates being stupid. I didn't tell you because I didn't want to worry you. Then I got another one showing her arriving home from school to our flat. This time there was

317

a text. It said if I told anyone, they'd take her. To stand by for further instructions."

Dark interrupts, his voice gentle. "What did they ask you to do to keep her safe?"

Josh looks at me and then at Ruby. "They said they'd hurt her. I had no choice. They told me if I did this one thing for them…"

"Let me guess," I say. "It had something to do with me?"

Josh sinks to the floor. He looks tired, defeated. "They asked me to break into your room. That night you ran into me outside your room, you were going for a run. They wanted me to search your room for a missing drive. Daisy – I didn't have any choice."

I put my hand up to the necklace that holds the drive. "But you couldn't find it because I always have it on me."

Josh nods. "I texted and said there was nothing there, just those weird boards. I took some photos of them. After that the videos and the texts stopped. I was so ashamed, worried about what would happen if I told anyone. I couldn't say anything to you. I'm so sorry."

Jones is shaking her head. "Someone messed with my team, my business, with all of us. Why?"

I take a deep breath. My heart is pumping way too fast, I need to do this right. "They were trying to find a data drive. All of this is about what Maya found out when she worked at Zu Tech. She was going to go public, become a whistle-blower about what Zu Tech were doing. It's why they killed her, killed her girlfriend Annie, tried to kill me."

Ruby looks up at me. "What do you mean?" There's a pause. "What is going on, Daisy?"

"My name's not Daisy."

And after that, I tell them *everything*.

When I finish, there is silence in the room. I stop and look at each of them. Dark, Augie, Jones, Josh and Ruby. All my secrets are out in the open now. There's nothing left to hide. No one says anything for a moment.

Jones is the first to speak. "That's a lot to take in, for me, for them. You only told me half the story, Asha."

I look at her. "You said it yourself. The people I confided in ended up dead. I didn't want to implicate any of you in this unless there was no other way."

Dark says, "We could still run, Asha." But even he seems unconvinced by his words now.

I give him a weak smile. "For ever? Knowing that they killed Maya, Annie, they threatened Dawn, a *little kid*? Knowing the consequences of letting this game into the world? That we had a chance to stop them and didn't. We can't run from this. You know that."

The look that passes over his face is heartbreaking. "The past always catches up with you, doesn't it?" he says. Then: "This virus. You're sure it needs to be planted in the final?"

"Yes, all the simulations I ran based on Maya's work gave me the same result. The final game is when the AI takes over. It's also when the game is vulnerable to attack. It has to be planted then." I swallow. "I don't know what will happen if I plant the virus," I say in a smaller voice.

"It might destroy the game. It could ruin our chances of getting the prize money. But if we don't, more lives will be ruined."

The silence stretches out. I look around at them all – Augie, lost in thought; Josh, sick with worry; Ruby, brows lowered; Dark, expressionless. And Jones, slowly tapping her fingers.

"There's only one thing we can do," says Ruby at last.

"What?" I ask.

"We have to win."

I look at them. I let go of the tension I had been holding in till now. My team. Whatever happens next I'm not alone any more.

"What about Dawn and our mum?" whispers Josh.

I look at Dark. "Bill?" I say.

He nods. "I think he can get them out. With help."

Josh shoots to his feet. "No offence but who even are you?"

"He's the guy who can get your little sister and your mum out, and he is my friend," I say.

Dark take a step towards Josh. "We can get you, your little sister and your mum out of here. My colleague Bill will take you all somewhere safe. You stay there until the tournament is over. After that we can do some more formal introductions."

Jones's fingernails drum on the side of her chair. "He's right, Josh. But, and I hate to point out the obvious, if Josh goes, we're down a player."

Dark looks towards her. "No, we're not."

Josh frowns. "Do you even play?"

Dark gives one of his rare smiles. "Yeah. Yeah, I do."

36

The atmosphere on the main arena floor is electric. However excited the crowd were before this, seeing the first round of matches has only amplified them. A large ticker-tape digital display board runs the entire length of the seated part of the arena showing the online viewing numbers. Previous eyeball counts are exceeded and still growing – billions of people are now watching via streams and old school broadcast sports coverage. This tournament is like nothing that came before. If anything, it's a throwback to the arenas of ancient Rome. Spectators are chanting now for their favourites. The arena lights start to lower, bright spotlights find three of us. The lights blind out everything as I take a step forward and almost trip. Ruby's hand reaches out to steady me. "We got this, remember?"

Augie walks in front of us – the eSports pro. The noise of the world begins to drain away, and all I can hear is the hammering inside my chest.

Dark is impersonating Josh, keeping his head low, a Tower team baseball cap hiding his face, a drive with a loop of Josh playing in his pod in his pocket, ready to hack into the internal camera system. He is already in his pod. If we pull this off, it will be a miracle.

Breathe, breathe. I've been in worse places. My mind flashes back to the night I found Maya. Images that just play over and over in my mind. I stare out into the darkness beyond the spotlights. My fingers instinctively reach for the pen drive and locket Annie gave me. I'm not giving up.

A giant thirty-metre screen in front of me lights up. My face fills it. My rankings, followed by Augie's and Ruby's. Josh's face fills the fourth screen – Dark has connected the live feed to the loop of Josh playing in his pod during the last match. A dull roar from the crowd and the online feeds. On the opposite side, another screen starts to project the stats of our rivals. The Panthers. Big eSports stars. I see another clip as I pass, a smaller screen of some presenters saying that the Panthers are favourites to win now the Dragons have been eliminated. Augie's pro record aside, it seems no one believes that lightning can strike twice, that we might somehow make it past this round. But we have to: this is a game of life or death.

323

Further away, another two other billboards light up with another two teams. One of them is Eliza's. We are the four that have made it to the semi-finals. The announcer goes into overdrive. Hype and more hype. This is what every kid dreams of when they watch eSport streams. That one day, they will be the ones here at the epicentre of everything.

I take my place inside my pod and wait for the game to load. Looking for a split second at the box at the top of the arena where Zu is. There is no choice.

"Let's play."

***

It's cold.

The graphics finish rendering, and I shiver as the pod's temperature lowers to match the projected environment: a vast wilderness of snow and ice. I am ready for this fight.

"Asha, find a vantage point." It's Augie.

I take off at speed over the empty white wasteland and climb up the glaciers surrounding us. Once on the top, I see a movement to my right. A super-soldier with a rifle and sword. The scout from the other team. We eye each other before pulling weapons. The other team's scout pulls a sword, deciding not to waste ammo on me. I fight like I never have before. Each bloody stroke brings me closer to a solution – I've made my peace with how much I am willing to risk to end this.

Afterwards, from the vantage point, I see the game's

world. The vast tundra of ice and snow surrounded by freezing waters. Movements in the sea. Think.

A memory surfaces: Maya and I are together, reading her book.

"But nothing could live in such cold water. Right, Maya?"

"Don't be so sure, Asha. It's home to a Tizheruk. A snake with a flipper and fangs. It can snatch people straight from the land."

Maya's hand mimicked snatching something as if her fingers were part of a giant snake mouth. I'd yelped, and it made her laugh.

"Don't worry, Asha, they're not real. They're just from the book."

I'd smiled. *"I think I'd prefer to stay on the land in this place."*

Maya had raised her eyebrows at me. *"Don't be so sure."* She made a howling sound. *"They have Amaroks here: wolf packs that can chase and eat you."*

She'd tickled me then as I flicked to the next page and an image of a green-coloured Qalupalik. *"What does that one do, Maya?"*

"That one" – Maya grinned – *"kidnaps naughty children who go too close to the water and drags them under."*

I snap back to the present. "Augie, I know how we can win this. We need to lure the other team towards the water and then let the monsters on this level take them out for us."

A pause. Then Augie replies. "Any ideas?"

I hear Dark's reply. "I have one."

I stand over the avatar of the scout I just killed and use

a small disguise mechanism to clone their avatar's skin. Impersonation in place, I climb down on to one of the ice flows and use a distress flare. A red shooting firework arches up into the sky. Once it's in the air, I run straight towards the water's edge.

Augie, Dark and Ruby line up hidden in the ridges around the flat-packed snow. The closer I get to the edge where the freezing waters lies, the more the surface of the snow seems to change. The ice underneath is fragile, weaker. I just need the other team to believe I'm one of them, a comrade in distress, and follow me. I sink to the ground and play dead.

The Panthers see their scout lying on the ice with a weakened life level. They come for me, and that's when Augie, Ruby and Dark spring the trap. Aiming their firepower not at the avatars but at the ice. It splinters and cracks until it breaks, and we are all plunged into the darkness of the water. The creatures that live there come quickly. Sharp teeth and claws are dragging the others down into the depths below. I keep my knife in front of me, slashing it at anything that comes near as I rise to the surface and then use the small blade like a pickaxe, crawling up and back on to the ice flow. I fall on to the surface just as the text *"GAME OVER"* appears. As the game fades, the stadium explodes into noise.

***

After the match, our pictures are projected into the winner's circle. We made it to the finals. The rank outsiders just defeated another of the favourites in under fifteen minutes. The energy is almost like a physical force. Tower team were the unrated group, headed by a washed-up pro player. As we walk out of the arena, I size up the remaining battle for a place in the final. Phoenix team. Thresher had said the note was from Eliza. Why did she send it, and how did she know that someone was betraying us?

As we move backstage, the Phoenix team goes into its final closing moves. Eliza glows under the spotlight as the match swings to her, Zahra, Noah and Mason. In the background, the announcers are talking about the final showdown. It will be "a clash of the underdogs". One that will "change the way we play for ever".

For once, they might be right.

In the darkness behind me, I see Jones raise her palm, the signal that Dawn, Josh and their mum are safe. One more match to go, and if we fail in what happens next, the world changes. I don't know why Zu Tech wants to control people. I only know that if they are willing to kill for this, to murder people like Maya and Annie, nothing good can come of it.

I wait backstage after the match ends. The fifteen-minute warning buzzer sounds just as Ruby finds me and pushes a paper bag into my hand. "Here, take this."

"What is it?"

Her voice goes low. "That guy Dark sent got my mum

and Dawn out. Dawn had made us matching shirts – she wanted us to wear them in the final."

I pull it out and look at it. It's the Tower team shirt but smothered in sequins and glitter. Ruby sees my look. "Custom design. It's stupid, but I'm wearing mine for good luck until we have to go out there."

I grab her hand. "Actually – it's kind of awesome."

Ruby and I hold each other's gaze, and then she throws her arms around me and hugs me. I hug her back. Somehow we don't need to say anything else.

When I get back to my dressing room, I shut the door on the shadows and then sink into the chair in front of the mirror. Penny's make-up bag is in front of me. I am staring at my reflection in the mirror. Slowly unwinding my space buns so that my coloured hair falls in waves around my shoulders.

"I never got a chance to say I like your hair. I miss the colour of your eyes, though."

Dark.

"Jones thought contacts would be best."

"I guessed. Asha, once this is over – did you mean what you said? About going after anyone involved in creating SHACKLE?"

I nod at him. "I meant it. Whoever was involved took my sister from me…"

He takes a step towards me. "Asha…" Outside, another warning bell sounds – five minutes to go.

Dark sighs. "Guess it's showtime."

"Yeah." I look at him in the mirror. Dark dressed in a Tower team shirt. Baseball cap hiding his face. Runners. Jeans. For once, he looks his age, maybe even younger than eighteen. "You're ready to do this?"

He nods. Silence. Then: "Just so you know, I would do anything for you, Asha. I'm sorry about before. All of it."

There. In those words, my eyes find his and I know. I know what this bond between us is. I'm cursing myself for not having seen it sooner. How much time we wasted, how many memories we'll never make because I was afraid to be vulnerable. Because he couldn't tell me the truth, and now it's out in front of us. That singular, rare thing. The reason why everything with Dark has always felt inevitable. Because I've always known, I just refused to admit it.

I stand up without saying anything and go into his arms. We just hold each other, and it's somehow more intimate than anything else. Then the knock comes on the door.

Jones. "The time has come."

I don't look back when we pull apart, because I can't. I go straight outside the door, walking past Jones. She looks at me and then over my shoulder at Dark.

"I put that insurance in place for you, Dark."

I don't even ask what they're talking about because, right now, I'm too scared. I don't want this to be our end.

37

None of us know what the landscape for the final battle will be. There's a tense hush among us as we wait for it to load — like the whole arena is just holding its breath with us. I glance around at the other screens as they load. At Eliza's stats. How did she know about Josh? But then the game starts to load around us, and I push everything else away as the terrain starts to appear. Mountains, snow, temples.

Augie calls the first play, and we all support him, even Dark, who has modified Josh's armour, so it's lighter and sleeker now. I look over and see that Ruby's armour is heavier than before, like she's planning on playing both sniper and defence. Her position and Josh's too. I go to higher ground to scout.

The air is cooler up here, where sky and mountaintop meet. I recognize this one as Maya's favourite chapters in the book. She designed this. I can see touches of my sister everywhere, in the intricate design of the gold temples, the gleaming white pure snow, and the endless blue sky. It's like seeing inside Maya's head, and I remember the first time she told me about this place.

"Where's that, Maya?"

"It's a special place, Asha, the axis mundi. The top of Mount Kailash is where you'll find them: the celestial poles, the centre of the world. The place where heaven meets earth. The legend says that's where the tree of all life is."

"Will you bring me there, Maya?" I'd asked as I snuggled in close to her.

She'd hugged me, held me tight as I'd started to fall asleep. Whispered, "One day, Asha. Sister promise."

I wipe a tear away. She'd kept her promise. Then I hit the team comms. "I know where we have to plant this."

Eliza and the Phoenix team are in the valley above. From what I can see, they're already laying a trap. We climb up, and they start to close in, confident that they can attack from the sides. A kill box framed by mountains. The other dangers in the game – the avalanches, the yeti, the snow leopards, wolves and blue bears – don't seem to worry them. Either that or they haven't spotted them yet.

I report back to the others. Then I hear another voice in my ear. Dark.

"Did you see it?"

He has hacked the comms system, so we can speak privately. "Yes."

He knows me too well. "What's the catch?"

I take a breath, remembering what I know. "It's on top of the mountain. Maya hid the access point in something she knew I'd remember from us being kids. We have to find *the tree of life*."

Silence.

We need to drop Maya's virus deep in this game to launch the kill code in the place in the memory where all the code branches converge, where the virus can replicate and spread to the entire codebase. Her code will attack and destroy all the game's programming, replicating as soon as it is introduced to the server till it overwrites everything.

The problem is the mountaintop towering above us. To get there, we're going to need to battle the Phoenix team and the game itself. The snow leopards, the bears, the wolves, the snow. All of them will be designed to protect the game's weak spot – and the clock is ticking.

Dark's voice interrupts my thoughts. "I don't need to remind you that whoever made this is going to be watching."

And trying to stop us. I know now that the game can adapt to our every move.

"I know. Let's start."

To begin with, we play in perfect harmony with Augie and Ruby. Our gameplay is better than anything we've managed in the past.

Dark talks little. He's in the zone now, the same way he gets when he hacks. Singular concentration on one goal only: getting both of us to that mountaintop.

He's the first over the edge, followed by Ruby and Augie. Avoiding the plain's centre, he heads straight towards the ridges and the Phoenix players hidden there. He takes out their scout first and then clears a path towards the mountain.

"Santos, Asha and I need to go up. You got this?"

Dark doesn't wait for the answer. He keeps moving, clearing a path upwards, slicing down wolves and bears who attack. But the game seems to sense that something is off because almost immediately a Phoenix player goes after us, blocking us with a volley of shots. Dark injures him and moves on.

My avatar sprints forward. Inside my pod, my body starts shaking, palms sweating, head aching. I can almost feel the game starting to try and exert its control over me.

I click my headset slightly. "Augie, you and Ruby OK?" If I am feeling this, they must be too.

Augie's voice is angry as he replies, "Nothing we can't deal with – go."

I run towards Dark. "Let's move. We can't give the game time to figure out what we're up to."

"Sure." He grits his teeth against the force we can all feel. "But I think it's deciding to play against us already." I follow his eyeline and see a cloud of white moving towards us at speed.

"Avalanche. We have to get to higher ground. Trees?"

The game tries to fight me as I will myself to speed up, hitting the trees and scaling them just as the snow rumbles down. By the time it lands where we were standing, our avatars are in the treetops, and my heart is beating out of control.

I can hear the grin in Dark's voice as he asks, "Want to go for a run?"

I dig deep, making my legs move again. We run using the treetops as our solid ground. A blur of sky and green till we reach past the snow and see the path to the mountaintop. In the distance, Augie and Ruby are battling, outnumbered in the pass below. Blocking the other players from advancing on us.

Dark notices my distraction. "You can't save them. They know what's at stake. It's just a game, Asha."

"I know." But it doesn't make it any easier leaving them behind – plus, we need them to keep us in the game, just a little bit longer. As we run forward, I spot it. Another snow bank. This one is anchored directly above where Ruby and Augie are battling it out.

"Look." I point, and Dark follows my eyeline.

"OK, I'll hit the bank. You alert the others, but we keep moving."

"But what if—"

"No time, Asha. We need to finish this, remember?"

I switch to our team mic. "Ruby, Augie, we are sending an avalanche your way. Get to higher ground now."

Dark opens fire on the snow bank as I climb up, sending the powdery snow downhill as Augie and Ruby scatter. The hit takes out another of the Phoenix team. We continue to scramble up. The wind around us picking up snow and ice, which it blasts at us. Is the game realizing what we are up to?

We land on the next ridge, and it gets worse. Wolves almost immediately surround us. Our avatars take position back-to-back, swords and guns trained on the growling beasts stalking through the snow, their number growing and growing.

"Damn it," I say.

"When the going gets tough…"

"Not funny," I shout back through the headset.

"Asha, Dark, you guys OK?" It's Augie.

"We're a little busy," I reply.

"We're dealing with the last two Phoenix players, and then we'll come—"

Dark cuts him off by overriding the channel, so it's just the two of us now. "Asha, there's no time. Both of us aren't going to make it. I'm boosting you up, and you're leaving me here."

I look around at the wolves closing in around us: their snarls, their bared fangs.

"You won't survive."

"No, but you will. Besides, I think my time is running out."

"What?"

A pause.

I understand, then. He's been unmasked. In the world

335

outside of the game, someone has realized he isn't Josh. We knew that was always a possibility, but I thought we would have more time. "How close are they?"

"Close. I kept a window open to my pod view. I can see them gathering outside the players' section." A moment. "They don't have Jones yet."

"You need to log off now. Run."

"Not until I know you can make it." His avatar draws a line in the snow against the advancing wolves and takes out his sword and shield.

"I'm charging up the shield. Then I'll take out as many wolves as I can so they can't follow you. Jump off the shield, and it will boost you to the next part." His voice is firm. "Now, Asha."

My eyes start to well up. "Dark."

His voice is calm above the sound of the battle all around us. "You need to stay, fight. End this. It's the only way."

And when I hear the tone of his voice, I don't argue. I do as he says, even as the tears run down my face in real life. My avatar turns as the wolves close in, ready to rush. I back up and then start to run towards his shield – I jump, using it to propel me up into the air. For a second, I'm flying above, looking down on Dark's avatar as it is overwhelmed by the wolves. He takes out a few more of them before he winks out of existence. Then I'm falling and dropping further up the path, away from the wolves.

I land. Augie and Ruby are still fighting below. Until the game ends, there is still a chance. I climb.

38

The game fights me every step of the way. The snow on this level hits me like small blades, leeching any warmth my body still had. My head pounds. Up ahead, more wolves howl, and I spot the movement of a terrifyingly giant yeti closing in.

Ahead of me, glimmering in the distance on the mountain peak, the axis – the centre of the world, of this game. I just need to make it a few more metres. I just have to—

Pain explodes on my back, sharp razor claws, a howling sound as teeth graze my right ear and dig into my shoulder. A flash of white fur, a snow leopard.

I go to fight it off, but everything is working against me. My headset is filled with the cries of Ruby and Augie.

The throbbing in my head that started behind my eyes is getting worse. The game is overtaking me, and I'm out of options. My destination, just a few hundred metres away, might as well be on the other side of the planet.

I can't make it.

Acceptance. Maya and Annie. I lost them. Dark is gone. The vision of the mountaintop still seems so close, but I can't play against these odds. I go to block the snow leopard's attack when it charges again, but I miss, and it sinks its teeth into my leg and I crumple. My vision starts to blur. I'm almost out of time. Alone. I call on the last of my strength and throw the animal away from me. It growls, calling to others who start to emerge from the trees. It starts to paw at the ground like it's preparing to charge.

Inside my pod, my fingers find the necklace Annie gave me. The photos and video footage I never finished watching of Maya. Images Maya gave to Annie for me. I connect the drive from the locket to my central console. If I am going out, I'm going out with my sister's image beside me. I have to see her one last time.

Maya's avatar — her take on a warrior princess — loads beside me. Swords rotating. I think it's a clip from one of her last games till the figure turns. A nod of the head, a careful flick of her hair. "Took you long enough, Ash."

I think I imagine it till I see the avatar move. Is she here? In this game? I choke on the word. "Maya?"

Her avatar turns, and I hear her voice, my sister's voice. "Go. Let's end this."

"Is it really you?"

"Not your Maya, but she promised not to leave you alone, and she's reliable. She created me." She fixes me with a stare. "You're smart enough when you want to be. Figure this out later. Right now, you have to end this. She trusted you, Asha. She always did. Go, now."

Maya's avatar turns her back to me and faces the snow leopards creeping up to us. "Run."

I don't understand. I try to touch her virtual arm before I do. "I'm sorry."

The avatar starts to rotate her swords, gaining momentum as she does and moves away, her words drifting over her shoulder as she advances. "The real Maya knew that, Asha. And she knew you'd find a way to finish what she'd started. She put me in this game to help you, but you have to end it. I can't. You know what you need to do."

I finally get it. Through the pain, I understand. Maya created a guardian in the game. She must have known that in the event of her death I, or Annie, would try and find answers. And she wasn't going to leave us to do it alone.

I start to run towards the mountain peak. The climb becomes almost vertical, but I power up using the last parts of my energy. The snow blinds me and the monsters attack, but I slash my way through. Their blood splatters on me.

Maya believed I could do this.

I keep holding on to that thought. My head and chest feel like they're caught in a vice. The golden glow comes closer – the axis is within my grasp.

I sprint while accessing my inventory in the game. Flicking past the weapons and landing on the two items I customized. The uploaded replica of Maya's book *World Myths and Legends*. The virus, the drive I had in the real world, is inside it. Beside it is a large sack. The logo on the outside of a Medusa's head. The Gorgon with snakes for hair. A few more metres and I can plant the virus – just a few seconds more… Then the shadow appears.

A sky god descending from above, and even though I can't see his face, I know who it is before he speaks.

It's Zu. Zu Thorp is in the game.

39

"You." Zu's avatar looks at me like a benevolent god, or a spider watching a fly that's already caught in his web, seconds from death. "I am glad it's you."

I draw a deep breath. My heart is pounding. "You were expecting me?"

"No. It was probable, but that was all. Your brain chemistry might have been different from your sister's. The only way to know for sure was to have you in the tournament."

"Maya," I say. My voice is hoarse. "Her name was Maya, and you killed her."

Zu looks at me, his head slightly to the side, puzzled. "You still haven't figured it out?" He raises his hand, and

I feel my knees buckle under me. They hit the snow, and I'm kneeling before his avatar. "I was the one who ensured that you made it here. I didn't kill Maya, Asha. I wanted her to live. She was *valuable* to me."

It doesn't make sense. I try to think, but the coldness from the snow is spreading through me like an icy frost. My head hurts; the pain behind my eyes stabs like a knife.

"It will be over soon, Asha. You will understand when I join you. All of this, the AI in the game, was about taking control to help mankind. But Maya — Maya was going to be used for something more than that, she was special. And now..." His image changes, becoming larger in front of me. "Now you're going to take her place."

I can feel myself getting weaker, the ice spreading, the blood rushing to my head. Zu smiles.

"W-why?" My teeth chatter. "What is happening to me?"

"SHACKLE is about saving the human race. You live in this world, Asha. You and your sister saw what it is like when you let people make choices by themselves. They can't be trusted to do the right thing. The planet is dying; resources are almost gone. Yet people surround themselves with engineered fake news and ignore the reality. If it stays on this path, the human race is destined to become extinct. I can prevent that. Take back control, correct this situation. Make people choose the right options. SHACKLE will save millions, and people won't even realize it. That's the beauty of this."

"You didn't s-save Annie…" I force the words out.

He inclines his head. "That was … unfortunate. An acceptable level of collateral damage, when weighed against the greater good. There was no choice."

I can't move. I can't speak. *Collateral damage.* "And my sister?"

Zu shakes his head. "I told you. I had nothing to do with Maya's death. I knew what she was trying to do, but I felt we could find the drive and keep her contained till needed. When she died, it created problems. I tried to find a replacement. At first, I used the initial test subjects like your friend Santos – but it didn't work. So I set up this tournament to find her substitute. To allow the AI in SHACKLE to search and find the perfect match for my brain chemistry through these battles."

Horror fills me, along with the icy cold. "Your brain chemistry?"

"There was no other way. I need to find a host. There is still so much more to be done. It would be wrong to abandon the world now. This game allows me to control its players – but, more than that, it enables me to download my brain, my own AI, into one of them. To live through them. Immortality means I can oversee this work properly and build a new future. Maya was supposed to be my vessel, but now it will be you. Don't you want to save people, Asha?"

"You wanted M–Maya to be your host? Your puppet?"

Zu looks down at me. I am almost at his feet now, his

image flickering in front of me. "It will be less painful for you if you just close your eyes and let go."

"No."

"You won't feel anything afterwards. It will be quick."

I need a little more time.

I collapse on to the snow. The coldness makes it so hard to move. I start to crawl.

"I'm not going to let you—"

Zu interrupts me, a terrible smile stretching across his face. "Win? But, Asha ... I *already have.*"

I grunt as I crawl another few inches. With my last bit of energy, I open the sack I took from my inventory just as Zu's giant avatar starts to lean over me. I close my eyes tight and grab the object from the bag with one hand, the hair on its head writhing around in my fingers. God I hate these things. I lift it firmly from the sack, holding it as high as my shaking arm can go. It has to be enough, please be enough.

It was the story that always stayed with me from Maya's book. *"The gorgons were sisters with wings, and snakes instead of hair."*

"Yuck!"

"That's what Perseus thought too, Asha, so he chopped off the head of one of the sisters, Medusa. But Medusa's power didn't end with her death; it lived on. He used her head as a weapon that could turn anyone who looked into her eyes into stone. He turned it into something that could deflect evil away."

I hold the head high and shut my eyes tight as my Medusa's eyes start to open and her mouth begins to scream.

344

I can feel the heat that radiates from her gaze as the air around me becomes a swirl of noise, screams and pain. One hand grasping the book, I move painfully forward. I adjust my headset so everyone can hear me. No more secrets.

When I speak, my voice is stronger. The gorgon's attack is buying me time.

"I'm not letting you win."

Zu's voice is annoyed, gasping. "You think you can stop me with a gorgon's head? You're just delaying your demise."

I use his confusion, the brief moments where his program combats Medusa's power. I hold it high, letting it draw his attention. Willing him to focus on it and not what is in my hand. I crawl another few precious inches.

Zu throws his head back. His voice booms as the gorgon's scream starts to die. "You hid a custom weapon in my game, Asha? Clever. But not smart enough."

I open my eyes fully then; the light from the head's eyes is almost extinguished. I see Zu's avatar start to shimmer in front of me. Around us, another storm has started to rage. Zu's AI is ready to transfer to me. I know it. This is it. The moment when the game is vulnerable. Play or be played.

Zu looks at me. "Clever, but not smart enough. This is the future, Asha, but not yours."

"You call your vision of the world the future? Where everyone is under your control till the end of time?"

Zu's voice rumbles now. "No more tricks. It's time, and I promise you, any more surprises and I will come for your friends. You made friends, didn't you, Asha? You never wanted to let people in, but they came anyway, didn't they? And the boy. I will come for him too. You'll never see him again." His expression becomes grim. "I see everything, you know. I know what's best for you, Asha."

I lie still. I let him see how beaten I am. I inch forward, and for the last time, he moves closer. We are now centimetres away from the tree at the axis mundi. I am begging him to underestimate me one last time. Just as he must have underestimated Maya if he thought that she would merely try to expose him and not also defeat him. The words I use to distract him are drenched in truth. "Please. Ruby, Josh, Augie ... Dark ... they mean everything to me."

Zu holds out his hand. His image assumes a kindly expression. "When this is done, you won't feel anything, and they will survive, otherwise..."

I bow my head low, and in that second, I roll past him and plunge the book straight into the snow at the tree's base.

His scream is instant, awful. "What did you do?" The horror in his voice makes me shiver. "Why?"

Then the landscape starts to shake. My avatar falls to her knees as I do in my pod. My vision is clouding over. I pray to whatever gods there are that Dark is all right, that Jones has found Augie and Ruby and got them out. I know I've done what they would have wanted.

346

The tree begins to change, growing faster from the ground. A glowing mess of code and branches join and combine until they blot out the sky. Maya's tree of life. It glimmers for a moment, and then all around me, the game starts to fade away till just the darkness remains.

40

I struggle out of my glasses and frantically tear off my gloves. My vision is blurred as I tumble out of the pod, stumbling into the chaos of the arena.

Dark. Zu knew about him. I have to find him.

Around me, no one seems quite sure what they've seen. It's not the ending they expected for the tournament. Presenters are unsure who won. Was Zu being in the game some sort of promotional stunt or something else? I see Jones herding Ruby and Augie away from the players' floor. I look up, and the massive countdown clock in the arena has stopped, frozen just minutes before the launch.

Hands reach out to stop me when they notice my blue

players' uniform, and I push past them to Josh's pod. It's empty.

Think. Where would they have taken him?

My skull feels like hot knives are being pushed into it — the after-effects of whatever the game was doing to me are getting worse.

I look up, and on the big screens across the stadium, my image starts to fill each one. Through blurry eyes, I can see the video I made for Dark, the one that was on the drive I gave to Bill. How? Then I remember the conversation between Jones and Dark about insurance. Jones must have found the broadcast booth on her way out. It looks like everyone is about to learn the truth.

But right now, only one person matters. I need to find him. I keep moving as my voice echoes off the screen.

Three main exits. I rule out the public one and the one for VIPs — Zu wouldn't smuggle Dark out that way. That leaves the players' area.

I run, bumping into people and slamming off walls like I'm in a pinball game. The pain doesn't even register. The players' area is in chaos; everyone is spooked despite the calming tones being broadcast, telling everyone to stay calm. I can see managers herding their teams out. Zu tech security guards trying to end the live streams and broadcasts. It's a mess of cars and people.

In the distance, I can see more security descending — I only have a short window before they shut this down. And then I see it. A car with blacked-out windows. A door slams. Headlights come on as the vehicle starts to move. I run towards it. Crashing into the front bumper as I do, causing the brakes to squeak as it stops. Pain explodes in my hip. I run to the front and start to hammer my fists on the front hood – hand banging into the metal. "Open up. *Open!*"

From out of nowhere, a firm hand reaches to cover mine. I go to fight against the owner, but then I stop.

"Easy now, Asha. I got you. He told me earlier to come back to make sure you got out."

I see the tattoos on the man's hands. Bill. "I think he's inside. Bill, help me. Please."

Bill produces a metal bar from his coat. Smashing the glass on the driver's side. He then reaches past the dazed security man and hits the auto-unlock button. "You heard the lady. We open up now, mate."

The car's security occupants start to spill out. They look confused. I run to the side door, pulling it open.

It's empty.

He's not there. Zu's words are ringing in my ears. "I promise you. I will come for your friends. I will come for him too. You'll never see him again."

What have I done?

The hollow inside me opens up, along with the slim hold I had on the effects of the AI. Everything starts to fade away as I crash on to the ground beside the vehicle. Bill's voice is loud in my ear. "Asha, Asha, are you OK?"

I struggle to draw breath, to get my lungs to pull air in.

"The code, I think it's poisoned me too. I can't breathe, can't breathe."

Arms wrap tight around me, a smell of coffee and cinnamon. Augie's voice. "Bill, we need a doctor, now."

He reaches up, putting his hand gently on my cheek. My body starts to feel like it's drifting away. "Stay with me, Asha, OK? Please stay with me."

I close my eyes as my body slumps against his.

41

I drift in and out of consciousness. I don't know how much time passes — whether it's hours or days. The others take it in turns by my side. Even when I'm asleep, I sense them there. Anchoring me. Occasionally, I hear their voices. The low beeping of machines.

In between, there are dreams. Images of Maya and Annie together, saying goodbye to me. Dark calling for me. I run after him, but I never catch up. Each time it ends the same way, with him fading into the distance.

"Why didn't you stay with me?" he asks. "Why did you let Zu take me?"

When I eventually wake and the world comes into focus, Augie is the first thing I see. Sprawled across a chair by the bed. Head resting in one hand. His other hand lies near mine. Eyes closed. I make my fingers move and let them brush against his, and he is instantly awake.

"Hi." His face lights up. "Asha."

I try to sit up, but my limbs still feel too heavy to move.

"You need to take it slowly. You were out for a while."

"How long?"

"Two days."

So long. And I realize then where I am. Dark's bedroom. Bill must have taken me here. I look towards the door. "Dark?"

Augie doesn't meet my gaze. "The others are safe. I'll call them; everyone was worried about you. No one has seen Zu since you destroyed the game, but the police say it's only a matter of time before they track him down."

Why isn't he answering my question? "Dark?"

Augie reaches for my hand, and I pull it away. Eventually, he shakes his head. "We're still looking."

I sink back against the bed. Augie is still talking, but I don't hear him. The emptiness creeps over me. Everything feels hollow again, like after I found Maya's body. Why, why did we waste so much time? Zu warned me. He told me what he would do if I destroyed the game.

What have I done?

***

353

Later, Ruby comes to see me as I lie in bed not knowing what to do or to try next.

"This won't help Dark, you know," she says.

"Where is he?" I ask helplessly.

"We don't know," she says. "But we think Zu had him taken somewhere. So wherever Zu is … that's where Dark is too."

I nod, and we fall silent. Then I take a deep breath, pulling back the bedding. I go to stand on shaking feet.

"Daisy – I mean Asha – what are you doing?"

"I'm going to find him," I say. "I'm going to find both of them."

***

We set up our investigation in Dark's office. Comb through private flight records, hotel CCTV, and local police sightings. The others join me. Josh and Ruby take it in shifts, but Augie almost never leaves my side.

"He should get some rest," I say one day to Ruby. "He's going to burn out. I didn't even think he cared about Dark."

She gives me an odd look. "He's not stupid, Asha. Of course he wants to find Dark. Then he'll want you to make a choice."

"What do you mean?"

She stares at me. "Really? Oh, come on! Augie likes you. But he's smart enough to know he can't compete with a ghost. He'll move heaven and earth to find your boy, but after that, he'll ask you to choose, and you'll need to be ready."

I don't ask her anything else after that, nor do I examine my feelings for Augie. I can't, not now. I numb it all out. But sometimes, when it's late, I find myself watching Augie more carefully. How, I wonder, could he like me after all I've done? I'm the reason Dark isn't here.

He asked me so many times to leave Zu Tech alone, and I never listened.

***

In the world outside my bubble, Zu Tech's empire begins to collapse. We keep the newsfeed rolling – shareholders and managers run like rats from a sinking ship, all claiming not to have known anything about the rotten heart of the corporation. An economic downturn starts. While in the background, other interested hungry parties begin to pick through the carcass of Zu Tech with sharp knives.

***

Murphy comes to see me, bringing with him updates and another box of funeral ashes: Annie's.

"Her family decided not to claim her," he says, setting down the box. "I thought … well, it felt like the right thing to do for her. She should be with your sister, shouldn't she?"

I cry when I hold the box.

"They're getting a memorial service," Murphy goes on. "There should be some substantial compensation."

Maya and Annie are heroes now. That's what the press and the government have called them anyway. Whistle-blowers who exposed how dangerous Zu Tech had become, even though some of the details must be kept under wraps until the trial.

It helps. But for the trial to happen, there needs to be someone to prosecute. I clutch Annie's box tighter.

"We have to find Zu."

Murphy nods. "We will. No one can hide for ever."

I don't know, though. Something tells me that Zu could.

***

With every day that passes, I feel that the thin thread that keeps me from breaking, the one that keeps me attached to Dark, is getting more and more frayed. At the same time, I'm becoming famous. Clips from my video message at the tournament go viral. It is Augie, with his years of pro gaming experience, who teaches me how to leverage this newly found fame, to use the connections the police can't to narrow the search. The police operate within the law, hackers don't. Cell phone information becomes crucial as we begin to track the movements of Zu's key team, including Emily Webber, who has also vanished. It turns out no one can hide for ever.

A day or two later, a lead emerges to a remote off-grid cottage purchased by a shell company tied to Emily four years ago. It has to be where they are. I hand over the information to the police. Then I spend the next few hours sitting by the phone. I can't move. I just need him to be OK. I wait for Murphy to call.

And then, that evening, he does in person.

Bill comes in with Murphy. He looks tired and rumpled like he hasn't had much sleep. Jones puts down her cup of herbal tea, and Josh and Ruby spin round from their screens. Augie stands in the doorway.

"Asha, I have news." Murphy's voice is strained. It sets off alarm bells inside me as I stand and face him.

"I am so sorry."

My stomach twists. "What did you find?"

He takes a deep breath. "We found Zu. We tracked him down to that off-grid cottage you found. Special forces and the police stormed the place this morning."

"Was Dark there? Is he hurt?"

Murphy shakes his head. "Dark wasn't there."

"What aren't you telling me?" I ask.

Murphy holds my gaze. "Zu's dead. They found a body. Dental records show it's him. But Asha … they estimate that the body has been dead for three years." The world around me starts to fall away.

"But – but I met him," I whisper. "At Zu Tech."

The tears start to roll down my face unchecked as I stand there and let everything sink in. For a moment, no one moves. Then Jones wraps her arms around me. "Asha, I'm so..."

"Don't."

Her voice breaks slightly, confused, as she stands back. "What do you mean? Don't what?"

I look at her and blink away the tears. "Don't. When I started this, I needed to know what killed Maya, and now we do. Dark was part of that; he helped me, all of us. Don't comfort me now like he's gone – because he isn't."

I swallow and look at them. Jones, Bill, Augie, the twins, and Murphy. "Zu Tech was responsible for killing my sister, for killing Annie, for threatening Dawn, for nearly taking down all of us in that tournament. They don't get to win. They *don't*."

I look at Murphy. His eyes are filled with unshed tears, which he blinks back when he sees me staring at him. He rolls his shoulder slightly.

"Was there a body? Other than Zu's?" I ask. "Was there any sign of another body?"

Murphy shakes his head. "No. Just Zu Thorp, no one else."

I swallow and take a deep breath. I look around the room. "Then Dark is still out there."

I look from one friend's face to another. "We're going to find him. Then I am going to hunt down whoever was behind SHACKLE. And when I do, they will wish they had never been born."

ACKNOWLEDGEMENTS

Thanks are due – first to you, reader. I hope you like the book because I really LOVED writing it. Also, Dark, Asha, Augie & co now refuse to leave. (So I hope you want more.)

It's an odd feeling getting a book published: equal parts exciting and terrifying. It comes too with its own set of notions. Like the image people have when you say the word "writer". The cliché of a person sitting alone in a tiny room, typing away into the night. Like with so many things, there is truth in this (especially when close to a deadline), but also in other truisms. Like: *it takes a village* (which means I owe "thanks" to many amazing people). And one of my other favourite phrases – *a rising tide lifts all boats* (meaning I was lucky enough to get support and advice when I was writing from some brilliant fellow creatives).

On my list of thanks:

My very gifted agent. I was fortunate to get signed by the best in the business, Marianne Gunn O'Connor. A true force of nature who can make dreams come true.

The simply fantastic Lauren Fortune at Scholastic, who believed in the book from day one. As well as the entire Scholastic team who made everything about this experience better: Sophie Cashell, Sarah Dutton, Hannah Love, Ellen Thomson, Eleanor Thomas, Genevieve Herr, Harriet Dunlea – and not forgetting the brilliant cover artwork of Jamie Gregory (huge apologies if I left anyone out, but, my thanks to you all).

My heart and soul. Thanks to my family – especially my incredible genius husband, Nuno (who will not like being mentioned). Also, my super kids. You inspire me daily (Martin, Sofia & João).

Teachers – because you never stop learning. Especially – the inspiring Louise O'Neill. Thanks to the team at Words Ireland & The National Mentoring Program, Louise was my mentor during lockdown when I was writing. She embodies the phrase *pay it forward* and is endlessly generous with her time and support.

Thanks, too, to my brilliant fellow writers and the teachers/organisers at the M Phil in creative writing at Trinity College (including Eoin McNamee, Kevin Power, Carlo Gébler, Harry Clifton and the lovely Sophia Ni Sheoin). As well as the amazing author (and teacher) Sarah

Webb, whose love of children's fiction and YA is contagious and who is always so incredibly kind. And thanks also to the brilliant Cynthia Murphy for her amazing blurb.

Thanks also to my Gamer Mode TV family (including Eimear O'Mahony & Suzanne Kelly in RTE for commissioning it) and all the fantastic guests (and behind-the-scenes crew). I miss you guys. Thanks as well to the lovely tech gurus Louise Daly and Kelley Pierse, who I met through the series.

Lastly — my forever friends. A massive thank you: Roisin Kearney, Helen Ennis, Anna Patterson, Eibhlin Curley, Helene McDermott, and Joanne Hayden — I've known you for so long, and I can't wait to hear what you think of the book — preferably over wine.

Finally — everyone starts somewhere — writing is a craft that gets better the more you do it (unless you are one of those rare geniuses, which I am not). So thanks to the writing for children's group run by Simone Schuemmelfeder at the Irish writers' centre. There is magic in writing groups (and if you want to write, I cannot recommend this group enough, as well as organisations like Children's Books Ireland).

On that note. To anyone reading this who is thinking of writing, here are my two cents: enjoy the process, the time alone with just you, the words, the story and an imagined reader. Believe, keep going and read (all books, not just this one — but if you could also put in a pre-order for book two, that would be great).

Jeff VanderMeer is the author of the Southern Reach trilogy, *Finch*, *Shriek* and *City of Saints and Madmen*. He has received the World Fantasy Award three times and has been a finalist for the Hugo, Nebula, Philip K. Dick and Shirley Jackson awards. He has written for the *New York Times Book Review*, the *Guardian* and the *Los Angeles Times*. Jeff VanderMeer grew up in Fiji and now lives in Florida.

Praise for *Acceptance* and the Southern Reach trilogy:

'A book about an intelligent, deadly fungus makes for an enthralling read – trust us'   TARA WANDA MERRIGAN, *GQ*

'Successfully creepy, an old-style gothic horror novel set in a not-too-distant future. The best bits turn your mind inside out'   SARA SKLAROFF, *Washington Post*

'The plot moves quickly and has all the fantastic elements you'd ever want – biological contaminants, peculiar creatures, mysterious deaths – but it's the novel's unbearable dread that lingers with me days after I've finished it'

JUSTIN ALVAREZ, *Paris Review*

'The prose is phenomenal ... it toyed with my imagination in ways that haven't happened since *A Wrinkle in Time*'

MADISON VAIN, *Entertainment Weekly*

ACCEPTANCE

TANCE

JEFF VANDERMEER

FOURTH ESTATE ● London

Fourth Estate
An imprint of HarperCollins*Publishers*
1 London Bridge Street
London SE1 9GF
4thestate.co.uk

HarperCollins*Publishers*
1st Floor, Watermarque Building, Ringsend Road
Dublin 4, Ireland

First published in Great Britain by Fourth Estate 2014
This paperback edition first published in Great Britain in 2015

11

Page design by Abby Kagan

Printed and bound by
CPI Group (UK)Ltd, Croydon, CR0 4YY

MIX
Paper from
responsible sources
FSC™ C007454

For Ann

ACCEPTANCE

000X: THE DIRECTOR, TWELFTH EXPEDITION

Just out of reach, just beyond you: the rush and froth of the surf, the sharp smell of the sea, the crisscrossing shape of the gulls, their sudden, jarring cries. An ordinary day in Area X, an extraordinary day—the day of your death—and there you are, propped up against a mound of sand, half sheltered by a crumbling wall. The warm sun against your face, and the dizzying view above of the lighthouse looming down through its own shadow. The sky has an intensity that admits to nothing beyond its blue prison. There's sticky sand glittering across a gash in your forehead; there's a tangy glottal *something* in your mouth, dripping out.

You feel numb and you feel broken, but there's a strange relief mixed in with the regret: to come such a long way, to come to a halt here, without knowing how it will turn out, and yet . . . *to rest*. To come to rest. Finally. All of your plans back at the Southern Reach, the agonizing and constant fear of failure or worse, the price of that . . . all of it leaking out into the sand beside you in gritty red pearls.

The landscape surges toward you, curling over from behind to peer at you; it flares in places, or swirls or reduces itself to a pinprick, before coming back into focus. Your hearing isn't what it once was, either—has weakened along with your balance. And yet there comes this impossible thing: a magician's trick of a voice rising out of the landscape and the suggestion of eyes upon you. The whisper is familiar: *Is your house in order?* But you think whoever is asking might be a stranger, and you ignore it, don't like what might be knocking at the door.

The throbbing of your shoulder from the encounter in the tower is much worse. The wound betrayed you, made you leap out into that blazing blue expanse even though you hadn't wanted to. Some communication, some trigger between the wound and the flame that came dancing across the reeds betrayed your sovereignty. Your house has rarely been in such disarray, and yet you know that no matter what leaves you in a few minutes something else will remain behind. Disappearing into the sky, the earth, the water, is no guarantee of death here.

A shadow joins the shadow of the lighthouse.

Soon after, there comes the crunch of boots, and, disoriented, you shout, "Annihilation! Annihilation!" and flail about until you realize the apparition kneeling before you is the one person impervious to the suggestion.

"It's just me, the biologist."

Just you. Just the biologist. Just your defiant weapon, hurled against the walls of Area X.

She props you up, presses water to your mouth, clearing some of the blood as you cough.

"Where is the surveyor?" you ask.

"Back at the base camp," she tells you.

"Wouldn't come with you?" Afraid of the biologist, afraid

of the burgeoning flame, just like you. "A slow-burning flame, a will-o'-the-wisp, floating across the marsh and the dunes, floating and floating, like nothing human but something free and floating." A hypnotic suggestion meant to calm her, even if it will have no more effect than a comforting nursery rhyme.

As the conversation unspools, you keep faltering and losing track of it. You say things you don't mean, trying to stay in character—the person the biologist knows you as, the construct you created for her. Maybe you shouldn't care about roles now, but there's still a role to play.

She's blaming you, but you can't blame her. "If it was a disaster, you helped create it. You just panicked, and you gave up." Not true—you never gave up—but you nod anyway, thinking of so many mistakes. "I did. I did. I should have recognized earlier that you had changed." True. "I should have sent you back to the border." Not true. "I shouldn't have gone down there with the anthropologist." Not true, not really. You had no choice, once she slipped away from base camp, intent on proving herself.

You're coughing up more blood, but it hardly matters now.

"What does the border look like?" A child's question. A question whose answer means nothing. There is nothing but border. There is no border.

I'll tell you when I get there.

"What really happens when we cross over?"

Not what you might expect.

"What did you hide from us about Area X?"

Nothing that would have helped you. Not really.

The sun is a weak halo with no center and the biologist's voice threads in and out, the sand both cold and hot in your clenched right hand. The pain that keeps returning in bursts is attacking every couple of microseconds, so present that it isn't even there anymore.

Eventually, you recognize that you have lost the ability to speak. But you are still there, muffled and distant, as if you're a kid lying on a blanket on this very beach, with a hat over your eyes. Lulled into drowsiness by the constant surging sound of the water and the sea breezes, balancing the heat that ripples over you, spreads through your limbs. The wind against your hair is a sensation as remote as the ruffling of weeds sprouting from a head-shaped rock.

"I'm sorry, but I have to do this," the biologist tells you, almost as if she knows you can still hear her. "I have no choice."

You feel the tug and pull on your skin, the brief incisive line, as the biologist takes a sample from your infected shoulder. From a great and insurmountable distance, searching hands descend as the biologist goes through your jacket pockets. She finds your journal. She finds your hidden gun. She finds your pathetic letter. What will she make of them? Maybe nothing at all. Maybe she'll just throw the letter into the sea, and the gun with it. Maybe she'll waste the rest of her life studying your journal.

She's still talking.

"I don't know what to say to you. I'm angry. I'm frightened. You put us here and you had a chance to tell me what you knew, and you didn't. You wouldn't. I'd say rest in peace, but I don't think you will."

Then she's gone, and you miss her, that weight of a human being beside you, the perverse blessing of those words, but you don't miss her for long because you are fading further still, fading into the landscape like a reluctant wraith, and you can hear a faint and delicate music in the distance, and something that whispered to you before is whispering again, and then you're dissolving into the wind. A kind of alien regard has twinned itself to you, easily mistaken for the atoms of the air if it did not seem somehow concentrated, purposeful. Joyful?

Taken up over the still lakes, rising up across the marsh, flickering up in green-glinting reflections against the sea and the shore in the late-afternoon sun . . . only to wheel and bank toward the interior and its cypress trees, its black water. Then sharply up into the sky again, taking aim for the sun, the lurch and spin of it, before free fall, twisting to stare down at the onrushing earth, stretched taut above the quick flash and slow wave of reeds. You half expect to see Lowry there, wounded survivor of the long-ago first expedition, crawling toward the safety of the border. But instead there is just the biologist trudging back down the darkening path . . . and waiting beyond her, mewling and in distress, the altered psychologist from the expedition before the twelfth. Your fault as much as anyone's, your fault, and irrevocable. Unforgivable.

As you curve back around, the lighthouse fast approaches. The air trembles as it pushes out from both sides of the lighthouse and then re-forms, ever questing, forever sampling, rising high only to come low yet again, and finally circling like a question mark so you can bear witness to your own immolation: a shape huddled there, leaking light. What a sad figure, sleeping there, dissolving there. A green flame, a distress signal, an opportunity. Are you still soaring? Are you still dying or dead? You can't tell anymore.

But the whisper isn't done with you yet.

You're not down there.

You're up here.

And there's still an interrogation going on.

One that will repeat until you have given up every answer.

PART I

RANGE LIGHT

0001: THE LIGHTHOUSE KEEPER

Overhauled the lens machinery and cleaned the lens. Fixed the water pipe in the garden. Small repair to the gate. Organized the tools and shovels etc. in the shed. S&SB visit. Need to requisition paint for daymark—black eroded on seaward side. Also need nails and to check the western siren again. Sighted: pelicans, moorhens, some kind of warbler, blackbirds beyond number, sanderlings, a royal tern, an osprey, flickers, cormorants, bluebirds, pigmy rattlesnake (at the fence—remember), rabbit or two, white-tailed deer, and near dawn, on the trail, many an armadillo.

That winter morning, the wind was cold against the collar of Saul Evans's coat as he trudged down the trail toward the lighthouse. There had been a storm the night before, and down and to his left, the ocean lay gray and roiling against the dull blue of the sky, seen through the rustle and sway of the sea oats. Driftwood and bottles and faded white buoys and a dead hammerhead shark had washed up in the aftermath, tangled among snarls of seaweed, but no real damage either here or in the village.

At his feet lay bramble and the thick gray of thistles that

would bloom purple in the spring and summer. To his right, the ponds were dark with the muttering complaints of grebes and buffleheads. Blackbirds plunged the thin branches of trees down, exploded upward in panic at his passage, settled back into garrulous communities. The brisk, fresh salt smell to the air had an edge of flame: a burning smell from some nearby house or still-smoldering bonfire.

Saul had lived in the lighthouse for four years before he'd met Charlie, and he lived there still, but last night he'd stayed in the village a half mile away, in Charlie's cottage. A new thing this, not agreed to with words, but with Charlie pulling him back to bed when he'd been about to put on his clothes and leave. A welcome thing that put an awkward half smile on Saul's face.

Charlie'd barely stirred as Saul had gotten up, dressed, made eggs for breakfast. He'd served Charlie a generous portion with a slice of orange, kept hot under a bowl, and left a little note beside the toaster, bread at the ready. As he'd left, he'd turned to look at the man sprawled on his back half in and half out of the sheets. Even into his late thirties, Charlie had the lean, muscular torso, strong shoulders, and stout legs of a man who had spent much of his adult life on boats, hauling in nets, and the flat belly of someone who didn't spend too many nights out drinking.

A quiet click of the door, then whistling into the wind like an idiot as soon as he'd taken a few steps—thanking the God who'd made him, in the end, so lucky, even if in such a delayed and unexpected way. Some things came to you late, but late was better than never.

Soon the lighthouse rose solid and tall above him. It served as a daymark so boats could navigate the shallows, but also was lit at night half the week, corresponding to the schedules of commercial traffic farther out to sea. He knew every step of its stairs, every room inside its stone-and-brick walls, every crack and bit of spackle. The spectacular four-ton lens, or beacon, at the top had its own unique signature, and he had hundreds of ways to adjust its light. A first-order lens, over a century old.

As a preacher he thought he had known a kind of peace, a kind of calling, but only after his self-exile, giving all of that up, had Saul truly found what he was looking for. It had taken more than a year for him to understand why: Preaching had been *projecting out,* imposing himself on the world, with the world then projecting onto him. But tending to the lighthouse—that was a way of looking inward and it felt less arrogant. Here, he knew nothing but the practical, learned from his predecessor: how to maintain the lens, the precise workings of the ventilator and the lens-access panel, how to maintain the grounds, how to fix all the things that broke—scores of daily tasks. He welcomed each part of the routine, relished how it gave him no time to think about the past, and didn't mind sometimes working long hours—especially now, in the afterglow of Charlie's embrace.

But that afterglow faded when he saw what awaited him in the gravel parking lot, inside the crisp white fence that surrounded the lighthouse and the grounds. A familiar beat-up station wagon stood there, and beside it the usual two Séance & Science Brigade recruits. They'd snuck up on him again, crept in to ruin his good mood, and even piled their equipment beside the car already—no doubt in a hurry to start. He waved to them from afar in a halfhearted way.

They were always present now, taking measurements

and photographs, dictating statements into their bulky tape recorders, making their amateur movies. Intent on finding . . . what? He knew the history of the coast here, the way that distance and silence magnified the mundane. How into those spaces and the fog and the empty line of the beach thoughts could turn to the uncanny and begin to create a story out of nothing.

Saul took his time because he found them tiresome and increasingly predictable. They traveled in pairs, so they could have their séance and their science both, and he sometimes wondered about their conversations—how full of contradictions they must be, like the arguments going on inside his head toward the end of his ministry. Lately the same two had come by: a man and a woman, both in their twenties, although sometimes they seemed more like teenagers, a boy and girl who'd run away from home dragging a store-bought chemistry set and a Ouija board behind them.

Henry and Suzanne. Although Saul had assumed the woman was the superstitious one, it turned out she was the scientist—of what?—and the man was the investigator of the uncanny. Henry spoke with a slight accent, one Saul couldn't place, that put an emphatic stamp of authority on everything he said. He was plump, as clean-shaven as Saul was bearded, with shadows under his pale blue eyes, black hair in a modified bowl cut with bangs that obscured a pale, unusually long forehead. Henry didn't seem to care about worldly things, like the winter weather, because he always wore some variation on a delicate blue button-down silk shirt with dress slacks. The shiny black boots with zippers down the side weren't for trails but for city streets.

Suzanne seemed more like what people today called a hippie but would've called a communist or bohemian when Saul was growing up. She had blond hair and wore a white embroidered peasant blouse and a brown suede skirt down below the knee, to meet the calf-high tan boots that completed her uniform. A few like her had wandered into his ministry from time to time—lost, living in their own heads, waiting for something to ignite them. The frailty of her form made her somehow more Henry's twin, not less.

The two had never given him their last names, although one or the other had said something that sounded like "Serumlist" once, which made no sense. Saul didn't really want to know them better, if he was honest, had taken to calling them "the Light Brigade" behind their backs, as in "lightweights."

When he finally stood in front of them, Saul greeted them with a nod and a gruff hello, and they acted, as they often did, like he was a clerk in the village grocery store and the lighthouse a business that offered some service to the public. Without the twins' permit from the parks service, he would have shut the door in their faces.

"Saul, you don't look very happy even though it is a beautiful day," Henry said.

"Saul, it's a *beautiful* day," Suzanne added.

He managed a nod and a sour smile, which set them both off into paroxysms of laughter. He ignored that.

But they continued to talk as Saul unlocked the door. They always wanted to talk, even though he'd have preferred that they just got on with their business. This time it was about something called "necromantic doubling," which had to do with building a room of mirrors and darkness as far as he could tell. It was a strange term and he ignored their explanations, saw no way in which it had any relationship to the beacon or his life at the lighthouse.

People weren't ignorant here, but they were superstitious, and given that the sea could claim lives, who could blame them. What was the harm of a good-luck charm worn on a necklace, or saying a few words in prayer to keep a loved one safe? Interlopers trying to make sense of things, trying to "analyze and survey" as Suzanne had put it, turned people off because it trivialized the tragedies to come. But like those annoying rats of the sky, the seagulls, you got used to the Light Brigade after a while. On dreary days he had almost learned not to begrudge the company. *Why do you see the speck in your neighbor's eye but not notice the log in your own eye?*

"Henry thinks the beacon could operate much like such a room," Suzanne said, as if this was some major and astounding discovery. Her enthusiasm struck him as serious and authentic and yet also frivolous and amateurish. Sometimes they reminded him of the traveling preachers who set up tents at the edges of small towns and had the fervor of their convictions but not much else. Sometimes he even believed they were charlatans. The first time he'd met them, Saul thought Henry had said they were studying the refraction of light in a prison.

"Are you familiar with these theories?" Suzanne asked as they started to climb; she was lightly adorned with a camera strapped around her neck and a suitcase in one hand. Henry was trying not to seem winded, and said nothing. He was wrestling with heavy equipment, some of it in a box: mics, headphones, UV light readers, 8mm film, and a couple of machines featuring dials, knobs, and other indicators.

"No," Saul said, mostly to be contrary, because Suzanne often treated him like someone without culture, mistook his brusqueness for ignorance, his casual clothes as belonging to a simple man. Besides, the less he said, the more relaxed they were around him. It'd been the same with potential donors as a preacher. And the truth was, he didn't know what she was talking about, just as he hadn't known what Henry meant when he'd said they were studying the "taywah" or "terror" of the region, even when he'd spelled it out as t-e-r-r-o-i-r.

"Prebiotic particles," Henry managed in a jovial if wheezy tone. "Ghost energy."

As Suzanne backed that up with a longish lecture about mirrors and things that could peer out of mirrors and how you might look at something sideways and know more about its true nature than head-on, he wondered if Henry and Suzanne were lovers; her sudden enthusiasm for the séance part of the brigade might have a fairly prosaic origin. That would also explain their hysterical laughter down below. An ungenerous thought, but he'd wanted to bask in the after-glow of the night with Charlie.

"Meet you up there," he said finally, having had enough, and leaped up the stairs, taking them two at a time while Henry and Suzanne labored below, soon out of sight. He wanted as much time at the top without them as possible. The government would retire him at fifty, mandatory, but he planned to be as in shape then as now. Despite the twinge in his joints.

At the top, hardly even breathing heavy, Saul was happy

to find the lantern room as he'd left it, with the lens bag placed over the beacon, to avoid both scratching and discoloration from the sun. All he had to do was open the lens curtains around the parapet to let in light. His concession to Henry, for just a few hours a day.

Once, from this vantage, he'd seen something vast rippling through the water beyond the sandbars, a kind of shadow, the grayness so dark and deep it had formed a thick, smooth shape against the blue. Even with his binoculars he could not tell what creature it was, or what it might become if he stared at it long enough. Didn't know if eventually it had scattered into a thousand shapes, revealed as a school of fish, or if the color of the water, the sharpness of the light, changed and made it disappear, revealed as an illusion. In that tension between what he could and couldn't know about even the mundane world, he felt at home in a way he would not have five years ago. He needed no greater mysteries now than those moments when the world seemed as miraculous as in his old sermons. And it was a good story for down at the village bar, the kind of story they expected from the lighthouse keeper, if anyone expected anything from him at all.

"So that's why it's of interest to us, what with the way the lens wound up here, and how that relates to the whole history of both lighthouses," Suzanne said from behind him. She had been having a conversation with Saul in his absence, apparently, and seemed to believe he had been responding. Behind her, Henry was about ready to collapse, although the trek had become a regular routine.

When he'd dropped the equipment and regained his breath, Henry said, "You have a marvelous view from up here." He always said this, and Saul had stopped giving a polite response, or any response.

"How long are you here for this time?" Saul asked. This particular stint had already lasted two weeks, and he'd put off asking, fearing the answer.

Henry's shadow-circled gaze narrowed. "This time our permit allows us access through the end of the year." Some old injury or accident of birth meant his head was bent to the right, especially when he spoke, right ear almost touching the upward slope of his shoulder. It gave him a mechanical aspect.

"Just a reminder: You can touch the beacon, but you can't in any way interfere with its function." Saul had repeated this warning every day since they'd come back. Sometimes in the past they'd had strange ideas about what they could and could not do.

"Relax, Saul," Suzanne said, and he gritted his teeth at her use of his first name. At the beginning, they'd called him Mr. Evans, which he preferred.

He took more than the usual juvenile pleasure in positioning them on the rug, beneath which lay a trapdoor and a converted watch room that had once held the supplies needed to maintain the light before the advent of automation. Keeping the room from them felt like keeping a compartment of his mind hidden from their experiments. Besides, if these two were as observant as they seemed to think they were, they would have realized what the sudden cramping of the stairs near the top meant.

When he was satisfied they had settled in and were unlikely to disturb anything, he gave them a nod and left. Halfway down, he thought he heard a breaking sound from above. It did not repeat. He hesitated, then shrugged it off, continued to the bottom of the spiral stairs.

Below, Saul busied himself with the grounds and organizing the toolshed, which had become a mess. More than one hiker wandering through had seemed surprised to find a lighthouse keeper walking the grounds around the tower as if he were a hermit crab without its shell, but in fact there was a lot of maintenance required due to the way storms and the salt air could wear down everything if he wasn't vigilant. In the summer, it was harder, with the heat and the biting flies.

The girl, Gloria, snuck up on him while he was inspecting the boat he kept behind the shed. The shed abutted a ridge of soil and coquina parallel to the beach and a line of rocks stretching out to sea. At high tide, the sea flowed up to reinvigorate tidal pools full of sea anemones, starfish, blue crabs, snails, and sea cucumbers.

She was a solid, tall presence for her age, big for nine— "Nine and a half!"—and although Gloria sometimes wobbled on those rocks there was rarely any wobble in her young mind, which Saul admired. His own middle-aged brain sometimes slipped a gear or two.

So there she was again, a sturdy figure on the rocks, in her winter-weather gear—jeans, hooded jacket and sweater underneath, thick boots for wide feet—as he finished with the boat and brought compost around back in the wheelbarrow. She was talking to him. She was always talking to him, ever since she'd started coming by about a year ago.

"You know my ancestors lived here," she said. "Mama says they lived right here, where the lighthouse is." She had a deep and level voice for one so young, which sometimes startled him.

"So did mine, child," Saul told her, upturning the wheelbarrow load into the compost pile. Although truth was, the other side of his family had been an odd combination of rumrunners and fanatics who he liked to say, down at the bar, "had come to this land fleeing religious freedom."

After considering Saul's assertion for a moment, Gloria said, "Not before mine."

"Does it matter?" He noticed he'd missed some caulking on the boat.

The child frowned; he could feel her frown at his back, it was that powerful. "I don't know." He looked over at her, saw she'd stopped hopping between rocks, had decided that teetering on a dangerously sharp one made more sense. The sight made his stomach lurch, but he knew she never slipped, even though she seemed in danger of it many times, and as many times as he'd talked to her about it, she'd always ignored him.

"I think so," she said, picking up the conversation. "I think it does."

"I'm one-eighth Indian," he said. "I was here, too. Part of me." For what that was worth. A distant relative had told him about the lighthouse keeper's job, it was true, but no one else had wanted it.

"So what," she said, jumping to another sharp rock, balancing atop it, arms for a moment flailing and Saul taking a couple of steps closer to her out of fear.

She annoyed him much of the time, but he hadn't yet been able to shake her loose. Her father lived in the middle of the country somewhere, and her mother worked two jobs from a bungalow up the coast. The mother had to drive to far-off Bleakersville at least once a week, and probably figured her kid could manage on her own every now and again. Especially if the lighthouse keeper was looking after her. And the lighthouse held a kind of fascination for Gloria that he hadn't been able to break with his boring shed maintenance and wheelbarrow runs to the compost pile.

In the winter, too, she would be by herself a lot anyway—out on the mudflats just to the west, poking at fiddler crab holes with a stick or chasing after a half-domesticated doe, or peering at coyote or bear scat as if it held some secret. Whatever was on offer.

"Who're those strange people, coming around here?" she asked.

That almost made him laugh. There were a lot of strange people hidden away on the forgotten coast, himself included. Some were hiding from the government, some from themselves, some from spouses. A few believed that they were creating their own sovereign states. A couple probably weren't in the country legally. People asked questions out here, but they didn't expect an honest answer. Just an inventive one.

"Who exactly do you mean?"

"The ones with the pipes?"

It took Saul a moment, during which he imagined Henry and Suzanne skipping along the beach, pipes in their mouths, smoking away furiously.

"Pipes. Oh, they weren't pipes. They were something else." More like huge translucent mosquito coils. He'd let the Light Brigade leave the coils in the back room on the ground floor for a few months last summer. How in the heck had she seen that, anyway?

"Who are they?" she persisted, as she balanced now on two rocks, which at least meant Saul could breathe again.

"They're from the island up the coast." Which was true—their base was still out on Failure Island, home to dozens of them, a regular warren. "Doing tests," as the rumors went down at the village bar, where they did indeed like a good story. Private researchers with government approval to take readings. But the rumors also insinuated that the S&SB had some more sinister agenda. Was it the orderliness, the precision, of some of them or the disorganization of the others that led to this rumor? Or just a couple of bored, drunk retirees emerging from their mobile homes to spin stories?

The truth was he didn't know what they were doing out on the island, or what they had planned to do with the equipment on the ground floor, or even what Henry and Suzanne were doing at the top of the lighthouse right now.

"They don't like me," she said. "And I don't like them."

That did make him chuckle, especially the brazen, arms-folded way she said it, like she'd decided they were her eternal enemy.

"Are you laughing at *me*?"

"No," he said. "No, I'm not. You're a curious person. You ask questions. That's why they don't like you. That's all." People who asked questions didn't necessarily like being asked questions.

"What's wrong with asking questions?"

"Nothing." Everything. Once the questions snuck in, whatever had been certain became uncertain. Questions opened the way for doubt. His father had told him that. "Don't let them ask questions. You're already giving them the answers, even if they don't know it."

"But you're curious, too," she said.

"Why do you say that?"

"You guard the light. And light sees everything."

The light might see everything, but he'd forgotten a few last tasks, a few last things that would keep him out of the lighthouse for longer than he liked. He moved the wheelbarrow onto the gravel next to the station wagon. He felt a vague urgency, as if he should check on Henry and Suzanne. What if they had found the trapdoor and done something stupid, like fallen in and broken their strange little necks? Staring up just then, he saw Henry staring down from the railing far above, and that made him feel foolish. Like he was being paranoid. Henry waved, or was it some other gesture? Dizzy, Saul looked away as he made a kind of wheeling turn, disoriented by the sun's glare.

Only to see something glittering from the lawn—half hidden by a plant rising from a tuft of weeds near where he'd found a dead squirrel a couple of days ago. Glass? A key? The dark green leaves formed a rough circle, obscuring whatever lay at its base. He knelt, shielded his gaze, but the glinting thing was still hidden by the leaves of the plant, or was it part of a leaf? Whatever it was, it was delicate beyond measure, yet perversely reminded him of the four-ton lens far above his head.

The sun was a whispering corona at his back. The heat had risen, but there was a breeze that lifted the leaves of the palmettos in a rattling stir. The girl was somewhere behind him singing a nonsense song, having come back off the rocks earlier than he'd expected.

Nothing existed in that moment except for the plant and the gleam he could not identify.

He had gloves on still, so he knelt beside the plant and reached for the glittering thing, brushing up against the leaves. Was it a tiny shifting spiral of light? It reminded him of what you might see staring into a kaleidoscope, except an intense white. But whatever it was swirled and glinted and eluded his rough grasp, and he began to feel faint.

Alarmed, he started to pull back.

But it was too late. He felt a sliver enter his thumb. There was no pain, only a pressure and then numbness, but he still jumped up in surprise, yowling and waving his hand back and forth. He frantically tore off the glove, examined his thumb. Aware that Gloria was watching him, not sure what to make of him.

Nothing now glittered on the ground in front of him. No light at the base of the plant. No pain in his thumb.

Slowly, Saul relaxed. Nothing throbbed in his thumb. There was no entry point, no puncture. He picked up the glove, checked it, couldn't find a tear.

"What's wrong?" Gloria asked. "Did you get stung?"

"I don't know," he said.

He felt other eyes upon him then, turned, and there stood Henry. How had he gotten down the stairs so fast? Had more time passed than he'd imagined?

"Yes—is something wrong, Saul?" Henry asked, but Saul could find no way to reconcile the concern expressed with any concern in the tone of his voice. Because there was none. Only a peculiar eagerness.

"Nothing is wrong," he said, uneasy but not knowing why he should be. "Just pricked my thumb."

"Through your gloves? That must have been quite the thorn." Henry was scanning the ground like someone who had lost a favorite watch or a wallet full of money.

"I'm fine, Henry. Don't worry about me." Angry more at looking silly over nothing, but also wanting Henry to believe him. "Maybe it was an electric shock."

"Maybe . . ." The gleam of the man's eyes was the light of a cold beacon coming to Saul from far off, as if Henry were broadcasting some other message entirely.

"Nothing is wrong," Saul said again.

Nothing was wrong.

Was it?

0002: GHOST BIRD

On the third day in Area X, with Control as her sullen companion, Ghost Bird found a skeleton in the reeds. It was winter in Area X now, and this had become more apparent once the trail meandered away from the sea that had been their entry point. The wind was cold and pushed against their faces, their jackets, the sky a watchful gray-blue that held back some essential secret. The alligators and the otters and the muskrats had retreated into the mud, ghosts somewhere beneath the dull slap and gurgle of water.

Far above, where the sky became a deeper blue, she caught a hint of some reflective surface, identified it as a wheeling cone of storks, the sun glinting silver from their white-and-gray feathers as they spun up into the sky at a great distance and with a stern authority, headed . . . where? She could not tell if they were testing the confines of their prison, able to recognize that invisible border before they crossed it, or like every other trapped thing here, simply operating on half-remembered instinct.

She stopped walking, and Control stopped with her. A man with prominent cheekbones, large eyes, an unobtrusive nose, and light brown skin. He was dressed in jeans and a red

27

flannel shirt, along with a black jacket and a brand of boots that wouldn't have been her first choice for walking through the wilderness. The director of the Southern Reach. The man who had been her interrogator. An athlete's build, perhaps, but as long as they'd been in Area X, he'd been stooped over, muttering, as he examined forever and always a few water-stained, wrinkled pages he'd saved from some useless Southern Reach report. Flotsam from the old world.

He barely noticed the interruption.

"What is it?" he asked.

"Birds."

"Birds?" As if the word was foreign to him, or held no meaning. Or significance. But who knew what held significance here.

"Yes. Birds." Further specificity might be lost on him.

She took up her binoculars, watched the way the storks turned this way and then that way but never lost their form: a kind of living, gliding vortex in the sky. The pattern reminded her of the circling school of fish into which they'd emerged in shock, their surprising entrance into Area X from the bottom of the ocean.

Staring down at her, did the storks recognize what they saw? Were they reporting back to someone or something? Two nights running, she had sensed animals gathering at the edge of their campfire, dull and remote sensors for Area X. Control wanted more urgency, as if a destination meant something, while she wanted more data.

There had already been some misunderstandings about their relationship since reaching the beach—especially about who was in charge—and in the aftermath he'd taken back his name, asked that she call him Control again rather than John, which she respected. Some animals' shells were vital to their survival. Some animals couldn't live for long without them.

His disorientation wasn't helped by a fever and a sense, from her own accounts of "a brightness," that he too was being assimilated and might soon be something not himself. So perhaps she understood why he buried himself in what he called "my terroir pages," why he had lied about wanting to find solutions when it was so clear to her that he just needed something familiar to hold on to.

At one point on the first day, she had asked him, "What would I be to you back in the world—you at one of your old jobs, me at my old job?" He had not had an answer, but she thought she knew: She would be a suspect, an enemy of the right and the true. So what were they to each other here? Sometime soon she would have to force a real conversation, provoke conflict.

But for now, she was more interested in something off in the reeds to their left. A flash of orange? Like a flag?

She must have stiffened, or something in her demeanor gave her away, because Control asked, "What's wrong? Is something wrong?"

"Nothing, probably," she said.

After a moment, she found the orange again—a scrap, a tattered rag tied to a reed, bending back and forth in the wind. About three hundred feet out in the reed-ocean, that treacherous marsh of sucking mud. There seemed to be a shadow or depression just beyond it, the reeds giving way to something that couldn't be seen from their vantage.

She loaned him the binoculars. "See it?"

"Yes. It's a . . . a surveyor's mark," he said, unimpressed.

"Because that's likely," she said, then regretted it.

"Okay. Then it's 'like' a surveyor's mark." He handed back the binoculars. "We should stay on the trail, get to the island." A sincere utterance of *island* for once, proportional to his dislike of the unspoken idea that they investigate the rag.

"You can stay here," she said, knowing he wouldn't. Knowing she would have preferred he remain behind so she could be alone in Area X for a few moments.

Except: Was anyone ever truly alone out here?

For a long time after she had woken in the empty lot, then been taken to the Southern Reach for processing, Ghost Bird had thought she was dead, that she was in purgatory, even though she didn't believe in an afterlife. This feeling hadn't abated even when she'd figured out that she had come back across the border into the real world by unknown means . . . that she wasn't even the original biologist from the twelfth expedition but a copy.

She had admitted as much to Control during the interrogation sessions: "It was quiet and so *empty* . . . I waited there, afraid to leave, afraid there might be some reason I was meant to be there."

But this didn't encompass the full arc of her thoughts, of her analysis. There was not just the question of whether she was really alive but, if so, *who* she was, made oblique by her seclusion in her quarters at the Southern Reach. Then, examining the sense that her memories were not her own, that they came to her secondhand and that she could not be sure whether this was because of some experiment by the Southern

Reach or an effect caused by Area X. Even through the intricacies of her escape on the way to Central, there was a sense of *projection*, of it happening to someone else, that she was only the interim solution, and perhaps that distance had aided her in avoiding capture, added a layer of absolute calm to her actions. When she'd reached the remote Rock Bay, so familiar to the biologist who had been there before her, she'd had peace for a while, let the landscape subsume her in a different way—let it break her down so she could be built up again.

But only when they had burst through into Area X had she truly gained the upper hand on her unease, her purpose-lessness. She had panicked for a second as the water pressed in on her, surrounded her, evoked her own drowning. But then something had *turned on*, or had come back, and raging against her own death, she had exulted in the sensation of the sea, welcomed having to fight her way to the surface— bursting through such a joyful hysteria of biomass—as a sort of proof that she was not the biologist, that she was some new thing that could, wanting to survive, cast out her fear of drowning as belonging to another.

In the aftermath, even resuscitating Control on the beach had seemed undeniable proof of her own sovereignty. As had her insistence on heading for the island, not the lighthouse. "Wherever the biologist would have gone, that is where I will go." The truth, the *rightness*, in that had given her hope, despite the sense that everything she remembered she had observed through a window opening onto another person's life. Not truly experienced. Or not experienced yet. "You want a lived-in life because you don't have one," Control had said to her, but that was a crude way to put it.

There had been little new to experience since. Nothing monstrous or unusual had yet erupted from the horizon in almost three full days of walking. Nothing unnatural, except for this hyperreal aspect to the landscape, these processes working beneath the surface. At dusk, sometimes, too, an image of the biologist's starfish came to her, dimly shining, like a compass in her head that drew her on, and she realized again that Control couldn't feel what she felt here. He couldn't navigate the dangers, recognize the opportunities. The brightness had left her, but something else had stepped in to replace it.

"Counter-shading," she'd said when he'd confessed his confusion that Area X looked so normal. "You can know a thing and not know a thing. A grebe's markings from above are obvious. You cannot miss a grebe from above. Seen from below, though, as it floats in the water, it is practically invisible."

"Grebe?"

"A bird." Another bird.

"All of this is a disguise?" He said it with a kind of disbelief, as if the reality were strange enough.

Ghost Bird had relented, because it wasn't his fault. "You've never walked through an ecosystem that wasn't compromised or dysfunctional, have you? You may think you have, but you haven't. So you might mistake what's right for what's wrong anyway."

That might not be true, but she wanted to hold on to the idea of authority—didn't want another argument about their destination. Insisting on heading for the island was protecting not just her life but his, too, she believed. She had no interest in last chances, last desperate charges into the guns of the enemy, and something in Control's affect made her believe he might be working toward that kind of solution. Whereas she was not yet committed to anything other than wanting to know—herself and Area X.

The light in that place was inescapable, so bright yet distant. It brought a rare clarity to the reeds and the mud and the water that mirrored and followed them in the canals. It was the light that made her feel as if she glided because it tricked her into losing track of her own steps. It was the light that kept replenishing the calm within her. The light explored and questioned everything in a way she wasn't sure Control would understand, then retreated to allow what it touched to exist apart from it.

Perhaps it was the light that got in the way, too, for theirs was a kind of backtracking, stuttering progress, using a stick to prod the ground in front of them for treachery, the thick reeds forming clumps that at times were impenetrable. Once, a limpkin, grainy brown and almost invisible against the reeds, rose so near and so silent it startled her almost more than it did Control.

But eventually they reached the rag tied to the reeds, saw the yellowing cathedral beyond, stuck in the mud and sunk halfway.

"What the hell is that?" Control asked.

"It's dead," she said. "It can't harm us." Because Control continued to overreact to what she considered insufficient stimuli. Skittish, or damaged from some other experience entirely.

But she knew all too well what it was. Sunken into the middle were the remains of a hideous skull and a bleached and hardened mask of a face that stared sightless up at them, fringed with mold and lichen.

"The moaning creature," she said. "The moaning creature we always heard at dusk." That had chased the biologist across the reeds.

The flesh had sloughed off, runneled down the sides of the bones, vanished into the soil. What remained was a skeleton that looked uncannily like the confluence of a giant hog and a human being, a set of smaller ribs suspended from the larger like a macabre internal chandelier, and tibias that ended in peculiar nub-like bits of gristle scavenged by birds and coyotes and rats.

"It's been here awhile," Control said.

"Yes, it has." Too long. Prickles of alarm made her scan the horizon for some intruder, as if the skeleton were a trap. Alive just eighteen months ago, and yet now in a state of advanced decay, the face plate all that saved it from being unidentifiable. Even if this creature, this transformation of the psychologist from what Control called "the last eleventh expedition," had died right after the biologist had encountered it alive . . . the rate of decomposition was unnatural.

Control hadn't caught on, though, so she decided not to share. He just kept pacing around the skeleton, staring at it.

"So this was a person, once," he said, and then said it again when she didn't respond.

"Possibly. It might also have been a failed double." She

didn't think she was a failed double like this creature. She had purpose, free will.

Perhaps a copy could also be superior to the original, create a new reality by avoiding old mistakes.

"I have your past in my head," he'd told her as soon as they'd left the beach, intent on trading information. "I can give it back to you." An ancient refrain by now, unworthy of him or of her.

Her silence had forced him to go first, and although she thought he still might be holding things back, his words, infused with urgency and a kind of passion, had a sincerity to them. Sometimes, too, a forlorn subtext crept in, one that she understood quite well and chose to ignore. She had identified it easily from the time he had visited her in her quarters back at the Southern Reach.

The news that the psychologist from the twelfth expedition had been the former director of the Southern Reach and that she had thought the biologist was her special project, her special hope, made Ghost Bird laugh. She felt a sudden affection for the psychologist, remembering their skirmishes during the induction interviews. The devious psychologist/director, trying to combat something as wide and deep as Area X with something as narrow and blunt as the biologist. As her. A sudden wren, quick-darting through brambles to flit out of sight, seemed to share her opinion.

When it was her turn, she conceded that she now remembered everything up to the point at which she had been scanned or atomized or replicated by the Crawler that lived in the tunnel/tower—the moment of her creation, which might have been the moment of the biologist's death. The Crawler and the lighthouse keeper's face, burning through the layered myths of its construction, made disbelief shine through Control as if he were a translucent deep-sea fish. Among all the impossible things he had already witnessed, what were a few more?

He asked no questions that had not been asked in some form by the biologist, the surveyor, the anthropologist, or the psychologist during the twelfth expedition.

Somehow that created an uncomfortable doubling effect, too, one that she argued about in her own head. Because she did not agree with her own decisions at times—the biologist's decisions. Why had her other self been so careless with the words on the wall? For example. Why hadn't she confronted the psychologist/director as soon as she knew about the hypnosis? What had been gained by going down to find the Crawler? Some things Ghost Bird could forgive, but others grated and drove her into spirals of might-have-beens that infuriated her.

The biologist's husband she rejected entirely, without ambivalence, for there came with the husband the desolation of living in the city. The biologist had been married but Ghost Bird wasn't, released from responsibility for any of that. She didn't really understand why her double had put up with it. Among the misunderstandings between her and Control: having to make clear that her need for lived-in experience to supplant memories not her own did not extend to their relationship, whatever image of her he carried in his head. She could not just plunge into something physical with him and overlay the unreal with the ordinary, the mechanical, not when her memories were of a husband who had come home stripped of memories. Any compromise would just hurt them both, was somehow beside the point.

Standing there in front of the skeleton of the moaning creature, Control said: "Then I might end up like this? Some version of me?"

"We all end up like this, Control. Eventually."

But not quite like this, because from those eye sockets, from the moldering bones, came a sense of a brightness still, a kind of life—a questing toward her that she rebuffed and that Control could not sense. Area X was looking at her through dead eyes. Area X was analyzing her from all sides. It made her feel like an outline created by the regard bearing down on her, one that moved only because the regard moved with her, held her constituent atoms together in a coherent shape. And yet, the eyes upon her felt familiar.

"The director might have been wrong about the biologist, but perhaps you're the answer." Said only half sarcastically, as if he almost knew what she was receiving.

"I'm not an answer," she said. "I'm a question." She might also be a message incarnate, a signal in the flesh, even if she hadn't yet figured out what story she was supposed to tell.

She was thinking, too, about what she had seen on the journey into Area X, how it had seemed as if to both sides there lay nothing around them but the terrible blackened ruins of vast cities and enormous beached ships, lit by the roaring red and orange of fires that did nothing but cast shadow and obscure the distant view of mewling things that crawled and hopped through the ash. How she had tried to block out Control's rambling confessions, the shocking things he said without knowing, so that she did not think he had a secret she did not now know. *Pick up the gun . . . Tell me a joke . . . I killed her, it was my fault . . .* Had whispered hypnotic incantations in his ear to shut out not only his words but also the horror show around them.

The skeleton before them had been picked clean. The discolored bones were rotting, the tips of the ribs already turned soft with moisture, most of them broken off, lost in the mud.

Above, the storks still banked and wheeled this way and that in an intricate, synchronized aerial dance more beautiful than anything ever created by human minds.

0003: THE DIRECTOR

On the weekends, your refuge is Chipper's Star Lanes, where you're not the director of the Southern Reach but just another customer at the bar. Chipper's lies off the highway well out of Bleakersville, one step up from being at the end of a dirt road. Jim Lowry's people back at Central might know the place, might be watching and listening, but you've never met anyone from the Southern Reach there. Even Grace Stevenson, your second-in-command, doesn't know about it. For a disguise, you wear a T-shirt for a local construction company or a charity event like a chili cook-off and an old pair of jeans from the last time you were fat, sometimes topped off with a baseball cap advertising your favorite barbecue joint.

You go bowling there, like you used to with your dad as a kid, but you usually start out front, solo, on Chipper's rotting but still functional Safari Adventure miniature golf course. The lions at the ninth hole are a sleeping huddle of dreamy plastic melted and blackened at the edges from some long-ago disaster. The huge hippo bestride the course-ending eighteenth has dainty ankles, and flaked-off splotches reveal blood-red paint beneath, as if its makers had been too obsessed with making it real.

Afterward you'll go inside and bowl a few pickup games with anyone who needs a fourth, under the fading universe painted on the ceiling—there's Earth, there's Jupiter, there's a purpling nebula with a red center, all of it lit up at night with a cheesy laser show. You're good for four or five games, rarely top two hundred. When done, you sit at the dark, comfortable bar. It's been shoved into a back corner as far from the room of stinking shoes as possible, and somehow the acoustics muffle the squeak, bump, and rumble of the bowling. Everything here is still too close to Area X, but as long as no one knows, that information can keep on killing the customers as slowly as it has over the past decades.

The Chipper's bar attracts mostly stalwart regulars, because it's really a dive, with dark felt stapled to the ceiling that's meant to be sprinkled with stars. But whatever the metal that's nailed up there, looking more like an endless series of sheriff's badges from old Westerns, it's been rusting for a long time, so now it's become a dull black punctuated by tiny reddish-brown starfish. A sign in the corner advertises the Star Lanes Lounge. The lounge part consists of half a dozen round wooden tables and chairs with black fake-leather upholstery that look like they were stolen long ago from a family-restaurant chain.

Most of your comrades at the bar are heavily invested in the sports leaking out of the silent, closed-caption TV; the old green carpet, which climbs the side walls, soaks up the murmur of conversations. The regulars are harmless and rarely raucous, including a Realtor who thinks she is the knower of all things but makes up for it by being able to tell a good story. Then there's the silver-bearded seventy-year-old man who's almost always standing at the end of the bar drinking a light beer. He's a veteran of some war, veers between laconic and neighborly.

Your psychologist cover story feels wrong here, and you don't like using it. Instead, you tell anyone who asks that you're a long-haul trucker between jobs and take a drag on your bottle of beer to end that part of the conversation. People find the idea of that line of work plausible; maybe something about your height and broad frame sells them on it. But most nights you can almost believe you *are* a trucker, and that these people are your sort-of friends.

The Realtor says the man's not a veteran, just "an alcoholic looking for sympathy," but you can tell she's not without sympathy for that. "I'm just going to opt out" is a favorite phrase of the veteran. So is "the hell there isn't." The rest are a cross-section of ER nurses, a couple of mechanics, a hairdresser, a few receptionists and office managers. What your dad would've called "people who're never allowed to see behind the curtain." You don't bother investigating them, or the oft-revolving bartenders, because it doesn't matter. You never say anything seditious or confidential at Chipper's.

But some nights, when you stay late and the bar crowd thins, you write down on a napkin or coaster a point or two you can't leave alone—some of the continual puzzle-questions thrown at you by Whitby Allen, a holistic environments expert who reports to Mike Cheney, the overly jovial head of the science division. You never asked for these questions, but that doesn't stop Whitby, who seems like his head's on fire and the only way to put the fire out is to douse it with his ideas. "What's outside the border when you're inside it?" "What's the border when you're inside it?" "What's the border when someone is outside it?" "Why can't the person inside see the person outside?"

"My statements aren't any better than my questions," Whitby admitted to you once, "but if you want easy, you should check out what they serve up over at Cheney's Science Shack."

An impressive document backs up Whitby's ideas, shining out from underneath the glossy invisible membrane of a piece of clear plastic. In a brand-new three-ring black binder, exquisitely hole-punched, not a typo in the entire twelve-page printout, with its immaculate title page: a masterpiece entitled "Combined Theories: A Complete Approach."

The report is as shiny, clever, and quick as Whitby. The questions it raises, the recommendations made, insinuate with little subtlety that Whitby thinks the Southern Reach can do better, that he can do better if he is only given the chance. It's a lot to digest, especially with the science department ambushing it and taking potshots in memos sent to you alone: "Suppositions in search of evidence, head on backward or sideways." Or, maybe even sprouting from his ass.

But to you it's deadly serious, especially a list of "conditions required for Area X to exist" that include

- an isolated place
- an inert but volatile trigger
- a catalyst to pull the trigger
- an element of luck or chance in how the trigger was deployed
- a context we do not understand

- an attitude toward energy that we do not understand
- an approach to language that we do not understand

"What's next?" Cheney says at one status meeting. "A careful study of the miracles of the saints, unexplained occurrences writ large, two-headed calves predicting the apocalypse, to see if anything rings a bell?"

Whitby at the time is a feisty debater, one who likes hot water, who leaps in with a rejoinder that he knows will not just get Cheney's goat but pen it up, butcher it, and roast it: "It acts a bit like an organism, like skin with a million greedy mouths instead of cells or pores. And the question isn't *what* it is but is the motive. Think of Area X as a murderer we're trying to catch."

"Oh great, that's just great, now we've got a detective on staff, too." Cheney muttering while you give him the hush-hand and Grace helps out with her best pained smile. Because the truth is, you told Whitby to act like a detective, in an attempt to "think outside the Southern Reach."

For a while, too, with Whitby's help, you are arrows shot straight at a target. Because it's not as if you don't have successes at first. Under your watch, there are breakthroughs in expedition equipment, like enhanced field microscopes and weaponry that doesn't trigger Area X's defenses. More expeditions begin to come back intact, and the refinements in making people into their functions—the tricks you've learned from living in your own disguise—seem to help.

You chart the progress of Area X's reclamation of the environment, begin to get some small sense of its parameters, and even create expedition cycles with shared metrics. You may not always control those criteria, but, for a while, the consensus is that the situation has stabilized, that the news is improving. The gleaming silver egg you imagine when you think of Central—those seamless, high-level thoughts so imperfectly expressed through your superiors there—hums and purrs and pulses out approval over all of you . . . even if it also emanates the sense that the Southern Reach is some kind of meat-brain corruption of a beautiful elegant algorithm Central has hidden deep inside itself.

But as the years pass, with Lowry's influence more and more corrosive, there's no solution forthcoming. Data pulled out of Area X duplicates itself and declines, or "declines to be interpreted," as Whitby puts it, and theories proliferate but nothing can be proven. "We lack the analogies," the linguists keep saying.

Grace starts to call them the "languists" as they falter, can't keep up, and as the grim joke goes, "fell by the side of a road that was like a mixed metaphor of a tongue that curled up and took them with it," Area X muddying the waters. Except it wasn't muddying waters or a tongue by the side of the road or anything else, muddled or not, that they could understand. "We lack the analogies" was itself somehow deficient as a diagnosis, linguists burning up during reentry into the Earth's atmosphere after encountering Area X. Making you think of all the dead and dying satellites sent hurtling down into the coordinates that comprised Area X, because it was easy, because space debris winking out of existence made a perverse kind of sense, even as turning Area X into a garbage can seemed like the kind of disrespect that might piss off an insecure deity. Except Area X never responded, even to that indignity.

ACCEPTANCE

The linguists aren't really the problem, nor even Central. Lowry's the problem because Lowry keeps your secret—that you grew up in what became Area X—and in return you have to try to give him what he wants, within reason. Lowry has invested other people's blood and sweat in the idea of the expeditions, and implied by that the idea of the border as an impenetrable barrier, which means he's safe on the right side of the divide. While Whitby keeps pushing against the traditional: "Whatever we think of the border, it's important to recognize it as a *limitation* of Area X." Was that important?

What seemed more important to you: The truth to rumors about Lowry's ruthlessness once he reached Central, that he's carved out his own soundproof shop. The whispers that came back to you distant but clear over the years, like hiking in a dark, still forest and hearing the faint sound of wind chimes. Something that beckons, promising all the comforts of civilization, but once the seeker reaches the end of that particular path, all she finds is a slaughterhouse piled high with corpses. The proof of it in the way he so easily overrules Pitman, your nominal boss at Central, and presses you harder for results.

By the time you're on the eleventh cycle of expeditions, you're more and more drained, and Central's plan has begun to change. The flow of new personnel, money, and equipment has been reduced to a trickle as Central spends most of its time crushing domestic terrorism and suppressing evidence of impending ecological destruction.

You return after long days to the house in Bleakersville, which is no refuge. The ghosts follow, sit on the couch or peer in through the windows. Thoughts you don't want creep in at odd moments—in the middle of status meetings, sitting down for lunch with Grace in the cafeteria, searching idly for Central's latest bugs in your office—that maybe none of this is worth it, that you're not getting anywhere. The weight of each expedition leaning in on you.

"I could've been director," Lowry boasted once, "but a warning light came on in the cockpit and I took the hint." The warning light is a fear that you know lives inside of him, but Lowry will never admit to it. The cruel jocularity to his goading, as if he knows he keeps asking you for the impossible.

Always worried, in a continual low-grade-fever sort of way, that someone at the Southern Reach or Central will discover your secret, that Lowry won't be able to bury the information forever—or he'll divulge it himself, having decided you're disposable. Security risk. A liar. Too emotionally invested. And yet compassion is what you most distrust, what you thrust away from you, preferring to project with everyone but Grace that you're cold, distant, even harsh, so that you can be clearheaded and objective . . . even if acting the part has made you a little cold, distant, and harsh.

In some unquantifiable way, too, you believe Lowry's approach is pushing the Southern Reach farther away from the answers. Like an astronaut headed into the oblivion of vast and empty space who, in flailing about, only speeds up the moment when he is beyond rescue. And worse, to your way of thinking, reliving without nostalgia the thrust of your days as a psychologist, Lowry has doomed himself to finding countless ways to relive his own horrifying experience in

Area X, so he can never be entirely free, the seeming attempt to cast it away turned into an endless embrace.

Your other sanctuary is the roof of the Southern Reach building—protected from view from below by the weird baffling, the wandering ridge, that circles the roof. Beyond Reach, BR for short, "Brr" in the winter and "Burr" or sometimes "Bee-arr!" or "Bear!" in the summer. Always "Bar" when you sneak up for drinks after work.

You share this sacred space with only one person: Grace. You bat around the ideas that pop up at Star Lanes, "shoot the shit," protected by the fact that only you, Grace, and the janitor have the key. Many times people will try to track you down, only to find you have evaporated, reappearing, unbeknownst to them, in Beyond Reach.

It's there, staring out at the prehistoric swamp, the miles of dark pine forest, that you and Grace come up with all the nicknames. The border you call "the moat" and the way in is "the front door," although both of you are always hoping you'll find a "side door" or a "trapdoor." The tunnel or topographical anomaly in Area X you refer to as "El Topoff," riffing on a strange film Grace once saw with her girlfriend.

A lot of it is stupid, but funny in the moment, especially if you've got a bottle of brandy, or if she brings cherry-flavored cigarettes, and you pull up a couple of lawn chairs and brainstorm or talk about the weekend to come. Grace knows about Chipper's, like you know about her canoe trips with her friends, "your addiction to paddles." You don't need to tell her not to show up at Chipper's, and you never invite yourself downriver. The circumference of your friendship is the length and breadth of the Southern Reach.

It's on the roof that you first mention to Grace your idea of sneaking across the border into Area X. Over time it has become more than a thought tingling at the edge of things—metastasizing as code, as "a road trip with Whitby," since the expeditions during the tenth and eleventh cycles have fared much better, even if there aren't any answers, either.

You can't take Grace, although you need her counsel. Because that would be like cutting off two heads at once if anything went wrong, and you've never thought Grace had the temperament for it; too many connections to the world. Children. Sisters. An ex-husband. A girlfriend. It's Grace who you joke is your "external moral compass" and knows better than you where the boundaries are. "Too normal," you wrote on a napkin once.

"Why do you let Lowry tell you what to do?" Grace says to you one afternoon, after you've directed the conversation that way. You deflect/refract. Lowry isn't your direct boss, is more like slant rhyme, not there at the end of things but still in control. Grace would have to know how Lowry's gotten his hooks in at Central, and how he got his hooks into you, and you've managed to shield her from that.

You remind Grace that there is a part of the kingdom you *do* control, that Lowry doesn't get to influence: what comes out of Area X from the expeditions. It's all processed through the Southern Reach, and so when the latest eleventh expedition came back with nothing to show for it except some blurry photographs left behind at base camp by the prior expedition, or perhaps one even earlier, you took them away and stared at them for hours. A collection of shadows against a black background. But was that a wall? Was that a texture that reminded you of another photograph from another expedition? So you pulled all of the photographs taken inside El Topoff. All thirteen of them, and, yes, these new ones could have been taken in the tunnel, too. That shadow, that faint outline of a face . . . is that familiar? Would it be wrong of you to believe it means something?

Confessing your simple plan to Grace, showing her some of the evidence, you're betting that she won't betray you to Central, but you know she might, out of a respect for the rules. Because behind all of your reasons, your data, you worry that it just boils down to being tired of the feeling in the pit of your stomach every time another expedition doesn't come back, or only half comes back, or comes back with nothing. Needing to somehow change the paradigm.

"It's just a quick jaunt over to El Topoff and back. No one will ever find out." Although Lowry might. What will he do if he finds out you crossed the border without his approval? Would his anger be directed just at you?

After a pause, Grace says, "What do you need from me?" Because she can see it is important, and that you'll do it whether she helps you or not.

The next thing she says is, "Do you think you can convince Whitby?"

"Yes, I do," you say, and Grace looks skeptical.

But Whitby's not a problem. Whitby's eager, like a yipping terrier wanting to go for a long, long walk. Whitby wants out of the science department for a while. Whitby's the one reassuring you by citing the survival rate of the last few expeditions. Whitby's so invigorated by the opportunity that you can almost forget the whole idea is dangerous.

It's a relief, because you realize that weekend, as you exchange small talk with the Realtor, that you were terrified of going alone. Realize, watching a football game on the bar TV, below that canopy of transfixed and rusting heavens, that if Whitby hadn't said yes, you might've called the whole thing off.

Through the door, on your way to Area X, you feel a kind of pressure that bends you low, see a black horizon full of shooting stars, their trails bleeding so rich and deep across the non-sky that you squint against the brilliance of that celestial welder's torch. A sense of teetering, of vertigo, but each time you lurch too far to one side or the other, something nudges you back toward the center, as if the edges, closer than they seem, curl up at a more severe angle. Your thoughts dart quick then slow, something stitching between them you cannot identify. The impulse comes to stop walking, to just stand there, in the corridor between the real world and Area X, for an eternity.

While hypnotized Whitby shuffles along, eyes closed, his face a twitching mass of tics as if he's having an intense dream. Whatever haunts him inside his own head, you've made sure he won't get lost, won't just come to a halt somewhere in transit. He's tied to you by the wrists with a nylon rope, and he stumbles along behind.

The molasses feeling Whitby told you to expect comes next, the sense of wading through thigh-high water, the resistance that means you are close to the end, a hint of the deep, spiraling door of light far ahead, and just in time, because stoic as you could be, Whitby's dream-walking has begun to get to you, makes you think *things* look in at you. You lose the sense of where you are in relation to anything, even your own body . . . Are you really walking, or are you standing still and your brain just thinks that your feet are lifting up, falling down, lifting up again?

Until the resistance falls away like a breath held too long and then released, and you both stumble through the door and out into Area X. With Whitby on all fours, hugging the ground, shaking convulsively, and you pulling him free and past, so he won't accidentally stagger in the wrong direction and disappear forever. He's gasping like you both are gasping, from the freshness of the air, acclimating to it.

Such a blue, cloudless sky. A trail that should be so familiar, but it has been decades since you saw the forgotten coast. It will take more than a moment to think of it as home. You recognize the trail more from photographs and the accounts of expedition members, know it was here before the first invaders, was used by some of your long-ago ancestors, and has even now survived, overgrown, as part of Area X.

"Can you walk?" you ask Whitby, once you've brought him back to his senses.

"Of course I can walk." Enthusiastic, but a kind of brittle sheen behind it, as if something has already been stripped away underneath.

You don't ask him what he dreamed, what he saw. You don't want to know until you're back across.

You had reviewed those toxic Area X video clips from the doomed first expedition not to seek answers but, with some measure of guilt, to seek a connection with the wilderness you'd known as a child. To reinforce your memories, to recall what you could not recall—pushing past the screams, the disorientation, and the lack of comprehension, past Lowry's weeping, past the darkness.

There you can see the line of rocks near the lighthouse, the shore already a little different then, as if Whitby's terroir could be traced through the patterns left by the surf. As if down there, amid the sand-crab holes and the tiny clams digging in every time the water reveals them, some sample might hold all the answers.

The trails, too: a dark stillness of the pine trees and thick underbrush mottled by a strangled light. The memory of being disoriented and lost in a thunderstorm at the age of six, of emerging from that forest not knowing where you were—brought out of you by the cautious quiet way the expedition leader noted looming clouds, as if they presaged something more than a need to find shelter.

After the storm, in the startling revelation of open space and sunlight, you'd encountered a huge alligator blocking the narrow path, with water on both sides. You'd taken a running start and jumped over it. Never told your mother about the exhilaration, the way you had in mid-leap dared a glance down to see that yellow eye, that dark vertical pupil, appraise you, take you in like Area X had taken in the first expedition, and then you were over and past, running for a

long time out of sheer joy, sheer adrenaline, like you'd con-
quered the world.

The running on the screen toward the end is away from
something, not toward something, and the screams later not
of triumph but of defeat—tired screams, as of weariness at
fighting against something that would not properly show
itself. In your more cynical moments you thought of them
as perfunctory screams: an organism that knows there is no
point in fighting back, the body capitulating and the mind
letting it. They were not lost as you were lost that day; they
had no cottage by the sea to return to, no mother pacing on
the deck, worried out of her mind, grateful for your sudden
grimy, soaked appearance.

Something on your face must have retained the memory
of your joy because she didn't punish you, just got you in dry
clothes and fed you, and asked no questions.

Bypassing the route to base camp, you head for the topographical anomaly with the urgency of a ticking clock driving
you. The knowledge—never discussed with Whitby—that the
longer you stay, the longer you seem to linger, the greater the
opportunity for disaster. That alligator eye staring up at you,
with more awareness behind its piercing gaze than you remember. Someone off-camera on the second day of the first
expedition saying, "I want to go home," and Lowry, goofing
around, so confident, saying, "What do ya mean? This is our
home now. We've got everything here. Everything we need.
Right?"

Nowhere is this sense of urgency more intense than while
passing through the swampy forest that lies a mile or two from
the border, where the woods meet a dank black-water gutter.

The place where you most often saw evidence of bears and heard things rustling in the darkness of the tree cover.

Whitby's often silent, and when he speaks his questions and concerns do nothing to alleviate the pressure of that gloom, the sense of *intent* eternal and everlasting that occupies this stretch of land, that predates Area X. The still, standing water, the oppressive blackness of a sky in which the blue peers down through the trees at startling intervals, only to be taken away again, and only ever seeming to come to you from a thousand miles off anyway. Is this the clearing where three men died during the fifth expedition? Does that pond hold the bodies of men and women from the first eighth? Sometimes, immersed in these overlays, Whitby's pale whispering form is a jolting shock to you, inseparable from these echoes of prior last days.

Eventually, though, you cross into a more optimistic landscape, one in which you can adapt, reconcile past and present into one vision. Here, a wider path separates the continuing dank swamp forest from open ground, allows you a horizon of a few tall pines scattered among the wild grass and palmetto circles. The lean of that forest means that the darkness ends at an angle casting half the trail in a slanted shade.

There are other borders within Area X, other gauntlets, and you have passed through one to get to the topographical anomaly.

Once there, you know immediately the tower isn't made of stone—and so does Whitby. Does he wish now, his expression unreadable, that you had put him through conditioning, that he'd been given all the training Central could bestow, not your half measures, your shoddy hypnotism?

The tower is breathing. There is no ambiguity about it: The flesh of the circular top of the anomaly rises and falls with the regular rhythm of a person deep in sleep. No one mentioned this aspect in the reports; you aren't prepared for it, but how easily you acclimate, give yourself up to it, can already imagine descending even as a part of you is floating, ascending to look down on the foolishness of this decision.

Will it wake up while you're inside it?

The opening leading into darkness resembles a maw more than a passageway, the underbrush around it pushed back, squashed in a rough framing circle, as if some now-absent serpent had once curled around it in a protective mode. The stairs form a curling snarl of crooked teeth, the air expelled smelling of thick rot.

"I can't go down there," Whitby says, in such a final way that he must be thinking that in the descent he would no longer be Whitby. The hollows of his face, even in that vibrant, late-summer light, make him look haunted by a memory he hasn't had yet.

"Then I'll go," you offer—down into the gullet of the beast. Others have, if rarely, and come back, so why not you? Wearing a breathing mask, just to be safe.

There is a dazed panic and coiled restraint behind your every movement that will come out later through the flesh, the bone. Months from now you will wake sore and bruised, as if your body cannot forget what happened, and this is the only way it can express the trauma.

Inside, it's different than in the fragmentary reports brought back by other expeditions. The living tissue curling down the wall is almost inert, the feeble wanderings of the tendrils that form the words so slow you think for a moment it's all necrotic tissue. Nor are the words a vibrant green as reported but a searing blue, almost the color of a flame on a stove top. The word *dormant* comes to mind, and with it a wild hope: that everything beneath you will be inert, normal, even if at the outer boundary of what that word means.

You keep to the middle, do not touch either wall, try to ignore the shuddering breath of the tower. You don't read the words because you have long seen that as a kind of trap, a way to become distracted . . . and still the sense that whatever will disorient and destabilize lies below you, deciding whether to be seen or remain unseen—around a corner, beyond the horizon, and with each new empty reveal, each curve of the steps lit by the blue flames of dead words, toward an unknown become shy, you are wound ever tighter, even though there is nothing to be seen. The hell of that, the hell of nothing at all, which feels as if you are reliving every moment of your life at the Southern Reach—descending for no reason, for nothing, to find nothing. No answers, no solution, no end in sight, the words on the wall not getting fresher but darker, seeming to wink out as you come upon them . . . until, finally, you glimpse a light far, far below—so far below it's like a glowing flower in a hole at the bottom of the sea, a glimmering, elusive light that through some magician's trick also hovers right in front of your face, giving you the illusion that you can reach out and touch it if you only can find the courage to extend your hand.

But that's not what makes your legs ropy, a rush of blood surging through your brain.

A figure sits hunched along the side of the left-hand wall, staring down the steps.

ACCEPTANCE

A figure with head bowed, turned away from you.

A prickling engulfs your head under your mask, a kind of smooth, seamless insertion of a million cold, painless needles, ever so subtle, ever so invisible, so that you can pretend it is just a spreading heat against your skin, a taut feeling across the sides of your nose, around your eyes, the quiet soft entry of needles into a pincushion, the return of something always meant to be there.

You tell yourself this is no less or more real than bowling at Chipper's, than the hippo with the red paint under the skin, than living in Bleakersville, working at the Southern Reach. That this moment is the same as every other moment, that it makes no difference to the atoms, to the air, to the creature whose walls breathe all around you. That you gave up the right to call anything impossible when you decided to enter Area X.

You come closer, drawn by this impossible thing, sit on the step next to him.

His eyes are shut. His face is illuminated by a dark blue glow that emanates from within, as if his skin has been taken over, and he is as porous as volcanic rock. He's fused to the wall, or jutting out from it, like an extension of the wall, something that protrudes but might be retracted at any moment.

"Are you real?" you ask, but he says nothing in reply.

Reaching out to him, extending a trembling hand, awestruck by this apparition, wanting to know what that skin feels like, even as you're afraid your touch will turn him to powder. Your fingers graze his forehead, a rough, moist feel, like touching sandpaper under a thick layer of water.

"Do you remember me?"

"You shouldn't be here," Saul Evans says under his breath. His eyes are closed; he cannot see you, and yet you know he sees you. "You need to get off the rocks. The tide's coming in."

You don't know what to say. You won't know what to say for a long time. Your reply was so many years ago.

Now you can hear the vast, all-consuming hum of some mighty engine from below, the swift revolving of strange orbits, and the light below, that impossible flowering light, is fluctuating, shifting, turning into something else.

His eyes snap open, white against the darkness. He's no different than when you last saw him, has not aged, and you're nine again and the light below is coming up toward you, coursing up the steps toward you, fast, and from above you can hear the distant echo of Whitby screaming, from the top of the tower, as if he's screaming for both of you.

0004: THE LIGHTHOUSE KEEPER

Armadillos ruining the garden, but don't really want to put out poison. Sea grape bushes must be pruned back. Will make a list of maintenance issues by tomorrow. Fire on Failure Island, but already reported and not major. Sighted: albatross, unidentified terns, bobcat (peering out of the palmetto grove to the east, staring at a hiker who didn't see him), flycatcher of some kind, pod of dolphins headed east in a frenzy as they chased a school of mullet through the sea grass in the shallows.

Bodies could be beacons, too, Saul knew. A lighthouse was a fixed beacon for a fixed purpose; a person was a moving one. But people still emanated light in their way, still shone across the miles as a warning, an invitation, or even just a static signal. People opened up so they became a brightness, or they went dark. They turned their light inward sometimes, so you couldn't see it, because they had no other choice.

"That's bullshit," Charlie said during the night, when Saul expressed something similar to him, after they'd had sex. "Don't ever become a poet." For once, Saul had convinced

Charlie to come to the lighthouse, a rare event because Charlie still had a skittish, flighty quality to him. Beaten by his father and kicked out by his family, and in the twenty years since he'd not entirely come out of his shell. So this was a halting step forward—something that made Saul happy, that he could provide a small sense of security.

"An idea in one of my father's sermons. The best he ever gave." Flexing his hand, trying to sense any residual discomfort from the incident with the plant. None to be found.

"Ever miss it? Being a preacher?" Charlie asked.

"No, I'm just working out something about the Light Brigade," he said. They still elicited in him a distant but sharp alarm. What were they projecting that he couldn't see?

"Oh, *them*, huh?" Charlie said with a simulated yawn as he turned over on his back. "You can't leave those Brigaders alone, can you? Bunch of crackpots. You, too." But said with affection.

Later, when he was drifting off, Charlie murmured, "It's not stupid. The beacon thing. It's kind of a nice thought. Maybe."

Maybe. Saul found it hard to tell when Charlie was sincere about such things. Sometimes their life between the sheets seemed mysterious, to have no relationship to life out in the world.

Sometimes, too, other people gave you their light, and could seem to flicker, to be hardly visible at all, if no one took care of them. Because they'd given you too much and had nothing left for themselves.

At the end, with his church, he'd felt like a beacon that had been drained of light, except for some guttering glimmer in the heart of him—the way the words shone out from his mouth, and it almost didn't matter what light they created, not to his congregation, because they were looking at him, not listening. At best, anyway, his ministry had been an odd assortment, attracting hippies and the straitlaced alike, because he'd pulled from the Old Testament and from deism, and the esoteric books available to him in his father's house. Something his father hadn't planned on: the bookshelves leading Saul to places the old man would rather he'd never gone. His father's library had been more liberal than the man himself.

The shock of going from being the center of attention to being out of it entirely—that still pulled at Saul at unexpected times. But there had been no drama to his collapsed ministry in the north, no shocking revelation, beyond the way he would be preaching one thing and thinking another, mistaking that conflict, for the longest time, as a manifestation of his guilt for sins both real and imagined. And one awful day he'd realized, betrayed by his passion, that *he* was becoming the message.

By the time Saul woke up, Charlie was gone, without even a note. But, then, a note might have seemed sentimental, and Charlie was the kind of beacon that wouldn't allow that kind of light.

In the afternoon, he saw Gloria walking up the beach, waved to her, wasn't sure she'd seen him until she corrected her course to slowly tack closer. It wouldn't do to seem too interested in talking to him, he knew. Might violate some girl code.

He was filling in holes from armadillos that had been rooting around in the garden. The holes, which roughly matched the shape of their snouts, amused him. He couldn't say why.

But the work made him happy in a formless, motiveless way. Even better, the twins, Henry and Suzanne, were very late.

It had become a stunning day after a cloudy start. The sea had an aquamarine sheen to it, vibrant against the dull shadows of submerged seaweed. At the very edge of a seamless, ever-deepening blue sky, the contrail of an airplane, showing its disdain for denizens of the forgotten coast. Much closer to home, he tried to ignore rocks slick with the white shit of cormorants.

"Why don't you do something about those armadillos?" Gloria asked when she'd finally reached the lighthouse grounds. She must have meandered, distracted by the treasures to be found in the seaweed washed up on the beach.

"I like armadillos," he told her.

"Old Jim says they're pests."

Old Jim. Sometimes he thought she made up a reference to Old Jim every time she wanted to get her way. Old Jim lived down one of the dozens of dirt roads, at the end of a maze of them, in a glorified shack near an illegal drop site for barrels of chemical waste. No one knew what he'd done before he'd washed up on the forgotten coast, but now he served as the ad hoc proprietor of the on-again, off-again village bar.

"Is that what Jim says, huh?" Making sure to pack the soil tight, even though he was already feeling strangely tired. Another storm and he'd have eroded divots all over instead.

"They are armored rats."

"Like seagulls are winged rats?"

"What? You know, you could set traps."

"They're much too smart for traps."

Slowly, staring at him sideways: "I don't think that's true, Saul."

When she called him Saul, he knew he might be in trouble. So why not get in a lot of trouble. Besides, he needed a break, was sweating too much.

"One day," he said, leaning on the shovel, "they got in through the kitchen window by standing on top of each other and jiggling the latch."

"Armadillo pyramid!" Then, recovering her youthful caution: "I don't think that's true, either."

Truth was, he did like the armadillos. He found them funny—bumbling yet sincere. He'd read in a nature guide that armadillos "swam" by walking across the bottoms of rivers and holding their breath, a detail that had captivated him.

"They can be a nuisance," he admitted. "So you're probably right." He knew if he didn't make some small concession, she'd drive the point into the ground.

"Old Jim said you were crazy because you saw a kangaroo around here."

"Maybe you need to stop hanging out with Old Jim."

"I wasn't. He lives in a dump. He came to see my mother."

Ah—gone to see the doctor. A sense of relief came over him, or maybe it was just the cold sweat of his exertion. Not that there was anything wrong with Jim, but the thought of her roving so widely and boldly bothered him. Even though Charlie had told Saul more than once that Gloria knew the area better than he did.

"So did you see a kangaroo?"

My God, is this what it would've been like having kids?

"Not exactly. I saw something that *looked* like a kangaroo."

The locals still joked about it, but he swore he'd seen it, just a glimpse that first year, exhilarated from the rush of exploring so many new and unfamiliar hiking trails.

"Oh, but I forgot. I came over here for a reason," she said.

"Yes?"

"Old Jim said he heard on his radio that the island's on fire, and I wanted to see it better from the top of the lighthouse. The telescope?"

"What?" Dropping his shovel. "What do you mean the island's on fire?" No one was over there now except members of the Light Brigade, as far as he knew, but part of his job was reporting incidents like fires.

"Not the *whole thing*," she said, "just part of it. Let me take a look. There's smoke and everything."

So up they went, Saul insisting she take his hand, her grip strong and clammy, telling her to be careful on the steps, while wondering if he should have called someone about the fire before he confirmed it.

At the top, after pulling back the lens curtain and peering through the telescope, mostly meant for stargazing, Saul discovered that she was right: The island was on fire. Or, rather, the top of the ruined lighthouse was in flames—several miles away, but clear through the telescope's eye. A hint of red, but mostly dark smoke. Like a funeral pyre.

"Do you think anyone died?"

"No one's over there." Except the "strange people," as Gloria had put it.

"Then who set the fire?"

"No one had to set it. It might have just happened." But he didn't believe that. He could see what looked like bonfires, too, black smoke rising from them. Was that part of a controlled burn?

"Can I look some more?"

"Sure."

Even after he had let Gloria take his position at the telescope, Saul thought he could still see the thin fractures of smoke tendrils on the horizon, but that had to be an illusion.

Strangeness was nothing new for Failure Island. If you listened to Old Jim, or some of the other locals, the myths of the forgotten coast had always included that island, even before the latest in a series of attempts at settlement had failed. The rough, unfinished stone and wood of the town's buildings, the island's isolation, the way the sea lanes had already begun to change while the lighthouse was under construction so long ago had seemed to presage its ultimate fate.

The lens in his lighthouse had previously graced the ruined tower on the island. In some people's eyes that meant some essential misfortune had followed the lens to the mainland, perhaps because of the epic story of moving the four-ton lens, with a sudden storm come up and lightning breaking the sky, how the lens had almost sunk the ship that carried it, run aground carrying the light that might have saved it.

While Gloria was still glued to the telescope, Saul noticed something odd on the floor near the base of the lens, on the side facing away from the sea. A tiny pile of glass flakes glinted against the dark wood planks. What the heck? Had the Light Brigade broken a bulb up here or something? Then another thought occurred, and stooping a bit, Saul pulled up the lens bag directly above the glass shavings. Sure enough, he found a fissure where the glass met the mount. It was almost like what he imagined the hole from a bullet might look like, except smaller. He examined the "exit wound," as he thought of it. The hairline cracks pushing out from that space resembled the roots of a plant. He saw no other damage to that smooth fractal surface.

He didn't know whether he should be angry or just add it to the list of repairs, since it wouldn't harm the functioning of the lens. Had Henry and Suzanne done this, deliberately or through some clumsiness or mistake? Unable to shake the irrational feeling of hidden connections, the sense that something had escaped from that space.

The reverberation of steps below him, the sound of voices—two sets of footsteps, two voices. The Light Brigade, Henry and Suzanne. On impulse, he pulled down the lens bag, dispersed the glass flakes with his boot, which made him feel oddly complicit.

When they finally appeared, Saul couldn't blame Gloria for the way she looked at them—staring like a feral cat with hackles up from her position at the telescope. He felt the same way.

Henry was again dressed like he was going out on the town. Suzanne looked tense, perhaps because this time she was carrying the bulk of the equipment.

"You're late," he said, unable to keep an edge of disapproval out of his voice. Henry held the handle of what looked like a metal tool kit in his left hand, was rocking it gently back and forth. "And what's that?" Saul hadn't seen it before.

"Oh, nothing, Saul," Henry said, smile as big as ever. "Just some tools. Screwdrivers, that kind of thing. Like a handyman." Or someone taking samples from a first-order lens that had managed to escape vandalism for more than a century.

Apparently noting Gloria's hostility, Suzanne put down the suitcase and cardboard box she was carrying, leaned over the telescope as she said, "You're such a sweet kid. Would you like a lollipop?" Which she produced as if by magic from Gloria's ear with the over-flourish of an amateur magician.

An appraising, hostile stare from Gloria. "No. We're watching the island burn." She dismissively put her eye to the telescope again.

"There's a fire, yes," Henry said, unperturbed, as Suzanne returned to his side. A tinny rattle as he set his tool kit next to the other equipment.

"What do you know about it?" Saul asked, although so many other questions now rose up.

"What would I know about it? An unfortunate accident. I guess we never got the right badges in the Boy Scouts, yes? No one has been hurt, luckily, on this glorious day, and we'll be gone from there very soon anyway."

"Gone?" Saul suddenly hopeful. "Closing up shop?"

Henry's expression was less friendly than it had been a moment ago. "Just on the island. What we're looking for isn't there."

Smug, like he enjoyed holding on to a secret that he wasn't going to share with Saul. Which rubbed Saul the wrong way, and then he *was* angry.

"What are you looking for? Something that would make you damage the lens?" His directness made Suzanne wince. She wouldn't meet Saul's gaze.

"We haven't touched the lens," Henry said. "You haven't, have you, Suzanne?"

"No, we'd never touch the lens," Suzanne said, in a horrified tone of voice. The thought occurred that Suzanne was protesting too much.

Saul hesitated. Should he show them the spot on the lens that had been damaged? He didn't really want to. If they'd done it, they'd just lie again. If they hadn't done it, he'd be drawing their attention to it. Nor did he want to get into an argument with Gloria around. So he relented and with difficulty tore Gloria away from the telescope, knowing she'd been listening the whole time.

Down below, in his kitchen, he called the fire department in Bleakersville, who told him they already knew about the fire on the island, it wasn't a threat to anything, and making him feel a little stupid in the process because that's how they treated people from the forgotten coast. Or they were just terminally bored.

Gloria was sitting in a chair at the table, absentmindedly gnawing on a candy bar he'd given her. He figured she probably had wanted the lollipop.

"Go home. Once you've finished." He couldn't put words to it, but he wanted her far away from the lighthouse right now. Charlie would've called him irrational, emotional, said he wasn't thinking straight. But in the confluence of the fire, the lens damage, and Suzanne's strange mood . . . he just didn't want Gloria there.

But Gloria held on to her stubbornness, like it was a kind of gift she'd been given along with the candy bar.

"Saul, you're my friend," she said, "but you're not the

boss of me." Matter-of-fact, like something he should've already known, that didn't need to be said.

He wondered if Gloria's mother had said that—more than once. Wryly, he had to admit that it was true. He wasn't the boss of Henry, either, or, apparently, anyone. The tedious yet true cliché came to mind. *Tend to your own garden.*

So he nodded, admitting defeat. She was going to do whatever she wanted to do. They all would, and he would just have to put up with it. At least the weekend was approaching fast. He'd drive to Bleakersville with Charlie, check out a new place called Chipper's Star Lanes that a friend of Charlie's liked a lot. It had the miniature golf Charlie enjoyed and he didn't mind the bowling, although what Saul liked most was that they had a liquor license and a bar in the back.

Only an hour later, Henry and Suzanne were downstairs again—he noticed first the creaking of their steps and then through the kitchen window their repetitive pacing as they roved across the lighthouse grounds.

He would have stayed inside and left them to it, but a few minutes later Brad Delfino, a volunteer who sometimes helped out around the lighthouse, pulled in to the driveway in his truck. Already, even before he'd come to a stop, Brad was waving to Henry, and somehow Saul didn't want Brad talking to the Light Brigade without him there. Brad was a musician in a local band who liked to drink and talked a lot, to anyone who'd listen. Sometimes he got into trouble; his spotty work at the lighthouse was what passed for community service on the forgotten coast.

"You heard about the fire?" Brad said as Saul headed him off in the parking lot.

"Yes," Saul said curtly. "I heard about it." Of course Brad knew; why else would he have come out?

Now he could see that Henry and Suzanne were ceaselessly snapping shots of every square inch of the grounds inside the fence. Adding to the chaos, Gloria had noticed him and was bounding toward him making barking noises like she sometimes did. Because she knew he hated it.

"Know what's going on?" Brad asked.

"Not any more than you do. Fire department says there's no problem, though." Something in his tone changed when he talked to Brad, a kind of southern twang entering, which irritated him.

"Can I go up and look through the telescope anyway?" As eager as Gloria to get a peek at the only excitement going on today.

But before Saul could respond to that, Henry and Suzanne bore down on them.

"Photo time," Suzanne said, smiling broadly. She had a rather bulky telephoto lens attached to her camera, the wide strap around her neck making her look even more childlike.

"Why do you want a photo?" Gloria asked.

That was Saul's question, too.

"It's just for our records," Suzanne said, with a wide, devouring smile. "We're creating a photo map of the area, and a record of the people who live here. And, you know, it's such a beautiful day." Except it was a little overcast now, the encroaching gray from clouds that would probably rain inland, not here.

"Yes, how about a photograph of you, your assistant—and the girl, I guess," Henry said, ignoring Gloria. He was studying Saul with an intensity that made him uncomfortable.

"I'm not sure," Saul said, reluctant if for no other reason than their insistence. He also wanted to find a way to extricate himself from Brad, who wasn't anything as formal as an "assistant."

"*I'm* sure," Gloria muttered, glaring at them. Suzanne tried to pat her head. Gloria looked at first as if she might bite that hand, then, in character, just growled and leaned away from it.

Henry stepped in close to Saul. "What would a photograph of the lighthouse be without its keeper?" he asked, but it wasn't really a question.

"A better picture?"

"You used to be a preacher up north, I know," Henry said. "But if you're worrying about the people you left behind, don't—it's not for publication."

That threw him off-balance.

"How do you know that?" Saul said.

But Brad had gotten a kick out of this revelation, waded in before Henry could answer. "Yeah, that Saul, man. He's a real desperado. He's wanted in ten states. If you take his picture, it's all over for him."

Did a picture really matter? Even though he'd left unfinished business up north, it wasn't like he'd fled, exactly, or as if this photo would wind up in the newspapers.

The wind had taken to gusting. Rather than argue, Saul pulled his cap out of his back pocket, figured wearing it might disguise him a bit, although why did he need a disguise? An irrational thought. Probably not the first irrational thought from a lighthouse keeper on the forgotten cost.

"Say 'cheese.' Say 'no secrets.' Count of three."

No secrets?

Brad had decided to assume a stoic pose that Saul supposed might be a way of poking fun at him. Gloria, seeking the dramatic, made them wait while she drew the hood of her jacket over her head and then ran to the rocks as her protest, certain Suzanne wouldn't be able to get her in the frame. Once at the rocks, she climbed away from them, and then turned around and began to climb back, shrieking with delight and shouting, for no good reason, "I'm a monster! I'm a monster!"

The count of three came, Suzanne grown still and silent, bending at the knees as if she were on the deck of a ship at sea. She gave the signal.

"No secrets!" Brad said prematurely, with an enthusiasm he might regret, given his drug record.

Then came the flash from the camera, and in the aftermath black motes drifted across the edges of Saul's vision, gathered there, lingered for longer than seemed normal.

0005: CONTROL

They had exploded through and up out of that terrible corridor between the world and Area X into a lack of air that had shocked Control, until the solid push of Ghost Bird's body against his, the weight of his backpack pulling him down, forced him to fight against the slapping pressure of what his burning eyes, strangled throat, told him was salt water. He had managed to shut his mouth against his surprise, to ignore the rush of bubbles pushing up and around the top of his head. Managed to clamp down on both his panic and his scream, to adjust as well to the ripping feel of a thousand rough-smooth surfaces against him, too much like the door that had become a wall cutting through his fingers, slashing against his arms, his legs, sure he had materialized into the middle of a tornado of shining knives—Whitby and Lowry and Grace and his mother the spy, the whole damned congregation of the Southern Reach calling out the word *Jump!* through those thousand silvery reflections. Even as his lungs flooded with water. Even as he struggled to lose the treacherous knapsack but still hold on to Whitby's document inside it, grappling, flailing for the pages, some of which exploded out into the water, the rest plummeting into the murk below with the knapsack: a slab of pulp, a soggy tombstone.

Ghost Bird, he recognized dimly, had already shot up and past him, toward a kind of glistening yellow egg of a reflected halo that might, or might not, be the sun. While he was still sucking water among the converging circles of the many swirling knives that stared at him with flat judgmental eyes. Confused by the swirl of pages that floated above or below, that stuck to his clothes, that came apart in miniature whirlpools to join the vortex. For a fading second, he was peering at a line of text and suffocating while blunt snouts bumped up against his chest.

Only when a true leviathan appeared did his oxygen-starved brain understand that they had emerged into a roiling school of some kind of barracuda-like fish now being disrupted by a larger predator. There came an awful free-falling emptiness . . . the quickly closing space where the enormous shark had sped through the vortex, annihilating fish in a crimson cloud. A megalodon of a kind. Lowry in yet another form . . . the air trickling out of his mouth like a series of tiny lies about the world that had decided to extinguish him.

"Lowry" left offal in its wake, so close to Control as he rose and it descended that the side of his face slid half raw against its gills. The frill and flutter sharper and harder than he could have imagined as it sculpted him, the expulsion of water a roaring, gushing piston in his ear, and the huge yet strangely delicate eye away to his left staring into him. Then his stomach was banging into its body, his bruised waist smacked by a swipe of the tail, and his head was ringing and he was drifting and he couldn't keep his mouth from beginning to open, the dot of the sun smaller and smaller above him. *"Pick up the gun, Control,"* said his grandfather. *"Pick it up from under the seat. Then jump."*

Did Lowry, or anyone, have a phrase that could save him?

Consolidation of authority.
There's no reward in the risk.
Floating and floating.
Paralysis is not a cogent analysis.

Except it was. And from the wash and churn, the thrashing around him, a familiar hand grasped his drifting wrist and yanked him upward. So that he was not just a swirl of confused memory, a bruised body, a cipher, but apparently something worth saving, someone in the process of being saved.

His feet had kicked out against nothing, like a hanging victim, while the fish again converged, his body buffeted by a hundred smooth-rough snouts as he rose, as he blacked out amid the torrent of upward-plunging bodies, the rough rebuke of continuous flesh that formed one wide maw from which he might or might not escape.

Then they were on the shore and Ghost Bird was kissing him for some reason. Kissing him with great, gulping kisses that bruised his lips, and touching his chest and, when he opened his eyes and looked up into her face, making him turn onto his side. Water gushed, then dribbled, from him, and he had propped himself up with both arms, staring down into the wet sand, the tiny bubbles of worm tunnels as the edge of the surf brushed against his hands and receded.

Lying there on his side, he could see the lighthouse in the distance. But as if she could tell his intent, Ghost Bird said, "We're not going there. We're going to the island."

And just like that, he'd lost control.

Now, on their fourth day in Area X, Control followed Ghost Bird through the long grass, puzzled, confused, sick, tired— the nights so alive with insects it was hard to sleep against their roar and chitter. While in his thoughts, a vast, invisible blot had begun to form across the world outside of Area X, like water seeping from the bottom of a leaky glass.

Worse still, the gravitational pull Ghost Bird exerted over him, even as she was indifferent to him, even as they some-times huddled together for warmth at night. The unexpected delicacy and delirium of that accidental touch. Yet her mes-sage to him, the moment he had crossed a kind of border and she'd moved away from him, had been unmistakable and absolute. So he'd retreated to thinking of himself as Control, from necessity, to try to regain some distance, some measure of the objective. To reimagine her in the interrogation room at the Southern Reach, and him watching her from behind the one-way glass.

"How can you be so cheerful?" he'd asked her, after she had noted their depleted food, water, in an energetic way, then pointed out a kind of sparrow she said was extinct in the wider world, an almost religious ecstasy animating her voice.

"Because I'm alive," she'd replied. "Because I'm walking through wilderness on a beautiful day." This with a sideways glance he took to mean that she wondered if he was holding up. One that made him realize that her goals might not be his, that they might converge only to diverge, and he had to be ready for that. Echoes of field assignments gone wrong. Of his mother saying, "The operational damage from an event can linger in the mind like a ghost." While he wondered if even the more banal things she had said had a hidden meaning or agenda.

Freedom could take you farther from what you sought, not closer. Something he was learning out here, beyond any standard intel, in a wilderness he didn't understand. About as prepared for Area X, he realized, as for Ghost Bird, and perhaps that was, in the end, the same thing. Because they existed alone together, walked a trail that threaded its way between reed-choked lakes that could be tar-black or as green as the reflected trees that congregated in islands among the reeds . . . and he was finally free to ask her anything he wanted to, but he didn't. Because it didn't really matter.

So, instead, he shoved his hand into his jacket pocket from time to time, clenched his fist around his father's carving, taken from the mantel in the little house on the hill in Hedley. The smooth lines of it, the way the grain of the wood under the paint threatened a splinter, soothed him. A carving of a cat, chosen to remind him of long-lost Chorry, no doubt blissfully hunting rats among the bushes.

So, instead, he dove, resentful at their pull, into reexamining over and over his rescued Whitby pages, the "terroir pages," although they were more personal than that. An anchor, a bridge to his memory of the rest of the manuscript, lost at sea. If he used those pages to talk to Ghost Bird, it was in part to bring relief or distraction from the closeness of her and the way that the endless reeds, the fresh air, the blue sky, all conspired to make the real world remote, unimportant, a dream. When it was the most important thing.

Somewhere back there his mother was fighting for her career at Central, that act synonymous with fighting against the encroachment of Area X. Somewhere, too, new fronts had opened up, Area X expanding in ways that might not even match its prior characteristics. How could he know? Planes might be falling from the skies, this non-mission, this *following* of his, already a failure.

Quoting Whitby's report as he remembered it, paraphrasing: "Had they, in fact, passed judgment without a trial? Decided there could be no treaty or negotiation?"

"That might be closer to the truth, to a kind of truth," Ghost Bird replied. It was now early afternoon and the sky had become a deeper blue with long narrow clouds sliding across it. The marsh was alive with rustlings and birdsong.

"Condemned by an alien jury," Control said.

"Not likely. Indifference."

"He covers that, too: 'Would that not be the final humbling of the human condition? That the trees and birds, the fox and the rabbit, the wolf and the deer . . . reach a point at which they do not even notice us, as we are transformed.'" Another half-remembered phrasing, the real becoming half real. But his father had never valued authenticity so much as boldness of expression.

"See that deer over there, beyond the canal? She's definitely noticing us."

"Is she noticing us or is she *noticing* us?"

Either scenario might have horrified his mother the spy,

who had never gotten along with nature. No one in his family had, not really. He couldn't remember any real outings into the woods, just fishing around lakes and sitting by fireplaces in cabins during the winter. Had he ever even been lost before?

"Pretend the former since we can't do anything about the latter."

"Or this," Control said. "Or this: 'Or are we back in time, some creature or impulse from the past replenishing us as we grind to a halt.'"

"A stupid thing to say," Ghost Bird said, unable to resist the bait. "Natural places are no different than human cities. The old exists next to the new. Invasive species integrate with or push out native species. The landscape you see around you is the same as seeing an old cathedral next to a skyscraper. You don't believe this crap, do you?"

He gave her what he hoped was a defiant expression, one that didn't hint at how he had begun to doubt Whitby even as he continued to recite the gospel of Whitby. He had held back the quotes that might lead to something more substantial so he could think on them a little longer, contaminate them with his own opinions.

"I'm trying to separate out the pointless from the useful. I'm trying to make some progress as we trudge on over to the island." Unable to avoid infusing the word *island* with venom. Grandpa Jack would've felt the same about the island, would be restless and pushing, for all the good it would've done against Ghost Bird.

"Did any expedition ever make it to the island?" she asked, Control recognizing her attempt at deflection.

"If they did, nothing came back to the Southern Reach about it," he said. "It wasn't a priority." Perhaps too much else to wonder about.

"Why all the focus on the lighthouse, the topographical anomaly, and not the island?"

"You'd have to ask the former director about that. Or you'd have to ask Lowry."

"I never met Lowry," she said, as if this disproved his existence.

Truth was, Lowry sounded unreal to Control when he said the name in this place. But Lowry also resisted being cast aside, disregarded, kept floating there at the edges of his vision like some majestic, demonic dust mote. Manifesting every time he worried he might still be on a mission that had lodged so deep inside his skull he couldn't draw it out. Unknown commands, messages, imperatives, impulses that were not his own, that could be activated by others.

"We think in terms of machines, not animals. The enemy doesn't acknowledge machines." He liked the word *enemy*—it crystallized and focused his attention more than "Area X." Area X was just a phenomenon visited upon humanity, like a weather event, but an *enemy* created intent and focus.

She laughed at *machines, not animals*. "It definitely understands and acknowledges machines. It understands them better than we do." She stopped to face him, to lend emphasis, and something like anger pulsed out from her. "Have you not understood yet that whatever's causing this can manipulate the genome, works miracles of mimicry and biology? Knows what to do with molecules and membranes, can *peer through things*, can surveil, and then withdraw. That, to it, a smartphone, say, is as basic as a flint arrowhead, that it's operating off of such refined and intricate senses that the tools we've bound ourselves with, the ways we record the universe, are probably evidence of our own primitive nature. Perhaps it doesn't even think that we have consciousness or free will—not in the ways it measures such things."

"If that's true, why does it pay us any attention at all?"

"It probably extends to us the least attention possible."

Is there something in the corner of your eye that you cannot get out?

"So we give up. We live on the island, make ourselves hats out of leaves, take bounty from the sea." Build a house from the ribs of one of the leviathans from his dreams. Listen to homemade dance music while drinking moonshine distilled from poisonous weeds. Turn away from the real world because it doesn't exist anymore.

Ignoring him, she said: "A whale can injure another whale with its sonar. A whale can speak to another whale across sixty miles of ocean. A whale is as intelligent as we are, just in a way we can't quite measure or understand. Because we're these incredibly blunt instruments." That idea again. "Or at least, you are." Maybe she hadn't muttered that under her breath, he'd only imagined it.

"You sympathize with It," he said. "You like It." A cheap shot that he couldn't help.

Too often over the past four days, he had felt like he was crossing one of the dioramas from the natural history museum he had loved so much—intriguing, fascinating, but not quite real, or not quite real to him. Even if the effects had not yet manifested, he was being invaded, infected, remade. Was it his fate to become a moaning creature in the reeds and then food for worms?

"There was a lot about fakes in Whitby's notes," he said a little later, slyly, to test her. Especially as her attention seemed elsewhere, always glued to the sky. To perhaps see just how dispassionate she could be about her own condition. With, he knew, just a sliver of payback in there, too, which he couldn't help. Because it made no sense to go to the island.

When she said nothing, he made up a quote, feeling guilty even as the words left his mouth: "'The sense in which the perfect fake becomes the thing it mimics, and this through some strange yet static process reveals some truth about the world. Even as it can't, by definition, be original.'"

Still no response. "No? How about 'When you meet yourself and see a double that is you, would you feel sympathy, or would the impulse be to destroy the copy? To judge it unreal and to tear it down like any cardboard construct?'" Another fake, because Whitby hadn't discussed doubles—not once in the whole damn document.

She stopped walking, faced him. As ever, he had trouble not looking away.

"Is that what you're afraid of, Control?" She said it with no particular cruelty or passion. "Because I could use hypnosis on you."

"You might be susceptible, too," he said, wanting to warn her off, even as he knew there might come a time when he would *need* her to use hypnosis just as she had in the tunnel leading into Area X. *Take my hand. Close your eyes.* It had felt as if he were continually crawling out of the mouth of a vast inky-black snake, that he could "see" a rasping sound from deep in its throat, and from all sides, through the infinite dark bruise that encircled him, leviathans stared in at him.

"I'm not."

"But you're the double—the copy," he said, pressing. "Maybe the copy doesn't have the same defenses. And you still don't know why." This much she had told him.

"Test me," she said, a snarl from deep in her throat. She stopped, faced him, threw down her pack. "Go ahead and test me. Say it. Say the words you think will destroy me."

"I don't want to destroy you," he said quietly, looking away.

"Are you sure?" she said, coming very close. He could smell her sweat, see the rise of her shoulders, the half-curled left hand. "Are you sure?" she repeated. "Why not inoculate me, if you're unsure? You're already caught between wanting me and not being sure I'm all human, is that it? Made by the enemy. Must be the enemy. But can't help yourself anyway."

"I helped you back at the Southern Reach," he said.

"Don't thank people for doing what they're supposed to. You told me that."

He took a stumbling step back. "I'm out here, Ghost Bird, traveling to a place I didn't want to go. Having followed someone I'm not sure I know." A beacon to him still, and he resented that, didn't want it. Couldn't help it.

"That's bullshit. You know exactly who I am—or you should have. You're afraid, just like me," she said, and he knew that he was. Had no defenses out here, for anything.

"I don't think you're with the enemy," he said, *enemy* sounding harsh and unreasonable now. "And I don't think of you as a copy. Not really."

Exasperation, even as she was relenting, or he thought she was: "I *am* a copy, John. But not a perfect one. I'm not her. She's not me. Do you know what I'd say if I came face-to-face with her?"

"What?"

"I'd tell her, 'You made a lot of fucking mistakes. You made a lot of mistakes, and yet I love you. You're a mess and a revelation, but I can't be any of that. All I can do is work out things myself.' And then, knowing her, she'd probably look at me funny and take a tissue sample from me."

A roaring laughter came out of him at that. He banged his hand on his knee. "You're right. You're probably right. She'd do exactly that." He sat on the ground, while she remained where she was, stiff as a sentinel. "I'm beyond my skill set out here. I'm totally fucked. Even if we'd gone to the lighthouse."

"Totally fucked," she said, smiling.

"Strange, isn't it? A strange place to be." Being drawn out of himself, even though he didn't want to be. Suddenly calmer than he'd been since he'd gotten here, all of his failures muffled and indistinct behind another kind of border.

She stared at him, appraising him.

"We should keep going," she said. "But you can keep reading."

She offered him a hand up, the strength of her grip as he got to his feet a greater reassurance than any words.

"But it's a fucking disaster," he said. "I'm reading you the last will and testament of a fool."

"What other entertainment do we have out here?"

"True."

Control hadn't told her about Whitby's strange room or

his suspicions about Whitby as a conduit for Area X. He hadn't told her about those last desperate moments at the Southern Reach as the border shifted. And in not telling Ghost Bird these things, he had come to understand his mother's lies better. She had wanted to cover up the core of her decisions by hiding facts or watering them down. But she must have been wise enough to realize, no matter her motivations, no matter the labyrinth, every omission left some sign of its presence.

"'How does It renew Itself if not through our actions? Our lives?'" Whitby asked, living on through Control when the man himself was probably dead or worse.

But she wasn't listening; something in the sky had caught her attention again, something he knew couldn't be storks, and he had the binoculars this time, scrambled to find what she was staring at. When he found it, he adjusted the focus a few times, not sure he'd seen correctly.

But he had.

Across the deepening blue, high up, something drifted that resembled ripped and tattered streamers. Long and wide and alien. Its progress so far up, so far away . . . Control thought of an invisible shredded plastic bag, eviscerated to elongate and drift through the sky . . . except it was thicker than that and *part* of the sky, too. The texture of it, the way it existed and didn't exist, made him recoil, made his hand twitch, become numb, skin cold, remembering a wall that was not a wall. A wall that had been breathing under his touch.

"Get down!" Ghost Bird said, and forced him to his knees beside her in a stand of reeds. He could feel the brightness in him now—tight, taut, pulling like it was his skin being pulled, drawn toward the sky that wasn't just the sky anymore. Drawn to it so much that he would have gotten up if Ghost Bird hadn't forced him down again. He lay there grateful for her weight beside him, grateful he wasn't out here alone.

Stitching through the sky, in a terrifying way—rippling, diving, rising again, and there came a terrible whispering that pierced not his ears but all of him, as if small particles of something physical had shot through him. He cursed, frozen there, watching, afraid. "The wavery lines that are there and not there." A line from Whitby's report he hadn't shared because he hadn't understood it. Images from the video of the first expedition coming back to him.

"Stay still," Ghost Bird whispered in his ear. "Stay still." She was sheltering his body with hers, she was trying to make it seem as if he wasn't there.

He tried not even to breathe, to become so motionless that he was no longer alive. As it curled in and through the sky, he could hear it rippling, diving, rising again, like traces of a sail until, as he risked a look, he saw some impact in the air freeze it in place, and for a moment it was stretched as taut as skin, almost brittle, unyielding.

Then, with a final plunge and ascent, coming far too close, the *presence* winked out of existence, or slipped out of the air, and the sky was the same as before.

He had no words for it, Whitby's or his own. This was no dead diorama. This was no beastly skeleton of a man he'd never known. Anything now seemed possible. Anything could happen. He clutched the carving of Chorry tight. So tight he almost punctured his skin.

They remained that way until a storm slipped across a sky Control now thought of as treacherous, and through the dark gray light there came lightning, thunder, and in amongst the raindrops that drenched them, dark, slippery tadpole-like things hurtled down and disappeared into the soil all around them while they tried to take shelter as best they could, soaked under a gnarled, blackened copse of trees with leaves like daggers. The tadpole things were more like living rivulets, about the size of his little finger. He could not help thinking of them as coming from the stitching in the sky, that somehow it had disintegrated into a million tiny pieces, and this, too, was somehow part of the ecosystem of Area X.

"What do you think that will become?" he asked her.

"Whatever everything else is becoming here," she said, and that was no answer at all.

When the storm passed, the marsh came alive with birdsong and the gurgle of water in the canals, nothing at all amiss. Perhaps the reeds seemed more vibrant, the trees greener, but this was just the quality of the light, from a sun that seemed as distant as the rest of the world.

After a time, they stood. After a time, in silence, they continued on, walking closer together than before.

0006: THE DIRECTOR

There's a place that as a kid you called the farthestmost point—the most distant you could get, the place that when you stood there you could pretend you were the only person in the world. Being there made you wary, but it also put a kind of peace into you, a sense of security. Beyond that point, in either direction, you were always returning, and are returning still. But for that moment, even now with Whitby by your side, you're so remote that there's nothing for miles—and you feel that. You feel it strongly. You've gone from being a little on edge to being a little tired, and you've come out on this perfectly still scene where the scrublands turn to wetlands, with a freshwater canal serving as a buffer to the salt marsh and, ultimately, the sea. Where once you saw otters, heard the call of curlews. You take a deep breath and relax into the landscape, walk along the shore of this lower heaven rejuvenated by its perfect stillness. Your legs are for a time no longer tired and you are afraid of nothing, not even Area X, and you have no room for memory or thought or anything except this moment, and this one, and the next.

Soon enough, though, that feeling falls away again, and you and Whitby—survivors of the topographical anomaly—

stand in the remains of your mother's cottage. It's just a floor and a couple of supporting walls with the wallpaper so faded you can't figure out the pattern. On the sunken splintered deck, a battered and smashed rot of wide planks that used to be the walkway leads to the dunes, and from there to a metallic-blue sea that tosses up whitecaps and drags them down again. Perhaps you shouldn't have come here, but you needed something like normalcy, some evocation of those days before it all went wrong—days that had seemed so ordinary at the time.

"Don't forget me," Saul had said back then, as if speaking not just for him but for your mother, too, and the rest of the forgotten coast. Now truly forgotten, Whitby standing at one end and you at the other, needing the space. He's unsure of you, and you're definitely unsure of him. Whitby wanted to abort the mission after the tower, but at no point did you think you should just leave. This was your home, and Whitby isn't going to stop you, though he might protest, though he might whimper and try to get free, though he might plead with you to return across the border immediately.

"Where's your optimism now?" you want to ask, but wherever he's wound up he's still not in your world.

Long ago, a fire or two was kindled on the cottage floor, in what used to be the living room, under the shelter of one sagging wall. Blackened splotches left behind provide the evidence, tell you that even after Area X, people lived here for a time. Did your mother make those fires?

Dead beetles litter the floor, crushed into glossy emerald pieces, teal moss and thick vines creating a chaotic green sea. Wrens and warblers hop through the underbrush outside, settle on the gaping window frame that looks out landward, then are gone again. The window you'd look through when expecting your dad to come for visits, driveway outside erased by a proliferation of bushes and weeds.

Cans of food, long since rusted and rotted, along with a thick layer of soil erupting out of the corners, through the insect-chewed floorboards, what's left of them. The anomaly of cracked, ancient dishes barely recognizable, and stacked in a sink that has fallen in on itself and been transformed by mold and lichen, the cupboards below rotted away.

There's a regret in you, a kind of daymark you've let become obscured. The expeditions are never told that people had lived here, worked here, got drunk here, and played music here. People who lived in mobile homes and bungalows and lighthouses. Better not to think of people living here, of it being empty . . . and yet now you want someone to remember, to understand what was lost, even if it was little enough.

Whitby stands there like an intruder as you explore, knows you're hiding something from him about the cottage. The flat, grim line of his mouth, the resentment in his gaze—is it natural, or is Area X already turning him against you? When you burst out of the tower, escaping whatever had risen up with such speed, you found him still screaming, babbling about something that had attacked him. "There wasn't any sound. Nothing. Then . . . a *wall* behind me, running through me. Then it was gone." But since then he hasn't said more, nor have you shared what you saw right before you leapt up those last steps into the light. Perhaps neither thinks the other would believe. Perhaps you both just want to be back in the world first.

No bodies here in the cottage, but what did you think?

That you would find her huddled inside this place, cocooned from disaster somehow as the world changed around her? That was never your mother's nature. If there had been something to fight, she would have fought it. If there had been someone to help, she would have helped them. If she could have struck out for safety, she would have. In your daydreams, she held on, like you have held on, hoping for rescue.

Sitting there at the Star Lanes Lounge, scribbling, you found the cottage coming back to you at odd moments, along with the lighthouse. Always that riptide compulsion dragging you down into the water, that need to know overriding the fear. The sound of the midnight waves at high tide, how from the window of your room in your mother's bungalow back then you could see the surf under the moonlight as a series of metallic-blue lines, dark water squeezed between them. Sometimes those lines had been broken by her figure as she walked the beach late at night, kept awake by thoughts she never shared, her face turned away from you. As if searching even then for the answer you seek now.

"What is this place?" Whitby asks, again. "Why are we here?" His voice giving away his stress.

You ignore him. You want to say, "This is where I grew up," but he's endured one shock too many already, and you still have to deal with Lowry, with the Southern Reach, when you get back. If you get back.

"That vine-strewn shadow there—that was my room," you would tell him if you could. "My parents divorced when I was two. My dad left—he's kind of a small-time crook—and my mom raised me, except I spent the winter holidays with him every year. Until I stayed with him for good because I couldn't go home anymore. And he lied to me about the reason why until I was older, which was probably the right thing to do. And I've been wondering my whole life what it would be like to come back here, to this place. Wondered what I would feel, what I would do. Sometimes even imagined there would be some message, something my mom had had the foresight to put in a metal box or under a rock. Some sign, because even now I need a message, a sign."

But there is nothing in the cottage, nothing you didn't already know, and there's the lighthouse at your back—laughing at you, saying, "I told you so."

"Don't worry, we'll go home soon," you say. "Just the lighthouse, and we'll go home." Saving the best for last, or the worst for last? How much of a childhood can be destroyed or twisted before the overlay replaces the memories?

You push past Whitby—abruptly—because you don't want him to see that you're upset, that Area X is closing in on you all over again.

The few remaining floorboards of the cottage creak and sigh, making a rough music. The birds chirp urgently in the bushes, chasing each other, spiraling up into the sky. It will rain soon, the horizon like a scowling forehead, a battering ram headed for the coast. Could they see it coming, even Henry? Was it visible? Did it sweep over them? All you could process as a child was that your mother was dead; it had taken you years to think of her death in other ways.

All you can see is the expression on Saul's face the last time you saw him as a child—and your last long look at the forgotten coast through the dusty back window of the car as you turned off the dirt road onto a paved state road, and the distant ripple of the sea passed from view.

ACCEPTANCE

0007: THE LIGHTHOUSE KEEPER

Two freighters and a coast guard vessel sighted last night. Something bigger out on horizon—oil tanker? "There is the sea, vast and spacious, and there the ships go to and fro." Western siren still not right—loose wire? Feeling a little sick, so visited doctor. Went on a hike late in the day. Sighted: a horned owl atop a tortoise, trying to eat it. Didn't know what I was seeing. Disturbed me at first. Thought it was something odd with a feathery body and an armored stump. The owl looked up at me and just stared, didn't fly away until I shooed it off the tortoise.

Acts of loving-kindness. The uselessness of guilt.

Sometimes Saul did miss the sermons, the cadence of them, the way he could raise the words up from within him and send them out, never severing the deep connection between them. Could name a thing and in naming it enter so many minds. But there had come a day during his ministry when he had no words left, when he knew he was enjoying the cadence of the sentences he spoke more than the meaning—and then he was lost for a time, swimming across an endless sea of doubt, certain he had failed. Because he had failed. Hellfire and apocalyptic visions, the coming destruction of the world by demons, could not sustain a man for long without robbing him of something, too. At the end, he did not know what he meant or what he believed, and so he had given it up in one prolonged shudder that cast off an entire life and fled as far south as he could, as far remote as well. Fleeing, too, his father, who had fed off that growing cult of personality, had been at once manipulative and envious, and that had been too much to bear for long: that a man so distant, who had projected so little light, should now reveal to Saul only those emotions he did not want.

Everything had shifted when he'd moved. There were ways in which he felt so different in the south than in the north, ways in which he was different because he was happier, and he didn't want to acknowledge sickness or anything that might hint at a change in what had been so ideal.

Yet there was a slight numbness when he lay in bed with Charlie a week after the incident in the yard, an episode of perhaps ten minutes during which his body seemed disconnected from him. Or the disconcerting moments on the walks he took along the coast near the lighthouse, supposedly to patrol for trespassers but that were really just about his joy in bird-watching.

He would look out to sea and find things swimming in the corners of his eyes that he could not quite explain away as black sun dots. Was this paranoia or some nagging doubt, some part of his brain trying to ruin everything, wanting him to be unhappy—to force him to deny himself the life he'd made here?

Next to these developments, the presence of the Light Brigade had become less and less real, and in the days since the photograph there had been a kind of truce, a mutual agreement not to accuse the other. He'd fixed the hole in the lens, cleaned up the glass, and told himself everyone deserved a second chance.

But their encounters were still fraught at times.

Today, he had walked into his own kitchen to find Suzanne making a sandwich there without any shame or embarrassment at being found out. His ham and his cheese slices in a pile on the counter, along with his wheat bread, his onion, and a tomato from the garden. Perched on the kitchen stool at such an extreme angle, one leg straight, foot on the floor, and the other bent, Suzanne and her posture had compounded his irritation. Because it almost looked as if she was clenched there, rigid, holding a position as artificial to her as it looked to him.

Henry had come in then and forestalled Saul's own questions, his lecture about not taking people's things for granted. About not making a sandwich without asking first, which seemed both invasive and ridiculously trivial later.

Henry said, almost conversationally, "There isn't any spooky action here, is there, Saul? Near or far?"

All that warranted was a pained smile. Everybody knew the ghost stories about the forgotten coast.

"And it's probably just a coincidence, but ever since your freak-out in the yard, our readings are off—distorted. Sometimes it is like the equipment is junk, doesn't work, but we've tested it. There's nothing wrong with it. I'm right, am I not, Saul?"

His "freak-out" in the yard. Henry definitely was trying to get a rise out of him.

"Oh yes, it's working, all right." Saul tried to sound cheery.

Anyone would have thought Henry, especially, a kind of buffoon and his stilted attempts at conversation signs of social awkwardness. But he was often unnerving to Saul, even just standing there.

So he kicked them both out, called Charlie to ask him if he could have lunch, locked up his living quarters, and drove to the village bar to take a break.

The village bar was an impromptu place, ad hoc style depending on who was around. Today it was a barbecue station out back and a cooler full of domestic beer. Paper plates from some kid's birthday party, cake with candles against a pink background. Saul and Charlie sat outside, on the worn deck that faced the sea, at a table under a faded blue umbrella.

They talked about Charlie's day on the boat and a new resident who'd bought a house half demolished by a hurricane, and how Old Jim really needed to refurbish the village bar because "it's not cool to have a dive bar in a place with no decent bars to compare it to." How maybe they'd check out that rock band Charlie'd been telling him about. How maybe instead they'd just stay in bed all day.

How the Light Brigade was getting on Saul's nerves.

"Henry's a freak," he said to Charlie. "He's got a stare like some kind of uncanny undertaker. And Suzanne just follows him everywhere."

"They can't come around forever," Charlie said. "One day they'll be gone. Little freaks. Freak Brigade." Testing out words for the fun of it, perhaps because they'd both had some beers already.

ACCEPTANCE

"Maybe, but in the meantime they're giving me the creeps."

"Could be they're undercover agents from forestry or environmental protection?"

"Sure, because I'm dumping chemicals all night long."

Charlie was joking, but the forgotten coast had suffered from a decade or two of lax regulations in what was an "unincorporated area." The wilderness hid its share of rotting barrels, some of them hidden on old abandoned farmsteads, half sunk into the pine loam.

They took up the conversation later, at Charlie's two-room cottage just down the street. A couple of photographs of his family, some books, not much in the fridge. Nothing Charlie couldn't toss in a knapsack if he ever decided to take off, or move in with someone.

"Are you sure they're not escapees from an insane asylum?"

Which made Saul laugh, because just the summer before two sanitarium residents had escaped from outside of Hedley and made their way down to the forgotten coast, managing to remain free for almost three weeks before being caught by the police.

"If you took away the insane people, no one would be left."

"Except me," Charlie said. "Except me and, maybe, you."

"Except the birds and the deer and the otters."

"Except the hills and the lakes."

"Except the snakes and the ladders."

"What?"

Except by then they had so lit each other up under the sheets that they could have been saying anything, and were.

It was Gloria who changed his mind about seeing a doctor. The next day, with Henry and Suzanne back up in the lighthouse, him down below, she appeared in the early afternoon to shadow him. He was so used to her that if she'd not shown up, he would've thought something was wrong.

"You're different," Gloria said, and he chewed on that for a bit.

This time she was leaning against the shed, watching him as he resodded part of the lawn. Volunteer Brad had promised to come in and help, but hadn't shown up. The sun above was a huge gob of runny yellow. The waves were a rushing vibration in his awareness, but muffled. One of his ears had been blocked since he'd woken up, no doubt because he'd slept on it funny. Maybe he was getting too old for this kind of work after all. Maybe there was a reason why lighthouse keepers had to retire at fifty.

"I'm a day older and wiser," he replied. "Shouldn't you be in school? Then you'd be wiser, too."

"Teacher work day."

"Lighthouse-keeper work day here," he said, grunting as he broke the soil with a shovel. His skin felt elastic, formless, and a tic under his left eye kept pulsing in and out.

"Then show me how to do your work and I'll help."

At that he stopped and, leaning on the shovel, took a good long look at her. If she kept growing, she might make a decent linebacker someday.

"You want to become a lighthouse keeper?"

"No, I want to use a shovel."

"The shovel is bigger than you."

"Get another one from the shed."

Yes. The mighty shed, which held all things . . . except when it did not. He took a glance up at the lighthouse tower where the Light Brigade was no doubt doing unimaginable things to his beacon.

"Okay," he said, and he got her a small shovel, more of a glorified spade.

Shaking off his attempt at shovel instruction, she stood beside him and awkwardly scuffed bits of dirt around, while he was careful to keep well away. He'd once been smacked in the head by a shovel handle wielded by a too-close, over-enthusiastic helper.

"Why are you different?" she asked, direct as ever.

"I told you, I'm not different." A little grumpier than he'd meant to be.

"But you are," she said, ignoring his tone.

"It's because of the splinter," he said, finally, to keep it simple.

"Splinters hurt but they just make you bleed."

"Not this one," he said, putting his back into his work. "This one was different. I don't really understand it, but I'm seeing things in the corner of my eye."

"You should go to the doctor."

"I will."

"My mother's a doctor."

"So she is." Her mother was, or had been, a pediatrician. Not quite the same thing. Even if she did give unlicensed advice to residents of the forgotten coast.

"If *I* was different, I'd go see her." Different. But different in what way?

"You live with her."

"So?"

"Why are you really here? To interrogate me?"

"You think I don't know what 'interrogate' means, but I do," she told him, walking away.

When Henry and Suzanne left for the day, Saul climbed to the top of the lighthouse and looked out onto the rich contrast of sea and beach, the deep bronze glint of afternoon sun. From this spot, a light had shone out through storms and human-made disasters, in calms and in crises. Light that cascaded or even interrupted itself. Light that pulsed and trembled, that pulled the darkness toward it and then cast it out.

He'd been standing in the lantern room the first time he'd seen Henry, so many months ago. Henry's trudging across the sand toward the lighthouse had been a kind of travesty of progress, as he sagged and lurched and fought for purchase. Henry squinting against the glare, the wind half ripping his shirt from him—so big on him that the back of it surged right and left off his shoulders like a sail, as if mad to get free. It obscured the lagging Suzanne, whom Saul hadn't even noticed at first. The sandpipers had hardly bothered with the usual nervous pitter-patter-glide away from Henry, choosing instead to poke around in the sand until the last moment and then take wing to escape the clumsy monster. Henry had looked in that moment like an awkward supplicant, a pilgrim come to worship.

They'd left their equipment—the metal boxes with the strange dials and readings. Almost like a threat. Squatters' rights. We will return. He didn't understand half of what he was looking at, even up close. And he didn't want to—didn't want to know what was on the séance side and what was on the science side. Prebiotic particles. Ghost energy. Mirror rooms. The lens was miraculous enough in what it could do without trying to find some further significance in it.

Saul's knee was acting up, putting too much creak in his step as he went through the Light Brigade's equipment. As he searched for something he knew he probably wouldn't recognize, he was reflecting that a man could fall apart from any number of ailments, and a bit of maintenance couldn't hurt. Especially since Charlie was seven years younger. But that just hid the thought that came now in little surges of panic: that something *was* wrong, that he was more and more a stranger in his own skin, that perhaps something was beginning to look out through his eyes. *Infestation* was a thought that crept in at moments between wakefulness and sleep, sleep and wakefulness, drifting down the passageway between the two.

There was the sense of something sliding more completely into place, and the feeling confused and frightened him.

Thankfully, Gloria's mother, Trudi Jenkins, agreed to see him on short notice about an hour before nightfall. She lived to the west, in a secluded bungalow, and Saul took his pickup truck. He parked on the dirt driveway, under oak and magnolia trees and a few palmettos. Around the corner, a deck peeked out that was almost as large as her home and had a view of the beach. If she'd wanted to, she could have rented a room to tourists in the summers.

It was rumored Trudi had come to the forgotten coast after plea-bargaining a drug-trafficking charge, this more than a decade ago. But whatever her past, she had a steady hand and a level head, and going to her was better than going to the clinic another fifty miles inland, or to the medical intern who visited the village.

"I had this sliver . . ." Another thing about Trudi was that he could talk about the sliver. He'd tried with Charlie, but, for reasons he couldn't quite figure out, the more he talked about it with Charlie, the more he felt like he was somehow putting it on Charlie, and he didn't yet know how much weight Charlie could take.

Thinking about that depressed him, though, and after a while he trailed off, without having mentioned the sensation of things floating at the edge of his vision.

"You believe something *bit* you?"

"Maybe not a bite so much as stuck me. I had a glove on my hand, but I still shouldn't have reached down. It might not have anything to do with how I've been feeling." Yet how could he have known? The moment of sensation, non-sensation, he kept returning to.

She nodded, said, "I understand. It's normal to worry, what with all of the mosquito- and tick-borne illnesses. So I can check your hand and arm, and take your vitals, and maybe put your fears to rest."

She might have been a pediatrician, but she didn't speak to him as if he were a child. She just had a way of simplifying things and getting to the point that made him grateful.

"Your kid wanders over the lighthouse quite a bit," he said, to make conversation as he took off his shirt and she examined him.

"Yeah, I know," she said. "I hope she's not a problem."

"No—she just climbs on the rocks a lot."

"She's a climber, all right. Gets into everything."

"Could be dangerous."

She gave him a sharp look. "I'd rather she go to the lighthouse and be around people I know than wander off on some trail or something."

"Yeah, true," he said, sorry he'd brought it up. "She's got a talent for identifying poop."

Trudi smiled. "She gets that from me. I taught her all about different kinds of poop."

"If a bear craps in the woods, she knows about it."

She laughed at that. "I think she might be a scientist when she grows up."

"Where is she now?" He'd assumed she would have walked home right after leaving the lighthouse.

"Grocery store. That girl likes to walk everywhere. So she might as well walk down to the grocery store and get us milk and some things for dinner." The grocery store adjacent to the village bar was pretty ad hoc, too.

"She calls me the defender of the light." He didn't know where that had come from, but he had liked it when she'd called him that.

"Mmm-hmm." Back to examining him.

At the end, she said, "I can't find any indication of anything abnormal on your arm or hand. I can't even find a mark. But if it's been a week it could've faded."

"So, nothing?" Relieved, and glad he hadn't gone into Bleakersville, thinking about how much time off he had coming, and how he'd prefer to spend it with Charlie. Peeling shrimp at some roadside café. Drinking beer and playing darts. Checking into a motel, careful to ask for double beds.

"Your blood pressure's elevated and you're running a

slight fever, but that's all. Eat less salt. Have more vegetables. See how you are in a few days."

He felt better when he left, after having worked out a barter-and-money payment of twenty bucks and a promise to hammer down some loose boards in the deck, maybe a couple of other things.

But as he headed back to the lighthouse, reviewing the checklist for the lens in his mind, the relief that had invigorated him faded away and doubt crept in. Underlying everything was the thought that he had gone to the doctor as a kind of half measure for a larger problem, that he'd only confirmed there would be no easy diagnosis, that this wasn't as simple as a tick bite or the flu.

Something told him to look back as he drove, toward Failure Island, which was a shadow to the west, appearing at that distance as if it were just a sharp curve to the coastline. A faint pulse of red light blinked on and off, too high to be coming from anything other than a container ship. But too irregular to be anything but handheld or jury-rigged. In the right location on the horizon to be coming from Failure Island, perhaps from the ruined lighthouse.

Blinking out a code he didn't recognize, a message from Henry that he didn't want to receive.

After he got back, he called Charlie but there was no answer, then remembered that Charlie'd signed up for a night shift, hunting octopus and squid and flounder—the kind of adventure Charlie liked best. So he made a quick dinner, cleaned up, and then prepped the beacon. No ship traffic was expected during the night and the weather report was for calm seas.

With sunset came a premonition of beauty: The pre-dusk

sky already had so many stars in it. Before he activated the lens, he sat there for a few minutes, staring up at them, at the deep blue of the sky that framed them. At such moments, he felt as if he really did live on the edge of the known world. As if he was alone, in the way he wanted to be alone: when he chose to be and not when the world imposed it on him. Yet he could not ignore that tiny dot of pulsing light still coming from Failure Island, even overshadowed as it was by so many distant suns.

Then the beam came on and obliterated it, with Saul retreating to sit on the top step to monitor the functioning of the lens for a few minutes before going back down to attend to other duties.

He wasn't supposed to sleep on nights when the lighthouse lens was on, but at some point he knew that he had fallen asleep on the top step, and that he was dreaming, too, and that he could not wake up and should not try. So he didn't.

The stars no longer shone but flew and scuttled across the sky, and the violence of their passage did not bear scrutiny. He had the sense that something distant had come close from far away, that the stars moved in this way because now they were close enough to be seen as more than tiny points of light.

He was walking toward the lighthouse along the trail, but the moon was hemorrhaging blood into its silver circle, and he knew that terrible things must have happened to Earth for the moon to be dying, to be about to fall out of the heavens. The oceans were filled with graveyards of trash and every pollutant that had ever been loosed against the natural world. Wars for scant resources had left entire countries nothing but deserts of death and suffering. Disease had spread in its legions and life had begun to mutate into other forms, moaning and mewling in the filthy, burning remnants of once mighty cities, lit by roaring fires that crackled with the smoldering bones of strange, distorted cadavers.

These bodies lay strewn across the grounds approaching the lighthouse. Visceral were their wounds, bright the red of their blood, loud the sound of their moans, as abrupt and useless as the violence they still visited upon one another. But Saul, as he walked among them, had the sense that they existed somewhere else, and it was only some hidden pull, like a celestial riptide, that drew them to manifest in that place, while the darkened tower of the lighthouse rose shrouded in a spiral of shadow and flame.

Out of this landscape Henry rose, too, at the lighthouse door, with a beatific smile on his face that kept growing larger until it curled off the edges of his jaw. Words erupted from him, but not aloud. *And God said, Let there be light. God said that, Saul, and He has come from so far away, and His home is gone, but His purpose remains. Would you deny Him His new kingdom?* There came with these words such a sense of sadness that Saul recoiled from them, from Henry. They spoke to all that he had put behind him.

Inside the lighthouse, Saul found not stairs leading up but a vast tunneling into the earth—an overwhelming spiral that wound down and down.

At his back, the moon had filled utterly with blood and was plummeting to the Earth, descending in the midst of a flame so hot he could feel it at his back. The dead and the dying had taken up the cry of approaching oblivion.

He slammed the door shut behind him, took that sudden

path traveling down, his hand trailing against an ice-cold wall, and saw the steps so very far below him, so that he was either watching himself from a great height or his body had become as tall as the lighthouse, and each footfall occurred stories below him.

But Henry remained at his side, unwanted, and the stairs were also filling with water with a great rush and growl of fury, and soon most of him was submerged, Henry's fine shirt billowing with water, while Saul still walked down, down, until his head was beneath water, taking no breath, teetering, and he opened his eyes to see the fiery green-gold of words on the wall, being wrought before his eyes by an invisible scribe.

Even as he knew the words came from him, had always come from him, and were being emitted soundlessly from his mouth. And that he had been speaking already for a very long time, and that each word had been unraveling his brain a little more, a little more, even as each word also offered relief from the pressure in his skull. While what lay below waited for his mind to peel away entirely. A blinding white light, a plant with leaves that formed a rough circle, a splinter that was not a splinter.

When he woke up, he was sitting in a chair outside the lighthouse, with no idea how he'd gotten there. The words still lived inside of him, a sermon now coming out whether he wanted it to or not. Whether it would destroy him or not.

Where lies the strangling fruit that came from the hand of the sinner I shall bring forth the seeds of the dead to share with the worms.

0008: GHOST BIRD

Soon after the storm, the trail they followed wound back to the sea along a slope of staggered hills running parallel to the water. The wet ground, the memory of those dark rivulets, made the newly seeded soil seem almost mirthful. Ahead lay the green outline of the island, illumined by the dark gold light of late afternoon. Nothing had returned to haunt the sky, but now they walked through a world of broken things, of half-destroyed silhouettes against that gleaming horizon.

"What happened here?" Ghost Bird asked him, pretending it was his domain. Perhaps it was.

Control said nothing, had said nothing for quite some time, as if he didn't trust words anymore. Or had begun to cherish the answers silence gave him.

But something bad had happened here.

Seeking a path down to the shore that didn't require lacerating themselves on rushes and sticker cactus, they had no choice but to encounter the memory of carnage. An old tire rut filled with mud, an abandoned boot sticking out from it. Dull glint of an automatic rifle hidden by the moist grass. Evidence of fires started and then hastily put out, tents raised and struck, then smashed apart—clear that command and control had been shattered into pieces.

"The storm didn't do this," she said. "This is old. Who were they?"

Still no answer.

They came to the top of a slight rise. Below lay the remains of a truck; two jeeps, one burned down almost to the wheels; a rocket launcher in a state of advanced decomposition. All of it gently cupped by, submerged in, moss and weeds and vines. Disturbing hints of yellowing bones amid rags of faded green uniforms. The only scent was a faint sweet tang from purple-and-white wildflowers nodding furious in the wind.

It was peaceful. She felt at peace.

Finally, Control spoke. "It couldn't be personnel trapped in Area X when it expanded, unless Area X somehow sped up the rate of decay."

She smiled, grateful to hear his voice.

"Yes, too old." But she was more interested in another feature of the tableau spread out before them.

The beach and the land directly parallel had been subject to some catastrophic event, gouged and reworked, so that a huge rut on the shore had filled with deep water, and across the grass-fringed soil beyond lay what could be enormous drag marks or just the effects of an accelerated erosion. She had a vision of something monstrous pulling itself ashore to attack.

He pointed to the huge gouges. "What did that?"

"A tornado?"

"Something that came out of the sea. Or . . . what we saw in the sky?"

The wind whipped a little ragged orange flag stuck via a stake into the ground near the ruined tents.

"Something very angry, I'd say," she said.

Curious. Down on the shore, they found a boat hidden against a rise of sea oats, a rowboat pulled up past the high-tide mark, complete with oars. It looked as if it had been there for a long time, waiting. A commingled sadness and nervousness came over Ghost Bird. Perhaps the boat had been left for the biologist to find, but instead they had found it. Or the biologist's husband had never made it to the island and this boat was proof of that. But regardless, she could not really know what it meant, except that it offered a way across.

"We have just enough time," she said.

"You want to cross now?" Control said, incredulous.

Perhaps it was foolish, but she didn't want to wait. They might have another hour of real light and then that halo of shadows before true darkness dropped down upon them.

"Would you rather spend the night sleeping next to skeletons?"

She knew he didn't much like sleeping at all anymore, had started having hallucinations. Shooting stars became white rabbits, the sky full of them, with smudges of darkness interrupting their leaping forms. Afraid his mind was playing tricks to disguise something even more disturbing that only she could see.

"What if whatever did this came from the island?"

Throwing it back at him: "What if whatever did this is somewhere behind us in the marshes? The boat's seaworthy. And there's time."

"You don't find it suspicious that a boat's just waiting for us?"

"Maybe it's the first piece of good luck we've had."

"And if something erupts out of the water?"

"We row back—very fast."

"Bold moves, Ghost Bird. Bold moves."

But she was just as afraid, if not of the same things.

By the time they cast off, over that enormous scooped-out part of the shoreline, and then past a series of sandbars, the sun had begun to set. The water was a burnished dark gold. The sky above shone a deep pink, the blue-gray of dusk encroaching at the edges. Pelicans flew overhead, while terns carved the air into sharp mathematical equations and seagulls hovered, pushing against the wind.

The slap and spray of their rowing sent little whirlpools of golden water swirling off to disappear into the reflecting current. The prow of the boat had a blunt pragmatism to it that, set against all of that light, seemed serious to Ghost Bird, as if what they were doing had substance. Patterns could suffice as purpose, and the synchronicity of their rowing reassured her. They were *meant* to be rowing toward the island—to be here, in this place. The anxiety she felt about possibly finding the biologist and her husband on the island, of standing there and facing them, reversed or erased itself, lost, at least for a time, in the water.

The long, wide swathe of green that was the island at that distance was made irregular and disheveled-looking by the few tall oaks and pines that, along with the shattered spire of the lighthouse, broke through into the skyline. Trapped between: the calm motionless sky and the always restless sea, the island shimmering in the middle distance, surrounded by distortion as if it emanated heat. Sliding in between them from either side, rangy, scruffy islets with pine trees contorted low upon them, the silhouettes of these outposts extended by the rough gray-black line of oyster beds shot through with a startling iridescent white from dead shells pried open by birds.

They did not speak, even when they needed a course correction slightly to the west to avoid a sudden shallows, or when a surge in the current—waves breaking over the bow— required that they row with vigor. There was just the leaky roar of his grunting, her heavy breathing, in rhythm with the motion of her oar, the slight tapping of his oar against the frame as Control couldn't match the fluidity of her strokes. There was in the smell of his sweat and the brine of the water, the sudden tangy smell, almost a flavor, a sense of honest effort. The tautness she felt in her triceps, her forearms as she put her back into it. The pleasing soreness that came after, letting her know this was effort, this was real.

As the light faded and the sea shed its golden glitter, the rough charcoal shadow of the boat merged with the deeper blue overtaking the waves, the stained and streaked purple of the sky. With dusk, something loosened in her chest, and her rowing became even more relaxed and powerful, so that Control glanced over with a frown. She felt his gaze upon her in little appraising glances, and sometimes she turned to blunt it or neutralize it.

The shattered lighthouse grew as the light deepened still further into night. Even ruined and ravaged and torn at by wind and erosion and storms, it was a beacon to them, had a sense of life she could not ignore. There was something almost noble about it, something about the cold and the shadows of the trees and yet this place still existing that made her both sad and proud—an unexpected feeling. Had the biologist felt this way, if she had come here? Ghost Bird didn't think so. The biologist would have seen everything that surrounded it first.

The lesser darkness between the lines of the island and sea had resolved into the wreckage of the dock, at a slight raised angle from the sea so the right half of it lay submerged, the shore to either side a human-made welter of broken concrete pilings and rocks. There was no hint of a beach, until a dull off-white grin became visible along the curve of the shore farther to the west.

No light came from the lighthouse, but raucous clusters of birds settling in for the night on the trees competed with the waves, their rude cries coming to her now over the wind. The trajectories of bats in the sky above seemed like something planned by a drunk navigator, their bodies obliterating stars in haphazard and unpredictable fashion.

"Do you feel like someone is watching us?" she whispered.

"No, I don't." His voice was hoarse, as if he'd been talking to her the whole time, some effect of the wind and the salt air.

"I feel like someone is watching us."

"Birds. Bats. Trees." But said with too much dismissal. He didn't believe it was just birds, bats, trees, either.

The gulping slosh under the dock as they lashed the rowboat to the pier, the lap-licking wash and retreat over the rocks below, the creak of the planks as they came up the causeway. The anonymous birds in the trees fell silent, but a throbbing series of croaks continued from various parts of the overgrown grounds of the lighthouse. Somewhere beyond that the deliberate footfalls of some medium-size mammal making its way through the underbrush. While above them the pale, almost luminous jagged spire of the lighthouse rose, framed by the dark sky and the stars arrayed around it as if it was the center of the universe.

"We'll spend the night in the lighthouse, and then forage in the morning." It was warmer here than on the sea, but still cold.

She knew it could not have escaped his notice—the worn little path through the long weeds, visible by the starlight. Only regular traffic or maintenance would cause the weeds not to grow there.

Control nodded, face unreadable in the darkness, and stooped to pick up a stick, brandished it. They had no guns—had long ago discarded their few modern supplies, acknowledgment of Area X's strange effects, keeping just one flashlight. Turning on that flashlight now would have felt unwise and foolish. But she had a gutting knife, and she took that out.

The lighthouse door lay on the landward side, and the path led right to it. The original door was missing, but in its place leaned a massive wooden barricade that she slowly realized was the door from a stable or something similar. With some effort, they moved it to the side, stood in the threshold. The inside smelled of decay and driftwood. It smelled fresher than she'd expected.

She lit a match, saw, obscured by shadows surging against

the walls, that the central spiral staircase lay naked, like a giant stone corkscrew, in the middle of the ground floor, and that it ascended into a giant hole above. Unstable at best. At worst, all of it about to come down.

As if reading her thoughts, Control said, "It could probably still hold our weight. They built it in such a way that the supporting walls take most of the burden. But that's pretty raw."

She nodded, could see the steel rods running through it now, a skeleton that inspired a little more confidence.

The match went out. She lit another.

The ground floor was covered in dead leaves and a smattering of branches, a catacomb of smaller rooms hidden from view at the back. A bare concrete floor, with the scars to show that someone had ripped up the floorboards.

The match went out. She thought she heard a sound.

"What was that?"

"The wind?" But he didn't seem certain.

She lit another match.

Nothing. No one.

"Only the wind." He sounded relieved. "Should we just sleep here, or explore the rooms in back?"

"Explore—I don't want any surprises."

The match went out from a gust of wind coming from the stairwell.

"We need to make these matches last longer," Control complained.

She lit another match, screamed, Control startled beside her.

A shadow sat halfway up the steps of the staircase, a rifle aimed at them. The shadow resolved into a black woman wearing army fatigues—compactly built, curly hair cut close to her head.

"Hello, Control," the woman said, ignoring her.

Ghost Bird recognized her from her first debriefing at the Southern Reach.

Grace Stevenson, the assistant director.

0009: THE DIRECTOR

owry's secret facility, on a dreary part of the east coast, with gravel beaches and stark yellowing grass, has been set up on the bones of an old military base. Here, Lowry has been perfecting his neurology and conditioning techniques—some would say brainwashing. From atop a mossy hill hollowed out for his command and control, he rules a strange world of decommissioned silver harbor mines lolling on the lawn below and rusting gun emplacements from wars fought seventy years ago. Lowry has had a replica of Area X's lighthouse built and a replica of the expedition base camp, and even a hole in the ground meant to approximate the little known about the "topographical anomaly." You knew this before you were summoned, and in your imagination this false lighthouse and false base camp were foreboding and almost supernatural in their effect. But, in truth, standing there with Lowry, looking out across his domain through a long plate of tinted glass, you feel more as if you're staring at a movie set: a collection of objects that without the animation of Lowry's paranoia and fear, his projection of a story upon them, are inert and pathetic. No, not even a movie set, you realize. More like a seaside carnival in the winter, in the off-season, when even the beach is a poem about loneliness. How lonely is Lowry out here, surrounded by all of this?

"Sit down and I'll get you a drink."

Very Lowry, but you don't sit and you politely decline the drink, staring out at the shore, the sea. It's a gray, crappy day and the weather reports say it may even snow. The water has an oily quality from offshore pollution, the dull light creating rainbows across its still surface.

"No? Well, I'll make you one anyway." Also very Lowry, and you're tenser than you were a moment ago.

The room is narrow, and you're standing at the window, behind you a long, low lime-green couch with a steel frame covered by psychedelic orange pillows. Shaped like crude downward-diving breasts, porcelain light fixtures hang in rows of twenty from a ceiling slanted to the curve of the hill. Their glow melts across the couches, tables, and wooden floor in soft overlapping circles. The whole back plate of glass sealing off the room from behind is a mirror, projecting your images and protecting you from the truth that this isn't really a lounge and you're here not by invitation but by order. That this is an interrogation room of sorts.

The refined Lowry, so unlike the uncouth Lowry—leaning forward from a chair catty-corner to the couch—has been spending a deliberate eternity prying ice cubes from a bowl on the glass table in front of you into the glasses, one by one, clink by clink. He opens a bottle of scotch with care, and, with a tap of the bottle neck against glass, pours out two fingers.

Lowry, bent over his task, letting the moment elongate

further. The mane of golden hair now silver, grown long. The determined, solid head on a thick neck, the landmarks of features upon a face that had served him well: craggy good looks, people say, like an astronaut or old-fashioned movie star. People who have never seen the photographs of Lowry after the first expedition into Area X, that dehydrated unshaven face still imprinted with an encounter with the horrific unknown, Lowry gone somewhere no one else had ever gone. "An honorable guy" back then, charismatic and direct. Even gone to fat a little, a thickness around the stomach, he retains some charm. Even with a left eye prone to wandering as if a tiny planet is straining out of alignment, being pulled to the side by the attraction of something just out of the frame. Those bright, piercing blue eyes. One scintilla more brilliant and all of his charisma would be wasted— the determined nose, the resolute jaw almost a parody, like the coastline of a confident country—undermined by a stare too glacial. But there is just enough warmth in that gaze to preserve the rest of the illusion.

"There, done," he says, and you're nervous to the inverse of his calm and reverential care for the drinks.

Lowry's replaced the bunkers hidden in the adjacent hills with secret labs. Full of higher-order animals, is the ridiculous rumor, brought here to bear the brunt of Lowry's imagination, as if to punish nature for having punished him. Experiments on neurons, neural linkage, synapse control. Boring, impossible things like that. You doubt he ever brings his fourth wife here, or his children, even though the family's summer house is conveniently nearby. No tours of Daddy's workplace.

You wonder what Lowry does for fun. Or maybe he's doing it now.

He turns, a drink in each hand, dressed in his expensive dark blue suit, his gold-tipped dress shoes. He smiles, holds both the drinks outstretched, the motion doubled, tripled, by the mirror at his back. The gleam of perfect teeth. The wide politician's smile. A dangerous smile.

It's hardly even a flick of the wrist, there's such economy of motion. So compact a movement of elbow and arm that for a moment you don't realize that your drink is being thrown at you.

The glass that was in his left hand smashes against the window near your head, shatters. As you recoil, sidestep, gaze never leaving Lowry, liquid splashes your shoes and splinters of glass needle your ankles. The window's bullet-proof glass, reinforced. It doesn't even reverberate. The drink in Lowry's right hand isn't even trembling. But, then, neither are you.

Lowry's still smiling.

He says, "Now that you've had your drink, maybe we can get the fuck down to it."

You recline, uncomfortable against the pillows, looking out at the sea, the lighthouse, the remains of the glass of scotch on the floor. You wonder if he has them specially made so they break easier. Lowry sits in his chair, leaning forward like a predator. You remain very still. Your heart is beating out some secret code you can't decrypt. Lowry's broad face up close, the ruddiness caused by alcohol, the abrupt lowering of the thick shoulders, the way the stomach spills onto his lap as he leans forward, his own drink still in hand. You haven't seen any sign of his staff, but you know security waits right outside the door.

"So you thought you'd take a closer look, huh, Cynthia? Thought you'd use my own security codes and bypass your superiors and take a quick peek. Couldn't resist seeing what's beyond the curtain."

It was a good plan; it should have worked. You should have been invisible coming back across. But Lowry had spies among the border command, had been alerted, and the best Grace could do was confiscate the materials they brought back, put them in the Southern Reach storage cathedral, mislabeled as from a prior expedition. Lowry'd had you held at the military base, top secret, before flying you up here. Whitby had been debriefed and then placed under a kind of house arrest.

"I already knew what was there."

A gigantic snort—of contempt, of disbelief. "Typical desk jockey. Thinks just because they've read the reports, just because they're in charge, they know something." Said without irony.

His breath is sweet, too sweet, as if something's on the verge of rotting inside him. The eyes are unstable, hostile, but otherwise his expression is unreadable. He looks like a man who, with just one more drink, is capable of almost anything.

"So you saunter across and have yourselves a great little holiday. Relax on the beach, right? Once you were across, got a little kinky thinking about being in that place with your boy toy, Whitby? Wanted a bit of lighthouse on the lighthouse steps?"

Silence is the best response. Central sees the sophisticated version of Lowry. You see the dregs, whatever he can get away with.

"You've got nothing to say to me, then. Nothing? No annotation? No further explanation?"

"I turned in my report."

He's half up out of his seat at that, but you don't move at all. Even at the age of nine on the forgotten coast you knew better than to run from a bear or wild dog. You stand your ground, face them down. Maybe even growl. Would you have done the same when the rules changed, when it became Area X? You don't know. You're sweating under all those ridiculous lights.

"I'm trying to get inside your head without getting inside your head, if you know what I mean," Lowry says. "I'm trying to understand how we got here. Trying to see if there's a good fucking reason I shouldn't just let Central fire you."

The Central egg opening up like a mouth to issue an order to make you spontaneously combust or, more likely, evaporate like mist. But this means Lowry's the main reason you haven't been fired yet, which gives you back a sense of hope.

"I couldn't keep sending in expeditions under my orders without going myself." You couldn't let them be the only ones to have the experience.

"*Your* orders? *My* orders, not *your* orders. You get that straight." He slams his glass down on the table between you. An ice cube escapes, slides across the surface onto the floor. You resist the urge to pick it up, put it back in his glass.

"And Whitby—you just had to recruit him for your sad little expedition, too?"

You could reveal that Whitby wanted to go, but you can't predict how Lowry would react. Whitby's always been beyond

Lowry, a fundamental misunderstanding between tragically different life-forms.

"I didn't want to go alone. I needed backup."

"*I'm* your backup. And involving the assistant director in all of this—that was a good idea, too?"

Grace might hate Lowry, but for some reason Lowry half liked Grace. Which, if she ever found out, would disgust her.

"None of it was a good idea. It was a lapse in judgment . . . But it's hard to send men into battle without going into battle yourself." Grace's idea for a defense. Keep it simple. Keep it old school.

"Cut the bullshit. Did Grace suggest you say that? I bet she did."

Have you missed a bug this time around, or is this just a guess?

Again: "You've got our reports."

Lowry is the only one who does have them. The army's border command knows this but Grace has concealed it from the Southern Reach, at Lowry's request—"for reasons of morale and security clearance"—pending a final decision. Officially you're still taking a very long vacation, and Whitby's on administrative leave.

"Fuck your reports. You're trying to hide Whitby from me"—not strictly true—"and your findings seem flimsy, incomplete. You were in there almost three weeks and your report is four pages long?"

"Nothing that unusual happened. Considering."

"Considering bullshit. What did Whitby see? Something real or just another fucking hallucination? Do you understand what could've happened by going there? Do you understand what you could've stirred up?" The words coming out of his mouth slur together so it sounds like *stirrups*.

"I understand." A toy lighthouse suddenly come to life.

Lowry, leaning in then, lurching in, to whisper, in a miasma of that sweet rotting breath, "You want to know what's funny. What's so fucking funny?"

"No." Here it comes. As if he's somebody's gramps at a holiday gathering. The same story almost every time.

"Back in the day. Back then, you got it all wrong. If you'd 'fessed up' to the old Ess Arr during the interview, the kicker is they might've taken you anyway. You might've gotten hired. They might have done it, knowing the old director. True, maybe a sick kind of fascination attached, like with some special, intelligent lab animal—a special, particularly magnificent white rabbit, say. True, you'd never have made director, but, fuck, that job sucks, right? As you're finding out. As you're going to keep finding out. Problem now, though, is the deception's gone on too long. So what the hell do we do."

The problem, from your point of view, is less the past than the present. The time when you could somehow have tried to contain Lowry or influence him is long gone. As soon as he'd ascended to Central, been canonized, you couldn't touch him.

That person, the person you'd been back before Ess Arr, had been careful—so careful trying to get to the point where you could do something reckless like cross the border into Area X.

Your father had been paranoid about the government,

every once in a while took on something shady to supplement the day job as a part-time bartender—a low-level grifter. He didn't want any involvement. He didn't want any trouble. So he kept the government out of it, didn't tell you your mother was probably dead and that you weren't going back to the forgotten coast ever again until he absolutely had to. Told you to give vague answers to the men who came to interview you about your mother—it would be better for your mother that way. Anything to avoid a light shining on his "business ventures."

"You don't know this, 'cause you're too young," came the usual lecture, "but politicians run all the big scams. Government's the thief of all time. That's why it tries so hard to catch thieves—it doesn't like the competition. You don't want *that* on your back your whole life just because you were in the wrong place at the wrong time."

When he did tell you that she was gone, you cried for a month, even as that look on your father's face, the gruff warning, the way everything in your constantly moving household operated on caution, indoctrinated you in the merits of silence.

Over time your memory of your mother faded, in the way of not knowing if an image or moment was something you'd experienced or seen going through the photographs your dad kept in a shoe box in the closet. Not in the way of keeping something close rather than pushing it away. You would stare at pictures of your mother—on the deck with friends, a drink in her hand or on the beach with your dad—and imagine that she was the one saying, "Don't forget me," feel ashamed when it was the lighthouse keeper's face that kept coming back to you.

Tentative and then with more determination, you started your own investigation. You learned there was something called the Southern Reach, devoted to cleaning up the "environmental devastation" in what had been the forgotten coast and was now Area X. Your scrapbook grew so fat it was hard to open, filled with clippings from books, newspapers, magazines, and, later, websites. Conspiracy theories dominated, or speculative recastings of the government's official story. The truth always something vague and out of focus that had nothing to do with what you'd seen, with the sense you'd had of the lighthouse keeper becoming *different*.

In your first year of college, you realized that you wanted to work for the Southern Reach, no matter what their role, and, with your grifter's sense of the truth, that your past would be a liability. So you changed your name, hired a private investigator to help you hide the rest, and went on to pursue a degree. Cognitive psychology, focused on perceptual psychology, with a minor in organizational psychology as well. You married a man you never really loved, for a variety of reasons, divorced him fifteen months later, and spent close to five years working as a consultant, applying and reapplying to Central with application-form answers tailor-made to give you a shot at the Southern Reach.

The director at the time, a navy man, loved by all but not hard enough by far, hadn't interviewed you. Lowry had— still at the Southern Reach back then and with his own agenda. He liked to acquire his power sideways. There had been the formal meeting in his office, and then you'd gone out to the edge of the courtyard and had a different kind of interview.

"We can't be overheard out here," he'd said, and alarm

bells had gone off. Irrational thought that he was going to proposition you, like some of Dad's friends. Something beyond his polite demeanor, his well-made clothes, his air of authority, must have warned you.

But Lowry had something more long-term in mind.

"I had my own people check you out. It was a good effort there, all that work to disguise yourself. A solid B for effort, all of that, sure. Not bad at all, considering. But I still found out, and that means Central would have, too, if I hadn't covered up your tracks. What was left of them." A broad smile, a genial manner. You could have been talking about sports or the swamp sweltering there in front of you, seeming to simmer in its own thick broth.

You cut to the important bit: "Are you going to turn me in?" Throat dry, it seeming hotter than it had a moment before. Memories of your father being taken off to jail for petty fraud, always with the bravado of a smile and a blown kiss, as if the point after all was to get caught, to have an audience, to be noticed.

A chuckle from Lowry, and you intimidated by what struck you back then as his sophistication despite his failings. His verve. The way he filled out the suit, and the way his face reflected experience, like he'd seen what you wanted to see, been where you wanted to be.

"Turn you in, Gloria . . . I mean, Cynthia. Turn you in? To whom? The guys in charge of keeping track of fake names and false identities? The forgotten coast truthers? No, I don't think so. I don't think I'm going to turn you in to anyone." The unspoken thought: *I'm going to keep you all for myself.*

"What do you want?" you asked. Thankful, for once, that

being your father's daughter meant sometimes you could cut right through the bullshit.

"Want?" Disingenuous to the core. "Nothing. Nothing yet, anyway. In fact, it's all about you . . . Cynthia. I'm going to walk back in there with you and recommend you for the job. And if you pass training at Central, then we'll see. As for all the rest of it . . . that'll just be our secret. Not really a little secret, but a secret."

"Why would you do that?" Incredulous, not sure you had heard right.

With a wink: "Oh, I only really trust people who've been to Area X. Even pre–Area X."

At first, the price wasn't so bad. All he wanted, off the record, told to him and him alone, was an account of your last days on the forgotten coast. The lighthouse keeper, the Séance & Science Brigade. "Describe the man and the woman," he said, meaning Henry and Suzanne, and all of his questions about the S&SB sounded as if you were filling in pieces of some story he'd already heard part of before.

Within months, the favors asked for and reluctantly given multiplied—support for this or that initiative or recommendation, and when you had more influence, to push against certain things, to be less than enthusiastic, to stall. Mostly, you realize, on certain committees connected to the science division, to undermine or curtail Central's influence within the Southern Reach. All of it clever and by degrees so that you didn't really notice the escalation until you were so mired in it that it was just part of your job.

Eventually, Lowry supported your bid to become director. Coming to the Southern Reach had been like being allowed to listen to the heartbeat of a mysterious beast. But as director you came even closer—terrifyingly closer, trapped within the chamber walls, needing time to adjust. Time exploited by Lowry, of course.

Tossed onto the table: the latest satellite footage from above Area X, images from on high reduced to 8½×11 glossies. Glamour shots of an inexhaustible resource. This blank mimicry of the normal, marred only by the blurs you might expect to find on photos taken by ghost hunters. Definitive proof of a change, this blurring. As if somehow the Southern Reach is losing the ability to see even the lie.

"Evil advances with good. But these terms have no meaning in Area X. Or to Area X. So why should they always apply to us in pursuit of an enemy to whom they go unrecognized? An indifferent context deserves equal indifference from us—if we want to survive."

You're not expected to answer, Lowry taking a break to philosophize as he fills up his drink for a second time. Nor would you know *what* to answer, for you would never characterize Lowry as *indifferent*, or as expressing indifference through his actions. As ever, this is part of the deception: the ability to convey authority by instilling in others his own confidence.

Lowry's already threatened to put you under hypnosis, but the one thing you have resolved, having lived on the outskirts of Lowry's experiments, is that you will never allow him that. Always hoping that Lowry must have limits, can't be untouchable, can't operate without some constraint from above. Surely every action he takes reveals something about his motives to someone somewhere with the power to intervene?

So you're at what appears to be an impasse.

Then he surprises you.

"I want you to meet someone else who has a stake in this. Someone you know already. Jackie Severance."

Not a name you expected to hear. But there she is—escorted in by Mary Phillips, one of Lowry's assistants, through the mirror door to your side of the glass, Severance oblivious to the way her heels are crunching broken glass. Dressed as impeccably as always, still addicted to scarves.

Has she been listening the whole time? The dynastic successor to the legendary Jack Severance. Jackie, about fifteen years removed from her last stint with the Southern Reach—a bright star still shining in the firmament of Central's personal cosmology, despite a dark star of a son in the service that she's had to rescue more than once. Lowry the outlaw and Severance the insider seem unlikely allies. One's holding the silver egg in her hand and petting it. The other is trying to smash it with an invisible hammer.

What's the play, here? Does Lowry hold something over her, or does she hold something over Lowry?

"Jackie is going to be my adviser on this situation. She's going to be *involved* from now on. And before we make a final decision on what to do with you, I want you to repeat for her everything that's in the report—everything that happened to you across the border. One last time."

Severance smiles the way a crocodile smiles and sits on the couch next to you while Lowry shuffles off to make her a drink. "Nothing too formal, Cynthia. Nothing you need to prep. And in no particular order. You can tell it in whatever order you like."

"That's kind of you, Jackie." It's not kind—it's just an attempt to get a different version. Which makes this a ritual of sorts, with a preordained outcome.

So you go back over it all again with Severance, who stops you from time to time with questions blunter than you expected, coming from someone you've always thought of as a political animal.

"You didn't go anywhere else? No shortcuts or other excursions?"

"Excursions?"

"It's easy to omit what doesn't seem relevant."

The same flat smile.

You don't bother to answer.

"Did you bring anything back with you?"

"Just the usual recovery along the way, of past expedition equipment, as happens with many expeditions." The story you and Whitby have decided on, because you want to hold on to the plant and phone, test them at the Southern Reach, not have them taken by Central. You're the experts, not Central.

"What sense did you get of the journals in the lighthouse? Was there an impression or idea you had about them, seeing them all like that? If that's not too vague."

No particular sense or impression or idea, you tell her. They were just journals. Because you don't want to go there, don't yet want to relive the end of your trip, the things that happened in the lighthouse.

"And nothing there seemed unusual or out of order?"

"No." You're selling the simpler story of danger in the tunnel.

Later, leaning in, conspiratorial, just you girls: "Gloria. Cynthia. Why'd you do it? Really?" As if Lowry's not in the room.

You shrug, give a pained smile.

At the end of your account, Severance smiles and says, "It's possible that we'll file this under 'never happened' and move on. And if so, you have Lowry to thank." A hand on your arm, though, as if to say, "Don't forget I helped." You get to keep Whitby, too, she says, if Whitby passes a psych eval you personally help conduct at Central, off the books. But. "You are vouching for him. You are responsible for him." Like you're a child asking to keep a pet.

The new border commander will be handpicked by Lowry and report to both Lowry and Severance, and they will institute procedures so that, as Lowry puts it, "You and Whitby and any other son of a bitch stupid enough to try another jailbreak thinks twice."

A few useless pleasantries and Jackie's left the room as fast as she got there, the encounter so brief you wonder why else she's here, what other business she has with Lowry. Has she walked into a trap, or has Lowry? Trying to remember the exact date when Severance came to the Southern Reach. Going through a list of her tasks, her duties, and where she was when. Thinking that there is some part of the puzzle you can't see, that you *need* to see.

Lowry, there at the center of his secret headquarters, overlooking the sea as snow in thick flakes begins to cover the grass, the sea mines, the little paths. With the geese and seagulls that will never care about Lowry's plans or your own huddled by the fake lighthouse, as deceived by it as the expeditions have been by the real one. But Severance is out there now, walking by the rocks, staring across the water. She's on her phone, but Lowry doesn't see her—just his own reflection, and she's trapped there, within his outline.

Lowry, pumping himself up, pacing in front of the glass, smacking his chest with one hand. "And what I want is this: The next expedition, they don't go to Central. They come here. They receive their training *here*. You want Area X to react? You want something to change? I'll change it. I'll coil things so far up inside Area X's brain, things that'll have a sting in the tail. That'll draw blood. That'll fucking make the enemy know we're the resistance. That we're on to them."

Some trails go cold fast; some trails take a long time to pick up and follow. Seeing Severance walking along the ridge of black rocks near the lighthouse, even a fake lighthouse, raises your hackles, makes you want to say, "That is *mine*, not yours."

Lowry's still standing over you and ranting about what will happen and how it's going to happen. Of course he wants more control. Of course he is going to get it.

But now you know, too, what you've only guessed at before: Beneath Lowry's bluster, he feels that your fates are intertwined. That he's more bound to you than ever.

After six months, you will be able to return to the Southern Reach. No one there will know why you were gone so long, and Grace won't tell them, promises she'll have pushed them so hard in the interim that "they won't have time to think about it."

While you wait out your suspension at home, you have this image in your head of Grace as a tall, stern black woman in a white lab coat and the tricornered hat of a general, holding a saber at arm's length, for some reason standing in the prow of a rowboat, crossing a strategically important river. When it's time for her to drop the hat, get rid of the boat, cede control back to you, how will she feel about that?

Single dim thought most nights, after a doctor's appointment or buying groceries for dinner: Which world am I really living in? The one in which you can hear Whitby's screams in the lighthouse intermingling with the screams from the first expedition, or the one in which you're putting cans of soup in the cupboard. Can you exist in both? Do you want to? When Grace calls to ask how your day is going, should you say "Same as usual" or "Awful, like conducting autopsies over and over again for no reason"?

Sitting on a stool in the bar at Chipper's—that's the same, isn't it, after you come back? Perhaps even more so, given you have more time to spend there. The Realtor's around a lot, too. She talks all the time—about a trip up north to visit her family, about a movie she saw, about local politics. Sometimes the veteran with the perpetual beer in hand dredges up a long-ago memory of his kids, trying to be part of the conversation.

As the Realtor and the drunk talk past and through you, you're nodding as if you know what they're talking about, as if you can relate, when all you can see now are two images of the lighthouse keeper superimposed, saying the same thing at different times, to two different versions of you. One in darkness and one in light.

ACCEPTANCE

"You're thinking of your own children, aren't you?" says the Realtor. "I can tell."

Your mind must have wandered. The mask must have slipped.

"Yes, you're right," you say. "Sure."

You have another beer, start to tell the Realtor all about your kids—where they go to school, how you wish you saw them more often, that they're studying to be doctors. That you hope to see them around the holidays. That they seem to belong to a different world now that they're all grown up. The veteran, standing at the end of the bar, staring past the Realtor at you, has a strange look on his face. A look of recognition, as if he knows what you're doing.

Hell, maybe you should play some songs on the jukebox, too. Maybe go take a turn at karaoke later, have a few more beers, make up a few more details of your life. Only, the Realtor left at some point, and it's just you and the veteran and some people trickling in late who you don't know, won't ever know. The floor's sticky, dark with old stains. The bottles behind the bar have water-cooler cups over them, to keep the fruit flies out. There's a sheen off the bar top that's not entirely natural. Behind you, the lanes are dark and the faded heavens have risen again, unimaginable wonders across the ceiling, some of them requiring a moment to recognize.

Because the other world always bleeds into this one. Because no matter how you try to keep what happened at the lighthouse between you and Whitby, you know it will leak out eventually, in some form, will have consequences.

At the lighthouse, Whitby had wandered, and you were still drifting through the downstairs when you realized that you couldn't hear him moving around in the next room anymore. In the stillness and the dust, the way the light through the broken front door made the darkness murky, you expected to find him standing in a corner, a figure luminous in shadow.

But soon enough you realized he'd gone up the lighthouse stairs, headed for the very top. There came the sounds of fighting and the splintering of wood. One voice rising above the other, both curiously similar, and how could there be a second voice at all? So you followed fast, and as you climbed, there was both a doubling and a dissonance, for in memory, the steps had been much wider, the trek much longer, the space inside the lighthouse conveying a kind of weightlessness, the walls once painted white, the windows open to receive the sky, the scent of cut grass brought by Saul. But in the darkness, worried about Whitby, you had become a giant or the lighthouse had become lost or *diminished*, not just undone by time, but contracting, like the spiraling fossil of a shell, leading you to a place no longer familiar. Erasing, with each step, what you thought you knew.

At the top, you discovered Whitby down in the watch room panting like an animal, his clothes torn and blood on his hands, and the strange impression that the edges of the journals were rippling, enveloping Whitby, trying to drown him. No one else there, just Whitby with an impossible story of encountering his doppelgänger, False Whitby, on the landing, chasing him up to the lantern room, until they had fallen through the open trapdoor onto the mound of journals, off-balance and awkward. The smell of them. The bulk of them. The feel of them around Real Whitby and False Whitby as they toiled in their essential opposition, now in and now out of the light coming through the open trapdoor.

How to verify this story of not one but two Whitbys? Not Whitby punching himself, kicking himself, biting himself, awash in flapping paper, but doing this to another version. His wounds were inconclusive.

But the tableau fascinates you, returns to you during your six months off, even while chopping onions for chili in your kitchen or mowing the lawn.

Sometimes you try to imagine what it would have been like if you had arrived earlier, not in the aftermath, and stopped there, at the top of the steps, peering down into that space, unable to move, watching the two Whitbys struggle. You can almost believe that Whitby birthed Whitby, that in exploring Area X, something in Whitby's own nature created this paradox, with one version, one collection of impulses, thoughts, and opinions, trying, once and for all, to exterminate the other.

Until two pale hands reach out to choke one pale throat, and two faces stare at each other, inches apart, the face above deformed by a paroxysm of rage while the face below remains calm, so calm, surrounded by the ripped and crumpled journals. The white paper with the red line of the margin, the blue lines to write on. The pages and pages of sometimes incomprehensible handwritten text. All of those journals without names but only functions noted, and sometimes not even that, as if Area X has snuck in its own accounts. Are they shifting and settling as if something huge sleeps beneath them, breathing in and out?

Is that a glow surrounding them, or surrounding Whitby? The Whitbys?

Until there is the crack. Of a neck? Of a spine? And the Whitby pinned against the mound goes slack and his head lolls to the side and the Whitby atop him, frozen, emits a kind of defeated sob and slides off Dead Whitby, awkwardly manages to wriggle and roll his way free . . . and sits there in the corner, staring at his own corpse.

Then, and only then, are you drawn to wonder whether your Whitby won—and who this other Whitby might have been, who in death would have seemed preternaturally calm, face smooth and unwrinkled, eyes wide and staring, only the angle of the body suggesting that some violence has been perpetrated upon it.

Afterward, you forced Whitby to come out of that space, to take some air by the railing, to look out on that gorgeous unknowable landscape. You pointed out old haunts disguised as your exhaustive encyclopedic knowledge of the forgotten coast. Whitby saying something to you—urgently, but you not really hearing him. You more intent on filling up the space between with your own script, your own interpretation—either to calm Whitby or to negate his experience. To forget about the mound of journals. A thing you don't want to consider for too long, that you put out of your mind because isn't that the way of things? To ignore the unreal so it doesn't become more real.

On the way down, you searched for Dead Whitby, but he still wasn't anywhere.

You may never know the truth.

But in what Whitby swore was Dead Whitby's backpack, you found two curious items: a strange plant and a damaged cell phone.

ACCEPTANCE

0010: CONTROL

Control woke to a boot and a foot, just six inches from where he lay on his side under some blankets. The black tread of the army-issue boot was worn down in tired ridges like the map of a slope of hills. Dried mud and sand commingled there and in the sporadic black studs meant to provide a better grip. A dragonfly wing had been broken along the axis of that tread, pulverized into rounded panes and an emerald glitter. Smudges of grass, a smear of seaweed that had dried on the side of the boot.

The landscape struck him as evidence of a lack of care not reflected by the tidy stacking of provisions, the regular sweeping out of leaves and debris from the landing. Next to the boot: the pale brown sole of a muscular foot that seemed to belong to a different person, the toenails clipped, the big toe wrapped tight in fresh gauze with a hint of dried blood staining through.

Both boot and foot belonged to Grace Stevenson.

Above the rise of her foot, he could see she held the three weathered, torn pages he'd rescued from Whitby's report. In her army fatigues, including a short-sleeved shirt,

Grace looked thinner, and gray had appeared at her temples. She looked as if she had endured a lot in a short time. A pistol lay in a holster by her side, along with a knapsack.

He twisted onto his back, sat up, and shoved up against the wall catty-corner to her, the window between them. The raucous birds that had briefly woken him at dawn were quiet now, probably out foraging or doing whatever birds did. Could it be as late as noon? Ghost Bird lay curled up in a camo-patterned sleeping bag, had throughout the night made little jerking motions and sounds that reminded Control of his cat in the grip of some vision.

"Why the hell did you go through my pockets?" Somehow the accusatory tone abandoned the words as he said them, relieved to find his dad's carving still in his jacket.

She ignored him, leafing through Whitby's last words, lingering between a smile and a frown, intense but uncommitted. "This has not changed since the last time I saw it. It's even more full of shit now . . . probably. Except back then the author was a crackpot. Singular. Now we're all fucking crackpots."

"Fuck?"

A quizzical look. "What's wrong with 'fuck'? Area X doesn't give a crap if I swear."

She continued to read and reread the pages, shaking her head at certain parts, while Control stared, still feeling possessive. He was more attached to those pages than he'd thought, afraid she might just ball them up and chuck them out the window.

"Can I have those back?"

A weary amusement, something in her smile that told him

he was transparent. "Not yet. Not just yet. Get some breakfast. Then file a formal request." She went back to reading again.

Frustrated, he looked around the space. Compulsively tidy, as he'd thought on first glance. Lock-action rifles in a precise row against the far wall, next to her sleeping space, which was a mattress covered with a sheet and blanket she had tucked in tight. A creased wallet photo of her girlfriend, propped on a ledge, curling edges smoothed out. Cans of food lined up against the long side wall, and protein bars. Cups and bottles of drinking water that she must have gotten from a stream or well. Knives. A portable stove. Pots, pans. Lugged all the way from the Southern Reach building or scavenged from the ambushed convoy on the shore? How much she had found on the island he wouldn't want to guess.

Control was just about to get up and pick out a can when she spilled the pages on the floor between them, right on a spot damp from rainwater.

"Dammit." He scrambled forward on all fours to retrieve them.

The muzzle of Grace's gun dug into the side of his head near his ear.

He remained extremely still, looking across at where Ghost Bird slept.

"Are you real?" she asked, in a kind of rasp, as if her voice had gone gray along with her hair. Should he have divined something more profound from her boot, her bandaged toe?

"Grace, I—"

She smacked him across the forehead with the muzzle, shoved the mouth of the gun harder into his skin, whispered in his ear, "Don't use my fucking name. Don't ever use my name! No names. It may still know names."

"*What* may know names?" Stifling the word *Grace*.

"Shouldn't you already know?" Contemptuous.

"Put the gun down."

"No."

"Can I sit up?"

"No. *Are you real?*"

"I don't know what that means," he said, as calmly as he could. Wondered if he could move fast enough to get out of the line of fire, push the gun from his temple before she blew his brains out.

"I think you do. Tampered with. Spoiled goods. A hallucination. An apparition."

"I'm as real as you," he said. But the secret fear behind that, the one he didn't want to voice. Along with the thought that he didn't know what Grace had endured since he'd seen her last. That he wasn't sure he knew her now. Any more than he knew himself now.

"What script are you running off of? Central or the L-word?"

"The L-word?" Absurd thoughts. *Lie? Lighthouse? Lesbian?* Then realized she meant Lowry. "Neither. I cut off hypnotic suggestion. I freed myself." Not sure he believed that.

"Should we run a test?"

"Don't try it. I really mean it—*don't*."

"I wouldn't," Grace said, as if he'd accused her of high crimes. "That's L's kink. But I know the signs by now. There is a pinched look you all get, a paleness. The hands curling into claws. His signature, written all over you."

"Residual. Just residual."

"Still, you admit it."

"I admit I don't know why the living fuck you're holding a gun to my head!" he shouted. Had Ghost Bird heard *nothing*, or was she pretending to sleep? And there, as if to call him a liar anyway: what Ghost Bird called "the brightness," curious, interested, questing. It rose now as a tightness in his chest, a spasm in his left thigh as he remained on all fours being interrogated by his assistant director.

A pause, an increased pressure of the muzzle at his head; he flinched. Then the pressure was gone, along with her shadow. He looked over. Grace was back against the wall, gun still in her hand.

He sat up, hands on his thighs, forced a deep breath in, out, and considered his options. It was the kind of field situation his mother would've called "an either without the or." He could either find some way to smooth it over or go for the rifles against the wall. Not a real choice. Not with Ghost Bird out of action.

Slowly, carefully, he picked his three Whitby pages off the floor, willed himself to move past the danger of the moment: "Is that your usual welcome?"

Her face a kind of impassive mask now, daring him to challenge her. "Sometimes it ends with me pulling the trigger. Control, I am not interested in bullshit. You don't have any idea what I've been through. What might be real . . . and what might not be real."

He slumped against the wall, holding Whitby's pages against his chest. Was there something in the corner of his eye?

"There's nothing to this world," he said, "but what our senses tell us about it, and all I can do is the best I can based on that information." Even though he didn't trust the world anymore.

"There was a time I would have shot first, before you even left the boat."

"Thank you?" Putting as much punch into that as possible.

A curt nod, like he was serious, and Grace shoved the gun back in its holster on her right side, away from him. "I always have to be careful." He noted the tension in her upper arm and heard the sharp click as she toyed with the clasp on the holster. Opening it. Closing it.

"Sure," he said. "I see someone got to your big toe. That kind of thing could make a person paranoid."

She ignored that, said, "When did you get here?"

"Five days ago."

"How long since the border shifted?"

Had Grace lost track of the days out here, by herself? "No more than two weeks."

"How did you get across?"

He told her, omitting any detail about where the door under the sea might lie. Omitting, too, that Ghost Bird had created it.

Grace considered all of that for a long moment, nursing a bitter smile that rejected interpretation. But he was on high alert again; she'd taken out her gutting knife with her left hand and was creating circles in the dust beside her. This wasn't just a paranoid debriefing. There were higher stakes and his own analysis to undertake: Had Grace just been rattled by something here on the island, or suffered the kind of shock that rearranged your thought processes, forever impaired your judgment?

ACCEPTANCE

With as much gentleness as he could muster: "Do you mind if I wake up Ghost Bird now?"

"I gave her a sedative with her water last night."

"You *what*?" Echoes of a dozen domestic terrorism interrogations, all the symbols and signs.

"Are you her new best friend now? Do you trust her? And do you even know what I mean?"

Trusted her not to be the enemy. Trusted her to be human. Wanted to say, *I trust her as much as I trust myself*, but that wouldn't satisfy Grace. Not this version of Grace.

"What has happened here?" He felt betrayed, sad. To have come so far, but that old dynamic—sharing a smoke in the courtyard of the Southern Reach—had turned to ash.

A shudder passed through Grace, some hidden stressor coming to the surface, moving through and past, as if waking only now from a nightmare.

"It takes getting used to," she said, staring down at the patterns she'd made in the dust. "It takes getting used to, knowing that everything we did meant nothing. That Central abandoned us. That our new director abandoned us."

"I tried to—" *I tried to stay; you told me to go.* But that clearly wasn't how she saw it. And now they were at the very edge of the world, and she was taking it out on him.

"I tried to blame you, at first, when I was getting things straight in my head. I did blame you. But what could you have done? Nothing. Central probably programmed you to do what they wanted."

Going over those horrific moments again, jammed together in his memory, wedged in there at odd angles. The look on Grace's face in that moment of extremes, as the border advanced on the Southern Reach, weighing the possibility that he'd said nothing to her at all. Hadn't been as close to her and hadn't put his hand on her arm. Just thought he had.

"Your face, Control. If you could have seen the expression on your face," she said, as if they were talking about his reaction to a surprise party. The wall of the building becoming flesh. The director returned in a wave of green light. The weight of that. The fingers of his left hand had curled around the carving of Chorry in his jacket pocket. He released his grip, pulled his hand out, let his fingers open up. Examined the white curved indentations, fringed with pink.

"What happened to the people in the science division?"

"They decided to barricade the basement. But that place was changing very fast. I didn't stay long." Said so casually, too casually, talking about the disappearance of the world they had both known. *I didn't stay long.* One sentence disguising a multitude of horrors. Control doubted the staff had had a choice about what happened to them, sealed off by that sudden wall.

And Whitby? But, remembering the last transmission from his spy cameras, he didn't want to know about the W-word yet, or perhaps ever.

"What about . . . the director?"

That level gaze, even in this new context, even with her on edge, twitchy, tired, and underfed. That unbreakable ability to take responsibility, for anything and everything, and to keep pressing forward.

"I put a bullet in its head. As per prior orders. Once I determined that what had returned was an intruder, a copy, a fake."

She could not continue or had thought of something that had distracted her from the narrative, or was just trying to hold it together. What it had cost her to kill even a version of the person she had been so devoted to, could be said to have loved, Control couldn't guess.

After a while, he asked the inevitable question: "And what then?"

A shrug, as she stared at the ground. "I did what I had to. I scavenged what I could, took along those who were willing, and, per orders, I headed for the lighthouse. I went where she said. I did exactly what she said and we accomplished nothing. We made no difference. So she was wrong, just wrong, and she had no plan. No plan at all."

Raw hurt, an intensity to all of it, everything she had told him in such a calm voice. He focused on the bottom of her boot. The disembodied thorax of a velvet ant lay somewhere south of five o'clock.

"Is that why you didn't go back across the border?" he asked. Because of the guilt?

"There is *no way back* across the border!" Shouting it at him. "There is no *door* anymore."

Choking on seawater, buffeted by fish. A vision of drowning all over again.

No door. Not anymore.

Just whatever lay at the bottom of the sea. Maybe.

Lost in the thought of that, while Grace continued to talk about grotesque and impossible things.

From the windows of the landing of the ruined lighthouse, the world looked different, and not just because Grace had reentered it. A thin wall of fog had crept in from the sea to obscure the view, and the temperature had plummeted. They would need a fire by nightfall if that didn't change. Vague through both fog and tree cover: the ghostlike remains of houses, walls like warped slabs of flesh sagging into other, even more rotted, flesh. Running parallel to the sea, a road, then hills covered in a dense pine-and-oak forest.

There was no door in the border, leading home.

Grace had terminated the director's doppelgänger.

Grace had felt the border move through and past her. "It was like being *seen*. Being naked. Being reduced. Down to nothing." As she stared with a fierce devotion at the fragile photo, so carefully repaired, of the woman she loved back in the world.

She had retreated in good order with a number of Southern Reach personnel, security and otherwise, to the lighthouse, per the director's prior directive, an order unknown to him and somehow reaching out of the past to be given validity. At the lighthouse, some of the soldiers had begun to change and could not handle that change. Some had struck out for the tunnel and never been seen again. A few had spoken of vast shadows approaching from the seaward side. A schism between factions, including an argument with the border commander, had made their position worse. "None of them survived, I don't think. None of them knew how to survive."

But she remained vague about her actions in the lighthouse, her retreat to the island. "I did what I had to do." "That's all in the past. I have made my peace with it." "I don't sleep much." All of that a jumbled mess. *In the past?* It had just happened.

He had held on to some hope or delusion of last redoubts, of hardened siege mentality, of making common cause to fight the enemy. But that had been a sick fantasy, a kind of abject denial. The Southern Reach was done even if they hunkered down in the science division for the next century, became the subterranean seeds for pale cave-dwelling people who lived in fear and whose children's children heard cautionary tales of the fucked-up surface world waiting for them above.

"You had expedition training?" A guess, but an educated one based on her supplies.

"The basic protection package, we called it," Grace said. "The director came up with it for department heads, management." Because she'd valued their safety so much, had hoped the head of their props department would survive the apocalypse. He was willing to bet "the basic protection package" had applied only to Cynthia and Grace. She'd never shared it with him.

"If you planned for this, that means there's a mission?"

"Does it look like there's a mission?" A terse, ironic grin. Her tone of voice different, as if aware Ghost Bird, who had begun to stir, might be listening. "The mission is survival, John. The mission is to take it day by day. I keep to myself. I follow certain protocols. I am careful and quiet." Grace was prepared to live out her days here. She had already resigned herself to that paradigm.

Ghost Bird propped herself up on one arm. She didn't look groggy. Her stare seemed like a weapon, as if she had no need of a gun or knife. Ghost Bird didn't look like someone who would appreciate being told she had been drugged, so Control didn't. A respectful, fearful look Grace gave her, now that she wasn't a sleeping lump on the floor.

"What attacked the convoy?" Ghost Bird asked.

No *Good morning* or even an interest in what they'd been discussing. How much had she overheard, lying there? What had seeped into her half-conscious mind about fakes and the director's doppelgänger?

A grim chuckle from Grace, followed by a shrug, but no other answer.

Ghost Bird shrugged, fell upon a protein bar, gutted it with her knife, wolfed down the contents. Between bites: "This is horrible and stale. Have you encountered anything unusual on the island?"

"It's all unusual here," Grace said, with a kind of exhaustion, as if the question had been asked too often before.

"Have you seen the biologist?" Direct speaking to direct, and Control tense, waiting for that answer.

"Have I seen the biologist?" Turning that question over and over, examining it from all angles. "Have I seen the biologist?" Grace's clicking of the holster strap came quicker now, the pattern in the dust drawn at knife point more complex. Was that a helix? Was that two intertwining spirals? A starfish or just a star?

"Well, answer me, Grace," Ghost Bird said, rising now, standing in front of them with her hands at her sides, in the kind of relaxed yet perfectly balanced stance someone took if they expected trouble. If they'd had combat training.

The light through the landing window faded into shadow as a cloud crossed over. A bird outside was muttering or whispering in time to the circling of the knife blade. Far distant came the suggestion of something sonorous, mournful, perhaps an echo off the lighthouse stones. A gecko scuttled up the wall. Control didn't know if he should be worried about the foreground or something in the background. This was the only question that mattered to Ghost Bird, and Control didn't know what she would do if Grace wouldn't answer.

Grace stared over at Control, said, "If I sat here and told this copy"—pointing at Ghost Bird—"everything I've found, we would still be sitting here when hell froze over."

"Just *answer* the question," Ghost Bird muttered.

"Are we just passing through?" Control asked. "Should we be moving on?" That's what this came down to, in a way. Not Ghost Bird's question but Grace's attitude, the constant suspicion that wore on him.

"Do you know how long I've been on this island? Did you ever ask me that?"

"Have you seen the biologist?" Ghost Bird demanded in a kind of staccato growl.

"Ask me." The knife stabbed, vibrating, into the wooden floor of the landing. The hand on the holster had gone still, resting on the gun.

Control gave Ghost Bird a quick look. Had he misread something vital?

"How long have you been on the island?" he asked.

"Three years. I've been here *three* years."

Outside, all seemed still, so impossibly still. The gecko frozen on the wall. Control frozen in his thoughts. Satisfaction, that Grace could not quite suppress, etched into her worn face. To have told them something they couldn't have known, couldn't have seen coming.

"Three *years*," Control said, a plea for her to recant.

"I don't believe you," Ghost Bird said.

A generous laugh. "I don't blame you much. I don't blame you at all. You're right. I must just be some crazy bitch who went mad out here all on her own. I must be unable to cope with my situation. I must be fucking nuts. Sure. Must be. Except for this . . ."

Grace pulled a sheaf of pages out of her knapsack. Brittle, yellowing, they had handwriting on them. A rusting clasp in the corner.

She flung the pages at Ghost Bird's feet. "Read it. Read it before I waste time telling you anything else. Just read it."

Ghost Bird picked it up, looked at the first page in confusion.

"What is it?" Control asked. Some part of him not wanting to know. Not wanting another dislocation.

"The biologist's last will and testament," Grace said.

PART II
FIXED LIGHT

Writing, for me, is like trying to restart an engine that has rested for years, silent and rusting, in an empty lot—choked with water and dirt, infiltrated by ants and spiders and cockroaches. Vines and weeds shoved into it and sprouting out of it. A kind of coughing splutter, an eruption of leaves and dust, a voice that sounds a little like mine but is not the same as it was before; I use my actual voice rarely enough.

A great deal of time has passed since I placed words on paper, and for so long I felt no urge to do so again. I have felt more acutely than ever that here on the island I should *never be taken out of the moment*. To be taken out of the moment is dangerous—that is when things sneak their way in and then there is no present moment to return to. Only very recently have I begun to feel something like a *lack*, or anything beyond the thought that I would in this place simply exist and live out whatever span was allotted to me. Neither have I had any interest in *recounting*, in *setting down*, in *communicating* in what has come to seem such a mundane way. Perhaps it's no surprise, then, that I have started to write this several times, and that I abandoned three or four drafts of this . . . this document? This letter? This . . . whatever *this* is.

Perhaps, too, hesitance overtakes me because when I think of writing I glimpse the world I left behind. The world beyond, that when my thoughts drift toward it at all, is a hazy, indistinct sphere radiating a weak light, riddled through with discordant voices and images that cut across eyes and minds like a razor blade, and none of us able to even blink. It seems a myth, a kind of mythic tragedy, a lie, that I once lived there or that anyone lives there still. Someday the fish and the falcon, the fox and the owl, will tell tales, in their way, of this disembodied globe of light and what it contained, all the poison and all the grief that leaked out of it. If human language meant anything, I might even recount it to the waves or to the sky, but what's the point?

Still, having decided to finally let the brightness take me, after holding out against it for so many years, I am giving it one more try. Who will read this? I don't know, nor do I really care. Perhaps I am just writing for myself, that some further record exist of this journey, even if I can only tell the first part of a much longer story. But if someone does read it, know that I didn't live here waiting for rescue, hoping for a thirteenth expedition. If the world beyond appears to have abandoned the entire idea of expeditions, perhaps that's evidence of the sudden appearance of sanity. But the world beyond, or even the dangers of this one I live in, will be even less of a concern in a few days.

ACCEPTANCE

01: THE BRIGHTNESS

At first, there was always the island ahead of me, somewhere, along the coast, and my husband's presence in the bread-crumb notes I thought I found along the way, that I hoped came from him. Under rocks, stabbed on branches, curling dead on the ground. They were all important to me, no matter which might be real and which nothing more than chance or coincidence. Making it to the island meant something to me then. I was still holding on to the idea of causality, of *purpose* as that word might be recognizable to the Southern Reach. But what if you discover that the price of purpose is to render invisible so many other things?

According to his journal, it took my husband six days to reach the island the first time. It took me somewhat longer. Because the rules had changed. Because the ground I found purchase on one day became the next uncertain, and at times seemed to fall away beneath me. Behind me at the lighthouse, a luminescence was growing in strength and a burnt haze had begun to dominate the sky, and through my binoculars for more days than should have been possible, there came the suggestion of something enormous rising from the sea in a continuous, slow-motion wave. Something I was not yet ready to see.

Ahead, the birds that shot through the sky trailed blurs of color that resembled other versions of themselves, that might have been hallucinations. The air seemed malleable, or like it could be *convinced* or *coerced*. I felt stuck in between, forever traveling, never arriving, so that soon I wanted a place to pretend was "base camp" for a while—a place that might quell the constant frustration of feeling that I couldn't trust the landscape I traveled through, my only anchor the trail itself, which, although it became ever more overgrown and twisty, never faltered, never petered out into nothing.

If it had led me to a cliff, would I have stood there or would I have followed it over the edge? Or would that lack have been enough that I might have turned back and tried to find the door in the border? It's difficult to predict what I might have done. The trajectories of my thoughts were scattered on that journey, twisted this way and that, like the swallows in the clear blue sky that, banking and circling back for a split second, would then return to their previous course, their fleeting digression a simple hunt for a speck of insect protein.

Nor do I know how much of these phenomena, these thoughts, I should attribute to the brightness within me. Some, but not all, based on everything that happened later, that is still happening. Just when I thought the brightness was one thing, it would become another. The fifth morning I rose from the grass and dirt and sand, the brightness had gathered to form a hushed second skin over me, that skin cracking from my opening eyes like the slightest, the briefest, touch of an impossibly thin layer of ice. I could hear the fracturing of its melting as if it came from miles and years away.

As the day progressed, the brightness manifested in my chest like a hot, red stone that pulsed next to my heart, unwelcome company. The scientist in me wanted to self-anesthetize and operate, remove the obstruction, even though I wasn't a surgeon and the brightness no tumor. I remember thinking that I might be talking to the animals by the next morning. I might be rolling in the dirt, laughing hysterically under that merciless blue sky. Or I might find the brightness rising curious out of the top of my head, like a periscope—independent and lively, with nothing left beneath it but a husk.

By dusk of that day, having ignored the biting flies and the huge reptiles that stared from the water, grinning up at me like the mindless carnivores they were . . . by then the brightness had come up to my head and lay behind all of my thoughts like a cooling piece of coal covered in icy ash. And I no longer could be sure that the brightness was a feeling, an impulse, an infection. Was I headed toward an island that might or might not give me answers because I *meant* to go there or because I was being directed somewhere by an invisible stranger? A companion. Was the brightness more *separate* than I knew? And why did the psychologist's words appear in my mind so often, and why could I not pry them out?

These were not speculative questions, a matter for idle debate, but concrete worries. At times, I felt as if those words, my final conversation with the psychologist, lay like a shield or wall between me and aspects of the brightness, that an intended peculiarity of those words had activated something in me. But no matter how I turned that exchange over and over in my thoughts, I came no closer to a conclusion. Some things you can be so close to that you never grasp their true nature.

That night, I made camp, started a fire, because I didn't care who saw me. If the brightness existed separate, and if every part of Area X saw me anyway, what did it matter? A kind of giddy recklessness was coming back to me again—and I welcomed it. The lighthouse had long since faded, but

I found I looked for it still, that great anchor, that great trap. Here, too, grew the purple thistles, in a greater abundance, which I could not help thinking of as spies for Area X. Even if everything here spied and was spied upon.

The wind came up strong from the shore, I remember, and it was cold. I held on to such details back then as a way of warding off the brightness—as superstitious as anyone else. Soon, too, a moaning came out of and through the dusk, along with a familiar thrashing, as something ponderous fought against the reeds. I shuddered, but I also laughed, and said aloud, "It's just an old friend!" Not so old, and not really a friend. Hideous presence. Simple beast. In that fearless moment, or maybe just in this one, I felt a deep affection for and kinship with it. I went out to meet it, my brightness muttering the whole way in a surly, almost petulant fashion. A monster? Yes, but after the monster that was the Crawler, I embraced this simpler source of mystery.

02: THE MOANING CREATURE

I'll spare you the search for this creature I had once fled; it was absurd trying to differentiate wind-blown reeds from those rattled by some force more specific, of sloshing through the muck and mire without breaking an ankle or getting stuck.

Eventually I came out into a kind of clearing, an island

of dirt covered in anemic grass and bounded by yet more reeds. At the far end, something pale and grub-like and monstrous flailed and moaned, its limbs pummeling the reed floor, the speed I had witnessed in the past seemingly now unavailable to it. I realized soon enough that it was sleeping.

The head was small compared to the body, but faced away from me, so all I could see was a thick wrinkled neck morphing into the skull. I still had a chance to leave. I had every reason to leave. I felt shaky, the resolve that had made me veer off the main trail evaporating. But something in its obliviousness made me stay.

I advanced, keeping my gun trained on the beast. This close, the moaning was deafening, the strange guttural tolling of a living cathedral bell. There was no way to be stealthy—the ground was strewn with dried reeds over the dirt and grass that crackled with my steps—and yet still it slept. I trained my flashlight on its bulk. The body had the consistency and form of a giant hog and a slug commingled, the pale skin mottled with mangy patches of light green moss. The arms and legs suggested the limbs of a pig but with three thick fingers at their ends. Positioned along the midsection near what I supposed was the stomach were two more append- ages, which resembled fleshy pseudopods. The creature used them to help lurch its bulk along, but they often writhed pa- thetically and beat at the ground as if not entirely under its control.

I shone the flashlight on the creature's head, that small pink oval backed by the too-thick neck. As the molting mask I'd found during my prior encounter suggested, it had the face of the psychologist from my husband's expedition. And this face in its slumber formed a mask of utter uncomprehending anguish, the mouth open in a perpetual O as it moaned out its distress, as its limbs gouged at the ground, as it made its wounded, halting progress in what amounted to circles. Its eyes had a white film over them that told me it was blind.

I should have felt something. I should have been moved or disgusted by this encounter. Yet after my descent into the tower, my annihilation by the Crawler, I felt nothing. No emotion at all, not even simple, common pity, despite this raw expression of trauma, some agony beyond comprehension.

This beast should have been a dolphin with an uncanny eye, a wild boar that acted as if it were new to its body. And perhaps it was part of an intentional pattern, and I just could not see those outlines. But it *looked* like a mistake, a misfire by an Area X that had assimilated so much so beautifully and so seamlessly. Which made me wonder if my brightness was a harbinger of some form of *this*. To disappear into the coastline, into the anonymous reaches of the beach and the wind, or the marshes, did not really disturb me, perhaps never had. But this did—this blind, relentless questing. Had I tricked myself into believing that letting the brightness overtake me would be a painless, even beautiful, process? There was nothing beautiful about the moaning creature, nothing that didn't seem a ghastly intervention.

In that context, I could not intervene, either, even as I watched the writhing of its perpetual distress. I would not end its misery, in part because I worked from incomplete data. I could not be sure of what it represented or what it was going through. Beneath what seemed to be pain might lie ecstasy—what remained of the human dreaming, and in that dream, comfort. There also came to me the thought that perhaps what this expedition member had *brought* to Area X had contributed to this final state.

This is what I can remember now, when memory begins to be interwoven with so many other considerations. In the end, I took a hair sample that proved as useless as any other—a consistency I suppose I should have admired but did not—and went back to my sad little fire out in the middle of a nowhere that was everywhere.

But this encounter did affect me in one way. I became resolved not to give in to the brightness, to give up my identity—not yet. I could not come to terms with the possibility that one day I might put aside my vigilance and become the moaning creature in the reeds.

Perhaps this was weakness. Perhaps this was just fear.

03: THE ISLAND

Soon enough, the island became a shadow or smudge on the seaward horizon, so I knew it was only a matter of days, even if I had trouble telling how much time was passing. The island that was as blank to me now as my husband had been upon his return. I knew nothing of what I might encounter there, and the reality of this sobered me, made me monitor the brightness more closely, fight it harder, as if, ridiculously, by the time I made it across, I had to be at my best, my most alert. For what? For a corpse I might find if I were lucky? For some memory of a life back in the world that we could now misremember as more placid and comfortable than it had been? I don't know the answer to those questions, except that an organism's primary directive is to continue to exist—to breathe and to eat and to shit and to sleep and to fuck, and to otherwise carry on with the joyous repetitions of its days.

I secured my backpack, and I dove into the water.

Anyone reading who likes stories about characters huddled around guttering fires with the wolves waiting just beyond will be disappointed to learn that I was not attacked by leviathans from the depths as I swam over to the island. That, although tired and cold, I easily set up living quarters in the ruined lighthouse waiting on the shore. That I found enough food there, over time, by catching fish and foraging for berries, digging up tubers that while bland were edible. I trapped small animals when I had to, planted my own garden using seeds from the fruit I found, fertilized it with homemade compost.

At first, the lighthouse perplexed me more than anything on the island. It kept striking me as a mirror of the lighthouse on the coast—the way the light glanced off of it—and that seemed to me like some kind of obscure and potentially ruthless joke. It could be just another detail in a host of them that brought me no closer to answers about Area X. Or this confluence, this incomplete synonym, the top caved in and the landing I chose as my stronghold languishing under a trough of wet dead leaves . . . it could be an unmistakable and massive indicator of some kind.

I took my time, later, exploring the lighthouse, the buildings nearby, the abandoned town, with a systematic and scientific thoroughness, but I felt that my first reconnaissance should be broader: to scour the island for threats, for food and water sources, for any sign of other human life. Not wanting to hope, for I had found no evidence of recent occupation of the lighthouse, which seemed the most likely shelter because most of the other buildings were, even at first glance, dilapidated, had rotted with astonishing swiftness once Area X had imposed its will on this place. There were also signs of pollution, of old scars, but faded so fast into the firmament that I could not gauge how long ago they had been inflicted. Whether Area X was accelerating the erasure of their effects.

This island is about fourteen miles long, six broad, and forty in circumference, containing what I would estimate as about eighty-four square miles or more than fifty thousand acres. The pine-and-oak forest comprises most of the interior, sprawling down toward the shore on the landward side, but the side facing the sea has been assaulted by storms, and there you will find mostly scrub and moss and gnarled bushes. Fresh springwater occurs more frequently than I had expected, from rivulets meandering down from the hills toward the shore. This probably explains the placement of the abandoned town, along with protection from storms blowing in from the sea. But I also found one faucet on the lighthouse grounds that, although spewing forth brown rust at first, eventually settled down to a trickle of something brackish but drinkable, from some hidden aquifer.

Farther afield, I found a rich ecosystem in which a wary rabbit population was held in check by raptors and island foxes, these latter the scrappy small sort that suggested an isolated initial breeding pair or pairs had adapted to the limited range and opportunities of their surroundings. The birdlife was robust as well, from tree swallows and purple martins to vireos and wrens, woodpeckers and nighthawks—along with too many types of shorebirds to catalog. At dusk, the sound of avian life triumphant forms a mighty bursting chorus of voices, such a contrast with the silence of the marshes, whose own richness is more muted, almost watchful.

I wandered the island for many days, both its perimeter and the interior, getting a feel for it and what it contained. As I recorded my observations, I cursed the Southern Reach for not providing us with a map, even if I also knew that I would have tested any map provided to me and wound up doing almost as much work. Not just because I distrusted the Southern Reach, but also because I distrusted Area X. Yet when I was done with this initial inspection, I could not say there was anything preternatural or unusual about the island itself.

Other, perhaps, than the owl.

04: THE OWL

Did I find my husband? In a way, if not in the form in which I had known him. On the far side of the island, in the late afternoon, after I had burst through nettles and scrub and sticker, lacerating long grasses, all of it overshadowed by close-knit copses of wind-gnarled black pines— burst through to a tranquil cove that cupped a white-sand beach and shallows that extended a fair distance before the darkness of deep water took over. On the beach, a scattering of low-lying concrete pilings and rocks, all that remained of an abandoned pier from another age, created a perch for more than a dozen cormorants.

A single stunted pine the height of a person stood defiant amid rocks and cormorants alike, blackened and almost bare of needles. On one outstretched branch, the unlikely silhouette of a common horned owl with sharp tufted ears: rust-brown face with white feathers at chin and throat, mottled gray-and-brown body. My loud approach should have alarmed it, but this owl just perched there, surrounded by the cormorants sunning themselves. An unnatural scene, to me, and it brought me up short.

I thought at first the owl must be hurt, more so when I came closer and it still didn't move, unlike the whirling circle of cormorants that, complaining bitterly, flew away, a long low line over the water, exiled to rove, restless. Any other owl would have taken wing and disappeared back into the forest. But instead, it remained glued to the ridged, scaly bark of the branch, staring out at the fading sun with enormous eyes.

Even when I stood right beside the tree, awkward on the rocks, the owl did not fly, did not look over at me. Injured or dying, I thought again, but cautious, ready to retreat, because an owl can be a dangerous animal. This one was huge, four pounds at least, despite its hollow bones, lightweight feathers. But nothing I had done had yet provoked it, and so I stood there as the sun began to set, the owl beside me.

I had studied owls early in my career and knew that neuroses were unknown among them as opposed to other, more intelligent bird species. Most owls are also beautiful, along with another quality that is hard to define but registers as calm in the observer. There was such a hush upon that beach, and one that didn't register with me as sinister.

At dusk, the owl turned its fierce yellow gaze upon me at last, and with the tip of its outstretched wing brushing against my face, the bird launched itself into the air in a smooth, silent arc that sent it off toward the forest behind me. Forever gone, or so I believed, with any of a number of reasons to account for its odd behavior. The lines between the eccentricities of wildlife and the awareness imposed by Area X are difficult to separate at times.

I needed to seek shelter for the night, and I found on the far western edge of the beach a small circle of rocks around the blackened ash of an old fire—above the high-tide mark, set back almost into the beginning of the forest. I found, too, in the last glimmers of light, an old tent, faded by the sun, weathered and crumpled by storms. Someone had lived here for a time, and without daring to think who it might have been, I made camp there, started my own fire, cooked a rabbit I had killed earlier that afternoon. Then, tired, I fell asleep to the sound of the waves, under a soft and subdued canopy of stars.

I woke only once during the night and saw the owl perched opposite me across the fire, atop my backpack. It had brought me another rabbit. I dozed again, and it was gone when I woke.

I stayed there three days, and I admit I did so because of the owl, and because the cove was near-perfect; I could see spending my life there. But also because I wanted to know more about the person who had made the fire, lived in the tent. Even in disarray and so old, it was clearly a standard-issue tent, although it carried no Southern Reach logo on it.

A little ways into the forest behind the tent, I found an expedition-issue sidearm, much like my own, in a rotting holster, amid wildflowers and sedge weeds and moss. I found the undershirt from an expedition uniform, and then the jacket and socks, strewn across that expanse as if given up willingly, even joyously . . . or as if some animal or person had thrown them there. I did not bother to gather them up, to try to re-create this exoskeleton of a person. I would not find a name, I knew that, and I did not find a letter, either. I would never really know if it might have been my husband who had camped there or some other person even more anonymous to me.

And yet there was the owl, always watching over me, always nearby. Always a little closer, a little tamer, but never completely tame. It would drop twigs at my feet, at random, more as if through some absentmindedness than on purpose.

It would bow at me, a typical owl behavior, then spend the next hours distant, almost sullen. Once or twice, it would perch at close to my height, and I would approach as an experiment, only for the owl to hiss at me almost like a cat, and beat its wings and fluff out its feathers until I had retreated. Other times, on a branch high up, the owl would sway and bob, bob and sway, moving its body from side to side while gripping its perch in the same place. Then look down at me stupidly.

I moved on, following the shore, sometimes also shadowed by the cormorants. I did not expect the owl to join me, but I am unashamed to say I was glad when it did. By the end of the second week, it ate from my hands at dusk, before going off to its nocturnal life. During the night I would hear its curious hollow hooting—a sound many find mysterious or threatening but that I have always found playful or deeply irreverent. The owl would reappear briefly toward dawn— once, in a tangle of feathers as it plunged its head into the sand and ruffled out its plumage, giving itself a dry bath and then picking at lice and other parasites.

The thought crept into my head when I wasn't careful, and then I would banish it. Was this my husband in altered form? Did he recognize me, or was this owl simply responding to the presence of a human being? Unlike the uncanny presence of other animals, there was no such feeling here—no sense of it to me, at least. But, I reasoned, perhaps I had become acclimated by then. Perhaps I'd reached a kind of balance with the brightness that normalized such indicators.

When I came full circle, back to the ruined lighthouse, the owl stayed with me. He tried even less for my attention, but in the twilight would appear in the branches of a tree outside the lighthouse, and we would stand there together. Sometimes he would already be there by midafternoon, if I walked through the shade of the dark trees, and follow me, making great hoot-hoots to warn of my coming. But never earlier, as if he remembered that I hated the unnatural in animals, as if he understood me. Besides, he had his own business—hunting. After a week, though, he roosted in the shattered upper spire of the lighthouse. The cormorants, too, reappeared there, or perhaps they were not the same cormorants, but I had not seen so many of the birds in that place before my explorations.

During the day, the owl would sun himself up there before falling into a sleep that sometimes was accompanied by a low and nasal snore. During the night, I would fall asleep on the landing and above me hear, so faint, the whisper as his wings caressed the air on his flight to the forest to seek prey. In those transitional moments, between day and night, when anything seemed possible, or I tricked myself into believing that this was true, I began to talk to the owl. Even though I dislike anthropomorphizing animals, it did not seem important to withhold this communication because the evidence of his eccentric behavior was self-evident. Either he understood or did not, but even if not, sound is more important to owls than to human beings. So I spoke to him in case he was other than what he seemed, and as common courtesy, and as a way to help with the welling up of the brightness.

Despite this, which might be foolishness, how could I ever truly recognize in him the one I'd sought, ever cross that divide? Yet there grew to be a useful symbiosis in our relationship. I continued to hunt for him, and he continued to hunt for me, although with a kind of sloppiness, as if unintentional—rabbits and squirrels falling from his perch down to mine. In some ways, wordless on his end and based on the most basic principles of friendship and survival, this arrangement worked better than anything back in the wider world. I had still seen no person on the island, but now I found more evidence of a prior presence.

It was not what I'd expected.

05: THE SEEKER & SURVEILLANCE BANDITS

Returned from my exploration, with the owl as my companion, I now slowly took the measure of my immediate surroundings: the lighthouse, the buildings around it, and the town beyond. The town, which must have been abandoned long before the creation of Area X, consisted of a main street and a few side streets that then faded into the impression of dirt roads, the tire ruts overgrown with weeds. All of it empty; I could be the ruler of this place by default, if I wanted to be.

"Main Street" had become a kind of facade, having fallen to a disheveled army of vines and flowering trees and bushes and weeds and wildflowers. Squirrels and badgers, skunks and raccoons, had taken over the remains, ospreys nesting on the ruins of rooftops. In the upper story of a house or former business pigeons and starlings perched on gaping windows, the glass broken and fallen inside. It all had the rich scent of the reclaimed, of sweet blossoms and fresh grass in the summer, with the pungent underlying odor of animals marking their territory. It had also a hint of the unexpected for me, a kind of lingering shock to see these rough, rude memorials to the lives of human beings in a place I had thought largely free of them.

Here and there, I found more signs of expeditions that had reached the island and either gone back across the water or died here and been transformed here. An abandoned backpack with the usual map in it. A flashlight. A rifle scope. A water canteen. These were tantalizing remnants—indicators that I tried to read too much into, for reasons that revealed a weakness in me. It should have been enough to know others had come here first, and that others had sought answers, whether they had found them or not.

But there were sedimentary layers to this information, and some of the older materials, which I believed dated back to just before and right after the creation of Area X, interested me more. People had taken up residence here within that narrow spectrum, and those people went by the initials of S&SB, although I never once found a fragment that told me what these initials stood for. Nor could I recall, either back in the world or during our training for the expedition, ever hearing of such an organization. Not, of course, that the island had been given any thought or attention in that training. By then, any betrayal by the Southern Reach struck me as just more of the same.

In lieu of any other evidence, I called them the Seeker & Surveillance Bandits. It suited what I knew about them from the scraps they'd left behind, and for a time, it occupied my days to try to reconstruct their identity and their purpose on the island.

The leavings of the S&SB, their detritus, took the form of damaged equipment that I identified as meant to record radio waves, to monitor infrared and other frequencies, along with more esoteric machines that defeated my attempts to decode their purpose. Along with such broken flotsam, I uncovered weathered (often unreadable) papers and photographs, and even a few recordings that croaked out incomprehensible too-slow words as I plugged them into a failing generator that gave me only about thirty seconds of power at a time before cutting out.

All of this I found inside the abandoned buildings on Main Street, remains protected by fallen-in supporting walls or in basements where certain corners had escaped flooding. Burn marks existed in places where controlled fires had been started indoors. But I couldn't tell if the S&SB had started these fires or if they had come later, during some desperate phase before everything had been assimilated by Area X. Looking at all of that ash, I realized that any attempt to reconstruct a sequence of events would be forever incomplete because someone had wanted to hide something.

I took what I found to the lighthouse and began to sort through it, such as it was, all under the watchful but unhelpful eye of the owl. Despite the oblique nature of what I had recovered, I began to piece together hints of purpose, suggestions of conspiracy. All of what I relate here is highly speculative but, I think, supported by the fragile evidence available to me.

The S&SB had begun their occupation of this island not with a mapping of the perimeter but with a thorough investigation of the ruined lighthouse, which meant they had come here with a specific purpose. That investigation had been twinned to establishing a kind of link between the light-house on the island and the one on the mainland. There were references to something that "might or might not" have been transferred, suggesting that perhaps the lens in the light-house I knew so well had originally come from here. But in context, this "might or might not" seemed almost certain to exist separate from the lens itself—or could exist separate. Torn pages from a book on the history of famous lighthouses, the lineage of lens manufacture and shipping, helped me little.

There also was debate as to whether they sought "an object or a recordable phenomenon," which seemed to return to the idea of linking the two lighthouses; if a "phenomenon," then this linkage was important. If an "object," then the linkage might not be important, and either the island or the lighthouse on the mainland would no longer be of interest. Further, the nature of these fragments was contradictory as to their organization and sophistication. Some S&SB members seemed to lack even a rudimentary understanding of science and wasted my time with scrawlings about ghosts and hauntings and copied-down passages from books about demonic possession. The listing of stages interested me only inasmuch as I could transfer it to the biological world of parasitic and symbiotic relationships. Others among them lay out under the stars at night and recorded their dreams as if they were transmissions from beyond. As a kind of fiction, it enlivened my reading but was otherwise worthless.

Along with this ephemeral superstition, I would also group the lesser scientific observations, which reflected the involvement of third- or fourth-rate minds. Here, it was not so much the accuracy of the observations but the banality of the conclusions. Into this category fell extrapolations about "prebiotic" materials and "spooky action at a distance," along with already debunked experiments from decades past.

What stood out from what I tossed on the compost heap seemed to come from a different sort of intelligence entirely. This mind or these minds asked questions and did not seem interested in hasty answers, did not care if one question birthed six more and if, in the end, none of those six questions led to anything concrete. There was a patience that seemed imposed and not at all a part of the swirling quicksilver consciousness that surrounded it. If I understood the scraps correctly, my pathetic attempt at playing oracle, this second type not only kept tabs on people living on the mainland, but on certain of its own fellow S&SB members. It did not have only experimentation on its collective mind.

Does the residue of a presence leave an identifiable trace? Although I could not be sure, I felt I had identified such a presence regardless—one that had infiltrated the S&SB late. A shift in command and control toward something more sophisticated, staring out at me from the pages I had found.

In among this detritus, these feeble guesses, the word *Found!* Handwritten, triumphant. Found what? But with so little data, even *Found!*, even the awareness of some more intelligent entity peering out from among the fragments led nowhere. Someone, somewhere had additional information, but the elements—Area X?—had so accelerated the decay of the documents that I could not glean much more, even though this was enough. Enough to suggest that there had been a kind of tampering with this coast before the creation of Area X, and my own experience to tell me that the Southern

Reach had deliberately excised knowledge of the island from our expedition maps and briefings. These two data points, although more to do with absence than with positive confirmation, made me redouble my efforts looking for S&SB scraps amid the rubble. But I never found anything more than what I uncovered on my first, thorough investigation.

06: THE PASSAGE OF TIME, AND PAIN

I never had a country, never had the choice; I was born into one. But over time, this island has become my country, and I need no other. I never thought to seek the way out, back into the world. As the years passed and no one else reached my island refuge, I began to wonder if the Southern Reach existed anymore—or if it had ever existed, that perhaps there had never been another world or an expedition, and I had suffered a delusion or trauma, a kind of memory loss. One day, perhaps, I would wake up and recall it all: some cataclysm that had left me the only person in this place, with just an owl to talk to.

I survived storms that gusted in suddenly, and drought, and a nail through my foot when I wasn't careful. I survived being bitten by many things, including a poisonous spider and a snake. I learned to become so attuned to my environment that after a time no animal, natural or unnatural, shied away at my presence, and for this reason I no longer hunted anything but fish unless forced to, relying more and more on vegetables and fruit. Although I thought I grew attuned to their messages as well.

In the lengthening silence and solitude, Area X sometimes would reveal itself in unexpected ways. I began to perceive infinitesimal shifts in the sky, as if the pieces did not quite fit together . . . and to acquire from the habitat around me a sense of invisible things stitching through, phantoms that almost made me reconsider my antipathy for the S&SB's emphasis on the supernatural.

Standing in a clearing one evening, as still as possible, I felt a kind of *breath* or thickness of molecules from behind that I could not identify, and I willed my heartbeat to slow so that for every one of mine the hearts of the tree frogs throating out their song might beat twenty thousand times. Hoping to be so quiet that without turning I might hear or in some other way glimpse what regarded me. But to my relief it fled or withdrew into the ground a moment later.

Once, the sky broke open with rain in an unnatural way, and through the murk an odd light burned at the limits of my vision. I imagined it was the far-off lighthouse, that other expeditions had been sent in after me. But the longer I stared the more the light appeared to be cracking open the darkness, through which I glimpsed for a moment dissipating shadows that could have been peculiar storm clouds or the reverse quickening of some type of vast organism. Such phenomena, experienced off and on these past thirty years, have also been accompanied by a changing of the night sky. On such nights, presaged only by a kind of tremor in the brightness within me, there is never a moon. There is never a moon, and the stars above are unfamiliar—they are foreign, belonging to a cosmology I cannot identify. On such nights, I wish I had decided to become an astronomer.

On at least two occasions, I would define this change as more significant, as a kind of celestial cataclysm, accompanied by what might be earthquakes, and cracks or rifts appearing in the fabric of the night, soon closing, and with nothing but a greater darkness seen shining through. Somewhere, out in the world or the universe, something must be happening to create these moments of dysfunction. At least, this is my belief. There is a sense of the world around me strengthened or *thickened*, the weight and waft of reality more focused or determined. As if the all-too-human dolphin eye I once glimpsed staring up at me is with each new phase further subsumed in the flesh that surrounds it.

Beyond these observations, I have a single question: What is the nature of my delusion? Am I hallucinating when I see the night sky that I know? Or when I see the one that is strange? Which stars should I trust and navigate by? I stand in the ruined lighthouse some nights and look out to sea and realize that in this form, this body, I will never know.

My survival has also, to put it bluntly, been predicated by hurting myself. By the time I stood on the shore opposite the island, about to swim over, I was using pain to push the brightness back. The ways were myriad and I was precise. You can find methods to almost drown, to almost suffocate, that are not as onerous as the thought might suggest. Ways to suggest the infliction of pain that can fool whatever lies within you. A rusty nail. A snake's venom. As a result, pain does not much bother me anymore; it gives me evidence of my ongoing existence, has saved me from those times when, otherwise, I might have stared so long at wind and rain and sea as to become nothing, to just disappear.

In a separate document, I have listed the best, least intrusive approaches, which I realize may seem morbid, even though I consider it an absurd method of chronicling my days. I have also noted the rotation of cycles that has proven most effective. Although, given the choice, I would not recommend this approach, you become acclimated to it, like doing the chores or foraging for food.

After so much time, pain has become such a familiar and revisited friend that I wonder if I will notice him more now that I have stopped my regimen. Will an absence of pain be harder to get used to? I suspect that this concern will be forgotten amid so many other adjustments that must be made. For, having found so many ways to put it off, I believe that my transformation will be more radical than it might have been, that I might indeed become something like the moaning creature. Will I see the real stars then?

Sometimes, too, pain comes at you unexpectedly; you don't have to generate it, don't have to will it consciously upon yourself. It's just there. The owl that has been my companion these thirty years died a week ago, without my being able to help, without knowing until too late. He had become an old owl, and although his eyes were still enormous and bright, his colors had faded, his camouflage tattered; he slept more and did not go out to hunt as often. I fed him mice by hand in his redoubt at the top of the ruined lighthouse.

I found him in the forest, after he had been missing for a few days, and I had finally gone out to search for him. From what I can reconstruct, he had become injured, perhaps from frailty or the onset of blindness, broken his wing, and settled on the forest floor. A fox or pair of foxes had probably gotten to him. He lay there splayed out in a mottled flurry of brown and dark red, eyes shut, head fallen to the side, all the life having left him.

My microscope had long since been abandoned in a corner of the lighthouse grounds, overtaken by mold, half buried there by the simple passage of years. I had no heart to take samples, to discover what I already knew: that, in the end, there was nothing a microscope could tell me about the owl that I had not learned from my many years of close interactions and observation.

What am I to say? That I do not miss him?

PART III

OCCULTING LIGHT

0011: GHOST BIRD

What kind of life was this, where you could read a letter from your own haunted twin? That you could live within the memories of another and think of them as real, a second skin, and yet so utterly false. This is who she had been. This is what she had thought, and how she had lived. Should that now be Ghost Bird's life, too, her thoughts? Anger and awe warred within—and no one to push either emotion onto, except herself. She had to let them battle like a second heartbeat and trust that her reaction was not just the mirror reflecting what it saw. That even if she was a mistake, she had become a viable mistake—a mutation, not an anomaly like the moaning creature. Long-moldering bones trapped in the marshes.

There were questions she did not want to ask, because if she did they would take on detail and weight and substance, flesh and skin reclothing the arch of ribs. Wonders and horrors alike she could compartmentalize, but Control, at least, might never be ready, and on some level it was wearying to push, to have that kind of purpose. It seemed to push against the reality of Area X, to say that even *she* had learned nothing from being her. Should she even try, knowing that it wasn't fair, that they had all traveled too far, too fast, even Grace with her three-year head start?

It was dusk now, almost nightfall, and into the silence and gathering shadows, Grace took the lead, said: "We're astronauts. All of the expedition members have been astronauts."

That should have been comforting in its way, a kind of anchor, but Control's face had become a resolute mask that said he didn't want to deal with this, that, defiantly, he wanted only to bury his nose in what was comfortable. He clutched the yellowing pages of the biologist's letter tight in his left hand, while the biologist's journal, which Grace had rescued from the lighthouse, lay on his lap. It had interested Ghost Bird to read it, to fill in the final gaps, and yet what gaps remained despite it. *The white light at the bottom of the tower. The manifestation of the lighthouse keeper within the Crawler.* These were things she distrusted without seeing them for herself. But to Control she knew it would just register as new evidence, new hope— information that might provide a solution, a sudden fix. As if Grace's scrutiny and thoughts about them were not enough.

"We're not on Earth," Ghost Bird said. We cannot be on Earth. "Not with that much distortion of time. Not with the things the biologist saw." Not if they wanted to pretend that there were rules in place, even if the rules had been obscured, made unclear, withheld. But was that true? Or had time just become irrational, inconsistent?

Still that reluctance, and the distance it created between her and them, until Grace finally said, "That was my conclusion, one of the theories put forward by the science division."

ACCEPTANCE

"A kind of wormhole," Control said. The limit of how far he could go; anything more would be pulled out of him by the brightness.

A disbelieving stare from Grace. "Do you think Area X builds spaceships, too? Do you think Area X traverses interstellar space? Wormholes? Think of something more subtle, something peering through what we think of as reality."

Flat, clipped words, stripped of the awe that should have animated them. Because she'd had those extra three years? Because she was thinking of loved ones back home?

Control, so slowly, almost as if in a hypnotized state: "Everything in Area X that we thought was degrading too rapidly . . . most of it was just getting old."

Some things were very old indeed—the remnants of the village and the various sedimentary layers of those journals under the trapdoor in the lighthouse. So much more time had passed in Area X after the border came down, before the first expedition had gone in. People could have *lived* in Area X for much, much longer after the border came down than anyone had thought.

"How was this not known before," Control said. "How was this not clear *before*." As if some elemental force of repetition might bring about a swift justice against those who had obstructed his access to the truth. Instead, repetition just underscored their ignorance.

"Corrupted data," Grace said. "Skewed samples. Incomplete information."

"I don't know how—"

"She means," Ghost Bird said, "that so many expeditions came back disoriented, damaged, or not at all, that the SR had no reliable samples." She meant that the time dilation must be more severe when Area X shifted or underwent a change, and otherwise must be almost unmeasurable.

"She's right," Grace said. "We never had anyone who lived long enough in Area X or saw so clearly and managed to write down their observations." Conflicting data, conflicting purposes. An opponent that didn't make it easy.

"But do we believe the biologist?" Control asked. Because the theories of the biologist's copy might be suspect? Because he wasn't built for this and Ghost Bird was.

"Do you believe *me*?" Grace said. "I've seen strange stars in the sky at night, too. I have seen the rifts in the sky. I have lived here *three years*."

"Then tell me—how can the sun shine, the stars, the moon? If we are not on Earth?"

"That's not the critical question," Ghost Bird said. "Not for organisms that are so masterful at camouflage."

"Then what is?" Control frustrated, trying to take in the enormity of the idea, and Ghost Bird found it painful to watch.

"The critical question," Grace said, "is what is the *purpose* of this organism or organisms. And how do we survive."

"We know its purpose," Control said. "Which is to kill us, to transform us, to get rid of us. Isn't that what we try to avoid thinking about? What the director, you"—pointing at Grace—"and Cheney and all the rest had to keep suppressing? The thought that it just wants to kill us all."

"You think we didn't have these conversations a thousand times?" Grace said. "You think we didn't go around and around trying to get out of our circles?"

"People make patterns all the time without realizing it," Ghost Bird said. "An organism can have a purpose and yet also make patterns that have little to do with that purpose."

"So fucking what," Control snarled, a trapped animal. "So fucking what?"

Ghost Bird exchanged a stare with Grace, who looked away. Control wasn't prepared to receive this knowledge. It was eating him from the inside out. Maybe something specific would distract him.

"There's a lot of energy being generated and discharged," she said. "If the border is a kind of membrane, it could be a case of dumping it somewhere else—think of how things disappear when they come into contact with the border."

"But they don't disappear, do they?" Grace said.

"I don't think so. I think they get sent somewhere."

"*Where?*" Control asked.

Ghost Bird shrugged, thinking about the journey into Area X, and the devastation and destruction she had seen. The ruined cities. Was that real? Something that gave them a clue? Or just a delusion?

Membranes and dimensions. Limitless amounts of space. Limitless amounts of energy. Effortless manipulation of molecules. Continual attempts to transform the human into the non-human. The ability to move an entire biosphere to another place. Right now, if the outside world existed, it would still be sending radio-wave messages into space and monitoring radio-wave frequencies to seek out other intelligent life in the universe. But Ghost Bird didn't think those messages were being received. Another way people were bound by their own view of consciousness. What if an infection was a message, a brightness a kind of symphony? As a defense? An odd form of communication? If so, the message had not been received, would probably never be received, the message buried in the transformation itself. Having to reach for such banal answers because of a lack of imagination, because human beings couldn't even put themselves in the mind of a cormorant or an owl or a whale or a bumblebee.

Did she want to ally herself to such a lack, and did she have a choice?

From the window the low buildings were revealed as facades: bruised and ruined cinder-block houses with the roofs gone, vines bursting out, and the worn white paint of the sides that lay in grainy despondency, unable to contain the tangled green. In among that unintended terrarium: a row of little crosses stuck in the soil, fresh enough to have been bodies buried by Grace. Perhaps she'd lied and a handful of others had followed her over to the island, only to meet some fate Grace had avoided. She'd heard almost the entire conversation between Control and Grace, had been ready to intervene if Grace had not taken the gun from Control's head. No one could drug her if her body didn't want it done. She wasn't built like that. Not anymore.

But she didn't like the view, felt some kind of instinctual discomfort at the sight of the damaged road, the "scrapes" on the forested hills that looked less like clearings in the late-afternoon sun and more like a kind of violence. The seaward window looked out on calm seas and a mainland rendered normal and perhaps even ordinary. Yet the distance disguised the havoc wreaked on the convoy.

Behind her, Grace and Control talked, but Ghost Bird had disengaged. It was a circular discussion, a loop that Control was creating to trap himself inside of, to dig the trenches, the moat, that would keep things out. How is this possible, how is that possible, and why—agonizing over both what he knew or thought he knew and what he could never, ever know.

She knew where it would all lead, what it always led to in human beings—a decision about what to do. What are we going to *do*? Where do we *go* from here? How do we *move forward*? What is our *mission* now? As if purpose could solve everything, could take the outlines of what was missing and by sheer will invoke it, make it appear, bring it back to life.

Even the biologist had done it, creating a pattern out of what might be random—correlating eccentric owl behavior with her lost husband. When it might have been the evidence of, the residue of, some other ritual entirely—and thus her account of the owl no more on target than her assertions about the S&SB. You could know the what of something forever and never discover the why.

The allure of the island lay in its negation of why—both for the biologist and, Ghost Bird guessed, for Grace, who had lived here with this knowledge for almost three years, as it ate at her. Ate at her still, the relief of companions having done nothing to take the edge off, Ghost Bird observing her from the window and wondering if she still withheld some vital piece of information—that her watchfulness and the evidence that she didn't sleep well provided the outline of a different, undisclosed *why*.

She felt so apart from both of them in that moment, as if the knowledge of how far they might be from Earth, of how time passed, ruthless, had pushed them away, and she was looking at them from the border—peering in through the shimmering door.

Control had started to return to safe ground of subjects like the lighthouse keeper, like Central. So there wouldn't be galaxies bursting in his brain like fireworks and the Southern Reach become a redoubt of Area X and humans turning into creatures with a purpose known only to the stitching in the sky, perhaps.

"Central kept the island a secret all this time. Central buried it, buried the island, just kept sending expeditions out here, to this . . . this fucking ugly place, this place that isn't really even where it's supposed to be, this fucking place that just keeps killing people and doesn't fucking even give you the chance to fight back because it's always going to win anyway and the . . ." Control couldn't stop. He wasn't going to stop. All he might do is pause, trail off, and then take it up again.

So after a time, Ghost Bird stopped him. She knelt beside him, gently took the biologist's letter and journal from him. She placed her arms around Control and held him, while Grace looked elsewhere in embarrassment, or a suppression of her own need for comfort. He thrashed in Ghost Bird's arms, resisting, her feeling the preternatural warmth of him, and then eventually he subsided, stopped fighting, held her loosely, then held her tightly while she said not a word because to say anything—anything at all—would be to humiliate him, and she cared more about him than that. And it cost her nothing.

When he was still, she disengaged, stood, directed her attention to Grace. There was still a question to ask. With no sound from the querulous nesting birds or, indeed, much sound at all intruding beyond the waves and wind, their own breathing, and Grace rolling a can of beans back and forth with her foot.

"Where is the biologist now?" Ghost Bird asked.

"Not important," Control said. "The least thing now. A fly or a bird or something. Or nothing. Dead?"

Grace laughed at that, in a way Ghost Bird didn't like.

"Grace?" Not about to let her get out from under an answer.

"Yes, she is definitely still alive."

"And where is she?"

"Somewhere out there."

The sonorous sound now rising. The distant sense of weight and movement and bulk and substance and intent, and something in Ghost Bird's mind linked to it, and no way to undo that.

"Not *somewhere* out there," Ghost Bird said.

Grace, nodding now, frightened now. This thing she couldn't tell them on top of all the impossible things she'd had to tell them.

"The biologist is coming here." Coming back to where the owl had once roosted. Coming down to the place where her doppelgänger now stood. That sound. Louder now. The snapping of tree branches, of tree trunks.

The biologist was coming down the hillside.

In all her glory and monstrosity.

Ghost Bird saw it from the landing window. How the biologist coalesced out of the night, her body flickering and stitching its way into existence, in the midst of a shimmering wave that imposed itself on the reality of forested hillside. The vast bulk seething down the hill through the forest with a crack and splinter as trees fell to that gliding yet ponderous and muffled darkness, reduced to kindling by the muscle behind the emerald luminescence that glinted through the black. The smell that presaged the biologist: thick brine and oil and some sharp, crushed herb. The sound that it made: as if the wind and sea had been smashed together and in the aftershock there reverberated that same sonorous moan. A seeking. A questing. A communication or communion. That, Ghost Bird recognized; that, she understood.

The hillside come alive and sliding down to the ruined lighthouse, at a steady pace like a lava flow. This intrusion. These darknesses that re-formed into a mighty shape against the darkness of the night sky, lightened by the reflections of clouds and the greater shadow of the tree line and the forests.

It bore down on the lighthouse, that strange weight, that leviathan, still somehow half here and half not, and Ghost Bird just stood at the window waiting for it, while Grace and Control screamed at her to come away, to get away, but she would not come, would not let them pull her from the window, and stood there like the captain of a ship facing a monumental storm, the waves rising huge against the window. Grace and Control gone, running down the stairs, and then that great bulk was shoved up against the window and smashing into the doorway below in a crack and crumble of stone and brick. Leaning against the lighthouse, and the lighthouse resisting, but only just.

The song had grown so loud as to be almost unbearable.

Now like deep cello strings, now like guttural clicking, now eerie and mournful.

The great slope of its wideness was spread out before Ghost Bird, the edges wavery, blurred, sliding off into some *other place*. The mountain that was the biologist came up almost to the windowsill, so close she could have jumped down onto what served as its back. The suggestion of a flat, broad head plunging directly into torso. The suggestion, far to the east, already overshooting the lighthouse, of a vast curve and curl of the mouth, and the flanks carved by dark ridges like a whale's, and the dried seaweed, the kelp, that clung there, and the overwhelming ocean smell that came with it. The green-and-white stars of barnacles on its back in the hundreds of miniature craters, of tidal pools from time spent motionless in deep water, time lost inside that enormous brain. The scars of conflict with other monsters pale and dull against the biologist's skin.

It had many, many glowing eyes that were also like flowers or sea anemones spread open, the blossoming of many eyes—normal, parietal, and simple—all across its body, a living constellation ripped from the night sky. Her eyes. Ghost Bird's eyes. Staring up at her in a vast and unblinking array.

As it smashed into the lower floor, seeking something.

As it sang and moaned and hollered.

Ghost Bird leaned out the window, reached out and pushed through the shimmering layer, so like breaking the surface of a tidal pool to touch what lay within . . . and her hands found purchase on that slick, thick skin, among all of those eyes, her eyes, staring up at her. She buried both hands there, felt the touch of thick, tough lashes, felt the curved, smooth surfaces and the rough, craggy ones. All of those eyes. In the multiplicity of that regard, Ghost Bird saw what they saw. She saw herself, standing there, looking down. She saw that the biologist now existed across locations and landscapes, those other horizons gathering in a blurred and rising wave. There passed between the two something wordless but deep. She understood the biologist in that moment, in a way she had not before, despite their shared memories. She might be stranded on a planet far from home. She might be observing an incarnation of herself she could not quite comprehend, and yet . . . there was connection, there was *recognition*.

Nothing monstrous existed here—only beauty, only the glory of good design, of intricate planning, from the lungs that allowed this creature to live on land or at sea, to the huge gill slits hinted at along the sides, shut tightly now, but which would open to breathe deeply of seawater when the biologist once again headed for the ocean. All of those eyes, all of those temporary tidal pools, the pockmarks and the ridges, the thick, sturdy quality of the skin. An animal, an organism that had never existed before or that might belong to an alien ecology. That could transition not just from land to water but from one remote *place* to another, with no need for a door in a border.

Staring up at her with her own eyes.

Seeing her.

0012: THE LIGHTHOUSE KEEPER

Repainted black daymark, seaward side; ladder may need to be replaced, rickety. Tended to the garden most of the day, ran errands. Went on a hike late in the day. Sighted: a muskrat, possum, raccoons, red foxes up a tree at dusk, resting in crooks like crooks. Downy woodpecker. Redheaded woodpecker.

A thousand lighthouses burned to columns of ash along the coastline of an endless island. A thousand blackened candles trailing white smoke from atop the broad, broken head of a monster rising from the sea. A thousand dark cormorants, wings awash in crimson flames, taking flight from the waves, eyes reflecting the wrath of their own extinction. *Who maketh his angels spirits; his ministers a flaming fire.*

Saul woke coughing in the darkness, sweating from a thin, flat heat that flared up in wings across the bridge of his nose and over his eyes. Leaning forward through his skull to kiss that heat came the now-familiar pressure, which he'd described to the doctor in Bleakersville a couple of days ago as "dull but intense, somehow like a second skin on the inside." That sounded bizarre, wasn't accurate, but he couldn't find the right words. The doctor had looked at him for a moment, almost as if Saul had said something offensive, and then diagnosed his condition as "an atypical cold, with a sinus infection," sent him on his way with useless medicine to "clear up your sinus cavity." *His word was in mine heart as a burning fire shut up in my bones.*

There came a whispering again, and instinctually he reached a hand out to find his lover's shoulder, chest, but gripped only the sheets. Charlie wasn't there, wouldn't be back from his night gig for another week at the earliest. Unable to tell him the truth: that he still didn't feel right, not a sickness in the normal way, not what the doctor had diagnosed, but something hiding inside, waiting for its moment. A paranoid thought, Saul knew. It was a cold, or maybe a sinus infection, like the doctor had said. A winter cold, like he'd had in the past, just with night sweats, nightmares, and verse spilling out of him, this strange sermon that spiraled up into his thoughts when he wasn't vigilant, was coiled there now. *And the hand of the sinner shall rejoice, for there is no sin in shadow or in light that the seeds of the dead cannot forgive.*

He sat up abruptly in bed, stifled another cough.

Someone was in his lighthouse. More than one person. Whispering. Or maybe even shouting, the sound by the time it infiltrated the brick and stone, the wood and steel, brought to him through a distance, a time, that he couldn't know. The irrational thought that he was hearing the ghosts of dozens of lighthouse keepers all at once, in a kind of threnody, the condensed chorus of a century. Another phantom sound?

The whispering, the mumbling, continued in a matter-of-fact way, without emotion, and this convinced him to investigate. He roused himself from bed, put on jeans and a sweater, and taking up the ax on the wall—a monstrous and unwieldy pendulum—he padded up the stairs in his bare feet.

The steps were cold and the spiral dark, but he didn't want to risk turning on the lights in case a real intruder waited above. At the landing, the moon shone in at an angle, making the chairs there, the table, look like angular creatures frozen by its glow. He paused, listening. The waves below, their soft hush, stitched through with the sudden chatter of bats, close and then gone, as their echo-location pushed them away from the lighthouse walls. There should have been a hum in the background, too, a kind of purr from above, but he could not hear it. Which meant no light shot out across twenty miles to guide the ships.

He continued up as fast as he could, fueled by an anger that cut through the haze of his sickness, wanted confrontation. *And he said unto me, My grace is sufficient for thee: for my strength is made perfect in weakness.*

When he barged into the lantern room, it was to the sight of the blue-black sky filled with stars—and to three figures, two standing, one bent over in front of the extinguished lens. All three holding tiny flashlights, the pinpricks of that illumination only intensifying his sense of their guilt, their complicity, but in what?

All three were staring at him.

He raised his ax in a threatening way and hit the switch, flooding the room with light.

Suzanne and a woman he didn't know stood by the door to the railing, dressed all in black, with Henry on his knees in front of them, almost as if he's been dealt a blow. Suzanne looked offended, as if he'd burst in on them in their own home. But the stranger hardly acknowledged his presence, stood there with arms crossed, oddly relaxed. Her hair was long and coiffed. She was dressed in an overcoat, dark slacks, and a long red scarf. Taller and older than Suzanne, she had a way of staring at him that made him concentrate on Henry instead.

"What the *hell* are you doing here?"

Their calm faced by a man with an ax baffled him, took some of the ire out of him, this delay between accusatory question and any response. Even Henry had composed himself, gone from a look almost of fear to a thin smile.

"Why don't you go back to sleep, Saul," Henry said, unmoving. "Why don't you go back to bed and let us finish up. We won't be long now."

Finish up with what? Henry's ritual humiliation? His usually perfect hair was mussed, his left eye twitching. Something had happened here, right before Saul had burst in. The condescension hit Saul hard, turned bewilderment and concern back into anger.

"The hell I will. You're trespassing. You broke in. *You turned off the light*. And who is *this*?" What was the woman to Suzanne and Henry? She did not seem to even belong to the same universe. He was more than sure that the bulge under her overcoat was a gun.

But he wasn't going to get an answer.

"We have a key, Saul," Henry said in a cloying tone, as if trying to soothe Saul. "We have a permit, Saul." Head turned a little to the side. Appraising. Quizzical. Telling Saul that he was the unreasonable one—the one interrupting Henry in his important studies.

"No, you *broke in*," he said, retreating to an even safer position, confused by Henry's inability to admit this basic fact, confused by the way the strange woman now regarded him with a kind of gunslinger's sangfroid. "You turned off the light, for Chrissake! And your permit says *nothing* about sneaking around at night while I'm asleep. Or bringing . . . guests . . ."

Henry ignored all of that, got up, and, with a quick glance at the woman and Suzanne, came closer than Saul wanted. If Saul took even two steps back he'd be stumbling down the stairwell.

"Go back to sleep." An urgency there, a whispered quality to the words, almost as if Henry was pleading with him, as if he didn't want the woman or Suzanne to see the concern on his face.

"You know, Saul," Suzanne said, "you really don't look well. You are sick and need to rest. You are sick and you want to put down that very heavy ax, this ax that just looks so heavy and hard to hold on to, and you want to put it down, this ax, and take a deep breath and relax, and turn around and go back to sleep, go to sleep . . ."

A sense of drifting, of sleepiness, began to overtake Saul. He panicked, took a step back, swung the ax over his head, and, as Henry brought his hands up to protect himself, buried the axhead in the floorboards. The impact reverberated through his hands, jamming one of his wrists.

"Get out. Now. All of you." Get out of the lighthouse. Get out of my head. *In the darkness of that which is golden, the*

fruit shall split open to reveal the revelation of the fatal soft-
ness in the earth.

Another long silence spread, and the stranger seemed to grow taller and straighter and somehow more serious, as if he had her full attention. Her coldness, her calm, scared the shit out of him.

"We're studying something unique, Saul," Henry said finally. "So perhaps you can forgive our eagerness, our need to go the extra mile—"

"Just *get the hell out*," Saul said, and wrenched the ax free, although it cost him. Held it high on the handle, because in such close quarters it would be no use to him otherwise. There was such a terror in him now—that they wouldn't go, that he couldn't make them *get the hell out*. While still in his head a thousand lighthouses burned.

But Henry just shrugged, said, "Suit yourself."

Staunch though he felt weak, to fill the silence they kept leaving like a trap: "You're done here. I'm calling the police if I ever see you here again." Curious, the words that came out of his mouth, that he meant them and yet was examining them already for their truth.

"But it is going to be a beautiful morning," Suzanne said, the words hurled at him with a knife's blade of sarcasm?

Henry almost contorted himself to avoid brushing against Saul as they passed by, as if Saul were made of the most delicate crystal. The woman gave him a mysterious smile as she turned into the spiral leading down, a smile full of teeth.

Then they disappeared down the steps.

When he was sure they weren't coming back, Saul leaned over to switch on the lens. It would need some time to warm up, and then he would have to go through the checklist of tests to ensure Henry and his acolytes hadn't changed the direction of the main reflective surfaces within the lens. In the meantime, still holding the ax, he decided he would go downstairs to make sure the odd three hadn't lingered.

When he reached the bottom, he found no sign of them. Opening the front door, he expected to see them walking across the lighthouse grounds or getting into a car. But even when he turned on the lawn lights, there was no sign of them or of a vehicle. Not enough time had passed. Had they run part of the way and disappeared into the hazy gloom of the beach? Or scattered into the pines, hidden in the marshes, become one with the shadows there?

Then he heard the faint sound of a motorboat over the waves. A boat that must be running without lights. The only illumination now besides the moon and stars came from the faint red dot still pulsing from the island.

Back at the front door, though, a shadow waited for him. Henry.

"Don't worry, it's just me," Henry said. "The other two are gone."

Saul sighed, leaned on his ax. "Will you never just leave, Henry? Will you continue to be *such* a burden?" But he was relieved Suzanne and the unknown woman hadn't remained behind.

"A burden? I'm a kind of gift, Saul. Because I *understand*. I know what's going on."

"I've told you I don't know what you're talking about."

"Saul, I made the hole in the lens, while Suzanne was away. I'm the one."

Saul almost laughed. "And that's why I should listen to you? Because you vandalized my lighthouse?"

"I did it because I knew something must be in there. Because there was this one spot where none of my equipment registered . . . anything."

"So what?" Didn't that just mean that trying to find strange things with uncertain instruments was a losing game?

"Saul, why would you look so haunted if this place wasn't haunted also? You know, just as I know. Even if no one else believes."

"Henry . . ." Should he launch into an explanation of why faith in a God did not automatically mean a faith in spirits?

"You don't need to say anything. But you know the truth—and I'll track it down, too. I'll find it."

The eagerness in Henry, the way he fairly thrummed with it, shocked Saul. It was as if Henry had thrown aside a disguise, laid bare his soul, and beneath that guarded exterior Saul had discovered one of the more virulently rigid of his flock from back north. The chosen ones who would never be dissuaded, the "Séance" side of their little brigade. He didn't want a follower.

"I still don't know what you're talking about." Obstinate, because he didn't want to be dragged into this, because he felt so ill. Because a few strange dreams did not add up to what Henry wanted them to add up to.

Henry ignored him, said, "Suzanne thinks the catalyst was something *they* brought with *them*. But that's not true, even if I can't tell you what combination of steps or processes brought us to this point. And yet, it happened. After we've spent so many years of searching in so many places with so little to show for it."

Against his better judgment, because more and more Henry looked like a victim to him, Saul said, "Do you need help? Tell me what's going on, and maybe I can help you. Tell me who that woman was."

"Forget you saw her, Saul. You'll never see her again. She doesn't care about the supernatural world or getting to the truth, not really."

Then Henry smiled and walked away, toward what destination Saul had no idea.

0013: CONTROL

Half the wall exploded and a thousand eyes peered in as Control sprawled from the impact in the dust and debris. His head throbbed and there was pain in his side and his left leg, but he forced himself to lie still. He was playing dead just to keep his head. He was playing dead to keep his head. A line from a book about monsters his father had read to him as a child. Rising out of a place long forgotten like a flare shot into the sky. Knocked into his brain, it kept looping. Playing dead to keep his head. The brick dust settling now, those eyes still an awful pressure. Even as the crunch of glass—the obliterating sound of that, the questing horror of that—sounded near his ear, and then the weight shifting near his legs. He fought the impulse to open his eyes, because he had to play dead to keep his head. Somewhere to his right, the knife he'd dropped, and his father's carving falling out of his pocket. Even sprawled as he was sprawled, seeking it with a trembling hand, reflexively. He was shivering, he was shaking, the reverberations of the creature's passage creating a pain like cracks and fissures in his bones, the brightness trying to escape, the part of him that was lonely, that wanted to reach out. Playing dead. To keep his head.

The glass crunch, the crunch glass, and its source beyond the wall, exploring inward, held his full attention. Boot? Shoe? Foot? No. Claws? Hooves? Cilia? Fins? Suppressed a shudder. Could he reach his knife? No. If he could have reached his knife in time, if his knife had been any help, it wouldn't have happened like this, except, yes, it was always going to be like this. Border breach, but there was no border here. It had all been moving so slow, like a journey that meant something, and now so fast. Too fast. Like breath that had become light, gone from mist to a ray, slashing out toward the horizon but not taking him with it. On the other side of the half-demolished wall, a new thing? An old thing? But not a mistake. Was there anything in it now of what he'd once known through its surrogate? Because he recognized its eyes.

Some part of it enveloped him, held him there, against the floor, while he screamed. Something like an eclipse in his head, a thick, tactile eclipse, pushing out his own intent. Questing through his mind for something else entirely, making him turn inward to see the things Lowry had put there, the terrible, irrevocable things, and how his mother must have helped Lowry. "Check the seats for loose change," Grandpa Jack had said, or had he? The heavy shape of the gun in his hands, Grandpa Jack's greedy gaze, and yet even that childhood memory seemed as hazy as smoke curling up from the cigarette of someone who stood in shadow at the far end of a long, darkened room.

Those thousands of eyes regarding him, *reading* him from across a vast expanse of space, as if the biologist existed simultaneously halfway across the universe. The sensation of being *seen* and then relief and a stabbing disappointment as it withdrew, spit him out. Rejected him.

There came a sound like a weight leaving the sky, a plunging toward the waves, and the awful weight of a pushing against the air lessened, and the restless agony in his bones receded, and he was just a dirty, spent figure weeping on the floor of a ruined lighthouse. With words like *collateral damage* and *containment* and *counterattacks* blossoming like old spells, incantations that worked in other, far distant, lands but not here. He was back in control, but control was meaningless. His father's sculptures in his old backyard were tipping over, one after the other. The chess moves between them in those last days before his father had died. The pressure of the piece between his fingers as he moved it, and the empty air as he let go.

Silence then. An absence into which the brightness again took up sentinel duty, swung around with ever-greater confidence to peer at him like the leviathans from his dreams. Perhaps unaware of what it protected, what it lived within.

Except *he* would never forget now.

Later, much later, familiar steps, and a familiar voice—Grace, extending a hand.

"Can you walk?"

Could he walk? He felt like an old man leveled by a blow from an invisible fist. He had fallen into a deep, dark, narrow fissure and now had to crawl up out of it.

"Yes, I can walk."

Grace handing him his father's carving, him taking it.

"Let's go back up to the landing."

There was a huge hole in the side of the first-floor wall. The night peered in from it. But the lighthouse had held.

"Yes, the landing."

He would be safe there.

He wouldn't be safe there.

Control lay there, back on the landing, sprawled across a blanket, looking up at the paint-peeled ceiling mottled by candlelight. Everything seemed so far away. Such an overwhelming psychic sense of their distance from Earth, that there might not now be astronomers, might never be astronomers who, all-knowing, could even make out the speck that was the star around which they must revolve. He found it hard to breathe, kept calling forth another passage from the pages of Whitby where the man almost waxed poetic: "Area X has been created by an organism left behind by a civilization so advanced and so ancient and so alien to us and our own intent and our own thought processes that it has long since left us behind, left everything behind."

Wondering, too, because of all that the biologist's intrusion had knocked loose in his head . . . if there was any evidence he'd ever sat in the backseat of his grandfather's muscle car—if somewhere at Central you would find black-and-white photos shot from farther down the street, through the windshield of a car or a van. An investment. A divestment. The start of it all. He'd had dreams of cliffs and leviathans and falling into the sea. But what if the leviathans were back at Central? The shadowy forms mere outlines of memories he could not quite recall, overlaid with those that he should not remember because they had never occurred. *Jump*, a voice had said, and he had jumped. Two days lost at Central before he came to the Southern Reach, and only his mother's word for it that he was being paranoid . . . But it was such a weight, so exhausting to analyze, as if the Southern Reach and Area X both interrogated him.

Hello, John, said some version of Lowry in his head. *Surprise.*

Fuck you.

Seriously, John? And here I thought you knew all along, the game we were playing. The game we've always been playing.

His lungs felt heavy, thick, as Grace checked him out, bandaged his elbow, told him, "You've bruised some ribs and your hip is bruised, too, but you seem able to move everything."

"The biologist . . . she's really gone?" *This leviathan that has taken the terroir of a place and made it its own.* Every moment that passed, the gospel of Whitby made more and less sense to him. Such an inconsistent heartbeat. Such simplicity to concentrate on those three pages, to focus on the parts so smudged he had to interpret the words or to smooth out a curled corner, than on the fact that the sun should not be shining above, that the sky could peel back to reveal a celestial landscape perhaps never dreamed of by humankind, the weight of that oppressive, a beast bearing down on the very center, which must be protected from that which did not bear contemplating.

"She's been gone for a while," Grace said. "You've been a little gone, for a while."

She stood next to the seaward window, along with Ghost Bird. Ghost Bird had her back to Control, staring out at the night. Was she charting her original's progress? Was that vast form now in open water, seeking depth and distance? Or had she departed for someplace stranger and more remote? He didn't want to know.

When Ghost Bird finally turned, the shadows made of her face an impression of a fading smile and wide, curious eyes.

"What did it share with you?" Control asked. "What did it take?" More caustic than he'd meant, but he was still in a kind of shock, knew that on some level. Wanted his experience to be the common one.

"Nothing. Nothing at all."

What side are you on? Lowry asked.

"What side are you on?" he asked.

"Enough!" Grace said. "Enough! Just shut the fuck up. That's not helping."

But he couldn't shut up. "No wonder you're on edge," he said. "No wonder you didn't tell us."

"The biologist took out the convoy," Ghost Bird said.

"Yes, she did," Grace admitted. "But I have been careful and quiet and not provoked her. I know when to stay away from the lighthouse or the shore. I know when to fade into the forest. Sometimes there's a kind of *foreshadowing* in the air. Sometimes she will make landfall where she found the owl, then push on through the interior, headed here. As if she remembers. Most times, I can avoid her. Most times, she isn't here."

"Remembers what? This place?"

"I don't know what she remembers or doesn't remember," Grace said. "I just know your presence here attracted her, made her curious." Not Control's presence, that much he knew. Ghost Bird's presence. The biologist was drawn to her as surely as he had been drawn to her.

"We could be just like the biologist," Control said. "Stay here. Wait it out. Wait her out. Just give in." Goading them.

But it was Ghost Bird who answered: "She earned the right to choose her fate. She earned the right."

"We're not her," Grace said. "I don't want to become her, or anything like her."

"Isn't that all you've been doing? Waiting?" Wanting to see just how well Grace had adjusted to living on an island with a monster.

"Not exactly. But what do you want me to do? Tell me what I should do, and I will do it!" Shouting now. "Do you think I *want* to wait here, die here? Do you think I like it?" The thought occurred that Grace had made use of the biologist's list of pain-inducers, that her thinness, the hollowed-out quality to her face, wasn't just about being haunted by a monster.

"You need a way out," Ghost Bird said.

"Through a hole in the sea that may not be there?"

"No. Another way out."

Control propped himself up with a groan. His side was on fire. "Are you sure the ribs are just bruised?"

"I can't be sure without an X-ray."

Another impossible thing. Yet another moment in his decline. A wall changing to the touch of his hand, the touch of the biologist in his head. Enough of this. Enough.

He took up Whitby's pages, began to read by candlelight even as he began to tear the corners off. Slowly.

We must trust our thoughts while we sleep. We must trust our hunches. We must begin to examine all of those things that we think of as irrational simply because we do not understand them. In other words, we must distrust the rational, the logical, the sane, in an attempt to reach for something higher, for something more worthy. Brilliance and bullshit both. A binary trapped in its single-minded focus on solutions.

"What?" he asked. He could feel the other two staring at him.

Ghost Bird said, "You need to rest."

"What I'd suggest isn't going to be popular anyway," he said. Tearing one full page into shreds. Letting the pieces fall to the floor. It felt good to tear something apart.

"Say it." Challenging him.

A pause, preparing himself. Aware of the conflicting voices in his head.

"What you call the Crawler—we have to try. We have to go back down into the tower and find some way to neutralize it."

Ghost Bird: "Have you been paying attention? Have you been listening?"

"Or we stay here."

"Staying here isn't going to work," Grace admitted. "Either the biologist will get us, or Area X will."

"There's a lot of open, vulnerable space for us between here and the tower," Ghost Bird said.

"There's a lot of everything between here and there."

"Control," Ghost Bird said, and he didn't want to look at her, didn't want to see those eyes that now reminded him of the creature the biologist had become. "Control, there's no reset. There's never going to be a reset. That's a suicide mission." Unspoken, that she thought it was a suicide mission for them. Who knew what it might be for her?

"But the director thought you could change its direction," he said. "That you could change it, if you tried hard enough." A halting kind of hope. A childish thrashing against the dictates of the real. *If you wished upon a star.* He was thinking of the light at the bottom of the tower, this new thing he hadn't known about before entering Area X. He was thinking about being sick, and now sicker, and what that meant. At least they were all out in the open now, clear to him. The brightness, Lowry, all of it. Everything in the mix, including the core he still thought of as John Rodriguez. The Rodriguez who didn't belong to anyone. Who clasped his father's carving tight in his pocket. Who remembered something beyond the wreck and ruin of all this.

"It's true we have one thing no one else had," Grace said.

"What?" Ghost Bird asked in a skeptical, doubting tone.

"You," Grace said. "The only photocopy of the director's last plan."

0014: THE DIRECTOR

When, eventually, you return to the Southern Reach, you find a gift waiting for you: a framed black-and-white photograph of the lighthouse keeper, his assistant, and a little girl playing on the rocks—head down, jacket hood disguising her features. The blood rushes to your head, and you almost black out, seeing that this photo you didn't know still existed.

"It's for your office," reads the pointed note that comes with it. "You should hang it on the wall there. In fact, you must keep it on the wall. As a reminder of how far you've come. For your years of service and for your loyalty. Love and Kisses, Jimmy Boy."

That's when you realize there is something very much more wrong with Lowry than you'd ever thought before. That he creates ever more spectacular and grandiose dysfunctions to test what the system might bear before it finds him out. He seems, year after year, to revel in his clandestine operations not because they are secret but for those tantalizing moments when, either by his own hand or by fate, the edges of them almost become known.

But where had the photograph come from?

"Pull everything we have on Jackie Severance," you tell Grace. "Pull every file that mentions *Jack* Severance. And the son—*John Rodriguez*. Even if it takes a year. We're looking for something that connects Severance—any Severance—to Lowry." You've got a sense of an unholy alliance, a devilish foundation. An inkling of bad faith. Something hidden in the grout between the stones.

Meanwhile, you have a plant and a cell phone, very early model, to deal with—all you have to show for your journey. Other than a new sense of being separate, remote, set apart from the staff.

When you see Whitby in the hallway now, sometimes you meet his gaze and nod and there is a sense of a secret shared. Other times, you must look away, stare at that worn green carpet that meanders through everything. Make some polite comment in the cafeteria, try to immerse yourself in meetings as they prep another expedition. Try to pretend everything is normal. Is Whitby broken? His smile flickers back into place at times. His old confident stance, the wit in Whitby, will reappear but not for long, and then a light winks out in his eyes and darkness comes back in.

There's nothing you could say to Whitby except "I'm sorry," but you can't even say that. You can't change the moments that changed him except in your memory, and even in memory that attempt is obscured by the fast-rising *thing* from below, the thing that terrified you so much you abandoned Saul there, on the tunnel steps. Said to yourself afterward that Saul wasn't real, couldn't be real, so you hadn't abandoned anyone. "Don't forget about me," he'd said, so long ago, and you won't ever forget him, but you might have to leave him behind. That apparition. The hallucination that, as you sit at the bar in Chipper's Star Lanes or debate policy with Grace on the Southern Reach rooftop, you still try to rationalize as not a hallucination at all.

In part because you came back with the plant. For a time, obsessed with each dark green leaf, the way looking at it from above it forms a kind of fanlike circle, but from the side the effect fades completely. If you focus on the plant, maybe you can forget Lowry, waiting out there, for a while. Maybe Saul won't matter. Maybe you can salvage something out of . . . nothing.

The plant will not die.

No parasites will touch the plant.

The plant will not die.

No extremes of temperature will affect it. Freeze it, it will thaw. Burn it, it will regenerate.

The plant will not die.

No matter what you try, no matter the experiments performed on it in the sterile, the blinding white environs of the storage cathedral . . . the plant won't die. It's not that you mean to order its execution, but that in the course of the samples taken, the researchers inform you that the plant refuses to die. That cutting—you could chop it up into five dozen tiny pieces, put those in a measuring cup, sprinkle it on a steak for seasoning . . . and in theory it would grow inside of you, eventually burst forth seeking sunlight.

So, relenting, you let samples be whisked away to Central, so that experts can solve the mystery of this simple, ordinary plant that looks like any number of temperate-climate perennials. Samples, too, to Lowry's secret headquarters, perhaps to reside next to cages in experimental bunkers, although none of their findings ever come back to you. All of this in the midst of a frenzied slicing and dicing of other specimens in the storage cathedral, just to make sure there hasn't been some domino effect, or something's been missed. But nothing has been missed.

"I don't think we're looking at a plant," Whitby says, tentative, at one status meeting, risking his new relationship with the science division, which he has embraced as a kind of sanctuary.

"Then why are we *seeing* a plant, Whitby?" Cheney, managing to convey an all-consuming exasperation. "Why are we seeing a plant that *looks like* a plant being a plant. Doing plant things, like photosynthesis and drawing water up through its roots. Why? That's not a tough question, is it, really? Or is it? Maybe it is a tough question, I don't know, for reasons beyond me. But that's going to be a problem, don't you think? Having to reassert that things we think are the things they are are actually are in fact the things they are and not *some other thing entirely.* Just think of all the fucking things we will have to reevaluate if you're right, Whitby—starting with you!" Cheney's blistered, reddening expression bears down on Whitby as if he were the receptacle of every evil thing that has ever afflicted Cheney since the day he was born. "Because," Cheney says, lowering his voice, "if that's a tough question, don't we have to reclassify all the *really* tough questions?"

Later Whitby will regale you with information on how quantum mechanics impacts photosynthesis, which is all about "antenna receiving light and antenna can be hacked," about how "one organism might *peer out* from another organism but not live there," of how plants "talk" to one another, how communication can occur in chemical form and through processes so invisible to human beings that the sudden visibility of it would be "an irreparable shock to the system."

For the Southern Reach? For humanity?

But Whitby's close-lipped about that, changes the subject. Abruptly.

You're less obsessed with the cell phone, which has been living with the techs down in the hardware department, the ones who have the right security clearance. But the techs can't make it work, are confused by it, perhaps even unnnerved. Nothing about it indicates a malfunction. It should work. It just doesn't. It should reveal who owned it. It just doesn't.

"As if it's not really made of the parts it should be made of. But it looks exactly that way—like a normal phone. Really old, though."

A bulky veteran of a phone, scarred and scraped and worn. It looks like you feel sometimes.

You offer it to Lowry during one of your calls, as a kind of sacrifice of a pawn. Give Lowry an exclusive, let him worry at it like a dog with a new bone, so the old bone can get some rest. But he doesn't want it—insists you keep it.

Something an expedition member had snuck in with them or inadvertently brought along? Something perhaps from a recent expedition that someone had thought was old enough not to disturb Area X's slumber? During the cycles that predated Lowry's intervention, your stewardship, techniques primitive and untested.

Recalling the very earliest photographs and video—of Lowry and the others in what amounted to deep-sea diving outfits to traverse the border, before they realized it was unnecessary. Lowry, returned, disoriented, babbling on videotape, words he would later recant, about how nothing would ever come out of the passage in the border, nothing, because they were waiting for ghosts, for something long dead, Area X a memorial, a gravestone.

"What made Area X spit it back up?" you ask Grace, safe on the roof in Beyond Reach.

"What made Whitby the one to find it?"

"A good question." A gift from Dead Whitby.

"Why did it allow itself to be found?"

That sounds like the right question, and some days you want to tell Grace . . . everything. But most days you want to shield her from information that will make no difference to her job, her life. Somehow Dead Whitby and the Saul apparition fall on the same side as telling her that your name is not your name. That all of the unimportant things about you are a lie.

Eventually, into the middle of all this comes the call you've been dreading: Lowry, with a purpose. While you're staring at the incriminating photograph on the wall: you on the rocks, shouting either before or after the shot was taken, "I'm a monster! I'm a monster!"

"Another eleventh expedition is a go."

"Already."

"Three months. We're almost there."

You want to say, but don't say, "It's time to stop tampering, not time to intensify the tampering." The fiddling. All the ways Lowry tries to control what cannot really be controlled.

"That's too soon," you say. Too soon by far. Nothing has changed, except that you interfered and went over the border and brought back two objects you can't explain.

"Maybe it's time for you to stop being a fucking coward," Lowry says. "Three months. Get ready, *Cynthia*." He bangs the phone down, and you imagine him banging it down into a housing that's a polished human skull.

They implant into the brain of the psychologist—on what will turn out to be the last eleventh—what Lowry calls "a pearl of surveillance and recall." Some tiny subset of the silver egg that is Central, passing first through Lowry's deforming grip. They make a man *not himself*, and you go along with it to keep your job, to stay close to what is important to you.

Twelve months later, the last eleventh expedition comes back, acting almost like zombies, memories cloudier than the drunk veteran's at the Star Lanes Lounge. Eighteen months later, they're all dead of cancer, and Lowry's back on the phone talking about the "next eleventh" and "making refinements to our process" and you realize something has to change. Again. And short of putting a gun to Lowry's head and pulling the trigger, it's going to come down to influencing the composition of the expeditions, how they are deployed, and a host of lesser factors. None of which may make a difference, but you have to try. Because you never want to see such lost, vacant faces ever again, never again want to see people who have been stripped of something so vital that it can't be expressed through words.

Morale at the Southern Reach becomes worse after the last eleventh returns and then, so quickly, passes on to the next place, wherever that might be. Numbness? A sense of having gone through so many crises that emotion must be hoarded, that it might not run out.

From the transcripts: "It was a beautiful day." "The

expedition was uneventful." "We had no problems in completing the mission."

What was the mission, in their eyes? But they'd never answer that question. Grace spoke of them in reverential tones, almost as if they'd become saints. Down in the science division, Cheney became more muted and subdued for a long time, as if the color TV of his commentary had been replaced by a black-and-white model with a single channel of pixelated fuzz. Ephemeral, ethereal Pitman called from Central with oblique condolences and a kind of calculated indifference to his tone that suggested misdirection.

But you were the one who had seen the curling worm of Lowry's corruption at work—that what he'd done, the bargain you had made that had allowed him to be so invasive and controlling, hadn't been worth it.

Even worse, Jackie Severance visits regularly afterward, as if maybe Central is concerned about something, takes to pacing around your office and gesticulating as she talks, rather than just sitting still. This emissary of Central you have to deal with in the flesh rather than just Lowry.

"She's my parole officer," you tell Grace.

"Then who is Lowry?"

"Lowry's the parole officer's partner? Boss? Employee?" Because you don't know.

"A riddle wrapped in a puzzle," Grace says. "Do you know what her father, Jack Severance, is up to?"

"No, what?"

"Everything." So much everything that Grace is still wading through all of it.

When Severance comes calling, there's a sense she's checking up on her investment, her shared risk.

"Does it ever get to you?" Severance asks you more than once, and you're fairly sure she's just making conversation.

"No," you lie, shoot back your own cliché: "We all have our jobs to do."

Back when she worked for the Southern Reach, you'd liked her—sharp, charming, and she'd done a good job of fine-tuning logistics, of diving in and getting work done. But since she's chained to Lowry, you can't risk that her presence isn't his presence. Sharing a swig of brandy with Grace: "A living bug—can't exactly just pull her out of the ceiling tiles." And the glamour has begun to fade: At times, Severance looks to you like a tired, faded clerk at a makeup counter in a department store.

Severance sits with you, observing the returnees through closed-circuit cameras for long minutes, coffee in hand, checking her phone every few minutes, often drawn off into some side conversation about some other project altogether, then coming back into focus to ask questions.

"You're sure they're not contaminated with something?"

"When do you send in the next expedition?"

"What do you think of Lowry's metrics?"

"If you had a bigger budget, what would you spend it on?"

"Do you know what you're looking for?"

No, you don't know. She knows you don't know. You don't even know what you're looking at, these people who became ever more gaunt until they were living skeletons, and then not even that. The psychologist perhaps even blanker than the rest, like a kind of warning to you, as if it were a side effect of his profession, encountering Area X. But a closer look at his history reveals Lowry probably leaned on him the most, thought, maybe, that his profession made him stronger than the rest. The bindings, the reconditioning sessions, the psychological tricks—surely a psychologist could absorb them, armed with foreknowledge. Except the man hadn't, and as far as they knew this "coiled sting" inside his brain had made no difference at all to Area X.

"There must be things you would have done differently," Severance says.

You make some noncommittal sound and pretend you're scribbling something on your notepad. A grocery list, maybe. A blank circle that's either a representation of the border or of Central. A plant rising out of a cell phone. Or maybe you should just write *Fuck you* and be done with it. Gnaw your way out of Lowry's trap.

At some point after the last of the last eleventh passes away, you get black paint from maintenance, along with thick black markers, and you open the useless door that gives you access to the blank wall—casualty of a clumsy corridor redesign. You write out the words collected from the topographical anomaly, the words that you know must have been written by the light-house keeper (this flash of intuition, unveiled at a status meeting, allowing you to order a deeper investigation into Saul's background than ever before).

You draw a map, too, of all the landmarks in Area X. There's the base camp, or as you call it now, the Mirage. There's the lighthouse, which should be some form of safety but too often isn't, the place that journals go to die. There's the topograph-ical anomaly, the hole in the ground into which all initiative and focus descended, only to become hazy and diffuse. There, too, is the island and, finally, the Southern Reach itself, looking either like the last defense against the enemy or its farthestmost outpost.

Lowry, drunk out of his mind at his going-away party, headed for Central, only three years after you had been hired, had said, "How goddamn boring. Fucking boring if they win. If we gotta live in that world." As if people would be living in "that world" at all, which wasn't what any of the evidence foretold, or kept foretelling, as if there were nothing worse than being bored and the only point of the world people already lived in was to find ways to combat boredom, to make sure "all the moments," as Whitby put it when he went on about parallel universes, might be accounted for in some way, so minds wouldn't fill up with emptiness that they bifurcated simply to have more capacity to be bored.

And Grace, fearless, an opposing voice from years later at some other party where a member of the staff had voiced an equally cynical, depressing opinion, but as if answering Lowry: "I'm still here because of my family. Because of my family and because of the director, and because I don't want to give up on them or you." Even if Grace could never share with her family the struggles she faced at the Southern Reach, being your "right-hand gal" as Lowry puts it, sarcastically. The profane voice of reason when yours is perceived as too esoteric, too distant.

Halfway through drawing the map, you feel eyes on you, and there's Grace, arms folded, giving you the stink eye. She closes the office door behind her, just keeps staring at you.

"Is there something I can help you with?" you ask, paint can in one hand and brush in the other.

"You can reassure me that everything is okay." For one of the first times, you sense doubt from her. Not disagreement but doubt, and given how much things rely on faith at the late-era Southern Reach, this worries you.

"I'm fine," you say. "I'm just fine. I just want a reminder."

"Of what? To the staff? That you're getting a little eccentric?"

A surge of anger at that, a faint echo of hurt, too. Lowry, for all of his faults, might not think it was strange. He'd understand. But also, if it were Lowry painting a map on the wall of his office, no one would be questioning him. They'd be asking if they could hold the brush, touch up this spot, that spot, get him more paint.

Going for the cumulative effect, to put more pressure on the breaking point, you say to Grace, "After I'm done here, I'm going to order the bodies of the last eleventh exhumed."

"Why?" Aghast, something in her background averse to such desecrations.

"Because I think it's necessary. Which is enough of a reason." Having what Grace will call "your Lowry moment," and it's not even that volcanic, just stubbornness.

"Cynthia," Grace says. "Cynthia, what I think or don't think doesn't matter, but the rest of the staff has to *want* to follow you."

More stubborn thought still: that all you really need is Lowry to follow you and Severance, and you could hold on here forever. Hideous thought, though, the image of another thirty-six expeditions being sent out, only some coming back, of you and Grace and Whitby, progressively more jaded and cynical, becoming ancient, going through motions that wouldn't help anyone, not even yourselves.

"I'm going to finish this up," you tell her in a conciliatory way. "Because I started it."

"Because it will look fucking stupid if you don't finish it now," she says, relenting as well.

"Yes, exactly. It will look fucking stupider if I don't finish."

"So let me help," she says, and something in the emphasis she puts on the words gets to you. Will always get to you.

Let me help.

"All right, then," you say gruffly, and hand her the extra brush.

But you're still going to dig up the dead, and you're still wondering how to change the paradigm like Lowry keeps trying to change the paradigm. Lost in the thought of that the next weekend at Chipper's while bowling, while home clipping coupons for the grocery store, while taking a bath, while going out for a ballroom dancing lesson because it's the kind of thing you would never do. So you do it, aware that if Severance has eyes on you, she'll find it evidence of being "erratic," but not caring. You put yourself here, set this trap for yourself, so if you feel trapped by it now, it's your own fault.

The day after painting the door, Grace follows up, as she always does, unable to leave it alone, but privately, on the rooftop, which by now you're pretty sure Cheney suspects exists, just as he suspects the involvement of "dark energy" in the maintenance of the invisible border . . . Grace saying, "You have a plan, right? This is all part of a plan. I'm relying on you to have a plan."

So you nod, smile, say, "Yes, Grace, I have a plan," because you don't want to betray that trust, because what's the good of saying "All I have is a feeling, an intuition, and a brief conversation with a man who should be dead. I have a plant and a phone."

In your dreams you stand on the sidelines, holding the plant in one hand and the cell phone in the other, watching a war between Central and Area X. In some fundamental way, you feel, they have been in conflict for far longer than thirty years—for ages and ages, centuries in secret. Central the ultimate void to counteract Area X: impersonal, antiseptic, labyrinthine, and unknowable. Against the facade, you cannot help but express a kind of terrible betrayal: Sometimes you admire Lowry's fatal liveliness next to *that*, a silhouette writhing against a dull white screen.

0015: THE LIGHTHOUSE KEEPER

Western siren finally fixed; touched up the white part of the daymark, seaward side; fixed the ladder, too, but still feels rickety, unsafe. Something knocked down a foot of fence and got into the garden, but couldn't tell what. No deer tracks, but likely culprit. S&SB? The shadows of the abyss are like the petals of a monstrous flower. Didn't feel up to a hike, but seen from lighthouse grounds, of note: flycatcher (not sure what kind), frigate birds, least terns, cormorants, black-throated stilt (!), a couple of yellow-throats. On the beach, found a large pipefish had washed up, a few sail jellyfish rotting in the sand.

There came an incandescent light. There came a star in motion, the sun plummeting to Earth. There fell from the heavens a huge burning torch, thick flames dripping out behind it. And this light, this star, shook the sky and the beach where he had walked a second ago under a clear blue sky. The scorched intensity of the sudden object hurtling down toward him battered his senses, sent him sprawling to his knees as he tried to run, and then dove face-first into the sand. He screamed as the rays, the sparks,

sprayed out all around, and the core of the light hit somewhere in front of him, his teeth smashed in his mouth, his
bones turned to powder. The reverberation lived within
him as he tried to regain his footing, even as the impact con-
jured up an enormous tidal wave like a living creature, aimed
at the beach. When it fell upon him the weight, the immen-
sity, destroyed him once more and washed away anything he
could have recognized, could have known. He gasped and
thrashed and hurt, dug his tortured hands into the shocking
cold sand. The sand had a different texture, and the tiny creatures living there were different. He didn't want to look up,
take in his surroundings, frightened that the landscape, too,
might have changed, might be so different he would not recognize it.

The tidal waves faded. The burning lights receded.

Saul managed to get to his feet, to stagger a step or
two, and as he did, he realized that everything around him
had been restored. The world he knew, the world he loved:
tranquil, unchanged, the lighthouse up the shore undam-
aged by the wave. Seagulls flew by, and far in the distance
someone walked, looking for shells. He brushed the sand
from his shirt, his shorts, stood there for a long moment bent
over with his hands on his thighs. The impact was still affect-
ing his hearing, still making him shake with the memory of
its power. Yet it had left no evidence behind except melan-
choly, as if he held within him the only memory of some lost
world.

He could not stop trembling in the aftermath, wondered
if he were going insane. That took less hubris than thinking
this was a message from on high. For in the center of the

light that had come storming down, an image had appeared, a pattern that he recognized: the eight leaves of the strange plant, each one like another spiraling step down into oblivion.

Midmorning. The rocks were slippery and sharp, encrusted with limpets and barnacles. Sea lice, ancient of days, traveled across those rocks on quests to scavenge whatever they could, and the seaweed that gathered there, in strands thin and thick and sometimes gelatinous, brought a tangy, moldy smell.

It was a relief to sit there, trying to recover—peering into the tidal pool that lay at his feet as the rock dug into his posterior. As he tried to control his shaking. There had been other visions, but none as powerful as this one. He had a perverse urge for Henry to appear, to confess all of his symptoms to a man who, once revealed as a passionate, delusional ghost-hunter, he recalled almost with fondness. But Saul hadn't seen Henry or Suzanne since the incident in the night, nor the strange woman. Sometimes he thought he was being watched, but that was probably nothing more than a reflection of believing Henry when he said he would "find it," implying a return.

The tidal pool directly in front of him became frustratingly occluded when a cloud passed overhead and changed the quality of the light, or when the wind picked up and created ripples. But when the sun broke through again and it wasn't just the reflection of his face and knees he saw, the pool became a kind of living cabinet of curiosities. He might prefer to hike, to bird-watch, but he could understand a fascination with tidal pools, too.

Fat orange starfish, either lumbering or slumbering, lay half in, half out of the water. Some bottom-dwelling fish contemplated him with a kind of bulging, jaded regard—a boxy, pursed-lipped creature whose body was the same color as the sand, except for bejeweled sapphire-and-gold eyes. A tiny red crab sidled across that expanse toward what to it must be a gaping chasm of a dark hole leading down, perhaps into an endless network of tiny caverns carved into the rocks over the years. If he stared long enough into the comforting oblivion of that microcosm, it washed away everything else, even the shadow of his reflection.

It was there, some minutes later, that Gloria found him, as Saul perhaps had known she would, the rocks to her what the lighthouse had become to him.

She dropped down beside him as if indestructible, corduroy-clad rump sliding hardly at all on the hard surface. Not so much perched as a rock atop another rock. The solid weight of her forced him a little to the side. She was breathing hard from clambering fast over the rocks, managed a kind of "uh-huh" of approval at his choice of entertainment and he gave her a brief smile and a nod in return.

For a long while, they just sat together, watching. He had decided he could not talk to her about what he had seen, that pushing that onto her was wrong. The only one he could tell was Charlie. Maybe.

The crab sifted through something in the sand. The camouflaged fish risked a slow walk on stickery fins like drab half-opened fans, making for the shadow-shelter of a tiny ledge of rock. One of the starfish, as if captured via time-lapse photography, withdrew at a hypnotically slow speed into the water, until only the tips of two arms lay exposed and glistening.

Finally Gloria said, "Why are you down here and not working by the shed or in the tower?"

"I don't feel like working today." Images from old illu-minated manuscripts, of comets hurtling through the sky, from the books in his father's house. The reverberation and recoil of the beach exploding under his feet. The strange creatures in the sand. What message should he take from that?

"Yeah, I don't always want to go to school," she said. "But at least you get money."

"I do get money, that's true," he said. "And they're never going to give you money to go to school."

"They should give me money. I have to put up with a lot." He wondered just how much. It might well be a lot.

"School's important," he said, because he felt he should say it, as if Gloria's mother stood right behind them, tapping her foot.

Gloria considered that a moment, nudged him in the ribs in a way as familiar as if they were drinking buddies down at the village bar.

"I told my mom this is a school, too, but that didn't work."

"What's 'this'?"

"The tidal pools. The forest. The trails. All of it. Most of the time it's true I'm just goofing off, but I'm learning things, too."

Saul could imagine how that conversation had gone. "You're not going to get any grades here." Warming to the idea: "Although I guess the bears might give you grades for watching out for them."

She kind of leaned back to get a better look at him, as if reappraising him. "That's stupid. Are you feeling okay?"

"Yeah, this whole conversation is stupid."

"Are you still feeling different?"

"What? No. No, I'm fine, Gloria."

They watched the fish for a bit after that. Something about their conversation, the way they'd moved too fast or been too loud, had made the fish retreat into the sand so now only its eyes looked up at them.

"There are things the lighthouse teaches me, though," Gloria said, wrenching Saul out of his thoughts.

"To stand up straight and tall and project light out of your head toward the sea?"

She giggled at that, giving him too much credit for an answer he'd meant at least half ironically.

"No. Here's what the lighthouse teaches me. Be quiet and let me tell you. The lighthouse teaches me to work hard, to keep my room clean, to be honest, and to be nice to people." Then, reflecting, looking down at her feet. "My room is a mess and I lie sometimes and I'm not always nice to people, but that's the idea."

A little embarrassed, he said, "That fish down there sure is frightened of you."

"Huh? It just doesn't know me. If it knew me, that fish would shake my hand."

"I don't think there's anything you could say to convince

it of that. And there are all kinds of ways you could hurt it without meaning to." Watching those unblinking blue eyes with the gold streaks—the dark vertical pupil—that seemed like a fundamental truth.

Ignoring him: "You like being a lighthouse keeper, don't you, Saul?" Saul. That was a new thing. When had they become Saul and Gloria rather than Mr. Evans and Gloria?

"Why, do you want my job when you grow up?"

"No. I never want to be a lighthouse keeper. Shoveling and making tomatoes and climbing all the time." Was that how it seemed he spent his time? He guessed it did.

"At least you're honest."

"Yep. Mom says I should be less honest."

"There's that, too." His father could have been less honest, because honesty was often just a way of being cruel.

"Anyway, I can't stay long." There was real regret in her voice.

"A shame, given how honest you're being."

"I know, right? But I gotta go. Mom's going to come by in the car soon. We're driving into town to meet my dad."

"Oh, he's picking you up for the holidays?" So this was the day.

A shadow had passed over the tidal pool again and all he could see were their two faces, peering down. He could've passed for her father, couldn't he? Or was he too old? But such thoughts were a form of weakness.

"It's longer this time," she said, clearly not happy about it. "Mom wants me up there for a couple of months at least. Because she's lost her second job and needs to look for another one. But that's only eight weeks. Or maybe sixty days."

He looked over at her, saw the serious expression on her face. Two months. That was an impossibly long time.

"You'll have fun. When you get back, you'll appreciate this place even more."

"I appreciate it now. And it won't be fun. Dad's girlfriend is a bitch."

"Don't use that word."

"Sorry. But she is."

"Did your mom say that?"

"No. I made it up myself. It wasn't hard."

"Well, try to get along," Saul said, having reached the end of any advice a lighthouse could convey. "It's just for a little while."

"Sure. And then I'll be back. Help me up, I think my mom's here." He couldn't hear a car, but that didn't mean anything.

He took her hand, braced himself so she could lean on him and get to her feet. She stood there, balanced against him, hand on his shoulder, and said, "Goodbye, Saul. Save this tidal pool for me."

"I'll put up a sign." He tried to smile.

She nodded, and then she was gone, scampering across the rocks like some kind of deranged daredevil—showing off.

On impulse he turned and shouted "Hey, Gloria!" at her before she was out of earshot.

She turned, balanced with both arms outstretched, waiting.

"Don't forget about me! Take care of yourself!" He tried to make it sound without weight, sentences that could float away into the air. Nothing that mattered.

She nodded and waved, and said something he couldn't hear, and then she was running up the lighthouse lawn and around the curve of the lighthouse wall, out of sight.

Below, the fish had its mouth around the small red crab, which was struggling in a slow, meditative way, almost like it didn't want to get free.

0016: GHOST BIRD

The lighthouse rose from fog and reflections like a mirror of itself, the beach gray and cold, the sand rasping against the hull of the boat as they abandoned it in the shallows. The waves came in small and half curling like the froth of malformed questions. The lighthouse did not resemble Ghost Bird's memory of it, for its sides had been scoured by fire. Discoloration extended all the way to the top, where the lens, the light within, lay extinguished. The fire had erupted from the landing windows as well, and in combination with the bits of broken glass, and all of the other talismans human beings had rendered up to it over the years, gave the lighthouse the appearance of something shamanistic. Reduced now to a daymark for their boat, the simplest of its functions, the one task that, unperformed, made a lighthouse no longer of use to anyone. Made it into a narrow, haunted redoubt.

"Burned by the border commander," Grace had told them. "Burned because they didn't understand it—and the journals with it."

But Ghost Bird caught the hesitation in Grace's voice, how she still would not tell them exactly what had happened within the lighthouse, what *slaughter* and *deception* consisted of, any detailed accounting of what had come at them from the seaward side.

All Grace could offer in its place was a localized pathology—the origin of the orange flags. The doing of the border commander, a cataloging of all that was unknowable to her. Perhaps the commander had been trying to keep separate the real from the imagined. If so, she had failed. Even common thistles had been so marked. Given more time, the commander might have marked the entire world.

Ghost Bird had a vision of the journals impervious, still up there, reconstituted, were they now to enter, walk up into the lantern room, undo the trapdoor, stare down as had the biologist, as had she, so many years ago. Would the reflected light from those frozen accounts irradiate their thoughts, contaminate their dreams, forever trap them? Or was there just a mountain of ashes in there now? Ghost Bird did not want to find out.

It was late afternoon already. They had left the island in the early morning, in a bigger boat Grace had hidden out of sight of the pier. The biologist had not reappeared, although Control had searched those waters with a kind of nervous anxiety. Ghost Bird would have sensed her presence long before there was any danger. She could not tell him, for his own sake, that the oceans through which the biologist now traveled were wider and deeper than the one that led them to the lighthouse.

They trudged up the beach toward the lighthouse, taking a path that minimized the possibility of sniper fire from above.

Grace believed everyone was dead, or long since had moved on, but there was always the chance. Nothing arose from the seaward side, ghostlike or otherwise. *Things came out of the sea, things like the biologist, but less kind.*

From the lip of the dunes, they came up to the level ground next to the lighthouse without incident, lingered at the edge of the overgrown, long-wild lawn beside it. Where nettle weed and snarls of blackberry plants grew: a thorny thicket for them, but a natural shelter for the wrens and sparrows that darted betwixt, between, their cheerful song a discordant element against the overcast quality of the light. The ever-present thistles looked to Ghost Bird like some kind of natural microphone, the stickery domes there to pick up and transmit sound instead of disseminate seeds.

A broken door yawned, beckoned to them with darkness, while the gray sky above, the way it could glint or waver at odd moments, made Control in particular jittery. He could not stand still, did not want Ghost Bird or Grace standing still, either. Ghost Bird could see the brightness flaring out from him like a halo of jagged knives, wondered if he would still be himself by the time they reached the tower. Perhaps he would, if nothing preternatural stitched its way through that sky.

"No point in going up," Grace said.

"Not even the least bit curious?"

"Do you like walking through charnel houses and cemeteries, too?"

Still evaluating her, and Ghost Bird unable to tell what she was thinking. Had Grace thrown in her lot with them, hoping Ghost Bird was indeed a secret weapon, or for some other purpose? What she did know was that with Grace there she'd had little time to talk to Control in private—any conversations were of necessity between the three of them. This disturbed her, because she knew Grace even less than she knew Control.

"I don't want to go up," Control said. "I don't. I want to cover the open ground as fast as possible. Get to where we're going as fast as possible."

"At least no one appears to be here," Grace said. "At least it appears as if Area X may have thinned out the opposition."

Yes, that was good, if a cold thing to say, but the look Control gave Grace indicated he could not jettison some essential sentimentality that was of no use here, some mechanism that belonged to the world outside.

"Well, let me add to the collection," Grace said, and tossed the biologist's island account and her journal through the open front door.

Control stared into that darkness as if she had committed a terrible act that he was thinking of setting right. But Ghost Bird knew that Grace was just trying to set them free.

"Never has a setting been so able to live without the souls traversing it." A sentence Ghost Bird remembered from a college text, one that had lingered with the biologist after her transition to the city, come back to her as she stood in the empty lot, following the silent launch of a sugar glider from one telephone pole to another. The text had been referring to urban landscapes, but the biologist had interpreted it as applying to the natural world, or at least what could be interpreted as wilderness, even though human beings had so transformed the world that even Area X had not been able to completely reduce those signs and symbols. The shrubs and trees that constituted invasive species were only one part of that; the other, how even the faint outline of a human-made path changed the topography of a place. "The only solution to the environment is neglect, which requires our collapse." A sentence the biologist had excised from her thesis, but one that had burned bright in her mind, and now in Ghost Bird's, where, even analyzed and kept at arm's length like all received memories, it had a kind of power. In the presence of the memory of a thousand eyes staring up at her.

As they headed inland, the larger things fell away, revealing the indelible: the dark line of a marsh hawk flying low over the water, the delicate fractures in the water where a water moccasin swam, the strangely satisfying long grass that cascaded like hair from the ground.

She was content with silence, but Grace and Control were less so.

"I miss hot showers," Control said. "I miss not itching all over."

"Boil water," Grace said, as if it provided the solution to both problems. As if Control's misses were wishes, and he should think bigger.

"Not the same thing."

"I miss standing on the roof of the Southern Reach and looking out over the forest," Grace said.

"You used to do that? How did you get up there?"

"The janitor let us go up. The director and me. We would stand up there and make our plans."

That catch in Grace's throat, that invisible connection, Ghost Bird contemplated it. What did *she* miss? There had been so little time to miss anything. Their conversation existed so apart from her that she wondered again what she might do when she met the Crawler. What if she was a sleeper cell for a cause much older than either the Southern Reach or Area X? Did her allegiance lie with the former director, or the director as a child, playing on those black rocks near the lighthouse? And what master did the lighthouse keeper serve? It would have been better if she could have thought of each person in the equation as just one thing, but none of them were that simple.

Perhaps the biologist's final response was the only response that mattered, and her entire letter a sop to expectations, to the reaction human beings were hardwired to have. A kind of final delay before she had come to embody that correct answer? Perhaps so many journals had piled up in the lighthouse because on some level most came, in time, to recognize the futility of language. Not just in Area X but against the rightness of the lived-in moment, the instant of touch, of connection, for which words were such a sorrowful disappointment, so inadequate an expression of both the finite and the infinite. Even as the Crawler wrote out its terrible message.

Back on the island, there had been one last, unanswerable question, and the weight of it had settled over each of them in different ways. If they now traversed a landscape transplanted from somewhere far remote, then what existed within the coordinates of the *real* Area X, back on Earth?

Grace had put forward the idea, had clearly been thinking about it, possibly for years now, haunted and frustrated by it.

"We are," Control had replied—distant, coming to her from afar with an unfocused stare. "*We* are. That's where we are." Although he wasn't stupid, must know Grace was right.

"If you go through the door, you come to Area X," Grace said. "If you walk across the border, you go to the other place. Whatever it is."

Grace's tone did not admit to doubt, or that she cared whether they believed her or not, an essential indifference to questions, as if Area X had worn her down. A pragmatism that meant she knew the conclusions she had reached would please no one.

But Ghost Bird knew what she had seen in the corridor leading into Area X, the detritus and trash she had seen there, the bodies, and wondered if it might be real and not summoned from her mind. Wondered what might have come through the twenty-foot door that Control had described to her, the door lost to them. What might still come through such a door? And her thought: Nothing, because if so, it would have happened long ago.

The marsh lakes had become such a deep, perfect blue in that uncertain light that the reflections of the surrounding scrub forest on that surface seemed as real as their root-bound doppelgängers. Their mud-encrusted boots churned up amid the rich sediment and plant roots a smell almost like crisp hay.

Control leaned against Ghost Bird more than once to keep his balance, almost pulling her down in the process. Ahead of them now came the smell of burning, and from above, something the others could not see stitched its way through the overcast sky, and Ghost Bird was not surprised.

0017: THE DIRECTOR

One spring day at the Southern Reach, you're taking a break, pacing across the courtyard tiles as you worry at a problem in your head, and you see something strange out by the swamp lake. At the edge of the black water, a figure squats, hunched over, hands you cannot see busy at some mysterious task. Your first impulse is to call security, but then you recognize the slight frame, the tuft of dark hair: It's Whitby, in his brown blazer, his navy slacks, his dress shoes.

Whitby, playing in the mud. Washing something? Strangling something? The level of concentration he displays, even at this distance, is of working on something that requires a jeweler's precision.

Instinct tells you to be silent, to walk slow, to take care with fallen branches and dead leaves. Whitby has been startled enough in the past, by the past, and you want your presence known by degrees. Halfway there, though, he turns long enough to acknowledge you and go back to what he's doing, and you walk faster after that.

The trees are as sullen as ever, looking like hunched-over priests with long beards of moss, or as Grace says, less respectfully, "Like a line of used-up old drug addicts." The water carries only the small, patient ripples made by Whitby, and your reflection as you come close and lean over his shoulder is distorted by widening rings and wavery gray light.

Whitby is washing a small brown mouse.

He holds the mouse, careful but firm, between the thumb and index finger of his left hand, the mouse's head and front legs circled by this fleshy restraint, the pale belly, back legs, and tail splayed out across his palm. The mouse seems hypnotized or for some other reason preternaturally calm while Whitby with his cupped right hand ladles water onto the mouse, then extends his little finger and rubs the water into the fur of the underbelly, the sides, then the furry cheeks, followed by anointment of the top of the head.

Whitby has draped a little white towel across his left forearm; it is monogrammed with a large cursive W in gold thread. Brought from home? He pinches the towel from his forearm and, using a single corner, delicately daubs the top of the mouse's head while its tiny black eyes stare off into the distance. There's a kind of febrile extremity of care here, as Whitby proceeds to wipe off one pink-clawed paw and then the other, before moving to the back paws and the thin tail. Whitby's hand is so pale and small that there is a sort of symmetry on display, an absurd yet somehow touching suggestion of a shared ancestry.

It has been four months since the last member of the last eleventh expedition died of cancer, six weeks since you had them exhumed. It has been more than two years since you came back across the border with Whitby. Over the past seven or eight months, you have had a sense of Whitby recovering—fewer transfer requests, more engagement in status meetings, a revival of self-interest in his "combined theories document," which he now calls "a thesis on terroir," evoking a "comprehensive ecosystem" approach based on an advanced theory of wine production. There has been nothing in the execution of his duties to indicate anything more than his usual eccentricity. Even Cheney has, grudgingly, admitted this, and you don't care that the man often uses Whitby as a wedge against you now. You don't care about reasons so long as it brings Whitby back closer to the center of things.

"What do you have there, Whitby?" Breaking the silence is sudden and intrusive. Nothing you say will sound like anything other than an adult talking to a child, but Whitby's put you in that position.

Whitby stops washing and drying the mouse, throws the towel over his left shoulder, stares at the mouse, examining it as if there might still be a spot of dirt here or there.

"A mouse," he says, as if it should be obvious.

"Where did you find her?"

"*Him*. In the attic. I found him in the attic." His tone like someone about to be reprimanded, but defiant, too.

"Oh—at home?" Bringing the safety of home to the dangerous place, the workplace, in physical form. You're trying to suppress the psychologist in you, not overanalyze, but it's difficult.

"In the attic."

"Why did you bring him out here?"

"To wash him."

You don't mean for it to seem like an interrogation, but you're sure it does. Is this a bad thing or a good thing in the progression of Whitby's recovery? There is no base score assigned to owning a mouse or washing a mouse that can confer an automatic rating of fit or unfit for duty.

"You couldn't wash him inside?"

Whitby gives you an upturned sideways glance. You're still stooping. He's still hunched. "That water's contaminated."

"Contaminated." An interesting choice of words. "But you use it, don't you?"

"Yes, I do . . ." Relenting, giving in a little, relaxing so that you're less concerned he's going to strangle the mouse by accident. "But I thought maybe he'd like to be outside for a while. It's a nice day."

Translation: Whitby needed a break. Just like you needed a break, pacing the courtyard tiles.

"What's his name?"

"He doesn't have a name."

"He doesn't have a name?"

"No."

Somehow this bothers you more than the washing, but it's an unease you can't put into words. "Well, he's a handsome mouse." Which sounds stupid even as you say it, but you're at a loss.

"Don't talk to me like I'm an idiot," he says. "I'm aware this looks strange, but think about some of the things you do for stress."

You'd gone across the border with this man. You'd sacrificed his peace of mind on the altar of your insatiable fascination, your curiosity, and your ambition. He doesn't deserve condescension on top of that.

"Sorry." You awkwardly lower yourself in the dead leaves and half-dried mud next to him. The truth is you don't want to go back inside yet, and Whitby doesn't seem to want to, either. "The only excuse I've got is that it's been a long day. Already."

"It's okay," Whitby says after a pause, and returns to cleaning his mouse. Then volunteers, "I've had him about five weeks. I had a dog and a cat growing up, but no pets since."

You've tried to imagine what Whitby's house looks like, and failed. You can only imagine an endless white space with white, modern furniture, and a computer screen in the corner as the only spot of color. Which probably means Whitby's house is an opulent, decadent free-for-all of styles and periods, all offered up in bright, saturated colors.

"The plant bloomed," Whitby says into the middle of your musings.

The sentence has no meaning at first. But when it takes on meaning, you sit up straighter.

Whitby looks over at you. "There's no emergency. It's already over."

You're quelling the impulse to pull Whitby to his feet and march him back inside to show you what *no emergency* means.

"Explain," you say, putting just enough pressure on the word to hold it there like an egg about to crack. "Be specific."

"It happened in the middle of the night. Last night," he says. "Everyone else had left. I work very late sometimes, and I like to spend time in the storage cathedral." He looks away, continues as if you've asked him something: "I just like it in there. It calms me down."

"And?"

"And last night, I came in and I just decided to check on the plant"—said too casually, as if he always checked on the plant—"and there was a flower. The plant was blooming. But it's gone now. It all happened very fast."

It's important to just keep talking, to keep Whitby calm and answering your questions.

"How long?"

"Maybe an hour. If I had thought it would disintegrate, I would have called someone."

"What did the blossom look like?"

"Like an ordinary flower, with seven or eight petals. Translucent, almost white."

"Did you take any photographs? Any video?"

"No," he says. "I thought it would still be there for a while. I didn't tell anyone because it's gone." Or because, with no evidence, it would be more evidence against *him*, against his state of mind, his suitability, when he is just now getting out from under that reputation.

"What did you do then?"

He shrugs, the mouse's tail twitching, as he transfers the animal to his right hand. "I scheduled a purification. Just to be sure. And I left."

"You were in a suit the whole time, right?"

"Sure. Yes. Of course."

"No strange readings after?"

"No, no strange readings. I checked."

"And nothing else I need to know?" Like, the possible connection between the plant having bloomed and Whitby, the next day, coming out here with his mouse.

"Nothing you don't already know."

A shade defiant again, a lifting of his gaze to tell you he's thinking about the trip into Area X, the one he can't tell anyone about, the one that made him unreliable to the rest of the staff. How to evaluate hallucinations that might be real? A paranoia that might be justified? Right after you came back, you remember Whitby saying wistfully to himself, as if something had been lost, "They didn't notice us at first. But, then, gradually, they began to peer in at us . . . because we just couldn't stop."

You get to your feet, look down at Whitby, say, "Give me a more extensive report on the plant—for my eyes only. And you cannot keep sneaking a mouse into the building, Whitby. For one thing, security will catch you eventually. Take it home."

Whitby and the mouse are both looking up at you now, Whitby harder to read than the mouse, which just wants to get out of Whitby's grasp and be on its way.

"I'll keep him in the attic," Whitby says.

"Do that."

Back inside, you visit the storage cathedral, putting on a purification suit so you don't contaminate that environment or it doesn't contaminate you. You find the plant, which has a false tag that designates it as belonging to the first eighth expedition. You examine the plant, the area around it, the floor, searching for any evidence of a dried-up flower. You find none, just a residue beside it that later comes back from testing as pine resin from some other sample that had sat there previously.

You look at those test results in your office and you wonder if the plant had only blossomed in Whitby's mind, and, if so, what that meant. Wonder for a good long while, before the thought becomes buried in the memos and the meeting minutes and the phone calls and a million minor emergencies. Should you ask Whitby if the mouse came with him into the storage cathedral? Perhaps. But what you do instead is put the immortal plant under round-the-clock surveillance, even though both Cheney and Grace give you grief about it.

Whitby just needs a companion. Whitby needs someone who won't judge or interrogate him, someone or something that depends on him. And as long as Whitby keeps the creature at home, in the attic, you won't tell anyone about the breach—have recognized by now that just as Lowry's tethered to you, you're chained to Whitby.

Playing pool with the Realtor and the veteran on an expedition to the Star Lanes a week later, you're listening to the Realtor describe some couple that had been squatting in a model home and refused to give her their names when you think again about Whitby not naming the mouse. As if he'd been following Southern Reach protocol for expeditions.

"They thought that so long as I didn't know their names, I couldn't call the police. Peering out from behind the curtains like ghosts. There was so much fail in that, not that I felt good about kicking them out. Except I have to sell the place—I'm not running a charity. I give to charities, sure, but why do they have homeless shelters anyway? And if I let them stay then someone else might get the same idea. Turns out the police had a file on them, so I made the right decision."

Waiting there back on your desk at the Southern Reach you already have the files of candidates for a twelfth expedition. Right on top is the most promising, to your mind: an antisocial biologist whose husband went on the last eleventh.

0018: THE LIGHTHOUSE KEEPER

Secured the lighthouse. Worked on the [illegible]. Fixed things. And shall cast them into a furnace of fire: there shall be wailing and gnashing of teeth. Came then the crying call of a curlew, and at dawn, too, I heard the hooting of an owl, the yap of foxes. Just a little ways up from the lighthouse, where I strayed for a bit, a bear cub poked its head out of the underbrush, looking around like any child might. And the hand of the sinner shall rejoice, for there is no sin in shadow or in light that the seeds of the dead cannot forgive.

By the time Saul made it to the village bar, everyone had already crammed inside, anticipating music by a few locals who called themselves the Monkey's Elbow. The deck, with its great view of the darkening ocean, was empty—it was too cold, for one thing—and he hurried inside with anticipation. He'd felt better with each day since the hallucination on the beach, and no one from the Light Brigade had returned to plague him. His temperature had receded, along with the pressure in his head, and with it the urge to burden Charlie with his problems. He hadn't dreamed for three nights. Even his hearing was fine, the moment his ears had popped like getting a jolt to his system: more energetic in every way. So everything seemed normal, as if he'd worried over nothing—and all he missed was the familiar sight of Gloria coming down the beach toward the lighthouse, or climbing on the rocks, or loitering near the shed.

Charlie had even promised to meet him at the bar for a short while before he went out night fishing again; despite the rough schedule, he seemed happy to be making money, but they'd hardly seen each other in several days.

Old Jim, with his ruddy beacon of a face and fuzzy white mutton-chop sideburns, had commandeered the rickety upright piano in the far corner of the main room. Monkey's Elbow was warming up around him, a discordant ramble of violin, accordion, acoustic guitar, and tambourine. The piano, a sea salvage, had been restored to its former undrowned glory—mother-of-pearl inlay preserved on the lid—but still retained a wheezy-tinny tone from its baptism, "sagging and soggy" on some of the keys, according to Old Jim.

The place smelled comfortingly of cigarettes and greasy fried fish, and some underlying hint of too-sweet honey. The oysters were fresh-caught, and the beers, served out of a cooler, were cheap. Saul always forgot the downside real quick. There was good cheer to be found here, if sometimes grudgingly given. Any prayers he offered up came from knowing that no health inspector had ever journeyed to the tiny kitchen or the grill out back where the seagulls gathered with irrepressible hope.

Charlie was already there, had gotten them a little round table with two stools that hugged the wall opposite the piano. Saul pushed through the press of bodies—maybe sixty people, practically a mob by forgotten-coast standards—and gave Charlie a squeeze of the shoulder before sitting.

"Hello there, stranger," Saul said, making it sound like an even worse pickup line than it would've been.

"Someone's in a better mood, jack," Charlie said. Then caught himself. "I mean—"

"I don't know any jack, unless you mean jack shit," Saul said. "No, I know what you mean. And I am. I feel a lot better." First evidence from Charlie that he had been dragged down by Saul's condition, which just deepened his affection for Charlie. He'd not complained once during all of Saul's moaning about his lethargy and symptoms, had only tried to help. Maybe they could get back to normal, once this night-fishing expedition came to its end.

"Good, good," Charlie said, smiling and looking around, still a little extra stutter-step of awkwardness from him when out in public.

"How was the fishing yesterday?" Charlie'd said something about a good catch, but they hadn't talked long.

"Best haul so far," Charlie said, his face lit up. "A lot of skates and rays and flounder. Some mullet and bass." Charlie got paid a flat rate per hour, but a bonus for catches over a certain weight.

"Anything odd?" A question Saul always asked. He liked hearing about strange sea creatures. Lately, thinking about what Henry had said, he took a special interest in the answer.

"Only a couple of things. Threw them both back 'cause they were so ugly. Some weird fish and a kind of sea squirt that looked like it was spewing blood."

"Fair enough."

"You look a lot better, you know. Calm at the light-house?" Which was Charlie's way of saying "Tell me why on the phone you said 'not a lot of fun around here recently.'"

Saul was about to launch into the story of his final confrontation with Henry and the Light Brigade when the piano cut off and Old Jim got up and introduced Monkey's Elbow, even though everybody already knew them. The band members were Sadi Dawkins, Betsey Pepine, and his erstwhile lighthouse volunteer, Brad. They all worked at the village bar on and off. Trudi, Gloria's mother, was on tambourine, the guest spot. Saul's turn would come someday.

Monkey's Elbow lurched into some sad thick song, the sea's bounty on display in its lyrics, and two ill-fated lovers, and a tragic hill overlooking a secret cove. The usual, but not so much chantey as influenced by what Charlie called "sand-encrusted sea-hippies," who had popularized a laid-back listener-friendly kind of folk-pop. Saul liked it live, even if Brad tended to ham it up a bit. But Charlie stared at his drink with a kind of pursed-lipped frown, then rolled his eyes secretively at Saul, while Saul shook his head in mock disapproval. Sure, they weren't great, but any performance took guts. He used to throw up before sermons, which might've been a sign from God, now that he thought about it. The worst nights, Saul had done push-ups beforehand and jumping jacks to sweat out the fear of performance.

Charlie leaned in, and Saul met him halfway. Charlie said in his ear, "You know that fire on the island?"

"Yeah?"

"A friend of mine was out there fishing that day, and he saw bonfires. People burning papers, for hours, like you said.

But when he came back around, they'd loaded a bunch of boxes into motorboats. You want to know where those boats headed?"

"Out to sea?"

"No. Due west, hugging the coast."

"Interesting." The only thing due west of Failure Island besides mosquito-infested inlets were a couple of small towns and the military base.

Saul sat back, just staring at Charlie, with Charlie nodding at him like "I told you so," although what he meant by that Saul didn't know. Told you they were strange? Told you they were up to no good?

The second song played out more like a traditional folk song, slow and deep, carrying along the baggage of a century or two of prior interpretations. The third was a rollicking but silly number, another original, this time about a crab that lost its shell and was traveling all over the place to find it. A few couples were dancing now. His ministry hadn't been one of those that banned dancing or other "earthly pleasures," but he'd never learned either. Dancing was Saul's secret fantasy, something he thought he'd enjoy but had to file under "too late now." Charlie'd never dance anyway, maybe not even in private.

Sadi came by during a short break between songs. She worked in a bar in Hedley during the summers, and she always had funny stories about the customers, many of them coming off the river walk "drunk as a skunk." Trudi came over, too, and they talked for a while, although not directly about Gloria. More about Gloria's dad, during which Saul gathered that Gloria and her dad had made it back to his place by now. So that was all right.

Then they mostly just listened, stealing moments between songs to talk or grab another beer. In scanning the room for people he knew, people he might give a nod to, claim a bond with, he'd felt for a while now not like the one watching but the one being watched. He put it down to some receding symptom of his non-condition, or to Charlie's skittishness rubbing off on him. But then, through the murky welter of bodies, the rising tide of loud conversations, the frenetic playing of the band, he spied an unwelcome figure across the room, near the door.

Henry.

He stood perfectly still, watching, without even a drink in his hand. Henry wore that ridiculous silk shirt and pretentious slacks, pressed just so, and yet, curiously, he blended in against the wall, as if he belonged there. No one but Saul seemed to notice him. That Suzanne wasn't with him struck Saul hard for some reason. It made him resist the urge to turn to Charlie and point Henry out to him. "That's the man who broke into my lighthouse a few nights ago."

The whole time Saul stared at Henry, the edges of the room had been growing darker and darker, and the sickly sweet smell intensified, and everyone around Henry grew more and more insubstantial—vague, unknowable silhouettes—and all the light came to Henry and gathered around him, and spilled back out from him.

A kind of vertigo washed over Saul, as if a vast pit had opened up beneath him and he was suspended above it, about to fall. There came back all of the old symptoms he'd thought were gone, as if they'd just been hiding. There was a comet dripping fire through his head, trailing flame down his back.

While the band kept playing through the darkness, their sound curdling into a song sung far too slow, and before they could vanish into a darkly glinting spiral, before everything not-Henry could disappear, Saul gripped the table with both hands and looked away.

The chatter, the rush and realignment of conversations came back, and the light came back, and the band sounded normal again, and Charlie was talking to him like nothing had happened, Saul's sense of relief so palpable the blood within him was rushing too hard and he felt faint.

When, after a stabilizing minute, he dared sneak a glance toward where Henry had stood, the man had vanished and someone else stood in his place. Someone Saul didn't know, who raised his beer to Saul awkwardly so that he realized he'd been staring across the room for too long.

"Did you hear what I said?" Charlie, in a voice loud enough to cut through the band. "Are you okay?" Reaching out to touch Saul's wrist, which meant he was concerned and that Saul had been acting odd. Saul smiled and nodded.

The song ended, and Charlie said, "It wasn't the stuff about the boats and the island, was it? I wasn't trying to worry you."

"No, not that. Nothing like that. I'm fine." Touched, because it was the kind of thing that might've secretly bothered Charlie if their roles had been reversed.

"And you'd tell me if you were feeling sick again."

"Of course I would." Half lying, trying to process what he'd just experienced. And, serious, struck by some form of premonition: "But, Charlie, I hate to say it—you should probably leave now, or you'll be late."

Charlie took that in stride, already half off his stool because he didn't like the music anyway.

"See ya tomorrow sometime, then," Charlie said, giving him a wink and a long last stare that wasn't entirely innocent.

Somehow Charlie looked so good in that moment, putting on his jacket. Saul clasped him tight before he could get away. The weight of the man in his arms. The feel of Charlie's rough shave that he loved so much. The tart surprise of Charlie's lip balm against his cheek. Held him for an extra moment, trying to preserve all of it, as a bulwark against whatever had just happened. Then, too soon, Charlie was gone, out the door, into the night, headed for the boat.

0019: CONTROL

The night was full of white rabbits streaking across the sky, instead of the stars, the moon—and Control knew that was wrong in some fevered part of his mind, some compartment holding out against the inquisitive brightness. Were they white rabbits or were they smudges of black motion rendered as photo negatives impeding his vision? Because he didn't want to see what was there. Because the biologist had unlocked something inside of him, and he returned now sometimes to the phantasmagorical art in Whitby's strange room in the Southern Reach, and then to his theory that to disappear into the border was to enter some purgatory where you would find every lost and forgotten thing: all of the rabbits herded across that invisible barrier, every beached destroyer and truck from the night Area X had been created. The missing in action from the expeditions. The thought a kind of annihilating abyss. Yet there was also the light blossoming from the place below the Crawler, detailed in the biologist's journal account. Where led that light?

Trying to pick out from all of those pieces what might be a reasonable, even an honorable, choice. One that his father would have agreed with; he no longer thought much of his mother, or what she might think.

Maybe I just wanted to be left alone. To remain in the little house on the hill in Hedley, with his cat Chorry and the chittering bats at night, not so far from where he had grown up, even if now so distant.

"It wouldn't have made a difference, Grace."

The three of them sleeping on the pine moss, the moist grass, less than a mile from the topographical anomaly, their final approach planned for the morning.

"What wouldn't?" Gentle, perhaps even kind. Which let him know the full manifestation of his distress. Kept seeing the biologist's many eyes, which became stars, which became the leaping white lights. Which became a chessboard with his father's last move frozen there. Along with Control's own last move, still forthcoming.

"If you had told me everything. Back at the Southern Reach."

"No. It wouldn't have."

Ghost Bird slept beside him, and this, too, helped him chart his decline. She slept at his back, guarding him, and with her arms wrapped tight around him. He was secure there, safe, and he loved her more for allowing that now, when she had less and less reason to. Or no reason at all.

The night had turned chilly and deep, and crowded at the edges with creatures staring in at them, just dark shapes silent and motionless. But he didn't mind them.

Things his dad had said to him stuck with him more clearly now, because they must've happened. His dad was saying to him, "If you don't know your passion, it confuses your mind, not your heart." In a moment of honesty after he had failed in the field and he could only talk to his dad in riddles about it, never tell him the truth: "Sometimes you need to know when to go on to the next thing—for the sake of other people."

The chill in that. The next thing. What was his next thing here? What was his passion? He didn't know the answer to either question, knew only that there was comfort in the scratchiness of the pine needles against his face and the sleep-drenched, smoky smell of the dirt beneath him.

Morning came, and he huddled in Ghost Bird's arms until she stirred, disengaged from him in a way that felt too final. Among the reeds, endless marsh, and mud, there came a suggestion on the horizon of burning, and a popping and rattling that could've been gunfire or some lingering memory of past conflict playing out in his head.

Yet still the blue heron in the estuary stalked tadpoles and tiny fish, the black vulture soared on the thermals high above. There came a thousand rustlings among the islands of trees. Behind them, on the horizon, the lighthouse could be seen, might always be seen, even through the fog that came with the dawn, here noncommittal and diffuse, there thick, rising like a natural defense where needed, a test and blessing against that landscape. To appreciate any of this was Ghost Bird's gift to him, as if it had seeped into him through her touch.

But the unnatural world intruded, as it always did, so long as will and purpose existed, and for a moment he resented that. Ghost Bird and Grace were debating what to do if they encountered any remnants of the border commander's troops. Debating what to do when they reached the tower.

"You and I go down," Grace said. "And Control can guard the entrance." This last stand, this hopeless task.

"I should go down alone," Ghost Bird said, "and you should both stand guard above."

"That would be against expedition protocols," Grace said.

"That's what you want to invoke here? Now?"

"What's left to invoke?" Grace asked.

"I go down alone," Ghost Bird said, and Grace gave her no answer.

Tactical not strategic, a phrase rising out of his back catalog of favorites. It seemed as obsolete as any of the rest, like the enormous frame of an old-fashioned bicycle.

He kept glancing up at that murky sky, waiting for the heavens to fall away and reveal their true position. But the mimicry remained in place, most convincing. What if the biologist had been wrong? What if the biologist in her writings had been a calmly raving lunatic? And then just a monster? What then?

They broke camp, used a stand of swamp trees as initial cover and surveyed the marsh, stared across the water of the estuaries. The smoke now billowed up at a sharp sixty-degree angle to add its own ash-silver roiling to the fog and form a heavier, weighted blankness. This alliance obscured the last of the blue sky and accentuated the crackling line of fire at the horizon parallel to them: waves of orange thrust upward from golden centers.

The pewter stillness of the channel of water in the foreground reflected the lines of the flames and the billowing of the smoke—reflected the nearest reeds, too, and doubled by reflection also the island that at its highest point showcased island oaks and palmetto trees, their trunks white lines lost in patches of fog.

There came shouting and screaming and gunfire—all too near, all from the island of trees, or, perhaps, something Lowry had placed in his head. Something that had happened here long ago only now coming to the surface. Control kept his eyes on the reflection, where men and women in military uniforms attacked one another while some impossible thing watched from the watery sky. At such a remove, distorted, it did not seem so harsh, so visceral.

"They are already somewhere else," Control said, although he knew Grace and Ghost Bird wouldn't understand. They were already in the reflection, through which an alligator now swam. Where swooped through the trees, oblivious, a flicker.

So they continued on, him with his sickness that he no longer wanted diagnosed, Grace with her limp, and Ghost Bird keeping her own counsel.

There was nothing to be done, and no reason to: their path would skirt the fire.

In Control's imagination, the entrance to the topographical anomaly was enormous, mixed with the biologist's vast bulk in his thoughts so that he had expected a kind of immense ziggurat upside down in the earth. But no, it was what it had always been: a little over sixty feet in diameter, circular, located in the middle of a small clearing. The entrance lay there open for them, as it had for so many others. No soldiers here, nothing more unusual than the thing itself.

On the threshold, he told them what would happen next. There was in his voice only the shadow of the authority of a director of the Southern Reach, but within that shadow a kind of resistance.

"Grace, you will stay here at the top, standing guard with the rifles. There are any number of dangers, and we do not want to be trapped down there. Ghost Bird, you will come with me, and you will lead the way. I'll follow at a little distance behind you. Grace, if we are down there longer than three hours"—the maximum time recorded by prior expeditions—"you are released of any responsibility for us." Because if there were a world to return to, the person to survive should be someone with something to return to.

They stared at him. They stared, and he thought they would object, would override him, and then he would be lost. Would be left out here, at the top.

But that moment never came and an almost debilitating relief settled over him as Grace nodded and said to be careful, rattled off advice he barely heard.

Ghost Bird stood off to the side, a curious expression on her face. Down there, she would experience the ultimate doubling of experience with the biologist, and he couldn't protect her from that.

"Whatever you have in your head now, hold on to it," Grace said. "Because there may be nothing left of it when you go down below."

What was coiled within his head, and how would it affect the outcome? Because his goal was not to reach the Crawler. Because he wondered what else might lie within the brightness that had come with him.

They descended into the tower.

0020: THE DIRECTOR

Whitby's worthless report on the blossom is on your desk by the time you go off to another pre-expedition interview of the biologist, the possible candidates for the twelfth whittled down to ten, and you and Grace, you and Lowry, pushing for your favorites, with members of the science department shadowboxing in the background as they whisper their own choices at you. Severance seems terminally uninterested in the question.

It's not a good time to interview anyone but you don't have a choice. The plant is blossoming again in your mind as you conduct the interview in a cramped little office in the biologist's town—a place you've borrowed and can pretend is your own, with all of the appropriate psychological and psychiatric texts on the bookshelves. The diplomas and family pictures of the room's true occupant have been removed. In a concession to Lowry, for his studies, you've allowed his people to swap out chairs, light fixtures, and other elements of the room, as if in redecorating and changing the color scheme from placid blues and greens to red, orange, and gray or silver there's some answer to a larger question.

Lowry claims his arrangements and recombinations can have a "subliminal or instinctual" effect on the candidates.

"To make them feel secure and at ease?" you asked, a rare moment of poking the beast with a stick, but he ignored you, and in your head he was saying, "To make them do what we want."

There's the smell of water damage still, from a burst pipe in the basement. There's a water stain in the corner, hidden by a little table, as if you need to cover up some crime. The only giveaway that it's not your office: you're cramped, stuffed into your chair.

The plant is blossoming in your mind, and each time it does there's less time to work with, less you can do. Is the plant a challenge or an invitation or a worthless distraction? A message? And if so, what did it mean, assuming Whitby didn't imagine it? The light at the bottom of a topographical anomaly, from a door into Area X, on the tarot card used by the Séance & Science Brigade. The blossoming light of an MRI body scan, the one you endured last week.

In the middle of all that blossoming in your brain, the kind of thing that would elicit a joke from Grace if only you could tell her, there, bestriding the world: the biologist, a talisman arriving just as everything is closing in again and your time has become more limited.

"State your name for the record."

"I did that last time."

"Nevertheless."

The biologist looks at you like you're an opponent, not the person who can send her where she so obviously wants to go. You note again not just the musculature of this woman but the fact that she's willing to complicate even the simple business of stating her name. That she has a kind of self-possession that comes not just from knowing who she is but from knowing that, if it comes down to it, she needs no one. Some professionals might diagnose that as a disorder, but in the biologist it comes across as an absolute and unbending clarity.

"Tell me about your parents."

"What are your earliest memories?"

"Did you have a happy childhood?"

All of the usual, boring questions, and her terse answers boring, too, in a way. But, after that, the more interesting ones.

"Do you ever have violent thoughts or tendencies?" you ask.

"What do you consider a violent act?" she replies. An attempt to evade, or genuine interest? You'd bet on the former.

"Harm toward other people or animals. Extreme property damage, like arson." The Realtor at Star Lanes has dozens of stories about violence against houses, relates them all with an edge to her voice. The biologist would probably classify the Realtor as an alien species.

"People are animals."

"Harm toward animals, then?"

"Only toward human animals."

She's trying to entangle you or provoke you, but the usual cross-referencing and analysis of intel turned up something interesting, something you can't confirm. While a grad student on the West Coast, she had worked as an intern at a forest ranger station in a national park. Her two years there had roughly coincided with a series of what some might call "tree-hugger terrorism." In the worst case, three men had been badly beaten by "an assailant wearing a mask." The motive, according to the police: "The victims had been tormenting an injured owl by poking at it with a stick and trying to light its wing on fire." No suspect had ever been identified, no arrest made.

"What would you do if your fellow expedition members exhibited violent tendencies?"

"Whatever I had to."

"Would that include killing someone?"

"If it came down to that, I would have to."

"Even if it was me?"

"Especially if it was you. Because these questions are so tedious."

"More tedious than your job working with plastics?"

That sobers her up. "I don't plan on killing anyone. I've never killed anyone. I plan on taking samples. I plan on learning as much as I can and circumventing anyone who doesn't follow the mission parameters." That hard edge again, the shoulder turned in toward you, to block you out. If this were a boxing match, the shoulder would be followed by an uppercut or body shot.

"And what if you turn out to be the threat?"

The biologist laughs at that question, and gives you a stare so direct you have to look away.

"If I'm the threat, then I won't be able to stop myself, will I? If I'm the threat, then I guess Area X has won."

"What about your husband?"

"What about my husband? He's dead."

"Do you hope to find out what happened to him in Area X?"

"I hope to find Area X in Area X. I hope to be of use."

"Isn't that heartless?"

She leans forward, fixes you again with that gaze, and it's a struggle to maintain your composure. But that's okay—antagonism is okay. In fact, anything helps you that helps her reject whatever traces of corruption you might have picked up, that might have adhered to you all unknowing.

She says, "It's a fallacy for you, a total stranger, to project onto me the motives and emotions you think are appropriate. To think you can get inside my head."

You can't share with her that the other candidates have been easy to read. The surveyor will be the meat-and-potatoes backbone of the expedition, without a trace of passive-aggressiveness. The anthropologist will provide empathy and nuance, although you're not sure whether her need to prove herself is a plus or a minus. She'll push herself further, harder because of that, but what will Area X think of that? The linguist talks too much, has too little introspection, but is a recruit from within the Southern Reach and has demonstrated absolute loyalty on more than occasion. Lowry's favorite, with all that entails.

Before the interview, you met with Whitby, who had rallied for this discussion, in your office, amid the increasing clutter. It was the biologist you talked about the most, the importance of keeping her paranoid and isolated and antisocial, how there's a shift in the biochemistry of the brain, naturally arrived at, that might be what Lowry's secret experiments are trying to induce artificially—and since her husband has already gone to Area X, "been read by it," this represents a unique opportunity "metrics-wise" because of "that connection," because "it's never happened before." That, in a sense, the biologist had forged a relationship with Area X before ever setting foot there. It might lead to what Whitby calls "a terroir precognition."

An expedition into Area X with the biologist would be different than with Whitby. You wouldn't lead, except in the way at the store as a teenager you sometimes walked ahead of your dad so you wouldn't seem to be with him, but always with a look back at him, to see where he was going.

As the questioning continues, you're more and more certain of what you feel in your gut. You are reminded of Area X somehow. The biologist reminds you of being in Area X.

The rest of the biologist's file is breathtaking in its focus, its narrowness, and yet fecund despite that. You're driving across the desert with her, in a tiny car, to check out the holes made by burrowing owls. You're lost on a plateau above an untouched coastline, stalked by a cougar, a place where the grass is the color of gold and reaches up to your knees and the trees are blackened by fire, silver-gray with ash. You're hiking up a mountain in scrubland, up huge blocks of stone, every muscle in your legs protesting even as you're possessed by a wild giddiness that keeps you moving past exhaustion. You're back with her during her first year of college, when she made a rare confession to a roommate that she wanted isolation and moved out the next day to her own apartment and walked the five miles from campus home in utter silence, receiving the world through a hole in her shoe.

You're certain you'll have to give up something to Lowry to keep him away from the biologist, but whatever the price you'll pay it, you decide as you order a whiskey for a change at the bar at Chipper's—order a whiskey for everyone at the bar, for a change, all four of them. Because it's late, because it's a weekday, because Chipper's is getting long in the tooth and the clientele is getting older and older. Like you. The doctor's told you cancer has blossomed in your ovaries and it's going to spread to your liver before you can even blink, even get used to the idea. Another thing no one needs to know.

"And before we could even think about selling that house," the Realtor's telling you, "we had to pull ten layers of wallpaper off. All this woman had done for a decade was keep re-wallpapering her house. It was a hell of a lot of wallpaper, and garish, like she was putting up warning signals. Wrapping her house from the inside out. I tell you, I've never seen that before."

You nod, smiling, with nothing to add, nothing to say, but happy to listen. Terminally interested.

It's plain old normal cancer, nothing like the accelerated all-out assault experienced by the last eleventh. It's just plain old life catching up with you, trying to kill you, and you can either take the aggressive chemo and leave the Southern Reach and die anyway, or you can hang on long enough to join the twelfth expedition and, with the biologist by your side, go across the border one last time. You've kept secrets before. What's one final one?

Besides, other, more interesting, secrets are opening up, because Grace has finally found something on Jackie Severance. There's been plenty of dirt, including the scandal involving her son—a blown assignment that resulted in a woman's death—but nothing until now that made any real difference. On a top-secret list, not of Jackie's open case files but Jack's closed ones, which makes sense because Jack is a little easier: He's retired, in his early seventies, and some of what he worked on exists only in paper form.

"Look at the fifth line item," Grace says, up on the rooftop, after a quick sweep for bugs. You've never found any there, but it's worth being cautious.

The line reads:

Payment request—SB, Project Serum Bliss

"Is there more?" It's not quite what you expected, but you think you know what it is.

"No, that's the only one. There might be more, but the rest of the files from the period are missing. This page wasn't even supposed to be there."

"What do you think 'Serum Bliss' means?"

"Protocol back then would've meant it wasn't supposed to mean anything. Probably generated at random."

"It's flimsy," you say. "That's not even 'S&SB.'"

"It's fucking rice paper," Grace says. "It might mean nothing, but . . ."

But if, somehow, the S&SB was on Central's payroll—even just a little bit, a side project—and Jack ran the operation, and Jackie knew about it, and the S&SB had anything at all to do with the creation of Area X . . .

A lot of ifs. A lot of leaps. A lot more research on Grace's plate.

Yet it's enough for you to begin to have an idea of why Lowry's new ally is Jackie Severance.

0021: THE LIGHTHOUSE KEEPER

. . . went back to the garden, [illegible], and kept the ax with me just in case. Unlikely, with black bears, but not unknown. Scrub jay, catbird, house sparrow, most humble of God's creatures. I sat there and fed it bread crumbs, for it was a scrawny thing and in need. I shall bring them forth, they said . . .

Saul stayed on to the bitter end at the village bar, not sure if it was because he wanted to test Brad's resolve or because he didn't want to walk outside only to encounter Henry. Or because he was sad Charlie'd had to leave.

So he knocked back a couple more beers, put down the way the room swayed to the booze, and ordered some oysters and fish-and-chips. He had a hunger in him that was rare. Food didn't interest him that much, but tonight he felt ravenous. The oysters were served in their own salt water, newly shucked and steamed, and he didn't bother dipping them in sauce but just gulped them down. Then he tore into the fish, which came away in thick flakes in his hands, the heat rising along with the saliva-inducing smell of the grease. The wedge fries he drowned in ketchup and they soon joined the fish. He was frantic at his feast, aware he was gobbling, stuffing his face, his hands moving at a frenzied, unnatural pace, but he couldn't stop.

He ordered another fish-and-chips. He ordered another round of oysters. Another beer.

After the last set, the musicians stuck around, but most of the others left, including Trudi. The black sea and sky outside the window peered in against the glass, smudged faces and the bottles of booze behind the bar reflected back at Saul. Now that it was just Old Jim at the piano, with the other musicians goofing around, and so few people he could just about hear the pulse of the sea again, could recognize it as a subtle message in the background. Or something was pulsing in his head. His sense of smell had intensified, the rotting sweetness that must be coming from the kitchen was like a perfume being sprayed in clouds throughout the room. A stitching beat beneath the striking of the piano keys twinned itself to the pulse.

Mundane details struck him as momentous. The worm of gray-white ash curling out of an ashtray on the table next to him, the individual flakes still fluming, fluttering, and at the buried core a pinprick of throbbing red that pulsed at him like a brake light. Beside the ash, the smudge of an old greasy thumbprint, immortalized by the gunk that had collected on the ashtray from hundreds of cigarette immolations. Beside the thumbprint, an attempt to etch something into the side of the ashtray, an effort that had ended after J and A.

The piano playing became discordant, or was he just hearing it better . . . or worse? On his stool against the wall, beer in hand, he contemplated that. Contemplated the way people's voices were getting confused, as if they'd become mixed up, and the thrum rising under his skin, the thrum and hum and the ringing in his ears. It felt like something was coming toward him from very far away—toward and into him. His throat was dry and chalky. His beer tasted funny. He put it down, looked around the room.

Old Jim couldn't stop playing the piano, although he did it so badly, fingers too hard against the keys, the keys smudged with his red blood as he now began to roar out a song Saul had never heard before, with lyrics that were incomprehensible. The other musicians, most of them seated around Old Jim, let their instruments fall from slack hands, and stared at one another as if shocked by something. What were they shocked by? Sadi was weeping and Brad was saying, "Why would you do that? Why in the hell would you be doing that?" But Brad's voice was coming out of Sadi's body, and blood was dripping out of Brad's left ear, and the people slumped at the bar proper . . . had they been slumped that way a moment before? Were they drunk or dead?

Old Jim erupted out of his seat to stand, still playing. He was reaching a chaotic crescendo on his shouting, shrieking, yowling song, his fingers destroyed joint by joint as blood smashed out from the piano onto his lap and down onto the floor.

Something was hovering above Saul. Something was emanating out of him, was broadcasting through him, on frequencies too high to hear.

"What are you doing to me?"

"Why are you staring at me?"

"Stop doing that."

"I'm not doing anything."

Someone was crawling across the floor, or pulling themselves across the floor because their legs didn't work. Some-one was bashing their head against the dark glass near the front door. Sadi spun and twitched and twisted on the floor, slamming into chairs and table legs, beginning to come to pieces.

Outside, utter night reigned. There was no light. There was no light. Saul got up. Saul walked to the door, the spray of Old Jim's incomprehensible song less a roar than a trick-ling scream.

What lay beyond the door he did not know, mistrusted the utter darkness as much as what lay behind him, but he could not stay there in the bar, whether it was all real or something he was hallucinating. He had to leave.

He turned the knob, went out into the cooling nighttime air of the parking lot.

Everything was in its rightful place, as normal as it could be, with no one in sight. But everything behind him, in there, was awry, wrong, too irrevocable to be fixed by anyone. The din had become worse, and now others were screaming, too, making sounds not capable of being made by human mouths. He managed to find his pickup truck. He managed to get his key in the ignition, put it in reverse, then drive out of the parking lot. The sanctuary of the lighthouse was only half a mile away.

He did not look in his rearview mirror, did not want to see anything that might spill out into the night. The stars were so distant and yet so close in the dark sky above.

0022: GHOST BIRD

During much of the descent, the strong feeling of a return to what was already known came to Ghost Bird, even if experienced by another—a memory of drowning, of endless drowning and, at the remove of those unreliable words from the biologist's journal, the end of what she had encountered, what she had suffered, what she had recovered. And Ghost Bird wanted none of it—didn't want Control, either, following behind. He wasn't suited for this, had not been meant to experience this. You couldn't martyr yourself to Area X; you could only disappear trying, and not even be sure of that.

If the biologist had not leaned in to stare at those words so long ago, the doppelgänger might not exist in this way: full of memories and sneaking down into the depths. She might have returned with a mind wiped clean, her difference not expressed through her role as the mirror of the biologist but instead as a function of the right time or the wrong place, the right place or the wrong time.

Such strange comfort: that the words on the wall were the same, the method of their expression the same, if now she might interpret it as a nostalgic hint of an alien ecosystem, an approach or stance that the Crawler and the tower, in concert, had failed to inflict upon Earth. Because it wasn't viable? Because that was not its purpose—and thus giving them instead these slim signs of where it came from, what it stood for, what it thought?

She had rejected a mask filter, and with it the idea that somehow Area X was only concentrated here, in this cramped space, on these stairs, in the phosphorescent words with which she had become too familiar. Area X was all around them; Area X was contained in no one place or figure. It was the dysfunction in the sky, it was the plant Control had spoken of. It was the heavens and earth. It could interrogate you from any position or no position at all, and you might not even recognize its actions as a form of questioning.

Ghost Bird did not feel powerful as they descended through the luminescent light, hugging the right-hand wall, but she was unafraid.

There came the overlay, in memory and in the moment, of the harsh revolution of a mighty engine or heartbeat, and she knew even Control could hear it, could guess at its identity. From there, they moved swiftly to that point from which there was no real return: the moment when they would see the monster and take its measure. It lay, all too soon, right around the corner.

"I want you to stay here," she said to Control, to John.

"No," he said, as she'd know he would. "No, I won't." An unexpected sweetness in his expression. A kind of weary resolve in the words.

"John Rodriguez, if you come with me, I won't be able to

spare you. You'll have to see everything. Your eyes will have to be open."

She could not deny him his name, here, at the end of it all. She could not deny him the right to die if it came to that. There was nothing left to say.

Trailing memory, trailing Control, Ghost Bird descended toward the light.

The Crawler was huge, seemed to rise and keep rising, to spread to the sides until it filled Ghost Bird's vision. There was none of the remembered distortion, no throwing back at her of her own fears or desires. It simply lay revealed before her, so immense, so shockingly concrete.

The surface of its roughly bell-shaped body was translucent but with a strange texture, like ice when it has frozen from flowing water into fingerlike polyps. Underneath a second surface slowly *revolved*, and across this centrifuge she could see patterns floating along, as if it had an interior skin, and the material on top of that might be some kind of *soft armor*.

There was a mesmerizing quality to that movement, distant cousin to the director's hypnotism, and she didn't dare let her gaze linger for long.

The Crawler had no discernible features, no discernible face. It moved so slowly as it perfected the letters on the wall that there was a strange impression of the delicate, the mysteries of its locomotion hidden beneath the fringe of flesh that extended to the ground. The left arm, the only arm, located halfway up its body, moved with unfailing precision, constant blurred motion, to create the message on the wall, more like a *wielder* than a *writer*—with a crash of sparks she knew was stray tissue igniting. Its arm was *the agent of the message*, and from that instrument flowed the letters. *Where lies the strangling fruit that came from the hand of the sinner I shall bring forth the seeds of the dead.* If ever it had been human, then that thick-scrawling arm, obscured by loam or moss, was all that was left of its humanity.

Three rings orbited the Crawler, circling clockwise, and at times waves and surges of energy discharged between them, rippled across the Crawler's body. The first ring spun in drunken dreamlike revolutions just below the arm: an irregular row of half-moons. They resembled delicate jellyfish, with feathery white tendrils descending that continually writhed in a wandering search for something never found. The second ring, spinning faster right above the writing arm, resembled a broad belt of tiny black stones grouped close together, but these stones, as they bumped into one another, *gave* with a sponginess that made her think of soft tadpoles and of the creatures that had rained from the sky on the way to the island. What function these entities performed, whether they were part of the Crawler's anatomy or a symbiotic species, she could not fathom. All she knew was that both rings were in their way reassuringly corporeal.

But the third ring, the halolike ring above the Crawler, did not reassure her at all. The swift-moving globes of gold numbered ten to twelve, appeared to be both lighter than air and yet heavier, too. They spun with a ferocious velocity, so that at first she almost could not tell what they were. But she knew that they were dangerous, that words like *defense* and *aggression* might apply.

Perhaps the lighthouse keeper had always been a delusion, a lie written by Area X and conveyed back to the biologist.

Yet she distrusted, too, this avatar, this monster costume, this rubber suit meant for a scientist's consumption: so precise, so specific. Or perhaps the truth, for it did not fluctuate in its aspect, morph into other forms.

"Nothing but a horror show," Ghost Bird said to Control, so still and silent behind her, absorbing or being absorbed.

What else was she to do? She stepped forward, into the gravitational field of its orbits. This close, the translucent layer was more like a microscope slide of certain kinds of long, irregularly shaped cells. The patterns beneath, on the second layer, she could almost read, but remained obscured, as if in shallows disturbed by wide ripples.

She reached out a hand, felt a delicate fluttering against her fingers as though encountering a porous layer, a veil.

Was this first contact, or last contact?

Her touch triggered a response.

The halo far above dissolved to allow one of its constituent parts to peel off like a drooping golden pearl as large as her head—and down it came to a halt in front of her, hovering there to assess her. Reading her, with a kind of warmth that felt like sunburn. Yet still she was not afraid. She would not be afraid. Area X had made her. Area X must have expected her.

Ghost Bird reached out and plucked the golden pearl from the air, held it warm and tender in her hand.

A brilliant gold-green light erupted from the globe and plunged into the heart of her and an icy calm came over her, and through the calm bled a kind of monumental light and in that light she could see all that could be revealed even as Area X peered in at her.

She saw or felt, deep within, the cataclysm like a rain of

comets that had annihilated an entire biosphere remote from Earth. Witnessed how one *made* organism had fragmented and dispersed, each minute part undertaking a long and perilous passage through spaces *between*, black and formless, punctuated by sudden light as they came to rest, scattered and lost—emerging only to be buried, inert, in the glass of a lighthouse lens. And how, when brought out of dormancy, the wire tripped, how it had, best as it could, regenerated, begun to perform a vast and preordained function, one compromised by time and context, by the terrible truth that the species that had given Area X its purpose was gone. She saw the membranes of Area X, this machine, this creature, saw the white rabbits leaping into the border, disappearing, and coming out into another place, the leviathans, the ghosts, watching from beyond. All of this in fragments through taste or smell or senses she didn't entirely understand.

While the Crawler continued in its writing as if she did not even exist, the words ablaze with a richer and more meaningful light than she had ever seen, and worlds shone out from them. So many worlds. So much light. That only she could see. Each word a world, a world bleeding through from some other place, a conduit and an entry point, if you only knew how to use them, the coordinates the biologist now used in her far journeying. Each sentence a merciless healing, a ruthless rebuilding that could not be denied.

Should she now say, "Stop!" Should she now plead for people she had never met who lived in her head, who the biologist had known? Should she somehow think that what came next would destroy the planet or save it? In its recognition of her, Ghost Bird knew that something would survive, that she would survive.

What could she do? Nothing. Nor did she want to. There was a choice in not making a choice. She released the sphere, let it hover there in the air.

She sensed Grace on the stairs behind them, sensed that Grace meant harm, and didn't care. It wasn't Grace's fault. Grace could not possibly understand what she was seeing, was seeing something else—something from back at the lighthouse or the island or her life before.

Grace shot Ghost Bird through the back. The bullet came out of her chest, lodged in the wall. The halo above the Crawler spun more furiously. Ghost Bird turned, shouted at her with the full force of the brightness. For she was not injured, had felt nothing, did not want Grace hurt.

Grace frozen there in the half-light, rifle poised, and now in her eyes the knowledge that this was futile, that this had always been futile, that there was no turning back, that there could be no return.

"Go back, Grace," Ghost Bird said, and Grace disappeared up the steps, as if she'd never been there.

Then Ghost Bird realized, too late, that Control was no longer there, had either gone back up or had snuck past, down the stairs, headed for the blinding white light far below.

0023: THE DIRECTOR

You return to what you knew, or thought you knew: the lighthouse and the Séance & Science Brigade, reinvigorated due to the line item linking the S&SB and Jack Severance. You comb through every file three or four times, force yourself to once again review the history of the lighthouse and its ruined sister on the island.

At odd moments, you see Henry's face, a pale circle from a great distance, moving closer and closer until you can catalog every unsavory detail. You don't know what he means, know only that Henry is not someone to be cast aside too quickly. He nags at you like an unopened letter that everyone has, with overconfidence, predicted will contain something banal.

Your antipathy toward them made you dismissive as a child. You hadn't been looking for ways to emblazon them in your memory, to capture details, but instead to banish them, edit them out, make them go away. This annoyance, this presence that you could tell made Saul uncomfortable, even uneasy. But what *about* them had made Saul feel that way?

No Henry, no Suzanne that looked like them appeared

on the lists of the S&SB members, no stray photos with members unidentified leaped out to reveal either of them. Prior investigations had tracked down the names and addresses of any member assigned to the forgotten coast, and exhaustive interviews had been conducted. The answers were the same: S&SB had been conducting standard research—the usual mix of the scientific and the preternatural. Anyone who knew anything else had been trapped inside and disappeared long before the first expedition stumbled through the corridor into Area X.

Worse, no further hint of Severance, Jack or Jackie, the latter also making herself scarce in the flesh, as if something new has caught her attention or she knows you want to question her, with each phone call fading into the backdrop, further subsumed by Central. So that you redouble your efforts to find her influence in the files, but if Lowry haunts you, Severance is the kind of ghost that's too smart to materialize.

Once again you watch the video from the first expedition, again study the background, the things out of focus, at the lighthouse. Through a flickering time lapse and sequencing, you review a kind of evolution and devolution of the lighthouse from inception through the last photograph taken by an expedition.

To the point that Grace takes you aside one day and says, "This is enough. You need to run this agency. Other people can review these files."

"What other people? What other people are you talking about?" you snap at her, and then instantly regret it.

But there are no "other people," and time is running out. You have to remember that, on some level, the entire Southern Reach has become a long con, and if you forget that you're not part of the solution, you're part of the problem.

"Maybe you need time off, some rest," Grace tells you. "Maybe you need to get some perspective."

"You can't have my job."

"I do not want your fucking job." She's simmering, she's about to boil over, and some part of you wants to see that, wants to know what Grace is like when she's totally lost it. But if you push her to that, she'll have lost you, too.

Later you go up to the rooftop with a bottle of bourbon, and Grace is already there, in one of the deck chairs. The Southern Reach building is nothing but a big, ponderous ship, and you don't know where the helm has gotten to, can't even lash yourself to the wheel.

"I don't mean anything I'm saying most of the time," you tell her. "Just remember I don't mean anything I say."

A dismissive sound, but also arms unfolding, grim frown loosening up. "This place is a fucking nuthouse." Grace rarely swears anywhere but on the roof.

"A nut job." Paraphrasing Cheney's latest puzzled, hurt soliloquy about lack of good data: "Even a falling acorn tells us something about where it fell from, Newton would tell us, wouldn't you say. There'd be a trajectory, for heck's sake, and then you'd backtrack, even if theoretical, find some point on the tree that acorn came from, or near enough." You can't say you've ever understood more than a third of his ellipticals.

"A White Tits nut job," Grace says, referring to the frozen white tents of the Southern Reach border command and control.

"Our White Tits nut job," you say sternly, wagging a finger. "But at least not nut jobs like the water-feature crew."

After Cheney's outburst, you went over yet another point-less, nonproductive report from the "water-feature crew," the agency studying radio waves for signals from extraterrestrial life. Central has suggested more than once that you "team up with" them. They listen for messages from the stars— across a sliver of two microwave regions unencumbered by radio waves from natural sources. These frequencies they call the water hole because they correspond to hydrogen and hydroxyl wavelengths. A fool's chance, to assume that other intelligent species would automatically gravitate to the "watering hole" as they called it.

"While what they were looking for snuck in the back door—"

"Set up the back door and walked through it—"

"You're looking up and meanwhile something walks by and steals your wallet," Grace says, cackling.

"Water feature built for nothing; they prefer the servants' entrance, thank you very much," you say grandly, passing the bourbon. "You don't just turn on the sprinklers and pump up the Slip 'N Slide."

You truly don't know what you're saying anymore, but Grace bursts into laughter, and then things are all right again with Grace, for a while, and you can go back to Henry and Suzanne, the talking mannequins, the deathly dull or just deathly twins.

But at some point that same week, Grace finds you throwing file folders against the far wall, and you've no excuse for it except a shrug. Bad day at the doctor's. Bad day prepping for the expedition. Bad day doing research. Just a bad day in a succession of bad days.

So you do something about it.

You fly out to Lowry's headquarters about one month before the twelfth expedition. Even though it's your idea, you're unhappy you have to travel, had hoped to lure Lowry to the Southern Reach one last time. Everything around you—your office, the conversation in the corridors, the view from Beyond Reach—has acquired a kind of compelling sheen to it, a clarity that comes from knowing you will soon be gone.

Lowry's in the final stages of his pre-expedition performance, has been exporting the less invasive of his techniques to Central. He enjoys impersonating an instructor for the benefit of expedition members, according to Severance. The biologist, she reassures you, has suffered "minimal meddling." The only thing you want ratcheted up in the biologist is her sense of alienation from other people. All you want is that she become as attuned inward to Area X as possible. You're not even sure she really needs your push in that regard, from all reports. No one in the history of the program has so willingly given up the use of her name.

Light hypnotic suggestion, conditioning that's more about Area X survival than any of Lowry's dubious "value adds," his claims to have found a way around the need, on some level, for the subject to want to perform the suggested action—"a kind of trickery and substitution." The stages you've seen described are identification, indoctrination, reinforcement, and deployment, but Grace has seen other documents that borrow the semiotics of the supernatural: "manifestation, infestation, oppression, and possession."

Most of Lowry's attention has accreted around the linguist, a volunteer with radicalized ideas about the value of free will. You wonder if Lowry prefers it when there's more or less resistance. So you absorb the brunt of his briefing, his report on progress, his teasing taunt about whether you've reconsidered his offer of hypnosis, of conditioning, with the hint behind it that you couldn't stop him if you tried.

Honestly, you don't give a shit about his briefing.

At some point, you steer Lowry toward the idea of a walk—down by the fake lighthouse. It's early summer, the weather still balmy, and there's no reason to sit there in Lowry's command-and-control lounge. You cajole him into it by appealing to his pride, asking for the full tour, taking just one thin file folder you've brought with you.

So he gives you the not-so-grand tour, through this miniaturized world of ever-decreasing wonder. There's the strange kitschy quality of piped-in music through speakers hidden around the grounds. A distant but cheery tune—not pop, not jazz, not classical, but something all the more menacing for being jaunty.

At the top of the quaint little lighthouse—what would Saul think of it?—he points out that the daymark is accurate, as well as "the fucking glass shards somebody added later." When he pulls the trapdoor open at the top, what's revealed in the room below are piles and piles of empty journals and loose, blank pages, as if he's bought a stationery store as a side business. The lens isn't functional, either, but as if by way of apology, you get a history lesson: "Back in the day—way back in the day—they used to just shove a big fucking fatty bird onto a stake and light it on fire for a beacon."

That "goddamn hole in the ground," as Lowry puts it, is the least accurate part—an old gunnery position with the gun unit ripped out, leaving the granite-lined dark circle that leads down a ladder to a tunnel that then doubles back to the hill behind you that houses most of Lowry's installations. You climb down only a little ways, enough to see, framed on the dank walls, Lowry's art gallery: the blurry, out-of-focus photographs, blown up, brought back by various expeditions. A kind of meta version of the tunnel brought to the faux tunnel, displaying with confidence something unknowable. Thinking of Saul on the steps of the real tunnel, turning toward you, and feeling such an acute contempt for Lowry that you have to remain there, looking down, for long moments, afraid it will show on your face.

After you've made the right noises about how impressive it all is, you suggest continuing along the shore, "fresh air and nature," and Lowry acquiesces, defeated by your tactic of asking a question about each new thing ahead because he just cannot shut up about his own cleverness. You take a side path that leads north along the water. There are geese nesting on a nearby rocky point that give you both the stink eye, an otter in the sea in the middle distance, shadowing you.

Eventually, you turn the conversation to the S&SB. You pull out a piece of paper—the line item linked to "Jack Severance." You point it out to him even though it's highlighted in hot pink. You present it as this funny thing, this thing Lowry must have known about, too. Given his secret debriefing of your childhood experiences when you first joined the Southern Reach.

"Is that the reason you and Jackie are working together?"

you ask. "That the S&SB had a link to Central—through Jack?"

Lowry considers that question, a kind of smirk on his craggy face. A smirk, and a look down at the ground and back up at you.

"Is that all we're out here for? For *that*? Jesus, I might've given you *that* in a fucking phone call."

"Not much, I guess," you say. Sheepish smile, offered up to a raging wolf of a narcissist. "But I'd like to know." Before you cross the border.

A hesitation, a sideways glance that's appraising you hard for some hidden motivation or some next move that maybe he can't see.

Prodding: "A side project? The S&SB a side project of Central, or . . . ?"

"Sure, why not," Lowry says, relaxing. "The usual kind of dependent clause that could be excised at any time, no harm done."

But sometimes the ancillary infected the primary. Sometimes the host and the parasite got confused about their roles, as the biologist might have put it.

"It's how you got the photograph of me at the lighthouse." Not a question.

"Very good!" he says, genuinely delighted. "Too fucking true! I was on a mission to find evidence to make sure you stayed true . . . and then I wondered how come that was in Central's files in the first place, and not over at the Southern Reach. Wondered where it originated—and then I found that very same line item." Except Lowry had a higher security clearance, could access information you and Grace couldn't get your hands on.

"That was smart of you. Really smart."

Lowry puffs up, chest sticking out, aware he's being flattered but can't help the self-parody that's not really parody at all, because where's the harm? You're on the way out. He's probably already thinking about replacements. You haven't bothered putting Grace's name forward, have been working on Jackie Severance in that regard instead.

"The idea was straightforward, the way Jack told it. The S&SB was kind of bat-shit crazy, low probability, but if there actually was anything uncanny or alien in the world, we should monitor it, should be aware of it. Maybe influence or nudge it a bit, provide the right materials and guidance. And if troublemakers or undesirables joined the group—that's a good way to monitor potential subversives, too . . . and also a good cover for getting into places 'hidden in plain sight' for surveillance, a methodology Central was keen on back then. A lot of antigovernment types along the forgotten coast."

"Did we recruit, or—"

"Some operatives embedded—and some folks we persuaded to work for us because they liked the idea of playing spy. Some folks who got a thrill out of it. Didn't need a deeper reason, like God and country. Probably just as well."

"Was Jackie involved, too?"

"Jack wasn't just protecting himself," Lowry says. "When Jackie was starting out, she helped him a bit—and then she came to the Southern Reach later and helped Jack again, to make sure none of this came out. Except I found out, as I do, sometimes. As you know."

"Ever come across a Henry or Suzanne in the files?"

"Never any names used in what I saw. Just code names

like, I dunno, 'Big Hawler' and 'Spooky Action' and 'Damned Porkchop.' That kind of crap."

But none of this is the real question, the first of the real questions.

"Did the S&SB facilitate, knowingly or unknowingly, the creation of Area X?"

Lowry looks both stunned and amused beyond reason or good sense. "No, of course not. No no no! That's why Jack could keep it secret, snuff it out. Strictly in the wrong place at the wrong time—because otherwise I would have . . . I would have taken measures." But you think he meant to say *would have killed them all.* "And it turns out Jack was running it mostly on his own initiative, which is something I think we can both appreciate, right?"

Above you loom the old barracks, the warrens, gun slits from concrete bunkers.

Do you believe Lowry? No, you don't.

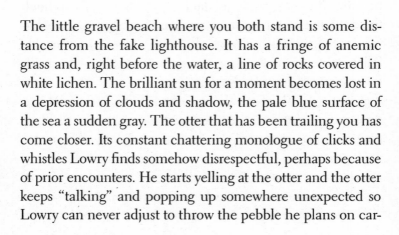

The little gravel beach where you both stand is some distance from the fake lighthouse. It has a fringe of anemic grass and, right before the water, a line of rocks covered in white lichen. The brilliant sun for a moment becomes lost in a depression of clouds and shadow, the pale blue surface of the sea a sudden gray. The otter that has been trailing you has come closer. Its constant chattering monologue of clicks and whistles Lowry finds somehow disrespectful, perhaps because of prior encounters. He starts yelling at the otter and the otter keeps "talking" and popping up somewhere unexpected so Lowry can never adjust to throw the pebble he plans on caroming off the otter's head. You sit down on the rocks, watch the show.

"Goddamn fucking creature. Goddamn stupid fucking animal."

The otter shows off a fish it's caught, swimming on its back, eyes full of a kind of laughter, if that's possible.

The otter skims and zags and disappears and comes back up. Lowry's pebbles skip and plop without effect, the otter apparently thinking it's a game.

But it's a game that bores the otter after a while, and it submerges for a long time, Lowry standing there with one hand on his hip, the other a fist around a rock, searching for a new ripple in the water, seeming to want to guess how long the otter can hold its breath, what range of options the animal has for where it can come up for air. Except it never reappears, and Lowry's left standing there, holding a rock.

Is Lowry a monster? He is monstrous in your eyes, because you know that by the time his hold on Central, the parts of Central he wants to make laugh and dance the way he wants them to laugh and dance . . . by the time this hold, the doubling and mirroring, has waned as most reigns of terror do, the signs of his hand, his will, will have irrevocably fallen across so many places. His ghost will haunt so much for so many years to come, imprint upon so many minds, that if the details about the man known as Lowry are suddenly purged from all the systems, those systems will still reconstruct his image from the very force and power of his impact.

You take out a photo of the cell phone, nudge his arm with it, make him take it. Lowry blanches, tries to hand back the photograph, but you're going to make him keep it.

He's stuck holding it and the rock meant for the otter. He drops the rock, but won't look at the photograph again.

"Lowry, I think you lied about this phone. I think this is your phone. From the first expedition." You've a sense as you say the words that you're going too far, but you'll be going even farther soon.

"You don't know that's my phone."

"It's got a long history now."

Lowry: "No." Stark. Final. Letting in no light. A kind of self-damnation. No protest. No outrage. None of the usual Lowry drama. "No." Without any way to pry loose some light between the letters of that word, so you'll have to try yourself, across the border.

"Are you working for them? Is that the problem?" You leave the "them" vague on purpose.

"For 'them'?" A laugh that burned. "Why, is there a problem with the phone?" Still not an admission.

"Does Area X have unfinished business with you? Is there something you haven't told us about the first expedition?"

"Nothing that would help you." Bitter now. Directed at you for ambushing him, or at someone else?

"Lowry, if you don't tell me whether or not this is your cell phone, I am going to go to Central and tell them all about the S&SB, all about where I came from, how you covered it up. I'm going to scuttle you for good."

"You'd be done for yourself then."

"I'm done for anyway—you know that."

Lowry gives you a look that's equal parts aggression and some secret hurt coming to the surface.

"I get it now, Gloria," he says. "You're going on a suicide

mission and you just want everything out in the open, even if it's unimportant. Well, you should know that if you share with anyone, I'll—"

"You're corrupted data," you tell him. "If we used your own techniques on you, Lowry, what would we find in your brain? Coiled up in there?"

"How the fuck dare you." He's trembling with anger, but he's not moving, he's not retreating one inch. It's not a denial, although it probably should be. Guilt? Does Lowry believe in guilt?

Pushing now, probing now, not certain if what you're saying is true: "While on the first expedition, did you communicate with them? With Area X?"

"I wouldn't call it communication. It's all in the files you've already seen."

"What did you see? How did you see it?" Were we doomed when you came back, or before?

"There will never be a grand unified theory, Gloria. We will never find it. Not in our lifetime, and it'll be too late." Lowry trying to confuse things, escape the spotlight. "You know, they're looking at water on the moons of Jupiter right now, out there, our not-so-secret sister organizations. There might be a secret sea out there. There might be life, right under our noses. But there's always been life right under our noses—we're just too blind to see it. These fucking questions—they don't matter."

"Jim, this is evidence of contact. Finding this particular cell phone in Area X." That it indicates recognition and understanding of some kind.

"No—random. Random. Random."

"It wants to talk to you, Jim. Area X wants to talk to you. It wants to ask you a question, doesn't it?" You don't know if this is true, but you're sure it'll scare the shit out of Lowry.

You have the sense of a time delay in Lowry, a gap or distance between the two of you that is very, very wide. Something ancient shines out of his eyes, peers out at you.

"I won't go back," he says.

"That's not an answer."

"Yes, it's my phone. It's my fucking phone."

Are you seeing Lowry as he was right after coming back from the first expedition? How long could a person hold to a pattern, a process, despite being fundamentally damaged? Whitby telling you, "I think this is an asylum. But so is the rest of the world."

"Don't you get tired after a while?" you ask him. "Of always moving forward but never reaching the end? Of never being able to tell the truth to anyone?"

"You know, Gloria," he says, "you'll *never* really understand what it was like that first time, going out through that door in the border, coming back. Not if you cross the border a thousand times. We were offered up and we were *lost*. We were passing through a door of ghosts, into a place of spirits. And asked to deal with that. For the rest of our lives."

"And what if Area X comes looking for you?"

There's still that remoteness to Lowry's gaze, as if he's not really there, standing in front of you, but he's done, pushed to his limit, stalks off without even a glance back.

You will never see him again, ever, and that temporary relief puts juice in your step as the sun returns, as the otter returns, and you sit by the shore and watch the animal cavort and frolic for a few minutes that you hope will never end.

ACCEPTANCE

0024: THE LIGHTHOUSE KEEPER

. . . bring forth the seeds of the dead to share with the worms
that gather in the darkness . . . Heard during the night:
screech owl, nighthawk, a few foxes. A blessing. A relief.

At the lighthouse, the beacon was dark. The beacon was
dark, and something was trying to spill out of him, or
course through him on its way to somewhere else. *The
shadows of the abyss are like the petals of a monstrous flower
that shall blossom within the skull and expand the mind
beyond what any man can bear, but whether it decays under
the earth or above on green fields, or out to sea or in the very air,
all shall come to revelation, and to revel, in the knowledge of
the strangling fruit.*

He was still in shock from the bar, kept believing that if he
went back it would prove to be some kind of waking vision or
even a terrible joke. The smashing of Old Jim's bloody fingers
against the piano keys. Sadi's look of being undone, betrayed
by her own words. Brad, standing there, gaze locked on the
wall as if someone had frozen him in place. Thank God
Trudi had already left. What would he tell Gloria when he
saw her again? What would he tell Charlie?

Saul parked the truck, stumbled to the lighthouse, unlocked the door, slammed it behind him, and stood in the entrance breathing hard. He'd call the police, tell them to come to the bar, to check on poor Old Jim and the others. He'd call the police, and then he'd try to get hold of Charlie out at sea, and then call anyone else he could think of. Because something terrible must be happening here, something beyond his illness.

But no one answered. No one answered. The phone was dead. He could run, but where to? The light had gone out. The light had gone out.

Armed with a flare gun, Saul stumbled up the stairs, one hand against the wall to keep his balance. The splinter was an insect bite. Or an overture. An intruder. Or nothing, nothing to do with this, as he slipped and almost fell, some kind of moisture on the steps, a fuzziness on the wall that came away in his hands, that he had to brush off against his jeans. The Light Brigade. They'd given him an experimental drug or exposed him to radiation with their equipment. *And the hand of the sinner shall rejoice, for there is no sin in shadow or in light that the seeds of the dead cannot forgive.*

Near the top, the wind whistled down briskly and he welcomed the chill, the way it told him a world existed outside of his mind, helped him deny these symptoms that had now crept back in. He felt a strong tidal pull, and a vibration that went with the pull, and he was burning up.

Or was the lighthouse burning up? Because a glow awaited him at the top of the stairs, and not the faint green phosphorescence that now arose from the walls, the steps. No, this was a sharp light that knew its purpose, he could tell that already.

ACCEPTANCE

But it was not the light from the lens, and he hesitated just below the lantern room for a moment. He sagged onto a step, not sure he wanted to see what new beacon had supplanted the old. His hands shook. He trembled. Could not get Old Jim's fingers out of his head, nor the words of the sermon that still uncurled all unbidden from his mind. That he could neither resist nor keep out.

But this was his place now, and he could not abandon it. He rose. He turned. He walked into the lantern room.

The rug had been moved.

The trapdoor lay open.

A light shone out from that space. A light that circled and curved even as it had the discipline not to trickle across the floor, or refract off the ceiling, but instead mimicked a door, a wall, rising from the watch room.

Quietly, flare gun held tight, Saul crept closer to the edge of the trapdoor and the source of the light, while the feeling increased that the stairs behind him had grown stranger still, that he should not look back. Bending at the knees, he peered down into the watch room, feeling the heat of that light crossing his face, his neck, singeing his beard.

At first all he saw was a vast mound of papers and what looked like notebooks that now rose from the watch room, a great behemoth, a disheveled library of shadow and reflection that leaped into and out of focus—ghosts and figments, curling and questing, there but not quite there, a record that he did not understand because it did not yet exist.

Then his eyes adjusted and the source of the light coalesced: a blossom. A pure white blossom with eight petals, which had unfurled from the top of a familiar plant, whose roots disappeared into the papers below. The plant that had enticed him on the lighthouse lawn, so long ago, to reach down, drawn by a glitter, a gleam.

An almost holy intensity rose from somewhere within and filled Saul up, along with a dizziness. Light was leaking out of him now, too, coursing down through the trapdoor to communicate with what lay below, and there came the sensation of something pulling him close, holding him tight . . . of recognizing him.

In rebellion against that, he rose from his crouch, arms out to the side for balance, teetering there on the edge of the trapdoor, staring down into that swirl of petals until he could resist no more, was falling into the pure white corona of a circle of fire, into a congregation of flames, a burning so pure that turning to ash was a kind of relief, engulfed by light that consecrated not just him but everything around him, anchoring receiver and received.

There shall be a fire that knows your name, and in the presence of the strangling fruit, its dark flame shall acquire every part of you.

When he regained consciousness, he was lying on the floor of the watch room, on his back, looking up. There was no mound of notebooks. There was no impossible flower.

Just the bodies of Henry and Suzanne, with no apparent wounds upon them, expressions blank and more haunting because of it. He recoiled from them, crawled away from them, staring. In the shadows there might have been what looked like the limp, desiccated remains of a plant, but he had no desire other than to leave that space.

He clambered up the ladder.

A figure in silhouette stood in front of the open door to the railing. A figure with a gun.

Impossibly, it was Henry.

"I thought you'd be gone longer, Saul," Henry said, in a distant tone. "I thought you might not even come back tonight. That maybe you'd go over to Charlie's, except Charlie is out fishing—and Gloria's staying with her father. Not that she would be out this late anyway, or be of much help to you. But just so you know where we stand."

"You killed Suzanne," Saul said, unbelieving even now.

"She wanted to kill me. She didn't believe in what I found. None of them believed. Not even you."

"You killed *yourself.*" Your twin. Knowing that even if it made a difference, he couldn't reach the flare gun in time, or even make it two steps into a headlong flight down the stairs before Henry would shoot him, too.

"A strange thing," Henry said. Where before he had been indistinct, hurting, in need of succor, now he had snapped back into focus. "A strange thing to kill yourself. I thought maybe it was a kind of wraith. But maybe Suzanne was right instead."

"Who *are* you?"

Ignoring him: "I found it, Saul, like I said I would. Or it found me. Only, it wasn't what I thought. Do you know what it is, Saul?" Almost pleading.

There was no good answer to Henry's question.

He took two steps toward Henry, as if he were watching someone else do it. He was an albatross, floating motionless in a high-above trough of air, gliding beneath the clouds with their dark underbellies, a coordinate of shadow and light that kept moving, a roving latitude and longitude, and far, far below, stood Saul and Henry, in the lantern room.

Saul took a third step, the plant a beacon in his head.

A fourth step and Henry shot him in the shoulder. The bullet penetrated and passed through, and Saul didn't feel a thing. Saul was still floating far above, intent on navigation, on riding thermals, an animal that hardly ever came down to land but just kept flying and flying.

Saul rushed Henry, rammed his bleeding shoulder into Henry's chest, and the two of them staggered, grappling out the door and toward the railing, Henry's gun spinning out of his hand and across the floor. So close, staring into Henry's eyes, Saul had the sense of the man being at a remove, a time delay—a gap or distance between receipt, acknowledgment, and response: a message coming to him from very far away. As if Henry were dealing with some other, completely different situation . . . while on some level still able to appraise him, to judge him. *When you hide your face, they are terrified; when you take away their breath, they die and return to the dust.*

Because Henry was drawing them both to the railing. Because Henry had a firm grip on him and was drawing them both to the railing. Except Henry was saying to Saul, "What are you doing?" But Saul wasn't doing it, Henry was and didn't seem to realize it.

"It's you," the albatross managed to say. "You're doing it, not me."

"No, I'm not." Henry beyond panic now, writhing and trying to get loose, but still leading them to the railing, fast now, and Henry begging him to stop what he could not stop.

Yet Henry's eyes did not send out the same message as his words.

Henry hit the railing—hard—and Saul a second later, swung to the side by momentum, and then they both went over, and only then, when it was too late, did Henry let go, the wind ripping screams from his throat, and Saul plummeted beside him through the cold empty air—falling too fast, too far, while a part of him still looked down from above.

The surf, like white flames surging and questing across the sand.

I am come to send fire on the earth; and what will I, if it be already kindled?

The awful thud and crack when he hit.

0025: CONTROL

There came to Control in that moment of extremity—almost unable to move, unable to speak—an overwhelming feeling of connection, that nothing was truly *apart* in the same way that he had found even the most random scrawl in the director's notes joined some greater pattern. And although the pressure was increasing and he was in a great deal of pain, the kind of pain that would not leave him soon, if ever, there arose a powerful music within him that he did not fully understand as he slipped and slid down the curving stairs, pulling himself at times, his left arm useless by his side, his father's carving clenched in a fist he could no longer feel, the brightness welling up through his mouth, his eyes, and filling him at the same time, as if the Crawler had accelerated the process. He was slipping in part because he was changing, he knew that, could tell that he was no longer entirely human.

Whitby was still with him, old friend, even if Lowry, too, chuckled and flailed somewhere in the background, and he clutched his father's carving to him as best as he was able, the only talisman he had left. *This machine or creature or some combination of both that can manipulate molecules,*

*that can store energy where it will, that can hide the bulk of
its intent and its machinations from us. That lives with angels
within it and with the vestiges of its own terroir, the hints of its
homeland, to which it can never return because it no longer
exists.*

And yet the Crawler had used such a cheap trick: Control had seen his mother standing there, taken a grim and
primal satisfaction in recognizing it as a delusion, one that
held no dominion over him—a person he forgave because
how could he not forgive her, finally, standing in such a
place? Free, then, free even before the Crawler had struck,
had hurt him so badly. And even in that hurting somehow
Control knew that pain was incidental, not the Crawler's intent, but nothing about language, about communication,
could bridge the divide between human beings and Area X.
That anything approaching a similarity would be some subset of Area X functioning at its most primitive level. A blade
of grass. A blue heron. A velvet ant.

He lost track of time and of the speed of his passage down,
and of his transformation. He no longer knew whether he was
still even a sliver of human by the time he—painfully, nause-
ated, crawling now, or was he loping?—came down the most
ancient of steps, of stairs, to the blinding white light at the
bottom shaped like the immortal plant, like a comet roaring
there but stationary, and now his decision to push himself
forward in the final extremity, to push through against that
agony and that outward radiating command to turn back,
and to enter . . . what? He did not know, except that the biologist had not made it this far, and he had. He had made it
this far.

Now "Control" fell away again. Now he was the son of a

man who had been a sculptor and of a woman who lived in a byzantine realm of secrets.

His father's carving fell from his hand, clattered onto a step, came to a halt, there on the stairs, alongside the signs and symbols left by his predecessors. A scrawling on the walls. An empty boot.

He sniffed the air, felt under his paws the burning and heat, the intensity.

This was all that was left to him, and he would not now die on the steps; he would not suffer that final defeat.

John Rodriguez elongated down the final stairs, jumped into the light.

0026: THE DIRECTOR

Two weeks before the twelfth expedition, the old battered cell phone comes home with you. You don't remember bringing it. You don't know why security didn't question it. It's just there, in your purse, and then on the kitchen counter. The usual suspects occur to you. Maybe Whitby's even stranger than you think or Lowry's having a laugh at your expense. But what does it matter? You'll just bring it back in the morning.

By then the divide between work and home is long gone—you've brought files home, you've done work at home, scribbled things on scraps of paper and sometimes on leaves, the way you used to do as a kid. In part because you take delight in imagining Lowry receiving photographs of them in his reports; but also using those materials seems somehow safer, although you can't say why, just a heightened sense of a "touch" roving among the files, a presence you can't pin down or quantify. An irrational thought, an idea that just came into your mind one night, working late. Going into the bathroom every so often to throw up—a side effect of the medication you are taking for the cancer. Apologizing to the janitor and saying any foolish thing you could think of other than that you were sick: "I'm pregnant." Pregnant with cancer. Pregnant with possibility. It makes you laugh sometimes. Dear alcoholic veteran at the end of the bar, do you think you'd like to be a father?

It's not a night for Chipper's, not a night for garrulous Realtors and nodding drunks. You're tired from the additional training, which has required more travel up north to Central to participate with the rest of the expedition and to receive your own training as expedition leader. To fully understand the use of hypnotic commands, to understand the importance—the specific details—of the black boxes with the red light that help to activate compliance.

So instead of going out, you put on some music, then decide on television for a while because your brain is cooked. You hear a sound in the hallway, beyond the kitchen—just something settling in the attic, but it makes you nervous. When you go look, there's nothing there, but you get your ax from where you keep it under the bed for home defense. Then return to the couch, to watch a thirty-year-old detective show filmed in the south. Lost places, locations that don't exist now, that will never come back. A landscape haunting you from the past—so many things gone, no longer there. During the car chases, you're watching the backgrounds like they're family photos you've never seen before.

You nod off. You come to. You nod off again. Then you hear something creeping low and soft across the tiles of the kitchen, just out of view. A kind of terrified lurching shudder burns through you. There's a slow scuttle to the sound, so you can't really identify it, get a sense of what has crept into your house. You don't move for a very long time, waiting to hear more, not wanting to hear more. You think you might not ever get up, go to the kitchen, see what animal awaits you there. But it's still moving, it's still making noise, and you can't sit there forever. You can't just sit there.

So you get up, you brandish the ax, you walk to the kitchen counter, lean on tiptoe to peer at the kitchen floor, but whatever it is has nudged up against the left side, out of view. You're going to have to walk around and confront it directly.

There, scuttling across the floor, blind and querulous, is the old cell phone—scrabbling and bulky, trying to get away from you. Or trying to burrow into the cabinets, to hide there. Except it isn't moving now. It hasn't moved the whole time you've been staring at it. You look at the phone in shock for so many moments. Maybe from the surprise of it or as a defense mechanism, all you can think is that your work has followed you home. All you can think of is the monstrous breach. Either in reality or in your mind.

With trembling hands, you retrieve the cell phone from the floor, ax held ready in your other hand. It feels warm, the melted nature of the leather against the phone creating the texture of skin. You get a metal box you use for tax receipts, toss them into a plastic bag, put the phone inside, lock it, put it on the kitchen counter. You resist the urge to toss the box into your backyard, or to drive with it to the river and fling it into the darkness.

Instead you fumble for a cigar from the humidor buried underneath some clothes in your bedroom. The cigar you pull out is dry and flaking, but you don't care. You light it, go into your home office, shove the notes you've brought home into a plastic bag. Every unsupportable theory. Every crazed journal rant rescued from old expedition accounts. Every incomprehensible scrawling. Shove them in there with a vengeance, for some reason shouting at Lowry as you do because he's peering into your thoughts on some mission of his own. You hiss at him. Stay the fuck away! Don't come in here. Except he already has, is the only person screwed up enough, knowing what he must know, to do this to you.

There are notes you weren't sure you remembered writing, that you couldn't be sure had been there before. Were there too many notes? And if so, who has written the others? Did Whitby sneak into your office and create them, trying to help you? Forging your handwriting? You resist the urge to take the notes out of the bag, sort through them again, be pulled down by that horrible weight. You take the bag of crazy outside with a glass of red wine, stand there on the stone patio smoking while you turn on the grill even though a storm's coming, even though you can feel the first raindrops, wait a minute or two, then with a snarl upend the bag onto the flames.

You're a large, authoritative woman, standing in her backyard, burning a crapload of secret papers, of receipts and other things that reflect the totality, the banality of your life—transformed into "evidence" by what you've scrawled there. Squirt lighter fluid over it to make it worse or better, toss this ceaseless, inane, stupid, ridiculous, pathetic detritus on top of it, light a match, watch it all go up in billowing, eye-watering, bile-like smoke. Curling and blackened, meaningless. It doesn't matter because there's still a flickering light in your head that you can't snuff out, a wavering candle distant in the darkness of a tunnel that was really a tower that was a topographical anomaly that was you reaching out to touch Saul Evans's face. It is all too much. You slump alongside the wall, watch as the flames rise up and then bank, and are gone.

It isn't enough. There're still more inside—on the side table by the couch, on the kitchen counter, on the mantel in the bedroom; you're awash in them, drowning in them.

Down the slant of your backyard, the windows are lit up and a television is on. A man, a woman, and a boy and a girl on a couch seem sublimely calm, just sitting there, watching sports. Not talking. Not doing anything but watching. Definitely not wanting to look in your direction, as the raindrops thicken, proliferate, and your burning papers sizzle.

What if you go back in, open that box, and the cell phone isn't a cell phone? What if containment is a joke? You can hardly contain yourself. What if you bring the cell phone back in and have it tested and nothing is out of the ordinary, again? What if you go back in, the cell phone isn't ordinary, and you report that to Lowry and he laughs and calls you crazy—or you tell Severance instead, and the cell phone is just sitting there, inert, and you're the compromised director of an agency that hasn't yet solved the central mystery around which its existence revolves? What if your cancer rises up and devours you before you get a chance to cross the border? Before you can escort the biologist across.

You with your cigar and your glass of wine and the music on the phonograph you turn up real loud, something you don't even remember buying, and the idea that somehow any of that will keep out the darkness, keep out the thoughts that churn through your head—the cold regard that holds you as if God herself had through some electrified beatific gaze pinned you like a butterfly in a collector's display case of mediocrity.

The storm comes on and you toss your cigar, stand there thinking about the invisible border and all the ceaseless hypotheses that amount to some psychotic religion . . . and you drink your wine, hell, get the whole bottle, and it's still not doing it, and you still don't want to go inside to face . . . anything.

"Tell me something I don't know! Tell me something I don't fucking know!" you scream at the darkness, and throw your glass into the night, and without meaning to you're on your knees in the rain and the lightning and the mud, and you don't know if this is an act of defiance or an act of pain or just some selfish reflexive grace note. You truly don't know, any more than you know if that cell phone in there had actually moved, been alive.

The burned notes are sopping now, falling in wet, stuck-together ash clumps off the edge of the overflowing grill. A few last sparks float in the air, winking out one by one.

That's when you rise, finally. You rise out of the mud, in the rain, and you go back inside and suddenly everything gets really cold and calm. The answer doesn't lie in your backyard because no one is going to come and save you even if you beg them to. Especially if you beg them to. You're on your own, like you've always been on your own. You have to keep going forward, until you can't go forward anymore.

You have to hang on. You're almost there. You can make it to the end.

You stop investigating the S&SB. You stop investigating the lighthouse. You leave the notes that remain in your office, which you're well aware are legion, many more than what you burned at home in your pointless effort at catharsis.

"Ever had anyone try to burn a house down?" you ask the Realtor later that night, ducking in for a quick drink, a couple of cocktails that'll put you to sleep and then wake you up again, restless and turning endlessly in your bed in the middle of the night.

The lights are dim, the TV a silent glow, a distant hum, the stars in the ceiling glinting on and off from the roving flash of spotlights on the bowling lanes. Someone's playing a dark country-western song on the jukebox, but it sounds distant, so far away: *Something's moving through my heart. Sometimes I just have to play the part.*

"Oh, sure," the Realtor says, "warming to her task" as the veteran, suddenly a wit, puts it. "The usual kind of thing, with arson for the insurance. Sometimes it's an ex trying to burn down the wife's house once her new boyfriend has moved in. But more times than you might think, you don't find any reason for it at all. I had one guy who got the urge to start a fire one day, and he let it all go up in smoke, and just stood there watching. Afterward he was crying and wondering why he'd done it. He didn't know. There must have been a reason why he did it, though, I've always thought. Something he couldn't admit to himself, or something that he just didn't know."

Anger tries to thrash its way free of you, manifests as a suspicion you've had for a while.

"You're not a Realtor," you tell the woman. "You're not really a Realtor at all." She's a touch on some notes, she's a cell phone that won't sit still.

You need some air, walk outside, stand there in the gravel parking lot, under the uncertain illumination of a cracked streetlamp. You can still hear the music blaring from inside. The streetlamp's shining down on you and the solid bulk of the hippo on the edge of the miniature golf course, its enormous shape casting a wide, oblong shadow. The hippo's eyes are blank glass, its gaping mouth a fathomless space you wouldn't put your hand into for all the free games Chipper's could give you.

The veteran comes outside.

"You're right—she's not a Realtor," he tells you. "She got fired. She hasn't had a job for more than a year."

"That's okay," you say. "I'm not a long-haul trucker, either."

Tragically, he asks if you want to go back inside and dance. No, you don't want to dance. But it's okay if he leans against the hippo with you to talk for a while. About nothing in particular. About the ordinary, everyday things that elude you.

The plant remains in the storage cathedral. Whitby's mouse remains in his attic for the most part. The last few days before the twelfth expedition, the phone migrates to your desk as a secret memento. You don't know whether you're more concerned when it is with you or when it is out of your sight.

0027: THE LIGHTHOUSE KEEPER

Saul woke on his back beneath the lighthouse, covered in sand, Henry crumpled beside him. It was still night, the sky a deep, rich blue bleeding into black, but full of stars against that vast expanse. He must be dying, he knew, must be broken in a hundred places, but he didn't feel broken. Instead, all he felt was a kind of restlessness, growing a hundredfold now and nothing else behind it. No agony from the fall, from the searing pain of what must be several broken bones. None of that. Was he in shock?

But still there was the rising brightness and the night staring down with thousands of glistening eyes, the comforting husk and hush of the surf, and as he turned on his side to face the sea, the faint dark shadows of night herons, with their distinctive raised crests, stabbing at the tiny silver fish writhing in the wet sand.

With a groan, anticipating a collapse that never came, Saul rose without a stagger or a swoon, a dreadful strength coursing through him. Even his shoulder felt fine. Uninjured, or so badly injured and disoriented that he was nearing the end. Whatever was coming into his head was being translated into words, his distress expressed as language, and he clamped down on it again, because he knew somehow that to let it out was to give in, and that he might not have much time left.

He looked up at the lantern room of the lighthouse, imagining again that fall. Something inside had saved him, protected him. By the time he'd hit the ground, he hadn't been himself—the plummet become a descent so gentle, so light, that it'd been like a cocoon tenderly plummeting, kissing the sand. Come to rest as if locking into a position preordained for him.

When he looked over at Henry, Saul could see even in the dull darkness that the man was still alive, that distant stare as locked and fixed on him as the stars above. That stare coming to Saul from across the centuries, across vast, unconquerable distances. Beatific and yet deadly. A scruffy assassin. A fallen angel ravaged by time.

Saul didn't want that gaze upon him, walked a short distance away from Henry, down the beach, closer to the water. Charlie was somewhere out there in the sea, night fishing. He wanted Charlie close now but also wanted him thrust far away, cast out, so that whatever had possessed him might not possess Charlie.

He made his way to the ridge of rocks that Gloria liked to explore, to the tidal pools, and sat there, silent, recovering his sense of self.

Out in the sea, he thought he could see the rippling backs of leviathans as they breached and then returned to the depths. There came the stench of oil and gasoline and chemicals, the sea coming almost up to his feet now. He could see that the beach was strewn with plastic and garbage and tarred bits of metal, barrels and culverts clotted with seaweed and barnacles. The remains of ships rising, too. Detritus that had never touched this coast but was here now.

Above, the stars seemed to be moving at a tremendous rate, through a moonless sky, and he could hear the thunderous screams of their passage—streaking faster and faster until the dark was dissolving into ribbons and streamers of light.

Henry, like an awkward shadow, appeared at his side. But Saul wasn't frightened of Henry.

"Am I dead?" he asked Henry.

Henry said nothing.

Then, after a moment, "You're not really Henry anymore, are you?"

No answer.

"Who are you?"

Henry looked over at Saul, looked away again.

Charlie, in a boat, offshore, night fishing, far away from whatever this was, this sensation pushing out of him like a live thing. Pushing harder and harder and harder.

"Will I ever see Charlie again?"

Henry turned away from Saul, began to walk down the beach, broken and stumbling. After a couple of steps, something further broke inside of him and he fell to the sand, crawling for a few feet before he lay still. *And the hand of the sinner shall rejoice, for there is no sin in shadow or in light that the seeds of the dead cannot forgive.*

Something was about to crest like a wave. Something was about to come out of him. He felt weak and invincible all at once. Was this how it happened? Was this one of the ways God came for you?

He did not want to leave the world, and yet he knew now that he was leaving it, or that it was leaving him.

Saul managed to get into his pickup truck, could feel the sickness overflowing, knew that whatever was about to happen he would be unable to control, was beyond anyone's ability to control. He did not want it to happen there, on the coast, next to his lighthouse. Didn't want it to happen at all, but knew the choice was not up to him. There were comets erupting in his head and a vision of a terrible door and what had come out of it. So he drove—down the rutted path, careening wildly at times, trying to escape himself even though that was impossible. Through the sleeping village. Past dirt road after dirt road. Charlie out at sea. Thankfully not here. Head pounding. The shadows begetting shadows, and the words trying to erupt from his mouth now, urgent to come out of his mouth, a code he couldn't decipher. Feeling as if something had its attention upon him. Unable to escape the sensation of interference and transmittal, a communication pressing in on the edges of his brain.

Until he couldn't drive anymore, there in the most remote part of the forgotten coast—the parts of the pine forest no one claimed or wanted or lived in. Stopped, stumbled out, the shapes of the dark trees, the sound of owls, innumerable rustlings, a fox pausing to stare at him, unafraid, the stars above still swirling and streaking.

Stumbling in the dark, scraping up against palmettos and tough scrub, pushing past the uprising of this undergrowth, a foot into black water and out again. The sharp scent of fox piss, the suggestion of an animal or animals watching him. Trying now to hold his balance. Trying to hold on to his wits. But a universe was opening up in his head, filled with images he didn't, couldn't understand.

A flowering plant that could never die.

A rain of white rabbits, cut off in mid-leap.

A woman reaching down to touch a starfish in a tidal pool.

Green dust from a corpse blowing away in the wind.

Henry, standing atop the lighthouse, jerking and twitching, receiving a signal from very, very far away.

A man stumbling through the forgotten coast in army fatigues, all of his comrades dead.

And a light that found him from above, pinning him there, some vital transaction complete.

The feel of wet dead leaves. The smell of a bonfire burning. The sound of a dog, distant, barking. The taste of dirt. And overhead, the interlocking branches of the pines.

There were strange ruined cities rising from his head, and with them a sliver that promised salvation. And God said it was good. And God said, "Don't fight it." Except that all he wanted to do was fight it. Holding on to Charlie, to Gloria, even to his father. His father, preaching, that inner glow, as of being taken up by something greater than himself, which language could not express.

Finally, in that wilderness, Saul could go no farther, he was done, and he knew it, and he wept as he fell, as he felt the thing within anchor him to the ground, as alien as any sensation he'd ever felt and yet as familiar as if it had happened a hundred times before. It was just a tiny thing. A splinter. And yet it was as large as entire worlds, and he was never going to understand it, even as it took him over. His last thoughts before the thoughts that were not his, that were never going to be his: Perhaps there is no shame in this, perhaps I can bear this, fight this. To give in but not give up. And projected back out behind him, toward the sea, Saul unable to say the name, just three simple words that seemed so inadequate, and yet they were all he had left to use.

Some time later, he woke up. That winter morning, the wind was cold against the collar of his coat as he trudged down the trail toward the lighthouse. There had been a storm the night before, and down and to his left, the ocean lay gray and roiling against the dull blue of the sky, seen through the rustle and sway of the sea oats. Driftwood and bottles and faded white buoys and a dead hammerhead shark had washed up in the aftermath, tangled among snarls of seaweed, but no real damage either here or in the village.

At his feet lay bramble and the thick gray of thistles that would bloom purple in the spring and summer. To his right, the ponds were dark with the muttering complaints of grebes and buffleheads. Blackbirds plunged the thin branches of trees down, exploded upward in panic at his passage, settled back into garrulous communities. The brisk, fresh salt smell to the air had an edge of flame: a burning smell from some nearby house or still-smoldering bonfire.

0028: GHOST BIRD

The Crawler was behind them. The words were behind them. It was just a submerged tunnel on a warm day. It was just a forest. It was just a place they were walking out of.

Ghost Bird and Grace did not talk much as they walked. There wasn't much to say, such a world lay between them now. She knew that Grace did not consider her quite human, yet something about her must reassure the woman enough to keep traveling with her, to trust her when she said that something had *changed* beyond the climate, that they should head for the border and see what that something was. The scent of pine pollen clung to the air, rich and golden and ripe. The wrens and yellow warblers chased each other through the bushes and trees.

They encountered no one and the animals while not tame seemed somehow unwary. Not wary of them, anyway. Ghost Bird thought of Control, back there, in the tunnel. What had he found down below? Had he found the true Area X, or had his death been the catalyst for the change she had felt, that manifested all around them? Even now she could not see Control clearly, knew only that his absence was a loss, a sadness, to her. He had been there almost her entire life—the real, lived-in life she had now, not the one she had inherited. That still meant something.

At the moment he had gone through the door so far below, she had seen him and had felt the Crawler's seekers fall away, the entire apparatus receding into the darkness after him. There had come a shuddering miniature earthquake, as the sides of the tunnel convulsed once, twice, and then were again still. Known that although nothing could be reversed, the director had been right: It could be changed, it could change, and that Control had added or subtracted something from an equation that was too complex for anyone to see the whole of. Perhaps the director had been right about the biologist, just not in the way she'd thought. The words from the wall still blazed across her thoughts, wrapped themselves around her like a shield.

Ghost Bird had walked up into the light to find Grace staring at her with fear, with suspicion, and she had smiled at Grace, had told her not to be afraid. Not to be afraid. Why be afraid of what you could not prevent? Did not want to prevent. Were they not evidence of survival? Were they not evidence of some kind? Both of them. There was nothing to warn anyone about. The world went on, even as it fell apart, changed irrevocably, became something strange and different.

They walked. They camped for the night. They walked again at first light, the world ablaze with sunrise and the awakening of the landscape around them. There were no soldiers, no suggestion of a ribbon stitching through the sky. The winter weather had lifted and it was hot, it was summer now in Area X.

ACCEPTANCE

The present moments elongated, once past still ponds and into the final miles. She lived in the present by dint of blistered feet and chafed ankles and biting flies drawn to the sweat on her ears or forehead and the parched feeling in her throat despite drinking water from her canteen. The sun had decided to lodge itself behind her eyes and shine out so that the inside of her head felt burned. Every beautiful thing that lay ahead she knew she had seen at least once behind her. Eternity found in the repetition of Grace's steps, her sometimes halting steps, and the constant way the light gripped the ground and sent its heat back up at her.

"Do you think the checkpoints are still manned?" Grace asked.

Ghost Bird did not reply. The question made no sense, but enough humanity remained to her that she didn't want to argue. The hegemony of what was real had been altered, or broken, forever. She would always know now the biologist's position, near or far, a beacon somewhere in her mind, a connection never closed.

In the final miles to the old position of the border, the sun was so bright and hot that she felt a little delirious, even though she knew it was a mirage—she had water and was still hobbling through blisters and petty aches. How could the sun be so oppressive and yet the scene so unbearably beautiful?

"If we do make it through, what do we tell them?"

Ghost Bird doubted there would be a "them" to tell. She longed now for Rock Bay, wished to see it through the eyes of Area X, wondered how it might have changed, how it might have remained the same. This was really her only goal: to return to a place that had been like the island was to the biologist.

They reached where the old border had been, on the lip of the giant sinkhole. The white tents of the Southern Reach had turned dark green with mold and other organisms. The brick of the army outpost was half pulled down and sunken in as if some giant creature had attacked it. There were no soldiers, there were no checkpoints.

She bent down to tighten the laces on her boots, a velvet ant beside her foot. From what seemed like a great distance, she heard a scrambling huff from the lush vegetation of the sinkhole. For an instant, some odd, broad-shouldered marmot pushed its face through the reeds. Then saw her and hurriedly disappeared with a plop into the creek behind it—while she rose, amused.

"What is it?" Grace asked from behind her.

"Nothing. Nothing at all."

Then she was walking again, laughing a bit, and everything was pressed out of her except a yearning for water and a clean shirt. Inexplicably, unaccountably happy, grinning even.

A day later, they reached the Southern Reach building. The swamp had crept up to the courtyard and seeped across the tiles, pushed up against the concrete steps leading inside. Storks and ibises had built nests on a roof that looked half caved in. The evidence of a fire that had burned itself out inside the building, somewhere near the science department, showed in scorch marks on the outer walls. From afar, they could see no signs of human life. No shadow of the people Grace had known there. Behind them lay the holding pond and the scrawny pine strung with lights, now two feet taller than when Ghost Bird had last seen it.

By mutual unspoken decision, they halted at the edge of the building. From there, a gash in the side showed them three floors of empty, debris-strewn rooms, and a greater darkness within. They stood for a moment, hidden by the trees, and peered at those remains.

Grace could not sense the way the building slowly took one breath and then another, the way it *sighed*. She could not sense the echo at the heart of the Southern Reach that told Ghost Bird that this place had built its own ecology, its own biosphere. To disturb that, to enter, would be a mistake. The time for expeditions was over.

They did not linger, look for survivors, or do any of the other usual or perhaps foolish things that they could have done.

But now came the crucible, now came the test.

"What if there is no world out there? Not as we know it? Or no way out to the world?" Grace saying this, while existing in that moment in a world that was so rich and full.

"We'll know soon enough," Ghost Bird said, and took Grace's hand for a moment, squeezed it.

Something in Ghost Bird's expression must have calmed her, for Grace smiled, said, "Yes, we will. We'll know." Between them, they might know more than any person still living on Earth.

It was just an ordinary day. Another ordinary summer day.

So they walked forward, throwing pebbles as they went, throwing pebbles to find the invisible outline of a border that might not exist anymore.

They walked for a long time, throwing pebbles at the air.

000X: THE DIRECTOR

You sit in the dark at your desk in the Southern Reach in the minutes before leaving for the twelfth expedition, your backpack beside you, the guns tucked into the outer mesh, safeties on, not loaded. You will leave it all a mess. The bookshelves have become overgrown, your notes nothing anyone would recognize as an organized pattern. So many things that make no sense, or only make sense to you. Like a plant and a battered cell phone. Like a photograph on the wall from when you knew Saul Evans.

Your letter to him is in your pocket. It feels awkward to you. It feels like trying to say something that needed to be said without words, to someone who may no longer be able to read it. But perhaps, too, it is like the script on the walls of the tower: The words aren't important but what's channeled through them is. Maybe the important thing is getting it out on the page so it can be there in your mind.

You agonize for the thousandth time that your course of action is poorly thought out. You have a choice. You can let it all go on as it has before. Or . . . you can do this thing that in just a short while will take you out of the dark, out of the silence, and on a path from which you cannot come back. Even if you make it back.

You have already said all the things to Grace that you had to say to make it seem like it would be all right. All the things said to the beloved mark, to reassure her. To keep up morale. And you almost believe she believed it, for your sake. *When I get back. When we solve this. When we . . .*

A pale, curious head peers in, turned at an angle: Whitby, the mouse peeking out from his shirt pocket, all ears and black little eyes and fragile handlike paws.

You feel suddenly old and helpless and everything seems very far from you—the chair, the door beyond, the hall, and Whitby a canyon yawning wide miles and miles away. You let out a little sob, a little attempt to draw in breath. Reeling there in momentary panic in the garbage heap of your notes. And yet, under that, a core that must not yield.

"Help me up, Whitby," you tell him, and he does, the man stronger than he looks, holding you up even as you lean into him, looming over his slight frame.

You sway there, looking down. Whitby has to stay behind, even as it all falls apart. As Whitby falls apart, because no one can withstand that vision for months, for years. But you have to ask it of him. You have no choice. Grace will run the agency. Whitby will be its recording, its witness.

"You have to write down whatever you see, your observations. It might still be important."

You can hear the surf in your ears. You can see the lighthouse. The words on the wall in the tower.

Whitby says nothing, just stares with his large eyes, but he doesn't need to. The fact that he stands there, silent, by your side, is enough.

ACCEPTANCE

When you take the first steps toward the door, you feel the weight on your back and the weight of your decision. But you ignore it. You walk into the hallway. It is very late. The fluorescent lights seem dim but a sickly heat comes off them, or from the vents, passing across the top of your head like a whisper. An unrecoverable reality.

The night will be cool and there might be the scent of honeysuckle in the air, even a half-remembered hint of salt spray, and it will seem to take no time at all, the familiar ride there, under the clear half-moon, and through the dark, submerged shapes of ruined buildings. With the other members of the twelfth expedition.

At the border, you enter the white tents of the Southern Reach mission control, and the linguist, the surveyor, the biologist, the anthropologist are escorted to their separate rooms for the final decontamination and conditioning process. Before long you will be at the border, will be headed with as much grace as your tall, broad shape can manage toward the luminescence of the enormous door.

You watch them all on the monitors. All but the linguist seem calm, movements relaxed and without evidence of jitters. The linguist is trembling and shivering. The linguist blinks at a rapid rate. Her lips move but no words come out.

The tech looks over at you for direction.

"Let me go in there," you say.

"We'll need to restart the process for her if you do."

"It's all right." And it is all right. You have enough resolve for both of you. For the moment.

Carefully, you sit down across from the linguist. You are trying to banish thoughts of your first trip across the border, of how it affected Whitby, but it's Whitby's face you see right now, not Saul's, not your mother's. The human cost across the years, the lives lost and broken, the long grift. The contortions and the subterfuge. All of the lies, and for what? Lowry, back at his headquarters, unable to see the irony, lecturing you: "Only by identifying the dysfunction and disease within a system can we begin to marshal a response whose logic would be to abolish the problems themselves."

The linguist has been placed on a regimen of psychotropic drugs. She has been operated on, reconditioned, broken down, brainwashed, fed false information that runs counter to her own safety, built back up again, and all of this she has on some level known about, volunteered for—Lowry finding in her story of lost family members on the forgotten coast the closest thing to a Gloria surrogate. It's a kind of taunt to you, a kind of petulant message, and, Lowry believes, the ultimate expression of his art. His coiled weapon—so tense that she's unraveling right here in front of you. The last eleventh's psychologist all over again, just from a different direction.

Her face reflects a confusion of impulses, the mouth ticking open, wanting to speak but not knowing what to say. The eyes are squinting as if expecting some kind of blow, and she will not meet your gaze. She's scared and she feels alone and she's been betrayed before she's ever even set foot in Area X.

You could still use her on the mission, could find a dozen ways to deploy her, even damaged. Fodder for whatever is waiting in the topographical anomaly. Fodder for Area X, a bit of misdirection for the other expedition members. But you want no distractions, not this way. It's just you. It's just the biologist. A plan that's really a guess in the dark, finding your way by feel.

You lean close and you take the linguist's hand in both of yours. You're not going to ask her if she still wants to go, if she can do that. You're not going to order her to go. And by the time Lowry finds out what you've done, it will be too late.

She stares at you with an eviscerated smile.

"You can stand down," you tell her. "You can go home. And it's going to be okay, it will all be okay."

With those words, the linguist recedes from you, gliding back into darkness, her and the chair and the room, as if they were merely props, and you're above Area X again, floating over the reeds, down toward the beach, the surf beyond. The wind and the sun, the warmth of the air.

The questioning is over. Area X is done with you, has taken every last little thing out of you, and there's a strange kind of peace in that. A backpack. The remains of a body. Your gun, tossed into the surf, your letter to Saul, crumpled and tumbling across the dried seaweed and the sand.

You are still there for a moment, looking out over the sea toward the lighthouse and the beautiful awful brightness of the world.

Before you are nowhere.

Before you are everywhere.

Dear Saul:

I doubt you will ever read this letter. I don't know by what means it might get to you or if you could even understand it now. But I wanted to write it. To make things clear, and so that you might know what you meant to me, even in such a short time.

That you might know that I appreciated your gruffness and your consistency and your concern. That I understood what those things meant, and it was important to me. That it would have been important even if all the rest of this had not occurred.

That you might know that it wasn't your fault. It wasn't anything you did. It wasn't anything other than bad luck, being in the wrong place at the wrong time—the same way it always happens, according to my dad. And I know this is true because it happened to me, too, even though I chose a lot of what's happened to me since.

Whatever occurred back then, I know you tried your best, because you always did try your best. And I am trying my best, too. Even if we don't always know what that means or how it will play out. You can get caught up in something that's beyond you, and never understand why.

The world we are a part of now is difficult to accept, unimaginably difficult. I don't know if I accept everything even now. I don't know how I can. But acceptance moves past denial, and maybe there's defiance in that, too.

I remember you, Saul. I remember the keeper of the light. I never did forget about you; I just took a long time coming back.

Love,

Gloria

(who lived dangerous on the rocks and pestered you true)

ACCEPTANCE

ACKNOWLEDGMENTS

Many thanks to my patient and brilliant editor, Sean Mc-
Donald, who made it possible for me to write these books
knowing someone really truly had my back. Thanks to everyone at FSG for making the experience of publishing
this trilogy so wonderful, including Taylor Sperry, Char-
lotte Strick, Devon Mazzone, Amber Hoover, Izabela
Wojciechowska, Abby Kagan, Debra Helfand, and Lenni
Wolff. Thanks to Karla Eoff, Chandra Wohleber, and Jus-
tine Gardner. Thanks as well to Alyson Sinclair for her ex-
cellent work on the publicity side and to Eric Nyquist for
great cover art. Thanks again to my stalwart agent, Sally
Harding, and the Cooke Agency. I'm also indebted to my
publishers in Canada, the U.K., and in other countries for
showing such imagination and energy in publishing the
Southern Reach trilogy. Blackstone Audio has also been a
delight to work with, and in particular Ryan Bradley. Many
thanks to the brilliant Bronson Pinchot and Carolyn Mc-
Cormick for great audiobook performances. Additional
thanks to Clubber Ace, Greg Bossert, Eric Schaller, Matthew
Cheney, Tessa Kum, Berit Ellingsen, Alistair Rennie, Brian
Evenson, Karin Tidbeck, Ashley Davis, Craig L. Gitney,

Kati Schardl, Mark Mustian, Diane Roberts, and the Fermentation Lounge. Appreciation for owl observations to Amal El-Mohtar and to Dave Davis for many kindnesses.

In thinking about and writing these books I've been grateful for ideas encountered in the Semiotext(e) Intervention Series, and in particular *The Coming Insurrection,* which had a tremendous influence on Ghost Bird's thinking throughout the novel and is quoted or paraphrased on pages 241, 242, and 336. I'm also grateful for the works of Rachel Carson and Jean Baudrillard; Taschen's *The Book of Miracles*; Philip Hoare's *The Sea Inside*; David Toomey's *Weird Life*; Iris Murdoch's novel *The Sea, The Sea*; the works of Tove Jansson (especially *The Summer Book* and *Moominland Midwinter*); *Tainaron,* by Leena Krohn; the nature poetry of Pattiann Rogers; *The Derrick Jensen Reader,* edited by Lierre Keith; Richard Jefferies's *After London*; and Elinor De Wire's *Guardians of the Light.* Finally, *The Seasons of Apalachicola Bay,* by John B. Spohrer, Jr., was like a revelation to me while writing *Acceptance*—a heartfelt, gorgeous, and wise book that kept me grounded in the places that made the Southern Reach trilogy personal.

Other research meant visiting, revisiting, or remembering landscapes that spoke to me in a way useful for the fiction: St. Marks National Wildlife Refuge, Apalachicola, rural Florida and Georgia, Botanical Beach Provincial Park and the Pacific Rim National Park Reserve on Vancouver Island, the coast of Northern California, and the Fiji Islands, which gave me a certain starfish.

I should also like to thank the many wonderful and creative booksellers I've met while on tour this year—you've been inspiring and energizing—as well as the enthusiastic readers willing to follow me on this somewhat strange journey. I really appreciate it.

Finally, I'm humbled and my heart made glad by my wife, Ann, who was my partner in all of this. She encouraged me, listened to me, helped me work out knots in drafts in progress, took other work off of my desk, went well beyond the call of duty or anything in the marriage vows to allow me the time and space to write these novels. It wouldn't have been possible without her.

Other books in the Southern Reach trilogy

Book 1: *Annihilation*

Area X has been cut off from the rest of the continent for decades. For thirty years, the secret agency known as the Southern Reach has monitored Area X and sent in expeditions to try to discover the truth about it. The first expedition returned with reports of a pristine, Edenic landscape; the second expedition ended in mass suicide; the members of the eleventh expedition all died of cancer within weeks of returning home. The twelfth expedition is made up of an anthropologist, a surveyor, a psychologist (the de facto leader) and a biologist. They discover a topographic anomaly and life forms that surpass understanding – but it's the surprises that came across the border with them and the secrets they are keeping from one another that change everything.

Book 2: *Authority*

John Rodriguez is the new head of the Southern Reach. He finds the agency in disarray. The previous director is lost; Area X remains a mystery. Undermined and under pressure to make sense of what happened to the twelfth expedition, Rodriguez retreats into the past in a labyrinthine search for answers. Yet the more he uncovers, the more he risks. What lies at stake is not just his sanity, for the secrets behind the Southern Reach are more sinister than anyone could have known.